Advance Praise for Nicole

A MAN DOWNSTAIRS

"A gripping story of troubled relationships, mental illness and buried secrets with a murder at its heart—who really killed young mother Edie Wynters in the small town of Aymes almost forty years ago? Her now grown daughter is about to find out. . . . *The Man Downstairs* is a clever, twisty and chilling read."—**Shari Lapena**, **international bestselling author of** *Everyone Here is Lying*

"A sharply observed, layered mystery about obsession, desperation, and the dark secrets small towns keep to protect their own."
—**Robyn Harding, bestselling author of** *The Drowning Woman*

"Combining sharp, assured prose with boundless humanity, this deftly plotted novel is a triumph. I stayed up all night racing toward a conclusion that provided more than just the deep satisfaction of a whodunit solved—it gave me chills, and made me think. Now all I want is another Nicole Lundrigan novel to become addicted to!"
—**Marissa Stapley,** *New York Times* **bestselling author of** *Lucky*

"Lundrigan is that rare breed of thriller writer who can weave a cunning plot twist while mesmerizing us all with her language. *A Man Downstairs* is a taut psychological nightmare with a poet's soul."—**Roz Nay, bestselling author of** *Our Little Secret* **and** *The Offing*

Praise for Nicole Lundrigan's
AN UNTHINKABLE THING
Shortlisted for the 2023 Crime Writers of
Canada Award for Best Crime Novel

"From the enticing first pages to the shocking last lines (don't peek!), Nicole Lundrigan's *An Unthinkable Thing* explores the trauma of loneliness and the power of belonging. . . . You'll be deeply moved by this thoughtful and atmospheric page-turner."—Ashley Audrain, #1 national bestselling author of *The Whispers*

"Gothic horror meets literary suspense . . . Flawlessly captivating, this is the book I've been waiting to read all year."—Karma Brown, #1 national bestselling author of *What Wild Women Do*

"This twisted suspense story's jaw-dropping events kept me glued to the pages until the ultimate satisfying surprise. A must read." —Hannah Mary McKinnon, bestselling author of *The Revenge List*

"This slow burn mystery builds to an inferno that will keep readers riveted until the final, satisfying page. Five enthusiastic stars!" —Nicole Baart, bestselling author of *Everything We Didn't Say*

"A magnificent example of all the elements of fine fiction—an engaging narrative voice, a profound evocation of time and place, a complex braiding of plot lines [and] a deeply compelling mystery that doesn't wholly reveal itself until the final page . . ."—William Kent Krueger, *New York Times* bestselling author of *This Tender Land*

"A superb read about helplessness, power, wealth, honesty, and truth—nightmarishly compelling."—*Booklist* (starred review)

A MAN DOWNSTAIRS

—

NICOLE LUNDRIGAN

VIKING

VIKING

an imprint of Penguin Canada, a division of
Penguin Random House Canada Limited

Canada • USA • UK • Ireland • Australia • New Zealand
• India • South Africa • China

First published 2024

LIBRARY AND ARCHIVES CANADA CATALOGUING IN PUBLICATION
Title: A man downstairs : a novel / Nicole Lundrigan.
Names: Lundrigan, Nicole, author.
Identifiers: Canadiana (print) 20230465846 | Canadiana (ebook) 20230465854 |
ISBN 9780735242722 (softcover) | ISBN 9780735242739 (EPUB)
Subjects: LCGFT: Novels. | LCGFT: Thrillers (Fiction)
Classification: LCC PS8573.U5436 M36 2024 | DDC C813/.6—dc23

Book design by Emma Dolan
Cover design by Emma Dolan
Cover images: (staircase) © Светлана Евграфова, Adobe Stock Images

Printed in Canada

10 9 8 7 6 5 4 3 2 1

Penguin
Random House
VIKING CANADA

For Simon Archer

"Do not fear autumn, if it has come. Although the flower falls, the branch remains. The branch remains to make the nest."

—LEOPOLDO LUGONES, "ETERNAL LOVE"

PROLOGUE

I'VE COME TO realize there is nothing sweeter than a second chance.

Of course, I knew I'd never see her again. But you and I are together now, and that's what counts. The first moment you smiled at me, all the missteps I'd made in the past were swept away. Forgiven and forgotten.

Most evenings, I am content to gaze at you through the window. My actions feel comfortably familiar, and each time I linger in the backyard, I automatically envision a dozen ways in. Cheap locks or forcible doors. That worthless plastic clip securing the bedroom window. But I won't do that this time. With her, I played a different role for different reasons, and now I have other ideas.

Though tonight, as I stand on the grass beneath a milk-white moon, I feel worried. You are pacing about the kitchen, a phone pressed to your ear and concern on your face. I wonder if you are safe. If you are happy. As I follow your steps, my left leg buckles from pain. Glancing down, I catch the glint of metal. Fingers gripping the splintery shaft of an axe, its dull blade jabbing my calf. I can't recall picking it up. And I take a moment to remind myself that I am like everyone else. Choking with apprehension. Prone to dark thoughts.

I rest the axe against the side of the house. I will remain measured this time, and not rush ahead. Second chances don't come along very often.

NOW

•

CHAPTER ONE

Molly

"what if it's a scam?"

"It's not a scam."

"But it could be, Mom. You don't know everything."

There was a sneer in Alex's tone, and Molly realized her teen-aged son was baiting her. Instead of responding, she gripped the steering wheel, focused on the curving road ahead. She still hated this stretch of the drive. These last few miles before they passed the mouth of that narrow dirt trail. When she was a child, some-one had erected a white cross in the ditch beside it. A glaring reminder for her, her father, and the entire town of what hap-pened there.

"If it's real, this place better not be a total dump," Alex mumbled as he unwrapped a hard candy, tossed it into his mouth.

This place was a cheap furnished rental that Molly had found online. Several overexposed snapshots suggested it was bright and clean. In no way luxurious, but choice was limited in a town this size. The owner was flexible with dates, mid-September to whenever, and the location was ideal, only about a twenty-minute walk from her childhood home.

"There's a roof and running water. How bad can it be?"

"Are you serious?" He slumped down in his seat. "I should've stayed with Dad."

A pain prickled through her chest. Since Leo left a year ago, Alex had seen him only a handful of times. At first calls were sporadic, unreliable, and before long they tapered off altogether. Then last spring, Leo purchased a one-bedroom condo with his latest girlfriend. Purposefully, Molly suspected, so there was zero room for a sweaty sullen teenager. Especially one who needed to monitor his food intake, his blood sugar, his insulin.

"I was joking," she said. "If it's awful, we'll pack up and head over to your grandfather's."

"We should have done that anyway."

She sighed. If they stayed with her father, she knew she'd be swallowed by the sadness of him. He'd had a massive stroke six weeks earlier. A passerby found him crumpled on the front step of his home and called for an ambulance. He was rushed to the hospital in the city, and when Molly arrived, doctors explained that the damage to his cerebellum was extensive. Even so, Molly had fully believed he'd recover. That he was simply hidden beneath some gauzy layers of confusion. But when he finally opened his watery eyes, there was no glimmer. No recognition. Just a blankness that broke her in two.

"I thought it was better," she said. "For us to have our own space. You'll hardly be around, anyway. What with school. And, well, your hours." Two hundred of them, to be exact. Community service for a terrible error in judgment involving his cellphone camera and a girl.

Alex turned his head toward the window, folded his arms over his ribs. "You always do that."

"Do what?"

"Bring it up when I'm trapped. Not like I can get out."

She glanced at the silver handle inches from his fist. Her mind spat out a scene. One fluid movement, unsnapping his seatbelt, shoving open the door, and rolling sideways. The dullest thud as his slender body hit blacktop.

"Fair point, darling. I'll try to speak only when you have a viable means of escape."

He didn't laugh, just unwrapped a second candy. The hard edges clinking against his teeth. She wondered if his blood sugar might be low. She wondered if she should ask. Nothing about their interactions seemed straightforward anymore.

Just ahead, a faded wooden sign said "Welcome to Aymes!" Beside the words was a ghost of a corncob with a bandana knotted around its kernel neck. Even though she tried to control her reaction, the sight still made her palms grow slick. They were nearly there.

Around the next bend, the yellowing fields gave way to a dense belt of trees. It was jarring, the sudden shift from vast openness to towering branches, rising up, pressing in, covering the road in leafy shadow. On the north side, the ground began to angle steeply, climbing higher and higher.

As though on cue, Alex bolted upright, pointed out the window. "And that's where it all went down."

The white cross had long ago decayed, and the once obvious road was now nothing more than an overgrown path, its entrance blocked by a red metal barricade. Years ago, men would drive through the brush to a drop-off point called the overhang. They'd lower their tailgates, toss trash into the deepest part of Rabey Lake. Bottomless, locals used to say. Things simply disappeared.

"I guess so," she said.

"Nobody really knows the whole story, but that dude still went to jail?"

Molly sighed again. They'd had this conversation innumerable times. "Yes, Alex, he went to jail. Until his conviction was reversed."

He was right, though, about no one knowing the entire story. A clear determination was never made about the location of her mother's death. It was possible she'd died in the garage at their home. Or was killed on the overhang. She could have been dumped over the side while still alive, drowning in the lake. And her skeleton remained there, bare bones tangled up with stained mattresses, pieces of scrap, torn chairs with wild rusted springs. Nearly forty years had passed, and Molly still thought of her mother every day.

"How's that fair?" he said. "All because you 'guessed so.'"

Her spine stiffened. He was being cruel now. Itching for a fight. He knew she'd witnessed her mother's death when she was a child. And that the following year she'd testified during the trial. Though proceedings were a blur, there was one moment she recalled with absolute clarity. The entire jury leaning forward as she'd whispered, "There was a man downstairs."

Later, of course, she understood that the individual who'd entered their home was not a man at all but a skinny boy. A year or two older than her own son was now. She could still picture Terry Kage, seated beside his attorney, shaggy hair and acne-scarred cheeks. His gangly form floating inside a beige suit with massive lapels. He might have worn that outfit to his high school prom. If he had gone.

When Alex was younger, he'd often peppered her with questions about his grandmother, the boy, the murder, but it was out of concern for Molly's well-being. Lately, though, his interest had intensified. He'd been snooping in her home office and found the one box she'd kept hidden. Her legs weakened when she discovered him sitting cross-legged on the floor, surrounded by pages of the police report, crime scene photos, trial transcripts. "Some of this is bullshit," he'd said. "You know that, right?"

As they rounded another turn, Molly slammed the car brakes. Alex lurched, smacking his palm on the dashboard.

"What the hell, Mom?"

"Oh, honey, look."

On the road in front of them, two deer had stopped. One larger, and one slightly smaller. Heads lifted to stare at them, the undersides of their tails white and flickering. Perhaps mother and son.

The doe stood her ground until her fawn had trotted down the shallow embankment on the other side. Then she darted behind him, the pair vanishing into the woods.

"Now you don't see that in the city, right?"

"Whatever," he growled. "Can we get going?"

"Doesn't hurt to pause and appre—"

"I told you a million times already. Quit trying your shrink garbage on me."

Annoyance bubbled inside her. How could this be the same boy she'd birthed, wore on her chest, played with for hours? Even slept on the floor of his bedroom when he was afraid of monsters. She'd desperately wanted to give him the intense dedication her own mother had once given her. Her father had often described it in detail when she was young, so Molly knew exactly how much she was loved. But instead of a similar bond, she could barely talk to her son.

Alex lay his cheek against his seatbelt. Hard crunch then, like crystal shattering, as his molars pulverized the sugar down to dust.

CHAPTER TWO

WHEN MOLLY PULLED into the driveway of the rental, a man was standing in the middle of the lawn. He was tall and gangly, the buttons of his plaid shirt misaligned. Behind him was the tiny bungalow she'd seen on the rental website. The wood siding had a deep chestnut stain, and the front was shaded by a steep roof.

As soon as she parked, the man began striding toward them.

"I guess that's our landlord, Mr. Farrell."

Alex groaned. "Why does he look pissed?"

"No clue." She rubbed at the dry patch on her left elbow. A tiny spot of psoriasis that persisted, no matter how many treatments she tried.

"Finally made it," the man said, as they stepped out. The lenses of his glasses were riddled with scratches, and it was difficult to see his eyes. "I'd expected you much earlier."

"Oh?" Though they'd been slow getting on the road, she couldn't recall giving him any indication of when they'd arrive. "Sorry about that."

"Well, we won't dwell. How was your trip?"

She glanced at Alex. "Blissfully quiet, thank you, Mr. Farrell."

"No need for formality, Molly." He tugged off his glasses and rubbed them with the hem of his shirt. "I prefer Russell. Or Russ. Not Rusty, though, if you don't mind."

"Got it," she said. "Russ, but not Rusty." She put her hands on her lower spine and stretched. A joint in her back popped.

Russell clapped his hands together. "Should we get you folks unpacked?"

"We can manage. Thank you though. We'll just need the keys."

He put up his palms and shook his head. His comb-over was a pale and unnatural color. Like butterscotch smeared on his scalp. "I wouldn't dream of it," he said. "Consider it part of services provided." Then he reached for the trunk latch.

When Russell turned his back, Alex rolled his eyes at her.

The screen door creaked when she opened it. The place was exactly as pictured online, though it appeared smaller. Cramped. The cupboards were basic brown, the countertop an uncluttered white. Pushed into a corner was a square table large enough for her and Alex to have dinner. It could also serve as a desk for when she connected with her young clients who'd opted to continue therapy through remote sessions.

When she walked through the kitchen and into the living room, she immediately took note of the oversized painting hanging above the couch. A basic landscape to most everyone else, but for Molly, the sight of the overhang on canvas was disturbing.

"Impressive, right?"

She jumped. Russell was right behind her, and she could feel the warmth of his breath on her skin.

"Did it myself," he continued. "I'm a beginner, as you can tell."

Molly could recall going there when she was a teenager. Traipsing through the woods until she reached that clearing. Always alone as friends were few and far between during those years. She'd usually stay until darkness rose around her, perched near the edge of the rock, wondering how it might feel to slip through the air the same as her mother had. Would she flail? Would there be a jolt of terror when she struck the water?

"You've certainly captured it," she said, turning her back to it.

"I hike over there fairly often. Set a few snares. Take in the view of Rabey Lake."

"I bet it's really something," she managed, as she envisioned a rabbit caught in a wire noose.

"Sure is. Especially in the fall."

"Which room's mine?" Alex yelled from the hallway.

"You choose," she called back.

While Russell went outside again, she continued exploring. Opened a closet to find a stackable laundry. Peeked into the bathroom. The fixtures were dated, but the shower curtain still had folds from the packaging.

"No pets, as I explained," Russell said over the top of the box he was carrying. "And I can't tolerate rowdiness." He glanced at Alex, who was dragging a bulging suitcase across the tiled floor. "If you could try to be light on your feet, that would be appreciated. Seeing as I'm in the apartment below."

He'd mentioned that in their email exchange. After his divorce, he'd created a "lower-level suite" and let out the upper level. Which was, he said, "much more appealing to clients."

"We'll do our best, won't we, Alex?"

Alex offered no reply as he went out for another load.

"Well, then. You'll notice I've provided a few basics so you won't have to rush out this evening. Seeing as you arrived late and all."

"That's very thoughtful, Russ."

Alex bustled back inside and dropped the last box on the ground. "Trunk's empty." Then he dug his phone out of his back pocket. "What's the Wi-Fi password?"

Russell pursed his lips, examined Alex over the top of his glasses. "A word about that, young man. As you may have surmised, the internet is shared by the entirety of the home. I expect you to be judicious with your streaming."

"Of course," Molly said, taking a step closer to Alex.

"And there are restrictions on the modem. Filters. To keep things appropriate, if you know what I mean."

"I'm sure that'll be fine, right?"

"Yeah, whatever. So, password?"

Russell nodded toward the fridge. There was a sticky note with writing on the front panel. Alex tore off the small paper, went into the bedroom on the left, pushed the door closed with the tip of his sneaker.

Russell raised his eyebrows. "I do hope we're not off on the wrong foot, Molly?"

"Don't worry. He's a good kid." Or he used to be. And she hoped he still was. "Besides, we're not in town to watch endless hours of porn."

Molly's attempt at lightness made Russell scowl, and he brought his hand to the highest shirt button, twisted. "I wasn't insinuating such a thing. I know you've got a lot on your plate. Regarding your father's health."

Her throat tightened. She'd have to get used to strangers with awareness. Aymes was no larger than a thimble, and most residents knew her father. He'd been the town pharmacist, retiring only a few years ago. As a teenager, she'd spent innumerable afternoons at his drugstore, retreating from the cruelty of her peers. Her mother's death had given her an indelible stamp of otherness that did not fade as she grew up. "You're right," she said. "I do have a lot on my plate."

"Well, keys are on the counter. Garbage day is Wednesday. Make a note because I don't do reminders." Russell's mouth widened into a line. A smile, perhaps. "I'll be close by if you need anything."

Then, instead of going outside, he opened the door beside the fridge.

"That's not your actual entrance, is it?" she asked.

"Oh, I'm just being lazy. I have a proper door on the far side of the house."

After he'd gone, she went behind him and pressed her ear to the wood. His footsteps grew softer and softer, and then a distant click from below. She turned the knob, eased the door open a crack. A steep set of steps with another door at the bottom. The light switch had to be in his apartment, as the single bulb suddenly flicked off and the space dissolved into blackness.

Grabbing the keys from the countertop, she locked the door.

When Alex came back to the kitchen, he'd changed into a different hoodie, different track pants. "Can we order an extra-large pepperoni? I'm starved."

Opening the fridge, she saw apples and juice, bread and eggs. A package of hot dogs and one of ground beef, dripping blood onto the empty shelf below. After Russell had gone through the trouble to make their first night comfortable, he'd surely be offended at the sight of a pizza delivery man. "Give me five minutes."

She filled a pot with water and put it on the stove. Slit open the hot dogs, dumped them in. Waited for it to boil.

"Mr. Farrell seems friendly." She peeled the safety foil off a bottle of ketchup.

"Yeah, if you vibe on weirdos."

"That's a bit harsh, Alex."

"So what?"

He flumped down at the kitchen table and screwed a needle cap onto the end of his insulin pen. Lifted his T-shirt, injected the clear liquid into his abdomen. They ate their hot dogs in weighted silence. The instant he'd shoved the last bite into his mouth, he scraped back his chair, cleared away his plate, and returned to his room. Molly kept chewing, swallowing. Barely managing half before discarding the rest.

Before getting up from the table, she took several slow, purposeful breaths. Hoping to calm the sensation inside her head. It reminded her of the rising hum in railway tracks, well before a train barreled into sight. As she taught her clients to do, she tried to identify a single concrete thought that was causing distress. Then examine the evidence to determine if the thought was fact, or if it was a distortion rooted in emotion.

What Alex said in the car had really bothered her. *"Because you 'guessed so.'"*

Perhaps he didn't realize that was a trigger point for her. Perhaps he did.

She'd attended many therapy sessions as part of her training and gone over and over the afternoon her mother died. Relayed the events, answered questions, processed feelings, and reviewed. Her recollection of what occurred was pristine. And therein lay the problem. Though the psychologist had not explicitly mentioned it, Molly believed her movie-like memory was suspicious. The way each detail neatly stacked on top of the one before, and nothing ever altered in her retellings. Based on Molly's experiences with her young patients, people often forgot aspects of a traumatic ordeal, or simply made mistakes. She, however, did not.

As she'd already completed the intensive work to heal, she tried to ignore baseless concerns when they crawled into her mind. That stone of grief hammocked inside her chest would be there for the rest of her life, but why continue to poke at it? Sometimes she told her patients that it was okay to simply accept aspects of a trauma and put those bits away. It was not avoidance; it was a strategy to cope.

Even so, she could still close her eyes and find her mother's killer there. In that moment he was standing in their driveway, he'd reminded Molly of a squirrel. A lock of black hair falling over his eyes, and both fists, like paws, pressed into his chest.

The trial made national news. Not so much for the murder; more for Molly's involvement. *Feisty girl takes down killer. Wonder child wows jury.* In newspapers, Terry Kage's droopy-eyed mug shot often appeared alongside her nursery school photo. Pigtails, plaid smock, crooked, nervous grin. The owner of a local diner clipped an article, slid it into a plastic frame, and hung it on the wall until Molly's father asked him to take it down.

Due to depth, debris, and murky conditions, divers had been unable to locate a body, but there had been overwhelming physical evidence. Copious amounts of blood in the garage, in the car, stains in the soil on the overhang. Even smeared on the boy's hands, face, neck, T-shirt. A clump of long dark hair was tangled in a button on his jacket, and two straight lines marked the dirt, where her mother's heels were undoubtedly dragged toward the edge.

But when it came to the decision those twelve people made in a stuffy room, were Molly's words the most damning? Did hearing those vivid details slipping from the innocent mouth of a four-year-old decide a young man's fate? It took less than an hour before Terry Jerome Kage was convicted in the death of Edie Margaret Wynters.

Several years later, that conviction was overturned. The appeal was based on the argument that the defendant had had ineffective counsel. Terry Kage's lawyer had opted not to cross-examine Molly. When prosecutors angled for a retrial, Molly's father refused to have her testify again, and they declined to proceed. Terry, then twenty-one years old, returned home to Aymes.

As she recalled what happened next, her muscles tightened. She was determined not to think about it, and took several additional deep breaths, exhales slightly longer than inhales. Then she got up, washed the few dishes from dinner, and made herself a cup of chamomile tea.

Carrying the mug into the living room, she sank into a worn wingback chair. Russell had placed a neatly folded wool blanket over the arm. Dry-cleaning tag still stapled to the frill. As she sipped her drink, she examined the enormous artwork again. When she'd told Russell he'd captured the overhang, she wasn't exaggerating. The glistening trees, the clearing, the sharp edge of rock in the foreground. And in the background, an expanse of murky water. A handful of colorful cottages dotting the shoreline on the other side.

Though Alex had labeled Russell a weirdo, she figured he was just a kind but quirky man. Still, she could not understand why he would choose this as his subject. If he knew her father, then surely he knew what had happened to her mother. What type of person would spend hours painting the exact place where a local boy had disposed of a dead woman's body?

CHAPTER THREE

"YOU DON'T HAVE to be here, you know."

"I actually think I do, though."

Molly was sitting in the high school's main office with Alex. Nothing much had changed since she'd attended all those years ago. The walls had been repainted the same mustard yellow. And the heavy curtains replaced with others in the same swampy green.

Alex's knee jiggled up and down. Molly's did, too. Her memories of being stuck inside this building were not positive ones. While some teachers were warm and empathetic, others were distant or dismissive. Her classmates were no better. Molly's mother had worked in the school cafeteria, and though she hadn't died there, students joked about her haunting the lunchroom. Girls would turn out the bathroom lights and pretend to conjure her mother in the mirrors above the sinks. Saying "Bloody Edie" instead of "Bloody Mary." One time, Molly was in a stall when it happened, and she burst out, sucker punching a ninth grade girl in the stomach. The two of them were sent to the office, and she'd likely sat in the exact chair she was perched in now.

"Look, they just need my signature, okay? And then I'm going to see your grandad."

Through the glass door in front of them, Molly recognized Shawna Springer. They'd been in the same graduating class, though she could not recall ever interacting with her.

The door swung open. "Welcome! Come in, come in!" Shawna pulled Molly into a tight embrace, as if they were old friends. "You haven't changed a bit."

Molly had not expected that. "You haven't either, Shawna." Which was true. Her face was plumper, but she moved in the same manner as she had all those years ago. Furtively and slightly hunched, dressed in billowy clothing. Earthy tones.

Shawna sat at her desk and leaned forward, clasping her fingers together. "So, I heard you're renting from Russell."

"You know Mr. Farrell?"

"Cousins," she said, nodding. Then she lowered her voice. "He might seem a bit stodgy, but that guy's got a heart of gold."

Molly thought of him carrying in the bags and boxes. Filling the fridge. Politely asking them not to stomp. "Certainly seems so."

"Now, on to you, young man." Shawna tugged a thin folder out of a pile, flicked open the cover. "How long are you planning to be with us, um, Alexander?"

Alex glanced at Molly, and she waited several seconds before responding. "It's tough to say. I'd anticipate a few months, but it could be more." She paused. "Or less."

"Of course," Shawna said. She made a note in his file. "I'm so sorry to hear about your dear dad. How's he getting on?"

Molly scratched at her neck. What could she say? Her father was not "getting on" in any sense. His movements were minimal. Communication was nonexistent. As he couldn't swallow, he relied on a feeding tube. "As well as can be expected."

"He was a wonderful pharmacist, you know. Never short of a funny story or an uplifting word." She turned her attention back to Alex. "You'll find we've got a bit of a slower pace here, which a lot of folks appreciate. Stop to smell the roses and all that jazz."

Molly followed Alex's distracted gaze. He was taking in the cutesy posters plastered on the walls. An image of a test with a red *X*. *Mistakes mean you're trying!* A soaring balloon with *The sky's the limit*. Two kittens, fur-cheek to fur-cheek. *There's nothing finer than a friend!* If the sight of them made Molly's forty-three-year-old jaw clench, she could only imagine what effect they might have on an anxious teen.

"That said," Shawna continued, "we've still got a wide range of after-school activities. Swimming, woodshop, debate club if that floats your boat?"

Nothing seemed to *float his boat* lately. Other than his cellphone. "He's pretty busy, actually," Molly said.

"Oh?"

"Commitments." She hoped Shawna would think family-related, chores around the house, not scraping gobs of chewing gum off sidewalks while wearing an orange vest.

"Of course, of course. Well, if things free up, Alexander, come see me. We'll get you sorted." She surveyed the paper in her hand. "Now that's exciting. First class is law. We're a couple of weeks into the term, but Mrs. Eliason will get you caught up, lickety-split." She stuck out her arm and handed the sheet to him. "Just give that to the nice lady right outside my door, dear, and she'll help you find your way."

As they were about to leave, Shawna cleared her throat, said, "Might you spare a minute of your time, Molly?"

"Um, sure?" Molly sat back down. Waved to Alex as he shuffled away. He didn't wave back.

"Something I wanted to run past you."

At once, she felt a surge of panic. She'd noticed that happening frequently now. Whenever anyone broached a topic without warning. Not surprising given how those little talks of late had changed her life. The telephone call from the emergency room doctor. The police officer who'd brought her son home in the back of a cruiser. The husband of eighteen years who announced over breakfast that he couldn't tolerate her a single second longer.

Shawna's smile was practically effervescent. "Oh my, you've gone pale. You can always decline."

"Decline?"

"You being a therapist, I thought you might want to roll up your sleeves and pitch in."

"Still lost," Molly said.

"Let me explain." She shifted left to right in her seat. "In recent years we've been exploring various initiatives to support the mental health of our residents here in Aymes. Given my background in guidance, I was the obvious choice to spearhead."

"Okay."

"We've organized activities, but let's say the response was mediocre at best. We can be a stubborn lot, Molly. In a small town, no one wants to air their dirty laundry."

"That makes sense, unfortunately." Molly immediately conjured up a poster for Shawna's wall. A clothesline laden with filthy socks.

"Long story short, we started a peer support line. Callers are completely anonymous. Discrete. They reach out, and all we do is use our listening ears"—she tapped the sides of her head—"and if needed, nudge them toward the right resource. It's all local and volunteer based."

Molly nodded. "That's a worthwhile initiative, Shawna. I've been involved with something similar."

"Figured as much." Shawna lifted her hands up, fingers spread. "Now I know you're stretched, but I'd be falling down on the job if I didn't beg for a few hours of your time. So far it's mostly been hang-ups and heavy breathers, but it's still important for someone to be available."

Molly's scalp was beginning to feel hot, as though she'd been standing too long in direct sunlight. She was stretched. Paper thin. She had to navigate everything related to her father's care and sort through the contents of the house. Plus, she was still working with over half of her young patients using phone and video conferencing. "I don't know. I mean, most of my—"

"Can I at least send you some information? Just for a peek?" She patted a palm on Alex's school file. "I have your email right here."

"Sure," Molly said, as she got up. "I'll let you know."

And before she'd reached her car, her phone was buzzing through her purse.

CHAPTER FOUR

MOLLY STARED AT the tarnished knocker on the front door of her childhood home. A fierce-looking lion clamped onto a brass circle. When Molly was little, the lion's expression had alarmed her. She'd ask her father if they could twist out the ring. "Maybe his teeth hurt. Maybe he wants to say something." And her father would chuckle, reply, "We better not. He might bite."

Lately, those memories had been fluttering up more and more often. Insignificant moments between her and her father. Like the sight of him reattaching a plastic eye to a cloth doll. Or the sensation of him wiping ice cream from her chin. The comfort of being carried firmly in his arms.

As she opened the door, a man hurried into the hallway, an apron tied around his waist, the fabric a pattern of apple halves. His face and head were shaved and shiny. "Nurse Glenn," she said, letting out a breath. "I'm glad you're here."

After the stroke, Molly knew her father would require continual care and that he'd want to remain at home, if possible. The same place he'd lived since the day he was married. Glenn came highly recommended as a local private nurse. And as he and his wife were in the process of separating, he was willing to live in.

Glenn smiled. "Where else would I be?"

She followed him into the kitchen. He plucked up a damp cloth and wiped flour from the countertops. Then flicked on the light in the oven, bent to peer inside. He'd been baking, the air filled with the scent of butter and sugar and delicate citrus. Though she was grateful for everything, it was still disconcerting to see a stranger so comfortable in her father's home.

"So, how's he doing?" she said, as she washed her hands in the sink.

"Good. He's verbalizing a lot."

"And that's progress, right?"

Glenn folded his arms across his barrel chest. "I mean, there are always unknowns with a stroke. But at the same time, we have to remain realistic."

She dried her hands. "So don't be the delusional daughter."

"That's not what I meant at all, Molly." He spoke with a calming authority. "He deserves to hear hope in our voices, doesn't he?"

"You're right." She coughed, hoping to loosen the knot in her throat. "And you two are getting along?"

"Like old chums," he said. "Did I mention your dad and I crossed paths when I was a teenager?"

"No?"

"There was a group of us. Used to hang out in the alleyway beside his pharmacy. Screaming and smoking and all kinds of shenanigans. We were such a bunch of degenerates. Most days, he'd open the door to his stockroom and holler at us."

"Really?"

"Totally. And all these years, I've been sheepish going into his pharmacy. He'd give me a look, you know. Like he thought I was up to something."

As Glenn spoke, Molly became aware of the acid in her empty stomach. She gazed at his hands, pale with neatly trimmed nails. A streak of flour across his left knuckles. She hadn't considered that Glenn might have interacted with her father prior to becoming his nurse. Which was ridiculous, of course, given they'd both lived in Aymes much of their lives. Not that it mattered. Glenn was competent, did not overcharge, and what teenager didn't go through a rebellious streak? She blinked, said, "I know that look." Though she didn't. Not really.

Glenn smirked, then tipped his head toward the window over the sink. "He's back, you know. Home with his mother."

When Molly leaned forward, she saw Bradley Fischer, the neighbor's adult son, pacing about at the end of their driveway. He was holding a phone to his ear and making jabbing gestures with his other hand. A flash of gold around his wrist.

"Yeah, I heard." Her father had mentioned Bradley's return the very last time they spoke. In the weeks since the stroke, she'd kept replaying their final conversation. The oddness of it. How he'd pleaded with her to drive back to Aymes. Insisting they needed to have a discussion.

"About what?" she'd said.

He was evasive. Told her there were things she needed to know.

Something in his hushed tone had made her muscles tense, and she had the childish urge to cover her ears. "Let's chat over the tablet. Remember Alex showed you how to set that up?"

"I don't want to talk to my daughter inside some contraption. This is important."

It can wait, she'd told herself. *It can wait*. Besides, what concerns could a relatively healthy, comfortably retired eighty-three-year-old possibly have? Had his mint plants choked out the roses? Or his favorite barber closed up shop? Perhaps his subscription to *Birds and Blooms* hadn't automatically renewed. Hardly worth a panic.

"Please, Molly." She could hear his breath, slightly labored. "And Bradley Fischer. He's come back."

"Okay? Surely he isn't bothering you in any way, is he?"

Molly had pressed her fingertips into her closed eyelids. Between a full caseload and juggling issues with Alex, she did not have time to entertain her father's whims. He'd always been antagonistic toward the neighbor's son. Bradley's presence put a crimp in the near-constant companionship her father shared with June Fischer. No matter the closeness that existed there, her primary focus would always be her beloved boy.

"I'll call you back, okay?"

It slipped her mind during a hectic week. Then, seven days later, her father collapsed. Now she wished she'd made a better effort. She'd tried to convince herself his reasons were trivial, but she couldn't shake the sense that something was legitimately wrong. And her excuse of busyness had been a cloak for cowardice.

Glenn lowered his voice. "He got caught with the housekeeper, you know. On the bathroom vanity. Toilet bowl still full of bleach."

"That's, um, unfortunate." Seeing Bradley in his bomber jacket and high-top sneakers, Molly found it both mortifying and comical that he had been her first crush.

"Yup. Third wife. Poor bastard was kicked out again."

"Well," she said. "Better luck on number four?"

Glenn was chuckling lightheartedly as she left the kitchen to go to her father. She found him in the family room at the back of the house. Seated in a wheelchair facing the sliding glass doors, a plaid blanket tucked in around his thin legs. Beside him, a bag of beige liquid hung from a metal pole. The thin plastic tube snaked across his shoulder and into his right nostril.

"Hey, Dad," she whispered, as she leaned down to kiss his dry cheek. "How are you doing?"

Molly pulled a chair closer, sat silently, waiting for the wave of sadness to subside. That was the worst part. Those first few minutes. Wondering if he recognized her face or her voice. Perhaps her perfume. Or if he was even in there at all. How badly she wanted to hear him say, "Oh, my lovely darling," as he always did. Looking at her with blind adoration, the kind only a parent could conjure for a child. One that ignored every shortcoming, every mistake.

Though he did not shift his head, his watery blue eyes found hers. "There you are." She reached over and gently squeezed his hand. "There you—" but she couldn't finish the sentence. In case it wasn't true.

She chattered nonstop through the afternoon. Told him everything that had been happening over the past few weeks. The details of her divorce settlement. A description of Alex's awful moods. The request to volunteer on a local peer support line. Though he gazed at her as she spoke, the flatness in his expression persisted. She was uncertain how she was going to manage one-sided conversations every day. Blathering about nothing. How long before she ran out of things to say?

"Nurse Glenn was telling me you used to yell at him when he was young. Do you remember that, Dad? Rowdy kids outside your drugstore?" She squeezed his hand again. His skin was cool. "I wonder if he knew . . ." The possibility had popped into her head. Glenn was some years older than Molly. Could he have known the teenager who'd murdered her mother? Could they have been friends?

Her father made a sound then. Wet. Guttural. And urgent.

"Dad? What is it?"

"That's what I was describing earlier." Glenn entered the family room with a muffin on a flower-rimmed plate. He placed it on a pedestal table next to Molly. "Those verbalizations."

"Do you think he's in pain?"

"Unlikely."

"Or trying to say something?"

Glenn's mouth tightened and then relaxed. "I truly doubt it, Molly. Given the results of his scans. But I can't answer with complete certainty." He checked the feeding bag, the tubing, patted her father's shoulder, and left.

Again, she was ignoring facts that had been explained multiple times. A blood vessel in his right hemisphere. Blocked and then ruptured. Full left-side paralysis. Loss of language and cognition. Possible vision loss. Inability to consume solids. Incontinence. The list went on and on. Unlike Glenn, the doctor had made his position clear. Her father's abilities to process, to function, to care for himself were irrevocably diminished.

She bit into the muffin, squishing a blueberry between her front teeth. A tiny spray of purple ink struck the cuff of her blouse, and she held her arm out. "Damnit." She stood up, walked out into the hallway, toward the basement.

At the bottom of the wooden stairs, she paused. As a child, she'd always felt nervous down there, as the space was damp and dreary. Minimal light came in through the window near the ceiling, and the glass in the basement door faced onto dull cement stairs. Even when she yanked a braided string hanging from the ceiling, the glow from the single bulb did little to banish the shadows.

She located some spot remover on the shelf above the washer and dryer. Slipped off her blouse, and pulled on one of her father's shirts that was hanging on a rod to dry. As she dabbed at the blueberry spatter, she surveyed the floor.

The area surrounding the laundry was even more cluttered than she recalled. Cement walls were lined with fishing rods and reels, photo albums, ancient medical textbooks, piles of dated magazines, holiday supplies, and sagging cardboard boxes taped closed. She could not grasp why her father never tossed anything out. Or why he'd clung to Aymes, for that matter. With all the reminders there, why hadn't he relocated for a fresh start?

Beyond that main area was a crawl space. Withdrawing her phone from her back pocket, she tapped for the flashlight, shone it into the alcove. Much of what was stored in that space had belonged to her mother. *Edie's Things* scrawled on the sides of collapsing cardboard boxes in faded marker. At some point, she'd ask Alex to shimmy in there and tug out those rotted containers.

Molly was surprised to see several lids torn open. Books and papers turned out onto the damp floor and a metal tin of photographs opened. An old item of clothing had been rolled into a ball, tossed to the side. As though her father was frantically searching for something. But what? She brought her fingers to her chin, trying to remember her last visit. Had she even gone down there? Surely she'd have noticed the mess. Hadn't the boxes been intact?

She went back up the stairs, and on her way down the hallway, she noticed a damp towel hanging on the doorknob of the first room on the left. Using the tip of her foot, she nudged open the door and stepped inside. Meant to be a main floor office or playroom, it was where she'd slept as a child. The daisy bedspread and macrame owl were long gone, but her father had kept it as a generic spare. Alex usually stayed there. And now Glenn. His pants and sweater were neatly folded on the end of the bed. Leaning against the lamp on the night table, there was a leather toiletries bag and an opened packet of cheese doodles.

"Okay that I've taken this room?" Glenn filled up the doorway behind her.

Molly's cheeks flushed. "Oh yes, absolutely," she stammered. "I'm sorry. I really wasn't snooping."

She slipped past him, out into the hallway, and he closed the door with a soft click.

"You know," he said in a near whisper, "this placement could not have come at a better time. I was sleeping at the motel over by the highway." He leaned his body a couple of inches closer to her. "Such a depressing place."

"You've been a godsend, Glenn. Really you have."

A phone began ringing, then. Loud and shrill. Glenn's hand jumped to his abdomen, covering the rectangular shape tucked inside his apron pocket.

"Do you need to answer that?"

"I'm sure it's nothing. I've probably won a cruise or am about to be arrested for tax fraud."

"I get those, too." She laughed. "Nothing some bitcoin won't fix." She took a few steps down the hallway, then turned. "Have you been searching for something in the basement?"

"What sort of something?"

"I don't know. Documents? Medical papers? Several boxes have been sorted through. Even some of my mother's old belongings."

Glenn frowned. "I've only been down there to wash clothes."

"Strange," she said, shrugging. "Probably it was Alex last time we visited."

After Molly said goodbye to her father, Glenn followed her to the front door. Out onto the step. "Just so you know," he said, "your neighbor keeps coming by."

"Bradley?"

"No, his mother."

She glanced at the house next door. Mrs. Fischer's face was in the window, but as soon as Molly raised her hand, the curtain dropped. She disappeared.

Another pang of guilt shot through her. In many ways, Mrs. Fischer had been the substitute mother of Molly's life. Teaching her to fry an egg or hem a skirt. Taking her to a department store to buy a training bra. Explaining menstruation and handing her a package of pads. Molly had welcomed it as a child, craved it even, but something shifted when she was a teenager. What once felt like care transformed into constriction. Constant questions. Constant interference. And the more Molly retreated, the more Mrs. Fischer encroached. Their interactions became strained and never quite recovered. Still, the neighbor had shared a close friendship with Molly's father. The news of his stroke should not have come via gossip.

"She insists she needs to see Dr. Wynters." With his feet spread, hands clasped in front of his hips, Glenn looked less like a nurse and more like a bouncer at a nightclub. "Wanted to know the severity of his condition. How well he could communicate, that sort of thing. Of course I didn't divulge a single detail."

"Thank you," Molly said. "I'll stop over. Let her know what to expect. You know, to minimize the shock."

After he went back inside, Molly stayed on the front stoop for a while, not quite ready to leave. Dark clouds covered the sky, and the grooves in the lion's face appeared deeper. He no longer wore that anxious expression, but instead appeared resolute. As if steeling himself against the inevitability of what was happening behind his door.

She needed to do the same. No matter how painful, she had to begin accepting reality. Her father might be sitting there. The shape of him, the smell of him was the same. But the person she loved, and every story or sadness or secret held within him, was gone.

THEN

·

CHAPTER FIVE

Gil

DR. GIL WYNTERS WATCHED a brown sedan skidding on the icy road. Wheels striking the curb. An older woman climbed out, and with deliberate steps, she shuffled along the sidewalk.

"Mrs. Paltry," he said as she came through the front door of his pharmacy. Then he brought his hand to his forehead. He'd completely forgotten. "I'm so sorry. I should have called."

She brushed snowflakes from the shoulders of her ill-fitting coat. "Called?"

"Your prescription is ready, but one of my shipments is late. I'm clean out of that ointment you need."

"Oh, dear. I guess the bad weather?"

"Likely. But I'm expecting the delivery later today."

"Well," she said with a bright smile. "I've been without it for weeks, so I can surely wait another while."

He scanned the brown bottles sitting on the counter. Located the one with her name typed on the label. *Methotrexate 2.5 mg.*

"I'm surprised you ventured out," he said, as he carried it to the front of the store. A cash register sat on an old oak table. "I don't think I've had a single customer all afternoon."

"No? I hope business is better on finer days."

"Usually is." He rapped his knuckles on the wood. "Much better."

She plucked a large container of cod liver oil from a shelf and a cake of Dove soap. Placed them beside her medication. "I'll take those, too," she said.

When she removed her knitted gloves to pay, she winced. Her hands were riddled with yellow crusts, red blotches, as though she'd been scalded by boiling water. Gil had to look away. In all his years at Wynters Even Drugs, he'd never seen a worse case of psoriasis.

"Let me reimburse you for your gas. Your bother." He pushed the paper bag toward her. "I insist."

Her cheeks flushed pink as she eased her gloves back on. But she laughed, said, "You'll do no such thing, Dr. Wynters."

The bell over the front door jangled as she left, and seconds later, jangled again. A man in a brown uniform was standing on the mat, carrying the missing box of supplies. Gil rushed past him, stomping through the sidewalk slush in his leather dress shoes. He called out, waved his arms, but Mrs. Paltry was already inside the idling sedan, gray exhaust chugging from the muffler. Wheels spitting slush as it drove away.

"Darnit," he said, as he went back inside. His striped socks soaked with dirty water.

That evening, he slipped on his coat, his rubber overshoes, and after locking up the pharmacy, he slowly drove through town. The sky was close and black, thick snow still tumbling, wipers barely beating it away. On the passenger seat beside him was a white paper bag. Opening neatly crimped, sealed with a single staple. Gil never did deliveries. But he could not stop thinking about Mrs. Paltry. How pain had shot across her face. And her steady pleasantness, even with those blistering sores.

He crossed the railway tracks. On that side of town, referred to as East Aymes, the homes were tiny, jammed together. Most of the front yards were a clutter of car parts and rusted bicycles. Soggy springless chairs. Tonight, though, everything was covered in a thick white blanket. The mounds of refuse had been transformed into something mysterious and strangely arresting.

Gil had made note of Mrs. Paltry's address from her file and found her home without issue. He pulled into her driveway, parked behind what was likely the brown sedan, though it was piled high with snow. He waded through a drift and tapped on her screen door. Beads of condensation trickled down on the inside of the glass.

"Dr. Wynters," she said. "What on earth?" She pushed the door, held it open with her slippered foot. Her dress had short sleeves, and the crook of her elbows were red and raw. "Come in, come in. Have you had dinner?"

Warm air billowed out into the night, heavy with moisture, the smell of boiling noodles. "No, thank you, I can't. I've just come to drop the ointment."

She took the paper bag in one hand and put the other hand over her heart. "Oh, you good man. You shouldn't have. And in this wretched weather."

Deeper inside the house, a television blared. The exaggerated voices of a soap opera. A girl was laughing, then. "Pitiable, Mom," she called out. "Quick. Come see."

"Well, I'll be on my way," Gil said, stepping backward.

"Thank you, Dr. Wynters." Mrs. Paltry lifted the paper bag, crinkling the paper. "I won't forget this."

With the sleeve of his coat, he swiped away the layer of fluff that had already accumulated on the windshield. Once inside the car, he twisted the key, but the engine would not turn over. Another twist. A clicking sound, but nothing else.

When he left his car for a second time, Mrs. Paltry was already opening her front door again, calling over her shoulder. "Dr. Wynters's battery is dead. Right in our driveway!"

Gil had expected a man, but a young woman appeared behind her mother. She had a round face, long dark hair parted in the middle, and was wearing a cardigan over a thin floral dress. She clomped down the wooden steps in a pair of enormous winter boots that surely did not belong to her. Without glancing in his direction, she lifted the trunk of the car that was nose-to-nose with Gil's. An explosion of snow, and she yanked out a tangle of cables. Hoisted the hood then. He moved toward her, reaching for the cables, but she twisted her body, blinking rapidly. "Excuse me? Did I ask for help?"

He found her attitude unusual. But amusing. He'd let her puzzle over the connections a moment or two until she threw up her hands, admitted her confusion. He propped open the hood of his car, then stepped aside, clasped his hands behind his back. How could a woman as short and thick as Mrs. Paltry produce a daughter who was a beautiful reed?

Instead of getting flustered, she began clipping the copper teeth to the terminals. Red to the dead. Black to the donor.

He was surprised. "Not your first time?"

She did not smile at him, just wiped her bare hands on her sweater after she'd finished. Got into her car and started it. When her engine was humming, she climbed out, and said, "Try now."

He slid into his car, cranked the key. Several coughs, and then his automobile growled to life. He revved it once, twice.

"Now don't turn it off," she said, hands on her hips. "You'll need to keep it running for twenty minutes. Half an hour, if possible."

He resisted saying *I know*. She unhooked the cables in reverse order, then slammed her hood shut. Slammed his as well.

He leaned out the window. "Well thank you—"

"Edie. It's Edie."

"Thank you, Edie. You've saved the day."

"Hardly," she said and pulled her sweater across her chest. Then she leaned closer. "You needn't have done that, you know."

"Done what?"

"Risked an accident, coming all the way out here with her stuff. I could have picked it up tomorrow."

The headlights shone straight through the fabric of her skirt. Above the openings of those ridiculous boots, her calves were like long twigs. Gil cleared his throat. "It was no trouble. Really. It was on my way."

Finally, she grinned. "I've learned two things about you tonight, Dr. Wynters. You're a kind person. And you're also a terrible liar."

On the drive home, her words circled around in his head. Not so much that he was an awful liar, but the part about being kind. To his knowledge, not a single person had ever said that to him before. As he replayed her voice, a pebble of warmth began to form in the very center of his chest.

CHAPTER SIX

GIL USUALLY ARRIVED at the pharmacy early in the mornings. He enjoyed working in silence, before customers filtered in
or the phone started ringing off the hook. With a silver blade, he
slid the last five pills across the counting tray and then dumped
the correct number into a glass bottle. Six weeks had passed, and
Mrs. Paltry was due to stop by for her refill. This time, he wanted
everything ready so they might have a few minutes to chat.

When the bell made its tinny jingle, Gil looked up and saw not
Mrs. Paltry but her daughter Edie striding through the door. She
was wearing a bright red coat and a matching hat with a pom-pom.
Her boots, this time, were properly sized.

Smoothing the front of his lab coat, he could feel his heart beating through the fabric. "What a surprise," he said. Though it wasn't.
He'd had an inkling that she would be the one picking up the prescription. He might even be so bold as to call it a premonition.
"How's your mother doing?"

"Better than your car, Dr. Wynters."

Gil was quiet for a moment. He was not used to that. A woman who was brazen. And clever. "It's old," he finally said. "But I'm attached."

"Well, there's no accounting for taste."

In the brighter light of the pharmacy, he realized how young she was. Perhaps nineteen or twenty. The tip of her nose was pink from the cold.

"You don't normally come in for your mother's medicine."

"She prefers to run her own errands. And I prefer to run mine."

"Of course." He slipped the prescriptions into a paper bag.

She jutted her chin toward the counter. "Where's the other one?"

"I'm sorry?"

"I usually see a different man behind the counter."

"That would be Dr. Even." Seth was Gil's partner at the pharmacy. They'd gone to high school together, then college, and now jointly owned the business. Gil worked the mornings, Seth covered evenings, and they usually split the afternoons. "I'm the early bird around here."

"Mmm," she said. She was peering over his shoulder at the wall of shelves, crowded with containers and boxes.

He walked around the counter and over to the register.

"That'll be . . ." He leaned closer to the machine, squinted. "Let me try that again. I messed up the numbers."

She tapped her foot, and her eyes narrowed. He could not explain why, but he found her obvious irritation enormously attractive.

"Do you often mess things up, Dr. Wynters?"

He chuckled lightly. "I actually pride myself on being precise."

"Useful trait, I suppose, for a pharmacist." More foot tapping.

"You're right about that," he said, trying to focus. He wondered if she could see the pulse in his neck. "Ah. Now we have it."

She handed him several bills, and he carefully withdrew the correct change. Dropped the coins into her gloved hand. The threads on the fingertips were coming loose, tiny gaps forming along the seams. She took the bag and stuffed it into her purse. Turned without so much as a thank-you.

"Pass on my best to your mom," he called.

"Yup."

She was already at the door. Fixing the knot in her scarf. Any second, she would disappear, and it would be weeks before he saw her. If he saw her. Realistically, he couldn't park outside her house, waiting for his battery to die again. Though he'd imagined doing just that multiple times.

"Miss Paltry? Edie?"

She stopped. "Did you make another mistake?"

"Nothing like that." He scratched his sideburn. "This may be a bit unexpected, but do you . . ." Why was he so nervous? Even though he was thirty-eight, he was still a fine-looking man. Tall, fit, with blue eyes and a decent head of dark brown hair. He was educated, earned a respectable living. All of that had to be appealing, and no woman had ever turned him down before. He cleared his throat. "What do you say about grabbing a bite?"

"A bite?"

"Dinner, I mean. To thank you for getting me out of a jam. You know, out at your place last month. I could've been stuck there all night, right? Frozen to death. Um, there's a great Italian place just two doors down." He was rambling, and he clasped his sweaty hands together.

For several seconds, she stood with her hand on the doorknob. Her expression was blank, jaw clenched. Was she going to decline? Whenever single women came into the pharmacy, it was often an effort to nudge them out. They'd chitter on about the forecast, a particular brand of canned tomatoes, a minor fender bender that happened a block away. Mind-numbing pointlessness.

Then it struck him. Perhaps Miss Paltry was not a single woman. Perhaps she was already spoken for.

"It's okay if you don't—"

"Fine," she said. "I'm free tonight. I'll meet you at six." Then without so much as a glance over her shoulder, she thrust open the door and stepped out onto the salt-covered sidewalk.

He grinned, a boyish delight spreading through him. "Not bad, old dog," he whispered to himself. "Not bad."

Since that first moment he saw her, he'd been existing within this warm floaty space. As though someone had clipped helium balloons to his wrists, the cuffs of his trousers. Edie Paltry was going to change the shape of his entire life.

•

When Seth appeared mid-afternoon, he took one look at Gil and said, "What the heck's wrong with you?"

"What do you mean?"

"You've got a weird smirk on your face."

"Nothing really. Just a date."

Seth removed his wool cap, smacked Gil's arm with it. "Finally, you're taking another swing at things. Andrea will be delighted." Seth had met his wife during the first semester of college. From that night forward, they'd been inseparable and had recently celebrated seventeen years of marriage.

"Tell her she needn't get ahead of herself. It's just one meal."

"And who's the lucky lady?"

"You know Mrs. Paltry? The woman with the—" Gil scraped at his arm with a fingernail.

Seth's eyebrows went up. "You're kidding me."

"No, not her," Gil said, smiling broadly. "Her daughter."

"Her daughter?" Beneath Seth's shuffling feet, a puddle of gray water had formed on the linoleum. "Are you certain?"

"Certain about what? I know she's young. But she's not that young."

"I don't mean her age. It's just." Even though the store was empty, he lowered his tone. "You know Andrea's in the office over at the high school, right? And Edie Paltry works in the cafeteria."

"Well, look at that. My date is gainfully employed, too."

"Sure, sure. But you know how women are. They like to talk. I usually tune it out, but . . ."

Gil bristled. Customers often wanted to gossip with him, and he prided himself on avoiding it. "And your point?"

"I mean." Seth sucked air through his teeth. "I guess you'd say she hasn't had an easy go of things. With her family."

"Seriously, who has?" Though Gil felt a twinge of shame when he said that. Both his parents were gone, and they'd given him nothing but a stable, loving home. Never an argument over the trash or the bills or the length of the lawn. There was always room for forgetfulness, for folly. Seth knew that, too. He had been at Gil's house practically every day.

"Maybe. I suppose. And just so you know, I've never said a word to Andrea about her." He nodded toward the tall metal filing cabinet. "Her business here is confidential."

Her business here?

"Yes, of course it is," Gil replied.

"Well then, that's that." A clap to the back. "Have a great time, pal." And Seth lumbered off toward the stock room.

Gil took a deep breath. Seth had always had periods when he was maudlin. Especially when Gil met someone new. He always thought his friend might be a little envious, and Gil's suspicions had been confirmed two years ago, when Seth was having a sleepless period after their fourth baby. Another boy. He'd complained to Gil that he'd married too young. Never had a chance to sow any oats, wild or otherwise. Though once the baby settled in, and his rest improved, Seth never mentioned it again. At their next anniversary party, he and Andrea seemed as in love as the moment they met.

Still, those questions nagged at Gil. *Her daughter? Are you certain?* And when he heard Seth chatting on the telephone behind the closed door, Gil did something he'd never done before. As a pharmacist, it was well within his right, but it still felt like the most minuscule of violations. He went to the cabinet and tugged open the second drawer from the bottom. Quickly leafing through, he found the correct folder and opened it. A few typed pages, notes in Seth's scratchy handwriting. Gil scanned them line by line. He could not identify the ailments with total certainty, but he now knew every prescription that Edie Paltry had ever filled at Wynters Even Drugs.

CHAPTER SEVEN

DIAZEPAM 2 MG. Gil took a single pill before he left home, and by the time he reached the restaurant, the prickles of anxiety in his stomach had subsided.

Edie was already waiting outside. Her breath making clouds in the icy air.

"You look lovely," he said as he opened the door for her. A forest-green skirt stuck out from beneath her coat.

"Okay," she replied.

The hostess led them to a table by the window. Edie tugged off her hat and poked it down the sleeve of her coat. As she unwrapped her scarf, Gil gazed at her in the glass reflection. Static fluffed her hair, and in the dip of her wool sweater, he could see her clavicles. Sharp and defined. Her face was pale, too. He wondered if she'd been taking the iron supplement her doctor had recently prescribed.

"Is this okay?" he asked, as they sat down. "If you're chilly, I could request something farther back."

"I don't really get cold." She touched the fork and spoon on the tablecloth. Straightening them. "I've never been here before."

"No? It's been around for ages, I think. Since I moved to town, anyway."

When the waiter appeared, he faced Edie with his white notepad, pen poised. "Miss? Something from the bar?"

"I don't know." She glanced at Gil. "If I'm, I mean . . ."

"Two glasses of chardonnay," Gil said. "Unless you prefer something else?"

"Um. That's good I guess." There was a genuine shyness about her that he hadn't anticipated. Confident with booster cables, less so with a wine list.

"I'm curious," she said, after the waiter retreated. "Why would you choose to live here?"

"In Aymes?"

"Yeah."

"Well, my business partner, Seth, suggested it. We always planned to open a pharmacy together. And with his family growing, he wanted a quiet place to settle down."

"I'm sure you'd prefer a city, though."

"Not really. I like the calm."

She frowned. "I'm the opposite. Quiet makes me itchy."

"That's because you're young," he said. "And I'm, well—"

"Not so young."

It was the first time he'd see her smile that evening. Gil exhaled. He hadn't realized he was holding his breath.

When the waiter brought the drinks, Edie still hadn't opened the menu, so Gil ordered for both of them. Leafy green salads, chicken Parmesan, and liqueur-soaked sponge cake with spiked cream for dessert.

"So," he said, sipping his wine. "You work at the high school?"

"How'd you know that?"

"Seth mentioned it. His wife's part-time in the office. Andrea Even?"

"Is she one who's always pregnant?"

"Yes, that's her. They've got four boys. She's determined to have a girl."

Edie shuddered. "Why? Because a girl is any better?"

Gil laughed, took another mouthful. The alcohol was mixing with the sedative and a calmness had diffused through his entire body. Pleasant numbness head to toe. "That's hectic, I bet. Your job in the lunchroom."

"Not really. Mostly I'm behind the counter. Passing out corn dogs or cartons of milk. I get to bring the leftovers home, though, but it's usually just carrots."

"And you enjoy being around teenagers?" He thought of the rowdy bunch that loitered in the alleyway between the pharmacy and the veterinary clinic. With their snug jackets and flared jeans, spindly moustaches, and unkempt hair. When he opened the back door to toss out the trash, one would usually holler, "You got any good shit in there, Pops?" And he'd inevitably reply, "Certainly do, boys. If you bring me a 'script from your doctors."

"Teenagers can be perfectly decent," she said. "You've never been one yourself?"

The waiter was back, his arms full. As soon as the plate was in front of her, Edie picked up her knife and fork and cut the entire chicken breast into bite-sized pieces.

"Well, Dr. Wynters?" she said as she chewed. "You didn't answer me."

He laughed again. "Edie, you need to call me Gil. And yes, of course I've been a teenager. But I don't think I was perfectly decent."

"Then how were you?" she said, stabbing another cube.

The first words that came to mind were *bashful, geeky, weak*. In high school, Seth had always been the cool, adventurous one. Lighting little fires, stealing packets of Certs. Gil had only followed. Seth was the one who was livid that they were too young to enlist, while Gil had been relieved. When they were older, Seth would run his fingers up the skirt of any girl who'd allow it. Gil would hesitate, his face burning when he asked permission to hold a hand. Finally, he replied, "I guess you could say I was typical."

"And 'typical' is code for boring, right?"

He grinned, crunched a piece of lettuce, and tried to change the topic. "You know, I've never met an Edie before."

"I was supposed to be an Eddie."

"After your father?"

"Yeah."

"So you two are close, I bet." His glass of wine was empty. His meal was mostly untouched. But he was enjoying watching Edie. The way she nibbled at a string of cheese. The way her long neck stretched and compressed as she swallowed.

"The other one with the wife didn't tell you?"

"Who, Seth? Tell me what?"

"That old man's a done deal. He's history."

"He left your family?"

She put down her fork. "No, like real history. Worm food."

"Oh." Gil understood. He'd passed away. "I'm so sorry to hear that, Edie. That must have been difficult."

"It's fine."

"Is it?"

"A relief actually. To be rid of him."

"I'm sorry," he said again. He hated to think what had happened for her to have such a dark attitude toward a parent. Perhaps that was what Seth had meant. She hadn't had *an easy go of things.* "I really shouldn't have pried."

She stared out the window. "Not being able to predict, that was the worst part. One day he was buying out a toy store, next day, burning every doll I owned. Our house was always torn up. All kinds of grand ideas, started and never finished." Her words were steaming up the cold glass. "He'd stay awake for days, then sleep nonstop. Once he bought a plow for his truck to clear snow. Worked a day and a half and then climbed to the top of our neighbor's roof, threatened to jump." She turned to face him. "'Come on, kids' was what he said. 'Watch me make a real snow angel.'"

"That sounds horrific, Edie." He could not fathom it. A defenseless child exposed to such behaviors.

"Yeah, but it's all over now. Last spring he broke into the motel near the highway ramp. Got himself a free room, you could say. Died there."

Gil leaned forward. "Was it unexpected? Sudden?"

"About as sudden as a bullet through the brain."

"Oh," he said again. Did she mean an aneurysm? A heart attack? An actual gun pressed to his skull? "In all those years, did he ever receive any type of help?"

"For what?" She scowled. "The man had a lifetime ticket on his own personal roller coaster. There's no fix for that."

"Yes," Gil said. "Yes, there surely was."

"Well, even if that's true, he didn't want any of it. And you can't force somebody to be better than they're meant to be."

Gil sighed. "No, I suppose not."

"So that's all our dirty wash. Figured I'd tell you, so you'd know what the Paltrys are all about."

He reached across the table, brushed his fingertips over hers. "Whoever your father was doesn't cast a shadow on you. You're your own distinct person."

She tilted her head. "How would you even know?"

"It's the same for everyone. Just take me as an example. My family's dull as dishwater. But I'm handsome. A crackerjack. Oozing so much charm, I'm basically a buoy in a pond of it."

She rolled her eyes. "To be honest, Dr. Wynters, you're quite bland. But my mother likes you immensely."

"It's Gil. If we're going to get along, you can't keep calling me Dr. Wynters."

"No?" She smirked. "You got a rule book hidden under the table?"

Was she teasing him?

After dessert, he drove her home. Some of the snow had melted, so the debris that riddled the front yards was poking through. Illuminated in the porch lights. A rusted barrel. Discarded tires. A child's wagon flipped on its side, wheels removed. When he pulled into her driveway, she leaned over and pecked him on the cheek. "Later days, then."

"Yes, Edie," he said as she climbed out of his car. "I hope so. Later days."

Gil drove away slowly.

When he was little, his mother always told him he'd know when he'd met the right woman. It would be a lightning strike, she'd said, like it was for her and his father. Gil realized, now, she had been right.

By the time he crossed over the railroad tracks, he'd decided that Edie Paltry would never feel another moment of uncertainty. Another moment of suffering. He'd do whatever it took to win her over. And then he was going to marry her.

Him

I NEVER KNEW the perfect woman existed before that chilly spring night when I was thirteen. When she appeared out of nowhere and saved my life. I'm certain that if she hadn't stopped her car, things would have taken a dark and dangerous turn.

One of the older boys had his license, and the evening started with seven of us packed into his parents' car. A brown station wagon with dark wood paneling. My friends and I liked to cruise around East Aymes while some of them smoked and drank. They relied on me to sneak my mom's cigarettes. That night I brought an extra surprise to share. A thermos full of stolen rum and fruit punch. It didn't last long, though. They each had a single gulp, and the container was empty.

"Can you snag more, pal?"

"No chance," I said. "She'd notice."

Then someone mentioned the skanky hag who worked at the cottages on the other side of Rabey Lake. She lived alone at the end of a dirt road, and everyone knew she supplied booze to teenagers in exchange for certain types of favors.

A wide U-turn, hands slapping the dashboard, and we were headed in her direction. When we pulled up beside her house, the lights were off, though the television screen glimmered green behind the sheer curtains in the window.

"Who's going in?" I asked. I knew they wouldn't make me do it. Or my friend sitting next to me. We were the youngest. Both still in middle school. What could either of us even give her?

"Well, I went last."

"No, I did. Couldn't get the stench off me for a week."

We played several rounds of rock, paper, scissors. And somehow, I emerged the obvious loser.

"Off you go, pal."

"But—but what am I supposed to say?"

"Just talk to her, buddy. See what she's in the mood for."

"What does that mean?" I stared out the car window. Hard rain pecked against the metal roof.

"Look, don't sweat it. She's fucking loaded by now."

"Whatever she wants, it'll go quick."

"Just diddle her with your hand, sure. But trust me, don't kiss her on the mouth. You'll puke."

The walkway leading to her front stoop was wet and glistening. A garden gnome sat with its chubby legs hanging over her bottom step. "I can't," I breathed.

"What? You lost the game fair and square. You gotta man up."

"I can't," I said again. "I can't do it."

Someone rolled down a window and spat. "You're such a loser."

"Yeah. Total chicken shit."

"Fucking pussy. Get out." Several sharp elbow jabs in my ribs. "And don't come back 'til you got something good."

I waited, but no one else volunteered. I left the car and crept up to the house on shaky legs. There was a wrinkled note taped above her doorbell that said "knock reel loud," but I didn't knock at all. Instead, I cracked open the door, slipped into the shadows of her entryway. The air reeked of sour sneakers and fryer grease. "Hello?" I said softly.

Two steps in, a cat appeared. Wound itself around my legs.

"Hello?" I whispered again. "Hey. Can I use your toilet?"

No one answered.

"Excuse me? Is anyone home?"

Another step, and when I turned to my left, I saw the lady spread out on the couch. Wearing only a bra and panties. Archie Bunker was on the television, and the glow from the screen danced over her chest, her stomach, making her skin gleam. The soles of her feet appeared stained.

I don't know how long I stood there, watching her. I realized my friends were right; she was likely drunk. And I could actually diddle her. If I wanted to. If I even knew what that meant. It probably wouldn't be that awful, and I'd get the whole weird experience out of the way.

I imagined myself tiptoeing over, squeezing her tits, sliding a steady hand down her front part. Wriggling my fingers through that fuzzy hair and whatever else was there. And because I did it all correctly, she'd sit up and say, "You're working some magic there, darling. What's your name?"

When she groaned and shifted her leg, I quickly swiped a bottle from the counter and blasted out the door. Leapt down the steps, accidentally kicking the gnome from its perch. When it struck the ground, its head spun one way, its stocky body, the other.

The car door was already wide open, frantic outstretched hands. I heaved myself in on top of my friends, and they were ready to receive me. Yelping, whooping, slaps on my back. The wheels of the car spitting up gravel as we tore away. My rib cage could have exploded from the joy.

"Shit man, you did it."

"Was it bad? Was it really fucking bad?"

"No." I shrugged. "Not really. I mean, nothing I haven't done before."

More yelps, more whoops, more slaps on my back.

"So, what'd you get? What'd you get?"

We drove along a dark stretch of road. "Not sure," I said. "I just grabbed one."

Then a snap, the yellow dome light illuminating everything.

"Here, give it over."

"Aw, fuck. It's the red shit."

"What?"

"Grenadine. You seriously screwed her for fucking grenadine?"

The car screeched to a halt.

"Get out!"

"Who?" I asked. "What?"

"Yeah, doofus. Get the fuck out."

"I didn't know," I stammered. "I couldn't see what I took. Wh-what she gave me."

One of my friends opened the door and stepped onto the road. He clutched at my clothes, yanking me from my seat and pulling me into the empty night. A fist in my spine, then, and my gangly legs stumbled. I tripped down the gravel slope, landing in the stagnant water in the bottom of the ditch.

"I made a mistake," I yelled, just as the grenadine bottle popped off my shoulder, landed beside me with a splash. "She screwed me over!"

But they just tore off.

It felt as though I knelt in the muck for hours. Rain kept striking my scalp, making me shiver. I was too afraid to move. Too afraid to go up to the road or back to the drunk lady's house. Thick woods rose up on both sides, branches scraping, shifting. I had the sense something was watching me. Perhaps a tiny bird. An animal? Or maybe even a lonely man with a scraggly beard, buck naked inside his survival suit.

I cried a little. My nose ran. I wiped it in the sleeve of the sweater my mother had knitted for me. Was she worried? Had her intuition alerted her to the fact I was in danger? Was she out searching for me?

Then bright headlights rolled over me. Reddish haze from the brake lights, and the sound of gears changing. At first, I thought my friends had returned, but the car reversing toward me was smaller. A girl leaned over from the driver's side, shoving at the passenger door so it opened.

"Are you actually stuck down there?" she called.

She wasn't that old. Her dark hair was loose, and her face was pale with wide-set eyes.

I crawled out of the ditch and got into her warm car. My teeth were chattering, and she must have noticed because she twisted a knob, snapped open a vent. Hot air shot onto my soaking body.

"Where can I drop you?"

I told her, and then she said, "I don't live too far from there. For a bit longer, anyway."

"You're moving?"

She didn't answer me.

As we turned onto a main road, I mumbled, "My mom's totally going to kill me."

"With the state you're in, you deserve it."

She was wearing an argyle skirt and a cropped top that hugged her ribs. It was tough to tell what color the outfit was, but I guessed yellow. Like buttercups. A girl like her could wear that sort of thing.

"Were you out to that lady's house, too?" I asked.

"The one who sells beer to boys?" She laughed. "No, I just like to drive around."

"Why's that?"

"You're real nosy, huh? I don't know. Maybe I like pretending I'm going somewhere?"

"Oh," I said. "That's cool, sure." Though I wanted to, I didn't ask her anything else. We drove along in silence, except for a song playing on the radio. Folk singer, twangy guitar. When she slowed near the end of my driveway, she said, "So what asshole left you like roadkill?"

"Just my friends." I tried to snicker a little. Like the whole thing was no big deal. "Playing a dumb joke."

"Dumb joke?" She clicked her tongue. "You should steer clear of them."

"Yeah," I said. "Probably I will."

I thanked her, got out of the car, and went up to my house. My mother was in her bedroom with the lights out, which was lucky. Discovering her thirteen-year-old son in such a filthy state would have sent her reeling. Her rant would be followed by a multitude of questions. Which would have led to a multitude of lies.

I didn't heed the girl's advice, of course. Right after lunch the next day, I stopped by the alleyway between the drugstore and the veterinarian. Sometimes our group liked to hang out there. I leaned against the cold brick, handed out more of my mother's cigarettes, and chuckled at my friends' stories. I never mentioned that the grenadine bottle had left a deep purple bruise on my shoulder blade. Or that I was so scared, I nearly pissed my pants. Or that the most gorgeous girl I'd ever seen had picked me up and drove me all the whole way home. The image of her was burned onto my mind.

No one asked either. Instead, they punched my upper arm. Took pretend shots at my jaw, my crotch. Caught me in a headlock and squeezed.

"Aw man, that was messed up last night. Can't believe you fell out of the fucking car."

"Yeah," I said. "It really was."

As the afternoon wore on, I began to rethink things. Perhaps I'd pressed too hard against the handle, and when the door sprung open, I'd tumbled into the ditch. With so many of us stuffed into the backseat, it would have taken them forever to realize I was gone. They'd probably circled and circled and couldn't find me.

Framing it like that was easier. Those boys were the only friends I had. And besides, I was grateful the whole thing happened. Clearly, Fate had been at work. Creating the circumstances for me and that girl to meet. As though we were star-crossed lovers.

I was glad I didn't do the diddling thing with that skanky hag. Now I had a reason to wait.

NOW

·

CHAPTER EIGHT

Molly

THE PIZZA WAS late. Alex still hadn't returned from community service. He'd gone straight there after he finished his first day of school. Molly grabbed a cardigan and went out into the front yard. Watching and waiting would not bring the boy or the delivery any quicker, but it eased her mind to walk back and forth over the lawn.

When she was a teenager, she had often wandered along this very street. She would cut across strangers' properties to get to the woods beyond their backyards. From there, she'd hike to the overhang and stay until cold penetrated her bones. She barely recognized it now. Perhaps the trees had grown, or the homes had been painted; enough change that it was completely unfamiliar.

Several minutes passed before she heard an engine. Yellow headlights came around the curve in the road, and then a patrol car stopped a few feet in front of her. Molly tensed; why was an officer, once again, bringing her son home? She caught a glimpse of the driver. A man, some years older than her, wearing a police uniform.

Alex climbed out of the passenger seat; he mumbled, "Uh, thanks," and slammed the door. The officer raised his hand and drove off.

He strolled toward her, knapsack slung over his shoulder. "Why're you standing outside like some stalker?"

She tried to keep her voice steady. "Waiting. For pizza."

"Delivery guys don't go to the door around here?"

At that moment, a tiny car sped up the driveway, slamming on its brakes. Window down and an elderly man thrust the flat box at Molly. Grabbed the cash she held out and peeled off without so much as a word.

"Woah," Alex said. "Dude needs some serious customer training."

Molly carried the pizza inside, heat from the bottom of the box offering a soothing burn on her forearms. She lingered in the doorway as Alex put his injection in his upper arm. When he was seated, he threw up his hands, said, "Mom? Food? Hungry, here."

"Sorry." She sat down and slid the box toward him. He opened the lid and grabbed the largest slice, chomped onto the drooping end. After he'd consumed several large bites, she said, "Alex? Who was that? Dropping you off." Her words sounded reed thin.

Alex mumbled around the mouthful of food. "Nobody. Just the guy overseeing my community service."

"Is that a common thing for *the guy* to do? Drive kids around?"

"First day on the job here, Mom. So how'd I know?"

She leaned forward, shifted the box. "What was his name?"

"Why does that matter?"

"I'm just making conversation." And yes, it totally mattered. In part because he looked very much like—

"Fine, then." Alex gulped his diet soda. "Officer Kage."

"Kage?"

"That's what I said."

"As in, a relative of Terry Kage?"

"Yup. Older brother. I don't get what's the big deal."

Lyle Kage. "The big deal is . . . the big deal is . . ." Her voice quavered, tone creeping upward. "What do you mean, 'What's the big deal?' I shouldn't need to explain."

Alex plucked out a second slice. "It's fine, Mom. He was cool. And this town is like a broom closet, so I don't have much choice."

She counted inside her head. One, two, three, four. *Fine. Cool. Everything is a-okay.* "You're right, it's not like the city." Then, casually, "What did you guys talk about anyway?"

"Nothing. He just complained about the shit weather."

"The weather? That's it?"

"I mean, mostly."

"What's that mean? *Mostly.*" She hadn't meant to snap.

Alex's jaw stopped. "I don't get why you're freaking out. He was just trying to be nice."

"You need to tell me. Now."

"Seriously?" He swallowed the lump of food in his mouth. "I asked him if people treated him different. Because of what happened with his brother. He said they used to, years ago, and some still did. And that it hurt too much to think about it a lot. He said his brother was really good in school. Best in his class for English. And even though he did dumb stuff, he wouldn't hurt a fly. He was always daydreaming, and he was super smart with cars. Their father owned a garage, and his brother knew what was wrong just by listening." Then he tossed the crust onto his plate. "Happy now?"

"Wow," she said. "Just wow." No surprise that Lyle didn't want to accept the truth about his brother. Even when Molly had witnessed the crime with her very own eyes. Though on some level she understood—what person could absorb such actions from someone they loved? The charges against Alex were miniscule in comparison, but Molly had fought hard against them. Until the moment her son had begun weeping. The memory of it always gave her a stab of anxiety. Alex was as tall as an adult man, but still a boy. Shaking, crying, when the severity of his actions had struck him. She'd wanted to crush him in her arms, so certain he was about to fly apart. "What on earth did you do?" she'd whispered. And as soon as she'd spoken those words, he'd shoved against her. His emotions contained. His face flat. "And that was it?" she said. "That was everything?"

"Nope. I asked him where his brother was now—"

"What?"

"Yeah. He told me he didn't stick around."

Molly looked at the pepperoni on her pizza. Each curled into a shallow cup, full of clear grease. "I suppose," she said. *Didn't stick around* was one way to phrase it.

"Doubt he got a fair shake. For his mistake."

Mistake? "You talk about it so casually, Alex. Killing a person is not some minor slip-up."

"I get it, Mom." Grating irritation, now. "But nobody really knows the whole truth. You said so yourself."

As he glared at her, she realized he could not fully grasp what had occurred. Perhaps he viewed it as similar to his own indiscretion and the fallout from that. Several of his friends back home being forced to limit contact. Their mothers, whom Molly had known for years, no longer pausing to chat when they saw her in the grocery store. Almost overnight, her son had been labeled a bad influence. Treated as though his legal problems were contagious.

Alex tore away a third slice. "Did you know he used to work at Grandad's pharmacy? Before your mother died. He quit right after, though. Obviously." Eye roll.

"Yes," she said, nodding. "I'd forgotten." But she hadn't known that. Out of all the teenagers in town, why had her father hired that particular one? Did he know the family? And why had he never told her? That new thread of connection made her mind swell with questions. Questions her father could no longer answer.

Alex jammed the pizza into his mouth, mumbled, "Inquisition finished?"

"It is. And I'm sorry." There was no reason she needed to react that severely. Terry Kage's brother had no more to do with her mother's murder than Molly did. "It's been a tough day," she said, bumping his elbow with hers. "Was it brutal, though? Community service?"

"Nah. There were a lot of kids there, hanging out and stuff. They had music playing over the speakers. I swept the gym floor with this enormous broom. Pulled staples out of the bulletin board with pliers. Which," he grinned, "was oddly satisfying."

And there it was. A rare instance when he forgot his anger and spoke with joviality. Those moments made Molly feel hopeful. Reminding her that the comfort and closeness they'd shared for so many years had not completely disintegrated. "I was worried you'd forgotten the address," she said. "Or that you were lost."

"I did, actually. But Officer Kage knew exactly where to go."

"Oh?"

Alex shook the can of diet soda over his open mouth. Last drops gone, and then he crushed the aluminum in his fist. "Yeah. He and our freaky landlord used to be friends."

•

After dinner, Alex retreated to his room. Earlier that day, she'd hung up his clothes and put sheets on his bed. Set up the narrow desk with a mug full of pencils and pens, a few highlighters. Collapsed the cardboard boxes. He'd closed his door with the heel of his sneaker and did not mention the effort she'd put in. The moment of connection already dissolved.

Settling on the couch, she opened her laptop. The painting of the overhang was still behind her, but at least she couldn't see it. She went to her patient files, transcribed her scribbly notes on the single patient she'd had that afternoon. A boy, eight years old, who'd been having night terrors since witnessing a convenience store robbery. He'd made incredible progress, and she was considering releasing him from care in the coming weeks.

Once she'd finished, she opened her email. At the top was the note from Shawna, with an attachment. *Aymes Peer Support Line: Training Manual.* Molly scrolled through the document. According to Shawna's "objectives," interactions on the peer support line were not meant to be therapeutic in nature. The goal was "empathetic listening" and, when needed, "to connect callers with professional resources available within the community." There were a series of flowcharts: how to answer the phone, how to assess the needs of the caller, how to direct them in an appropriate way. Molly had to admit, Shawna had done an admirable job pulling it together.

At the end of the instruction manual, Molly discovered a username and password assigned specifically to her. Out of curiosity, she went to the website, clicked the "Volunteer" button, and logged in. The format of the page was clean and simple. All white, and in the very center, a cartoon drawing of a rotary telephone and receiver. Beneath that was a basic text box where the volunteer was meant to include a note about the call.

She slid her headphones over her ears and waited. Staring at the page. After a minute or two, the top of the phone lifted slightly and began to shudder. An old-fashioned *brrrriiinng*. She hesitated for a moment, then moved the cursor and clicked.

"Aymes Peer Support Line, Molly speaking."

Silence. She tapped at the keyboard to increase the volume. "Hello? Is anyone there?"

Breathing. Slow and deep. Molly closed her eyes, and her head filled with the eerie sounds of the person on the other end of the connection. Possibly a man. She could see him sitting on a wooden chair in a darkened empty room. Before Molly could say anything else, the call ended.

The time had already been captured in the text box, and she typed: "No contact. Caller disconnected."

As soon as she pressed "Enter," her screen refreshed, and the phone receiver was shaking again. She introduced herself, and was met with staticky silence at first. Then a masculine voice, impossibly deep. "Hello, Molly."

"How can I help you?"

"I have to be quiet because my girlfriend's asleep beside me. She gets angry if I wake her up."

"That's okay. I can hear you just fine."

"Good, that's good, Molly. You can't sleep either?"

She straightened her back. Then said, "Is there anything you'd like to talk about?"

"I'm a little nervous, actually. I don't usually turn to someone for help like this."

"Well, I'm here to listen. Or I can share resources that are available."

"Let me just grab a blanket, Molly. My bedroom's chilly. Are you in your bedroom too?"

"I'm happy to wait for you."

Rustling in the background. "Ah, all better now." He sighed. "There is something I'd like to run by you. It's her," he said quietly. "We're having problems."

"Do you mean your girlfriend?"

"Yeah."

"Are you comfortable communicating with her about these problems?"

"She won't do things I like."

Molly's thoughts went to camping or backgammon, but then he cleared his throat, said, "With her mouth. It's so wet. And pink. A perfect hole. What sort of things can you do with your mouth, Molly?"

She should have guessed it was one of those calls. The way he'd tried to establish common ground with her, repeating her name over and over. A man, likely no girlfriend beside him, likely bored, likely lonely.

A commotion in the background. A woman's voice, now. "I told you to shut that damn computer down and go to sleep, mister. You got school tomorrow."

"Oh, shit, shit." A click. The virtual receiver slid back onto its cradle, and the ambient noise in her headphones disappeared.

Molly scowled. Not a man at all. Just some high school twit up past his bedtime.

She flicked the lid on her laptop, snapping it closed. Despite her annoyance, she thought she could easily volunteer during an occasional evening. She knew she would usually be on her own, as Nurse Glenn put her father to bed right after dinner and Alex would be doing homework or on his phone. Perhaps it would offer a distraction from the uneasiness that had begun expanding within her. She sensed that the past was drifting closer and closer. Her mother's ghost was part of it. And Terry Kage's ghost, too.

CHAPTER NINE

MAIN STREET WAS busy for midweek at lunchtime, and Molly had to park two blocks away from the pharmacy. Glenn had called to ask if she could pick up her father's prescriptions on her way. Blood thinners and blood pressure pills.

She tightened the thin wool scarf around her neck. The sun was shining, but over the past couple of days, the temperature had dropped. Autumn leaves were already falling, and threads of wood-smoke hung in the air. As she walked along the sidewalk, she noticed a new store here or there, but nothing had really changed. The same red brick buildings, narrow alleyways, chalkboard signs. Worn fabric awnings jutting out overhead. On the opposite side of the road, the village green. A shady expanse of grass and trees with a fountain in the center that spurted murky water. She could recall balancing on the stone lip as a child, tossing in penny after penny, wishing for a mother. Wishing for a family.

When she entered the pharmacy, an old-fashioned bell tinkled above her head. Her father had owned the place since before she was born, and in all those years, he'd rarely missed a day. People referred to him as a "fixture" in Aymes, and he'd only agreed to sell on his seventy-eighth birthday. Dr. Jacobs, the young pharmacist who'd purchased the business a few years earlier, had not changed the name. Or the sign. Or the bell. Molly went to the back counter.

"Dr. Wynters's medications are ready to go," Dr. Jacobs said, smoothing a label onto an orange plastic container. "How's he faring?"

After tapping her credit card on the machine, she dropped the pills into her purse. "Spirits are high," she lied. That was the concise phrase she'd begun using whenever anyone asked. What else could she say? Nobody wanted to hear the truth. She wasn't even sure she could verbalize it.

"Any questions at all, give me a ring. Our number hasn't changed."

"Thank you, I will," Molly said and left, the bell tinkling again as she walked away.

She was about to start the car when a face suddenly appeared in her driver's side window. She flinched, dropping her keys into her lap. An elderly man, wearing a beige overcoat, tapped sharply at the glass with the handle of his cane and gestured for her to lower her window. She did, assuming he was going to ask if the parking spot would be free.

"I'm leaving," she stammered. "Just give me a minute."

After gazing at her for several seconds, he said, "You're—you're Molly Wynters."

She hesitated before replying, "Yes, I am."

With both hands, he leaned on his cane. "The resemblance to your mother is uncanny."

That happened occasionally when she was in Aymes. Older strangers remarking that her appearance was eerily similar to her mother's.

Molly did not quite agree, as in the photos she'd seen, her mother had been strikingly beautiful. Even so, she usually sensed that the observation was not meant to be complimentary. As though the sight of her mother's face, emerging through Molly, was unnerving for some.

A gust of wind played with his comb-over, and he reached up to smooth the strands. "Your dad and I are old pals. We lost touch some years ago when my wife and I moved away. But I got word—he's not doing so well?"

She'd not expected that. Her father had always been something of a loner. Many casual acquaintances, but she could not recall a single trusted friend. Except Mrs. Fischer, of course. "That's true," she replied. "We're taking things day by day."

"Could you tell him I was asking after him? Wishing him a speedy recovery?"

"Sure. And you are?"

"You don't remember me?"

She tilted her head. His eyes and voice were familiar. *Maybe?* "I'm sorry. No."

"You were a youngster, I suppose." He touched his chin with his index finger. "Well, tell him you spoke to Seth. Seth Even. He'll know who you mean."

When she arrived at her father's house, Glenn was perched on a stool in the kitchen, head bent, tapping furtively on his phone.

"Sorry to interrupt," she said, as she slid the paper bag across the countertop.

"Thanks for that," he said, looking up. There was a sheen of sweat on his forehead. "Saves me a trip."

"No trouble. I pass right by." Molly paused, then asked, "I'm curious. How does he manage to swallow them?"

"He doesn't. I administer the dosage through his gastrostomy tube. Dissolved in a little water. It's pretty straightforward, and no discomfort at all for Dr. Wynters." Glenn turned his phone over, covered the black case with his hand. "I can show you later, if you like?"

"That's really okay," she said. "I trust you know what you're doing."

Molly crossed the hallway and went into the dining room. As her father's second-floor bedroom was no longer an option, a hospital bed had replaced the wooden table. Today, his wheelchair was positioned in front of the bay window, facing the street and the strip of grass that divided the two lanes. Classical music was playing on low volume. The mournful sounds of a cello.

"Hello again," she said as she sat down beside him. She fixed the collar of his shirt and smoothed the wrinkles. "You know what I was just thinking about, Dad? When Mom used to dress me. Helping me with tights. Or tugging a turtleneck over my head. The relief when I popped out the top." She adjusted the blanket that was slipping off his knees, tucked it in around his hips. "Isn't that peculiar? How vivid those memories are?"

Her father's head was slumped to the side, jaw hanging open. Inside of his mouth a chalky pink.

She wondered if the impending loss of him was causing her brain to scour every crevice of their family history. Strange, though, that it kicked up moments with her mother. Tea parties and hand puppets, bath time and storybooks. All occurring before she was three. As though secured in her mind like insects in amber.

"Oh, I saw a gentleman today as I was leaving the pharmacy. Said he was one of your friends?" Had her parents known him when Molly was a baby? She took a moment to consider it. Her mother and father happily hosting another couple. Serving some finger foods. Deviled eggs. Maybe a cheese fondue. Molly would be in a playpen or dandled on Mrs. Even's knee. It was pleasant to imagine comfort and contentment within the walls of her childhood home. "He looked about your age. Does Seth Even ring a bell?"

A watery noise erupted from her father's throat.

"He wishes you well."

Another groan. Then his arm fell off the armrest of the wheelchair, dropped into his lap. Hand buckling. Molly straightened his wrist, gently uncoiled his fingers. Each day he seemed thinner and thinner. As though his weight was melting away. Even the gold watch he'd worn forever was now dangling.

She lowered her voice. "Do you hear me, Dad?" She paused. "I wish you could talk back. I miss you so much."

He groaned again.

"Here. Let me help." She undid the clasp on the watch strap. Slipped it over his bony hand. "You don't need to wear that chunk of metal. I'll put it somewhere safe."

Molly carried the watch upstairs to his bedroom. When she stepped into his closet, the scent of his cologne caught her off guard. As though she was surrounded by him. Or who he used to be. She looked at the hangers full of shirts and shelves piled with precisely folded sweaters. The box that held a dapper hat he used to wear on Sundays.

She leaned against the wall, light-headed. Soon this would all be sorted through and boxed up. Whatever was salvageable would be sent off for donation. Blankets, linens, towels. Did anyone even take towels? The remaining items stuffed into black garbage bags, abandoned on the curb. An entire life dismantled.

She located her father's jewelry box on an upper shelf. Inside was a pair of cufflinks, his wedding band, and the sleek box that once held his watch. She carried it over to the bed. When she cracked open the lid, revealing the forest-green interior, she discovered a piece of paper. Slightly yellowed, folded into an uneven square.

Molly sat down on the comforter and carefully opened it. A personal letter, the ink blooming in spots. The handwriting was juvenile, a sloppy half-print-half-cursive, and the words leaned sharply backward.

Dear Dr. Wynters, I know I'm the very last person you want to hear from. But prison gave me lots of time to think about my mistakes. I'm being honest when I say I still don't know what happened that night. Somebody gave me something. Drugs, I suppose. I don't want to say who, but I was stupid enough to swallow them. I don't blame them though. It was my choice, and maybe in the end its a better thing. It messed up my head, but at least I don't got to remember what I did. Mrs. Wynters was always a real kind lady at school and I was an idiot kid.

I don't deserve to be out. I don't deserve nothing. I didn't mean to ruin your life or your little girls life. I'm so full up with regret, sometimes I can't even breath.

I wanted you to know. I'm sorry for everything. Real sorry.

Terry Kage

Molly eased the band of her father's watch around the miniature pillow and then refolded the paper. Slid it behind the watch. For some time, she remained on the side of the bed, the open box in her hands. Waiting for the leaden weight on her shoulders to lift. She hadn't known that letter existed. A letter that essentially amounted to a confession.

She wondered if Terry Kage wrote it after her mother's skull washed up on the other side of Rabey Lake. Soft frontal bones and crowded teeth. Every molar jammed with mercury and silver. By that time, he'd have been out of jail for around four months. Likely telling people his story, his lies. But when dental X-rays confirmed the identity, every awful rumor was erased, every doubt obliterated.

Molly clicked the lid closed. Her father had kept that letter hidden away for a reason. Never uttered a word about it. She was reminded then of the two times she'd seen him cry. The first was the evening her mother was murdered. The second, when he'd learned that twenty-one-year-old Terry Kage had hanged himself from a light post up behind the high school.

CHAPTER TEN

AS MOLLY RANG the bell to the neighbors' home, she recalled the last time she'd stood on those steps. She was a teenager, arguing with Mrs. Fischer about college. Mrs. Fischer had insisted that Molly stay in Aymes. "There's a perfectly decent school nearby." But Molly was adamant about going away and resented the continued over-involvement in her life. When she announced she was already packing, was leaving the loneliness and stigma behind, Mrs. Fischer had scowled. "After all your father's done for you, you're still selfish. How could you turn out like your mother?" Immediately she began apologizing, but Molly was already storming away. Reeling from the sting of that altercation. The confusion of it.

She rang the bell again, and finally heard a man's voice from inside. "I'm coming, I'm coming, for shit's sakes." Footsteps clomping closer. Bradley Fischer yanked open the door.

Molly hadn't seen him up close in years. Other than a few wrinkles around his eyes, a streak of gray at the temples, he looked much the same as when he was young. And she should know. As a child, she'd spied on him constantly. Used to marvel at how he could eat an apple, core and all, in two bites. And how he glistened in the sunshine while lifting weights in his backyard. She'd cried into her pillow the day he moved away.

"Hi," she stammered. "Um. I'm from next door. I was wondering if your mom—"

"Little Molly Wynters! Of course, you're from next door." He grinned at her and stepped to the side. He was wearing the same loose gray joggers and gleaming white sneakers she'd seen him in a few days earlier. "Come on in, neighbor. She'll be back soon. You'll wait."

As she followed Bradley into the house, she was unnerved by the decor. It appeared frozen in time. She remembered the leaf-and-raspberry wallpaper in the entryway, the photo of long-dead Mr. Fischer hanging in the hallway. In the living room, the same sofa was sun-bleached and threadbare, the same coffee tables scratched. With the exception of a brand-new leather chair, Mrs. Fischer had not updated a single element of her home in decades.

Molly sat on the sofa and crossed her legs. Her fingernails found the tiny patch of dry skin on her arm, and she caught herself scratching.

"My mother had to loop back to the grocery store," Bradley said as he plopped down in the new chair. "Last thing I told the old woman was 'Don't forget limes.' And what does she do?" He ran his palms over the leather, the color of cocoa. "She forgets the limes."

"I guess that happens. More so as people age?"

"I mean, sure, but seriously. What's a G and T without them?"

"That's fair," she said, trying to smile.

"I'm expecting her any minute." Then he narrowed his eyes. "Unless of course she's stopped for a rendezvous. With a lover, or something."

Laughter burst from Molly's mouth. Mrs. Fischer was only a few years younger than her father. Seventy-eight? Maybe seventy-nine? "I'd be very surprised."

He leaned forward, hands gripping his knees now. "You never know, Moll. My mother always kept a secret or two."

"Don't we all?" Everyone hid things. Like the fact that being around Bradley Fischer was making her slightly nervous. But not exactly in a bad way.

"Sure, sure." Then he tilted his head, low-whistled. "I don't remember you looking so hot, Miss Wynters. What happened?"

She shifted on the couch. "Nothing." Other than enormous amounts of stress, and honey highlights in her usually dark hair. "I'm exactly the same."

"Well, how come I never noticed?"

"Maybe because you left home when I was in primary school. So that would've been kind of peculiar."

"True, true," he said. "But you're all grown up now." When he grinned, his teeth were bright white and perfectly aligned. She wondered if perhaps he'd had them capped. "Besides, you and me are in the same boat, right? Moving back here."

She nodded in agreement, but thought, *Not the same boat at all.* Her father had had a devastating stroke, and she was there to make decisions about his care, his house, his belongings. And if what Glenn had told her was true, Bradley's wife had tossed him out for screwing around.

"I'm not actually staying there," she said. "I rented the floor of a house, a couple of streets over. Do you know Russell Farrell?"

He emitted a hoot. "Old Rusty Nail? Never gets banged?"

Molly put her hand over her mouth to cover the smile. "You're terrible. Let's hope your mother brings home a filter with those limes."

"Where's the fun in that? Besides, that guy was such a prick in high school. Total asshat."

"High school? We're a long way from there, aren't we?"

Bradley's tongue moved to the corner of his mouth. "You probably don't remember when I lost my eyebrows."

Molly shook her head. In her silly child's mind, he'd been sublime.

"We were up at the overhang, you know, me and Rusty and that whole gang. Hyped up on something illegal, I'm sure. Russ put a lighter to an aerosol can, and the flame shot out and scared him so bad, but the twerp wouldn't lift his finger off the knob. I tried to grab it, and he aimed it right in my face. Took the works clean off."

Molly was laughing again. With everything going on, it felt good to think about something so innocent as burnt eyebrows.

"You're amused, but that's serious damage, you know. A person don't look right without their eyebrows. Ruined my grad photos. Couldn't even get a date for prom."

"I think you managed okay."

"Did I? Three marriages. None of them lasted long. I blame it all on the trauma I experienced at the hands of Rusty fucking Nail. Shook my confidence." He slapped the arms of his chair. "But you're separated too, aren't you? Mom said something about that."

"Divorced actually," she said, clearing her throat. "Things have been . . . a lot lately. With my dad and all. I'm here with Alex."

"That's right. You got a son. And how's that working out for you?"

"For the most part, it's been really easy."

"Teenage boy, easy? So basically, you don't got a clue what's going on in his life."

"I'd like to think I do." But he was right. For the most part, she had no idea. She'd been completely unaware Alex had a serious girlfriend. Would never have fathomed he'd have naked snapshots of her on his cellphone. That after their messy breakup, his response was to blast those images out to his classmates. And then the police were involved. Charges laid.

The front door opened and closed. Mrs. Fischer sang out, "Limes are in hand, Bradley, dear. You can rest easy now."

"Finally. Took you long enough." He winked at Molly.

When Mrs. Fischer came into the room, her hand jumped to her chest. "Molly sweetheart. I wasn't expecting company." She handed a plastic bag to Bradley and dropped her car keys on the piano stool. Even her keychain was the same. A now-tarnished metal octopus that Molly had given her as a gift when she was ten or eleven years old.

"Sorry. I should have called first."

"Nonsense, dear."

As Bradley drifted off toward the kitchen, she gave Molly a loose hug. Molly could feel the frailness of Mrs. Fischer's ribs, the stoop in her bony shoulders. Time had taken its inevitable toll.

"Tell me," she said. "How are things with you? Your life?"

"Keeping busy. Still working with my patients, and I've started volunteering on a local peer support line in the evenings. Mostly minutiae, but it fills some time."

"And Gil?" She touched Molly's arm. "I've tried to visit, but I can't get past that terrible man. Acts like I never knew him when he was a youngster. Glenn sat at my table with Bradley more times than I can remember." She brought her hand to her mouth, spoke through the shaky cage of fingers. "And now he won't even give me basic courtesy."

Molly counted inside her head. One. Two. Three. Timed her breath, waiting for the emotion to settle. Then, "That's my fault, Mrs. Fischer. I am sorry, I should have been in touch earlier. The stroke was quite . . . debilitating."

"Oh goodness. I can't believe it. Your father was always so full of life." She pulled her cardigan around her body. "Is he communicating? Can he talk?"

"I'm afraid not."

Mrs. Fischer plucked a dead leaf from a plant, crumpled it into the soil. "It was Bradley who found him, you know."

"I'm sorry?"

"I was going to make an olive oil cake. Some new recipe, and I didn't have quite enough sugar. I sent Bradley over to borrow, as we do, and the door was ajar. Your dad had fallen."

"Oh my." Molly was told her father had collapsed on the front step. That a passerby had noticed and called an ambulance. She hadn't realized that person was Bradley. "Well, I'm grateful. Really, I am. And I'll mention it to Glenn, okay? So he understands you're welcome anytime. Those moments together still mean something."

"Yes, yes of course they do. Might help him recover?"

Molly badly wanted to say yes. That, of course, he was going to recover. He was strong and capable, and nothing in this world would ever keep him down. "I don't think so."

"Goodness," she said again. "I love your father. I always have, you know. I always wanted to sort everything out with him."

"Sort everything out about what?"

"Oh, I don't know." Another dried leaf disintegrating between her fingers. "A matter we discussed ages ago. Though I guess it's irrelevant now."

Molly had an inkling it was related to the strip of land at the back of their properties. Mrs. Fischer's plot narrowed, while her father's widened. For years, Mrs. Fischer had used that area for a vegetable garden, sharing whatever she grew. At some point she'd offered to purchase it from Molly's father, but he told her it already belonged to her. Perhaps she wanted it documented. Perhaps she was updating her will and would be leaving her home to Bradley. Whatever the case, Molly's father had given his word, and she would honor it.

"Things will work themselves out. Don't worry."

"I'm not worried. But I'm sad, dear." Her raspy voice cracking. "Things ending on this note."

As Molly was leaving, Bradley fake-jogged toward her. "Hey," he said, picking away a fleck of pulp stuck to his upper lip. "Leaving already?"

She smiled at him. "Your mom told me. What you did for my dad. Thank you." Hand to her chest. "I hate to think—"

"All in a day, Moll. Seriously, though. How about grabbing a drink sometime?"

"A drink?"

"Yeah. You know the deal. Meet someplace that reeks of cigarettes and spilled booze. I'll probably flirt with you. You'll find me irresistible."

She felt a warmth rise in her cheeks. Even though Bradley had made a dozen ridiculous statements in a matter of minutes, it had been a long time since a man was playful with her. "People don't smoke indoors anymore. And besides, I've got a lot—"

"I get it. But come on. You're wound tighter than a spring. You need a break. Especially from that loser, Glenn the Hen."

With every interaction, Aymes kept shrinking around her. "Is everyone an asshole or a loser in your book? I don't know what I'd do without Glenn."

He clapped his hands together. "So that's a yes, then."

"Maybe, okay? It depends. I mean, everything depends these days."

CHAPTER ELEVEN

THE WIDE BODY of Shawna Springer was on the other side of the screen door, blocking the early evening light. She held a cardboard tray, two large drink containers.

"Care for a coffee?" she said through the wire mesh. "I brought it for Russell, but he's probably out tromping in the woods."

"I'd love one." Molly pushed open the door.

"It's decaf, so it won't keep you up." She placed the tray on the kitchen table, wiggled one cup out and handed it to Molly.

"Perfect," Molly said, though she was unconcerned about caffeine. These days she was usually tired. And usually unable to sleep. As she sat down, she gestured for Shawna to join her. "You stop by to see your cousin often?"

"More so lately. He was the one who built the platform for the support line. I've got a few more tweaks to suggest, and he doesn't mind obliging me."

"That's generous of him." She took a sip. The coffee was lukewarm but still delicious. "And he's lucky to have you, too. I'm sure he appreciates the company after his divorce."

"Divorce?" Shawna shook her head. "Russell's never been married."

Molly tried to recall the exact words of his email. "Appears I misunderstood."

"Well, I suppose it sounds safer than 'single white man living in the basement.'" With a tissue from her pocket, she dabbed the corners of her lips. "Though in fairness, it probably felt like divorce. He was tangled up with this woman when he lived away. On and off for years. She took his heart, his confidence, and finally his money. We didn't hear from him for ages."

"Wow, that's difficult."

"Yup. Despicable. He's such a soft soul, too. Mostly on his own as my aunt is gone, and he doesn't have much contact with other family. Relatives can be complicated, right?" She playfully rolled her eyes. "I'm just glad he's back home where he belongs."

Even though Molly was back, too, she had the opposite sense. She did not belong. Had it ever felt like home to her? Had that tension in her spine always been there?

"So," Shawna continued, "how has Alex found his first couple of weeks? All caught up?"

"I think so. No complaints."

"Snug as a bug, then. I'm sure he'll find some good pals in no time."

She hoped so. "All depends on how long we stay."

Shawna brought a hand to her cheeks, tilted her head. "I can't believe that would slip my mind. I do apologize, Molly."

"No need. It slips mine, too. Regular life keeps chugging along and then all at once I remember."

Like a splinter. Forgotten sometimes, until it was nudged in the wrong direction.

Shawna flicked her hair, then began chatting about the beautiful fall weather. "When it's not raining cats and dogs out there!" She detailed her husband's lower back pain. Described the clarity of the crab apple jelly she'd made. And how grateful she was for Molly's help on the support line.

"I don't think I'm making much of a contribution. It's mostly quiet."

"Still. You're an important cog in our little wheel," she said, lifting and dropping her shoulders.

Molly's head began to ache. Occasionally she felt that way after an afternoon of back-to-back therapy sessions with particularly difficult cases. As though too much had been funneled into her skull, and she wanted to drill the tiniest hole to let it seep back out. She often talked to her young clients about doing what was healthy for them. Setting boundaries, though she never used that particular phrase. Molly pushed back her chair, stood up. "Well, it's been lovely. I enjoyed the coffee and the chat."

Molly waited, but Shawna did not move. Instead she shook her cup, and a drop sloshed from the tiny hole onto the table.

"We'll do this again soon?" A second attempt to wrap things up.

Shawna gazed at Molly and then picked at her fingernails for several seconds. Finally, her face brightened and she stood up. "Yes, of course. Such a treat to chat." She pushed in the chair with her hip. "Before I go, did you have a chance to connect with Mrs. Eliason?"

"Who?"

"Alex's law teacher. She was a little concerned over the subject he chose for his assignment."

"And why would that be?"

Even before Shawna could reply, a staticky feeling had arrived in Molly's limbs. As though her body understood before her mind caught on.

"Clearly Alex didn't obtain your consent like she'd asked. It's—"

"My mother." Molly squeezed her cup, indentations forming in the cardboard.

"Exactly. A case study. Basically researching and presenting the details and outcome to the class. Mrs. Eliason takes a discussion-based approach. She—"

"No, it's fine. It's all good." Molly swallowed the hard knot that suddenly appeared in the middle of her throat. What was Alex doing? He knew what had happened to his grandmother. Wasn't that enough? "Tell his teacher it's his choice. My son can knock himself out."

Grimacing, Shawna said, "I've never been a fan of that phrase."

No. That idiom wouldn't be an appropriate poster for her office wall. A teenager, ball cap turned backward, banging his bloodied forehead against a cinderblock wall.

She stepped out the door, then turned. "Oh and very last thing. I nearly forgot to tell you you're volunteer of the month!"

"For?"

"On the support line, silly." A light slap to Molly's hand. "It's nothing really. A short write-up on our community website to show appreciation. I assume that's okay?"

On calls, Molly introduced herself only with her first name and imagined there was some degree of anonymity. But she nodded, said, "Of course. Yes. It's a lovely gesture."

Once Shawna was gone, Molly took the last inch of cold coffee and carried it outside. Russell had created a seating area on the stone patio with a bistro table and two chairs. In the center of the table, a terra-cotta pot held a stubborn begonia that was still in bloom.

She picked up her cellphone and called her best friend, Casey. A therapist as well, working at the same clinic. Though Casey had a different area of expertise—teenaged girls and dialectic behavioral therapy.

Casey answered on the first ring. "Hey, you!"

"How are my plants?" Molly asked.

"Climbing the walls. Like they're supposed to do."

"I'm missing them. Missing everything."

"Listen. I've got it all under control, okay?"

"I wish I could say the same. Work is okay at least. The video sessions are going smoothly for the most part. Kids take to technology." Molly sighed. "Alex is barely talking."

"Haven't you heard? Language loss during the teenage years is well documented."

She pressed a fingernail into a flower petal. "I just thought I'd be able to find a way in, you know. To connect."

"You're his mother, Molly. Not his confidant. And you need to cut yourself some slack. I mean, your plate is overflowing."

"And get this. He's decided to present on my mother's case for his law class. I don't understand it."

Silence on the other end for a moment. Then, "I understand it. It's part of his family history."

"To a degree, sure. But he never met his grandmother. He's never lived here. It's all just words on paper. Details he already knows."

Another silence. "I don't think that's quite right, Moll."

She gulped the last drops of coffee. "Illuminate me, then."

"Well, what happened shaped you, didn't it? In a very profound way. And you're a huge part of his world. His one parent, essentially. So while you experienced the tragedy directly, it has also impacted his life in significant ways."

Molly leaned back in the chair. The evening air was cool, and it was shot through with threads of dampness. She'd never considered that before. "You're right," she said. "You're completely right."

"All you can do is support, and at the same time respect and value your own limitations."

"Good reminders. Thank you."

"Now," she said, laughing, "tell me what I really want to know. Is your landlord the sizzly sort of divorcé?"

Groaning. "Not even close."

"Really? I'm envisioning him shirtless, working a backyard garden on a charming plot of land. A sheen of sweat. Come-hither gaze."

Molly shook her head. "That's a stretch, Case. You're too ridiculous right now."

"Whatever lightens the mood."

A twig snapped. Molly twisted in her chair, discovered Russell a few feet behind her in the darkened backyard. He was wearing a beige cardigan, and his glasses had fallen to the tip of his nose. Two long rabbits were resting against his right thigh, furry feet lashed to his belt.

"Oh hi," Molly said, then whispered into the phone, "I better go."

"Gotcha. Call me soon." Casey hung up.

"Beautiful evening, Mr. Farrell."

He stepped closer. "Russ, I told you."

"Sorry. I forgot."

"I didn't mean to interrupt your call, Molly. I was out checking my snares."

"At night?"

"It's as good a time as any."

"Well, you've had some success, I see."

He ran a hand down over the fur legs, the cotton ball tails. "They're for the farmers' market. I used to make sausages, but now everyone wants those little slider things. Most annoying to prepare."

"I'd imagine." She smiled. "But you have to please your customers."

As he passed her on the patio, he stopped. "You know," he said. "I remember when your mother worked at the school."

A shiver crept across her shoulders, and she felt the hair on the back of her neck lift.

"Really?" she replied. A closer look revealed that Russell was not as old as she'd first thought. Though he dressed like an elderly man, he was likely mid-fifties. Same as Bradley. *Rusty Nail.* They'd been high school friends.

"Mrs. Wynters was a thoughtful lady. If ever I forgot my lunch money, she'd still put something on my tray. She did that for all of us."

Molly reached up, smoothed her skin with a clammy palm. "That's kind of you to tell me, Russ."

"You look so like her, you know. Even your mannerisms."

"So I've been told."

He scuffed the ground with his boot. "Any evening plans for yourself?"

"If I admit I'm free, you're not going to ask for help with the rabbits, are you?" There was a faint odor coming from them. Not foul, exactly, but still reminding her of death.

"Wouldn't dream of it."

"Then not much really. Maybe I'll join the support line for an hour or two. Occasionally I seem to do some good."

"Ah, that's right. Shawna's online venture."

A puff of wind knocked the empty coffee cup off the table, and Molly reached to retrieve it. "She stopped by to see you earlier. She mentioned your mother. I'm not sure if that's recent?"

"Mentioned how."

"That's she's gone."

He clicked his tongue. "Yes, gone, Molly. Gone away. Assisted living, where she gets a great deal more sunshine than we're getting here."

"Oh, I misunderstood. I thought—"

"And did she want anything else? My nosy cousin. Or just to talk out of turn?"

"Um. Something about altering some features?"

"I forgot about that," he said, groaning. "Now she wants a new phone icon. Thinks the rotary dial alienates the youth."

"Isn't retro hip nowadays?"

"You'd expect Shawna to know that. Working with teens. Is it a useful resource, at least?"

"Can't say. Last lady who called was distraught over burnt cookies. I suggested aluminum pans and a lower temperature."

"Sage wisdom. It may seem trivial to us, but perhaps she had nobody else."

Molly nodded. "That's a perfect way to frame it, Russ. I shouldn't be so quick to dismiss."

"No," he said as he continued toward the side of the house, rabbits swinging. Then over his shoulder, he called, "But that's part of life, isn't it? Being dismissed."

•

When Alex arrived home, he mumbled, "Before you say anything, already ate, everything's good, I've got no homework, and I'm wiped," and then he closed his bedroom door. Molly's mouth tightened. What even was that? Ten seconds of interaction? Though she was tempted, she would not go knock. Or call out to him. If that was all the communication he could muster, she would have to accept it.

Over the past two years, he'd grown so fast, sometimes she couldn't clearly envision his face. She'd never admit this to anyone, but occasionally she'd open the photo gallery on her phone and scroll through the images when he was in a room only a few feet away. There were traces of her in his appearance, traces of her mother. He looked nothing like his father, which quietly pleased her.

At the end of the hallway, his door was in shadow. Only a narrow line of light glowed at the gap near the bottom. She really should discuss his law assignment with him. While she'd told Shawna it was fine, she was having second thoughts. If she explained to him that it unsettled her, and there was nothing new to learn about her mother's death, perhaps he might reconsider. Choose another topic. Though if Molly were honest with herself, that change of mindset was unlikely no matter how she broached it.

To distract herself, she opened up her laptop and slipped the headphones over her ears. Logged into the support line website. Lately, this had become her nightly routine. Writing up her reports or watching a show, then pausing if a call came in. Usually, an hour or two of mostly silence, a few crank calls, and an occasional moment that made her feel useful.

The telephone icon appeared in the middle of the screen, and she was surprised to see that within seconds the receiver was shuddering. She clicked. "Aymes Peer Support Line, Molly speaking."

"Hey there. I got a quick question for you. About bowling."

"Like the activity?"

"Yeah. Sorta. Specifically, about the balls."

"A bit out of my depth, to be honest. Someone who works at an alley could better assist you."

"Do you think they got ten-pound ones?"

Perhaps the person had carpal tunnel syndrome. Wanting to enjoy the sport but suffering from pain in his wrists. "Well, I suppose so."

"Really? Ten-pound balls? How do you think the guy walks?" Then multiple peals of raucous laughter, and the caller disconnected.

Molly couldn't help but grin. She'd strolled right into that trap. Who'd have guessed those sorts of innocent pranks still existed? She summarized the call in the text box. "Nostalgic tween wisecracker."

Aymes was having a quiet evening. Nearly an hour passed with no further activity, and she was about to log off when the receiver lifted again. One last one, she thought, and then she'd get a bath and go to bed. Read the boring novel that was sitting on the night table. Perhaps it would help her sleep.

After she introduced herself, there was a strange hollowness inside her headphones. Almost like the caller was inside a cavern. She heard several steady breaths.

"Hello? Is anyone there?"

A dry mouth, peeling opening. "Do you ever think about what happened, Molly?"

She sat up on the couch. The voice was gravelly. Distorted. As though it was forced through the spinning blades of a fan.

"I'm sorry?"

"Do you ever think about what happened that day?"

She was unsure if it was a man on the other end. Or a woman. "You've reached a peer support line. Is there anything I can do to help?"

"Yes, you can, Molly. But we'll get to that shortly."

"I don't—"

"I understand if you're confused. We all deceive ourselves, don't we?" Was that a sigh? "You, especially."

"Who is this?" She should disconnect, but instead she pressed the headphones closer to her ears. Straining to listen. A ping in the background, like a cellphone notification.

"But guilt eats away at you. It consumes from the inside out."

"What are you—"

"We'll talk later, Molly. Good night."

Then the soft click. And the text box appeared with the cursor flashing. Indicating she needed to enter the details. When she glanced down at her hands, they were shaking. For no reason whatsoever, she told herself. It was a disturbed individual, who surely recognized her name due to the volunteer of the month post. Just a gag. Though this one was not at all funny.

She got up and stood in front of the bay window that offered a view of the road. Offered anyone on the road a view of her, as well. Outside, the wind lifted the branches of a nearly naked tree, and the streetlamp appeared to flicker. She yanked the curtains across, blocking out the darkness. For a moment, she remained there, polyester fabric gripped in her fists. What sort of person would find that entertaining? Use her tragedy for a sick thrill? She took a deep breath and tried to relax her muscles. Refusing to allow her mind to twist and turn on pointlessness when she had too many other legitimate things to tackle. Like Alex. His assignment.

Molly went to his door. Tapped. When he didn't answer, she turned the knob and cracked it open an inch. He had earbuds in, was focused on his screen. When she caught his eye, he flinched, clapped his laptop closed.

"Hey," she said.

"What the hell, Mom." He tore the bud from his right ear. "Can't you knock?"

"I did."

"What do you want?"

His hair was ruffled up, soft around his face. "I thought you might like a snack."

"Seriously? If I want a snack, I'll get a snack. I'm not two."

"True." She shrugged. "Sorry."

Not so many years ago, he'd have invited her in. Made her sit on the bed as he wrapped a blanket around her shoulders, tying the ends in front of her chest. He'd clutch the knot of fleece with both hands and yell, "I've caught you now, Mom. You're mine forever."

Alex lifted his eyebrows, bugged out his eyes. "Anything else?"

Do you ever think about what happened?

That eerie voice from the call was still with her. Circling around inside her mind. She hesitated, then. Part of her wanting to tell Alex to leave her mother's tragedy alone. To keep away from dark and scary places, in case he discovered something lurking there.

And another part, strangely more forceful, wanting him to carry on.

She said, "Nope. All good," and closed the door.

THEN

•

CHAPTER TWELVE

Gil

EVERYTHING WAS BLURRY. But that was not Gil's fault. Since early morning, Seth had been serving him whiskey, two innocent fingers at a time.

"You won't survive the day on an empty stomach," Andrea said, but Gil could barely touch the jiggly poached eggs she'd made. He rushed to the bathroom. As he gripped a towel rack to steady himself, a curious memory appeared. Playing hide-and-seek as a small boy with his mother. Folding his body down inside a box, limbs and head pressed into his trunk. That childish swirl of fear and elation, wondering when he would be found. If.

"Come on, buddy," Seth said, when Gil emerged from the bathroom. "Let's get you to the other side." He pressed a pill into Gil's palm. *Benzedrine 10 mg.* Gil tossed it to the back of his throat and swallowed.

Seth was a great friend. Through all the years of thick and thin, he'd never once judged Gil's anxiety. That morning, he'd been offering up small but necessary tweaks to alleviate Gil's stress. A few sips of booze. A low-dosage sedative. Enough to calm the nerves without making him sloppy. Though nothing more today, Gil thought as he saw himself in the hallway mirror. Slightly glazed eyes. Goofy grin.

Fretfulness was part of his nature, and the nerves he felt today were in no way connected to doubt. After that first date, he knew getting hitched was in his future. While Seth hinted he should "slow his roll," Gil bought Edie a diamond after six weeks. Finally gave it to her at four months. He'd meticulously planned a romantic evening, but instead proposed on the spur of the moment in Mrs. Paltry's kitchen. Down on one knee, interrupting Edie's game of solitaire. She was thrilled, of course, but it was Mrs. Paltry's face that Gil remembered the most. Her delight so intense, the expression almost akin to pain. She nearly dropped the pot roast when he pushed the ring onto Edie's third finger.

Neither of them wanted a long engagement, and Edie did not want the fuss of a church gathering, so they'd made arrangements for a few guests to join them at city hall.

When they arrived, Gil gazed around the room. A small space with mint walls, blond wood floors, artificial flowers in a ceramic vase. Edie was wearing her mother's dress. Off-white, it draped over the bones of her shoulders. Her hair was covered by a lacy wide-brimmed hat.

As he said his vows, he was swaying slightly. Then he lowered his head while he listened to Edie say hers. On the ruffles of his shirt, there was a thick drip of yolk. He was about to scratch it away when someone clapped him on the back. Grabbed his hand tightly, and he felt the dull ache of a ring around his finger. Gil looked up. The ceremony was over, and he was flooded with relief. As though the lid was torn from the box where he was hiding. And he'd burst out, stretching tall. Still the same, but also completely different.

On the stone steps out front, Gil snaked his hand around his bride's waist, leaned close to her. Whispered, "We're married, you know."

"I know."

"Well, then, hello to you, Mrs. Gil Wynters."

He expected her to say something similar back to him, but she wrenched away. Plopped down on the top step. Repeated in a flat tone, "Mrs. Gil Wynters. Mrs. Gil Wynters."

"Yes. That's who you are now."

Suddenly her shoulders hunched, and she was sobbing. Her makeup, thickly applied, dribbled down her cheeks.

He sat down beside her. Placed his hand on her lower back. "What's wrong? What could possibly be wrong?"

When she replied, her tone had shifted. No longer distressed but weighted with irritation. Almost aggression. "And Edie Paltry? What about her?"

"I don't understand." Gil knew he was slurring. There was a sour taste on his tongue.

"Is she meant to simply disappear?"

"Who?"

"Me!"

Chuckling, he slapped his thigh. "Of course she's not. Of course you're not. It's just the custom, Edie."

She threw her bouquet then, with some force, and it shot down over the stairs. "Well, I don't like that custom. In fact, I hate it. And I won't let you smother me into some—into some—" She stood up and stomped off. Her flowers in a torn heap on the sidewalk.

Gil was speechless. And as he was also drunk and jittery, he wondered if the words that were firing into his ears had actually come out of her mouth. Perhaps he was imagining things. Misinterpreting. She was acting like a spoiled child. But then again, she was barely twenty years old. Spent her days with teenagers in a cafeteria. She'd never traveled beyond the borders of Aymes. What should he expect?

Mrs. Paltry appeared beside him, in a peach-colored suit. "That was a lovely ceremony," she said. "It makes me so sad Edie's sister isn't here."

Gil placed both hands flat on the stone for balance and managed to get to his feet. "Sister?"

"And Calvin, of course. Her poor brother couldn't get away from work, unfortunately."

Edie had two siblings? Gil scratched the back of his head. Not once had she ever mentioned them. "For sure," he said. "That's really too bad."

Mrs. Paltry touched his sleeve and smiled. "All this stress puts her in a mood, Dr. Wynters. I wouldn't take it seriously. She'll be fine once the day is done."

She made her way down the stairs and collected the bouquet. Cleaned up every loose rose petal, the torn clusters of baby breath, that were scattered in a wide radius. Then she tucked the entire mess into her oversized purse. Out of sight.

·

The reception was held at the same restaurant where he and Edie had their first date. Gil booked the entire place, selecting the menu, the wines. The evening passed in a blink of eating and drinking and long-winded speeches. Seth's dragged on the most. He spoke of Edie having some enchanting quality, able to lock down a wrinkly old bachelor. That he hoped she could help Gil to match his socks and root the parsley out of his teeth. And he was grateful his best buddy could now join the period of life he'd dubbed "the long suffering."

A club exclusively for married men. With each joke, Andrea gasped playfully, while Edie pressed her hands into her thighs, clutching at the fabric of her dress.

For Gil, the end of the evening could not come quickly enough, and minutes after cutting the layered fruitcake, they said goodbye to everyone and hurried out the door. As he drove, his heart was thumping and his hands were shaking. Likely a combination of the wedding stress, the booze, and the medication. When they arrived at the house, Edie's foul mood vanished, just as Mrs. Paltry had said it would. He put the car in park, and instead of waiting for him to open her door, she darted out, ran around, and flung open the driver's side.

"Hurry," she said. "Hurry."

"What's the rush?"

"I can't wait any longer."

She grabbed his wrist and yanked him toward the front step. Giggled as she bumped the nose on the brass lion knocker. He opened the door and swept her into his arms. "And now you're home," he said as he carried her over the threshold. She was a feather and had her arms wrapped around his neck.

"This is all yours?"

"All ours now, Edie." He'd bought the place a week after she'd agreed to marry him. Since the sale was finalized, she'd refused to visit. Wanted to wait. Keep it for a surprise.

As she raced about, exploring every corner, he poured himself a final lick of whiskey. Undid his top button and sunk into the couch. The windows were open and the scent from the neighbor's blooming gardenia drifted in on the breeze. He lay his head back and his entire body began to spin. Had the surreal sensation of being pinned in place. Sitting up slightly, he blinked, tried to orient himself. Edie was standing in front of him.

"Do you want one?" He lifted the glass an inch.

"No," she replied.

"Okay. What about a record?" He gestured toward the credenza. "Shall we put on Joni Mitchell?"

"No, to that too."

Now that the night had finally arrived, he didn't want her to feel any pressure. Though they'd been a couple for six months, they had not yet slept together. She'd laughed, called him a hard hat, but he understood that Mrs. Paltry was old-fashioned. And he was adamant about doing things right.

"Come," he said, taking a deep breath and closing his eyes. "Sit with me."

He heard the opening of zipper's teeth. Slitting one eye open, he saw Edie's dress as it was falling, crumbling on the floor. With a bare foot, she kicked it away. A second later, his body tilted as the cushion beside him lowered. She'd climbed onto the couch. "Now there you are," he whispered. "We can relax together." She had to be as exhausted as he was. Things could wait one more night.

But instead of resting against his side, laying her head on his shoulder, she knelt, leaned forward. The front of her slip gaped, and he could see her breasts, two perfect cups.

"We can—"

"Shut up," she said.

She took his whiskey and set it on the coffee table. Then her fingers worked on his leather belt, tugging out the tongue, the silver buckle falling to the side. He shifted slightly as she pulled his pants down over hips. All he could see was the back of her head, her long hair splayed over his lap. He felt her mouth, warm and tight.

His eyes were wide open now. "Oh, god, Edie. What are you doing?"

While her head moved up and down, her other hand disappeared beneath the hem of her slip. The low hum of her moaning moved through him. Her breath was catching, and she released him suddenly, shoved him backward, then flung a pale leg over his hips. As she eased herself down, he slipped inside her, and she guided his hands to her nipples as she rocked back and forth. Grasping the back of the couch.

Gil had had relations with eight, maybe nine, women over the years. Three one-nighters, a couple of short-lived romances in college. A few ladies in Aymes. Most experiences were the same. Usually, the woman lying quietly beneath him. Sometimes he'd make awkward attempts at mixing things up. But nothing so bold as this.

It was over too quickly. Edie had done all the work and he'd barely had the pleasure of touching her. He immediately wanted to apologize for his speed. His sloppiness. His animal grunts. But she rolled back onto the couch, then stood up, stepped over the mound of her wedding dress, and walked away.

He peered down at himself. Lower half shiny and limp. Band of his trousers cutting into his thighs. The drip from the egg yolk was still on his shirt ruffle. As he picked at it with his thumbnail, a sick feeling bubbled up inside him. In her drug file at the pharmacy, he'd seen the prescription. *Ortho-Novum 5 mg.* Hormonal birth control. She was using it before they even met. What if she'd done that same exact thing with someone else?

He tried to tamp down that pointy shard of jealousy. The past was the past. All of those thrills, all that exhilaration, now belonged to him.

CHAPTER THIRTEEN

THEY LEFT FOR the honeymoon the day after the wedding. Gil
had rented a one-bedroom cottage for seven nights on the other side
of Rabey Lake. Not exactly the luxury vacation he'd envisioned, but
with the wedding, new house purchase, and funds set aside for a
reliable vehicle for Edie, they had to be cautious with their finances.
The pamphlet described charming accommodations, an abundance
of nature, and plenty of privacy. *"A haven for newlyweds."* It would
have to do.

Gil slowed the car at the entrance to the park. There was a
wooden shelter off to the side, and a woman stepped out with a
worn clipboard. Her straggly hair was pulled back in a tight ponytail and her skin was brown and cracked.

"How do you do?" Gil said, leaning his elbow out the window.
"I made a reservation over the phone?"

"Yep," she said, scanning the single piece of paper. "Dr. Wynters.
Only visitors checking in today."

As she stepped closer, he could smell the sweetness of alcohol in the air around her. She handed him a silver key, a dangling miniature Coke can as the keychain.

"You mean to say you've been sitting there waiting for a single guest?"

"That's why they pay me the big bucks, pal." She checked her watch, made an enormous check mark on her sheet of paper. "Name's Winnie. Holler if you need anything. You'd be real surprised how voices carry 'round here."

As Gil drove down the trail, branches scraped against the sides of the car, and the wheels dipped into deep potholes. He drove slowly, while Edie edged forward in her seat, both hands flat on the dashboard. "Now this is a real forest," she said. "This is a real getaway."

When they arrived at Number 16, he was instantly disappointed. It was nothing like the gleaming photographs. The place was just a functional box facing the lake, peeling clapboard, tattered shingled roof. Two rickety lawn chairs on a square of patchy grass.

"Well," he said, as they stepped out. "Can we manage with this?"

Edie was already flitting about the yard. She was wearing lemon-yellow shorts and a matching crocheted top that tied behind her neck. "Oh, it's heavenly. We've got a fire pit and a log pile. Even our own dock for sitting and reading. And the lake is like blue glass. I could almost walk on it."

When he entered the cottage, all he could smell was earthy dampness, like the underside of a decaying log. The rooms were full of shadows, and the tiniest bathroom had a line of black mold clinging to the sealant around the tub.

"Edie? Can you come see this?" He braced for her reaction. Expected her mouth to twist when she realized the decrepit level of accommodations. But when she rushed inside, she twirled around, and a boyish whistle escaped her lips. "Will you get a load of this place! It's so rustic. Is that the correct word?"

He pulled her into a tight embrace. How was it that she could look beyond the multitude of flaws and identify only the charm? "Yes, that's the exact word," he whispered into her ear. "Rustic."

She darted into the bedroom and leapt onto the bed. "Now you come see this," she said, laughing. He watched her through the doorway. Feet planted in the middle of the mattress, hips wiggling side to side, she unsnapped her shorts and let them slip down. Untied her top and tugged it over her head. She wasn't wearing a bra and he could see the dark hair behind her sheer white panties. Then she tugged those down, too.

Gil could not be rid of his khakis quickly enough. She lay back on the plaid comforter, parted her legs for him, and he climbed on top of her without even removing his shirt. He moved inside her, sliding his hands up around her back and clutching the slender bones of her shoulders. He curled his body over hers and pushed harder. But as he edged closer, a panicky feeling began to develop in his throat. As though he were having an allergic reaction. His lungs would not accept a full breath, and his mind began churning at a dizzying speed. What if she became unhappy? What if she decided to leave him? What if he lifted his head and gazed at the mattress, and she was already gone?

Moments later, Gil lay back on the bed, gasping. The fears that had seized him so fiercely had already evaporated. Everything was fine. His insecurities, his vulnerabilities were only trying to surface. Edie belonged to him. They loved each other. He'd have to force those worries down.

"What a way to kick things off," he said.

Edie crawled off the bed, rummaged around for her clothes. Her hair was like a bird's nest and her cheeks were flushed. To Gil, she'd never been more gorgeous, and he said so.

As she leaned against the wood-paneled wall, she yanked on her panties. "Never tell a girl she's hot after you just screwed her."

"What? Why?"

"Because it's an insult. At that moment, a man would find beauty in anything. A tree stump, if it had a proper hole in it."

Gil was about to tell her she was being crass. What they did was not "screwing," and clearly she couldn't comprehend the depth of his emotions. But he closed his mouth. If that was how she felt, then so be it. Part of marriage was learning about the other person, those idiosyncrasies that shaped who they were. Gil would figure it out, and he'd find better moments to express himself.

Edie wasted no time in getting them settled. She tugged open the sun-bleached curtains. Cracked all the windows. Carried in their bags and arranged their clothing on the shelves. Hung his shirts and her dresses on the metal hangers. Gil lugged in the cooler full of food, the bags from the grocer, and Edie organized the kitchenette. Putting milk and juice in the miniature fridge. Pasta and sauce on the shelf. A jar of instant coffee on the windowsill.

Gil carried the emptied cooler outside and placed it against the side of the cottage. Hidden in the trees above him, chickadees chirped, and cicadas produced their piercing buzz.

When he came back around the corner, he discovered Edie sitting on the shaded ground. She'd changed into a floral skirt and had a mound of sunflower seeds in the dip of the fabric.

"Aren't they adorable?" She kept very still as a red squirrel approached, then reached out its clawed paws and stole the seed from her palm.

Gil frowned. He'd never been fond of rodents. "Watch it doesn't bite."

"Why would it bite? I'm being friendly."

"Because, Edie. You can't trust something wild."

She lifted her face. "You'd better not become a drag, Dr. Wynters."

He chuckled. "If I even get close, let me know." He had to be mindful. He didn't want to morph into a husband like Seth, tied down with a squalling brood of youngsters, always striving to identify the downside of any situation. No, there'd be no "long suffering" for Gil. He carried the entire package of seeds over to Edie and dropped it in her lap. "Here you go. Why don't you fatten those buggers up."

•

Later, he cooked hamburger patties on the grill. They ate while seated at the very end of the dock. Gil drank lager from a can, and Edie had a Diet Dr Pepper. The heat of the day had not relented, and they kept their feet dipped in the cool water.

"I was thinking," he said, as he licked ketchup off a finger. "About you not going back."

"Going back where?"

"To the school. To the cafeteria."

She swallowed her mouthful. "You mean quit?"

"I wouldn't phrase it like that. You just don't have to keep a job, Edie. I can take care of everything."

"And what do you expect I'll do all day, huh?" She tossed the remains of her bun into the lake. It floated for a second, then a fish darted up and snapped it off the surface. "Climb the walls inside your house?"

"As I already said, it's *our* house." He was taken aback by her sudden shift in mood. He'd assumed it was his role to earn the money, same as his father had. "And you'll find there's plenty to do. What with groceries and meals and decorating." Weren't those the tasks most women enjoyed? And in a year, they'd surely have their first baby. She'd need extra rest while expecting, and besides, why would she want to spend all day slopping sawdust meatballs and swollen noodles at belligerent teenagers?

Edie wiggled her feet through the water. "I'll be keeping my job, Dr. Wynters."

"I never meant—" he started, but his words were interrupted by a rumbling engine. The noise so distinct, he braced for the stench of exhaust. "Is there a motorboat coming?" He peered up and down the lake.

Edie put her hand to her forehead, pointed across the lake. "Nope. Over there. Look up high."

Gil followed the angle of her arm. On the opposite side of the water, a flat wall of stone rose several stories. The gray rock was featureless, topped with a forest of trees like unkempt hair. In a clearing, he could make out a beige pickup truck. Revving its engine. Then it spun around and slowly began backing up toward the edge. When it was close, a man leapt from the cab, dropped the tailgate, hauled several large hunks of debris onto the ground. Gil even heard him straining seconds before the crunch of metal striking dirt.

"What's he doing?"

"Probably cleaned up his yard. Watch."

And sure enough, the man dragged one of the items to the rocky lip. Lifted his boot and tipped it over. Down, down it fell, a violent splash, and the dark lake swallowed it up.

"Shameful," Gil said. "Poisoning nature like that."

"Why? My dad used to do it. Cal, too. They dump stuff there because the lake's bottomless. It just disappears."

"Nothing's bottomless, Edie," Gil said. "And nothing disappears."

"I didn't mean for real. Though it might as well be. Half the trash from East Aymes is down there."

The tailgate slammed. Then the man cleared his throat and spat on the ground.

"It's uncanny," he said. "How close he sounds. He could be right between us." He reached over and wiped grease from her chin. Sunlight was catching in strands of her hair. Flickers of auburn. "You truly are lovely."

"Am I?"

"Yes, you are. Was that appropriate timing?"

She reached down and cupped a handful of lake water, splashed him in the face. "Yes, that was perfectly appropriate timing, Dr. Wynters."

The days of their honeymoon passed like that. Hour after hour of easy living. Not a single drop of rain fell the entire time. Edie swam every morning, and sometimes Gil paddled out in the rowboat for trout fishing, but never caught a thing. Other than some animals, a couple of trucks, and Winnie the gatekeeper occasionally bringing towels, there was no other sign of life. He and Edie were alone, and if Gil could manage it, he'd keep things that way forever.

CHAPTER FOURTEEN

EARLY EVENING ON their last day at Rabey Lake, Winnie appeared in the driveway with a wicker basket. Dull apples and spotted bananas. A dozen grapes left on near-naked stems. Fig Newtons, a box of Ganong chocolates. Dented tin of sour lemon drops. "This came a couple of days ago," she said as she handed it to him. "But darn, if I forgot."

Gil opened the already opened card. "Some snacks and bubbly to toast your nuptials. Regards, Seth and Andrea." He did not see any bubbly.

Winnie grinned shyly, plucked up an empty wrapper that had fallen to the ground. "I'll leave you to it."

Down on the dock, Edie was napping on a towel. The orange trim on her white T-shirt matched her short shorts. In that outfit, Gil thought she looked like a student, ready for gym class.

"Look what Seth sent," he said as he placed the basket on the warm wood slats.

She opened her eyes and sat up. "What?"

"Some goodies. A bit picked over, but a few treats left."

She started sorting through. "Let's eat it all. Lie here in the sunshine and fill ourselves up with sugar."

Gil settled in beside her. Could life get any smoother? Other than the mildest friction in their conversation about the school cafeteria, he and Edie had not exchanged a tense word. She was the calmest woman he'd ever known.

He plucked up an apple, shined it in his shirt, and bit into it. It didn't crunch, but it was still juicy. Edie tore open a packet of honeyed peanuts. Flung them in the air and leaned this way and that, catching them in her mouth. "You know, when we were kids and being awful, my father always promised he'd take us here."

"You've been before?"

"Of course I haven't. It was just a thing he'd say, to shut us up. But oh, we'd love him so hard for that minute when it seemed like a possibility."

"That's pretty rotten."

"And my mother would say, 'Do you hear that, children? Won't it be wonderful?' Even though she knew it'd never come true."

He reached over, dug a few peanuts from her packet, and chewed them into paste. After he swallowed, he said, "That was you and your brother and sister?"

"Yup."

"How come you never mentioned them?"

"I didn't?"

"Not a word. I didn't know they existed until your mother said they couldn't make the wedding."

Edie missed the last peanut, and it landed in the lake with a tiny plop. "Well, Connie is dead, so there's that."

"What? How?"

"She got in a fight with her boyfriend."

"How do you die from an argument?"

"No, like a fistfight," Edie said flatly. "He drove her home afterward, though. We found her the next morning in the neighbor's front yard. He got the driveway wrong."

"My god," Gil said, touching her arm. "That's absolutely awful. How did I miss that in the news?"

"Really? No one in Aymes proper would want to read about that?" She laughed. "And then there's Cal. I guess he slipped my mind. He's been away for a while." Leaning back on her elbows, she pointed at the sky. "Do you see how many stars are coming out. It's nice, huh?"

Gil tilted his head back. The black sheet above them was sprayed with endless pricks of white light. "Sure is. So where does he live now?"

"A few hours away." With her fingertip, she was tracing the patterns. "There's the Big Dipper. That's easy, though. My dad knew every single one."

"Did he?" Gil was not interested in stars, or Mr. Paltry's astronomy skills. "And Cal didn't want to come to our wedding?"

"I didn't invite him. I didn't bother."

"Why not?"

Edie dropped her arm, turned to face him. "Do you want to get your flashlight and shine it in my face, Detective Wynters?"

"I just meant I'd love to meet him. He'd be welcome to visit. Anytime."

"Well sometimes it's not all so easy, is it? He stormed off two years ago, and I haven't seen him since. Broke my mother's heart."

"I'm sorry," he said.

"Yeah. Well. I told her I'd never do that. Hurt her."

"Of course you won't. How could you possibly?"

Gil got up and collected some logs for a final campfire. Found the perfect stick so Edie could roast marshmallows from a safe distance. He wouldn't ask about her siblings again. There was no need to dredge up painful memories from a past that no longer mattered. When some doors closed, they should simply remain closed.

They passed the evening that way. Sitting cross-legged beside a dancing fire, the water lapping at the shore. Gil had never felt this contented in his entire life. He leaned over and kissed her. Her tongue tasted of burnt sugar.

"I'm heading inside," he said. "You coming?"

"In a minute or two. This is our last night."

Gil stood up, arched his spine, vertebrae popping. "We can always come back, you know. This place isn't going to vanish."

"Don't you see? It won't ever be the same as it is right now."

He smiled in the darkness. "And why might that be?"

"I just know, that's why. Everything's going to change.

Him

I COULDN'T STOP thinking about the girl who'd saved me. All summer, whenever I was out, I searched for her, just hoping to catch a glimpse of her face.

My legs turned rubbery when I finally spied her. It wasn't until September, on my very first day of high school. She was standing behind the counter in the cafeteria, a stained apron covering her chest. She was serving up meatloaf and gluey potatoes.

I'd been anticipating this moment for months. Wondering if she'd remember me, even though I looked different. Taller, wearing dry clothes, with straight shoulders and a cool demeanor. When I reached the front of the line, I silently willed her to meet my gaze. I was all set to say, "Hey there. Thanks a bunch for saving me last spring." I'd practiced that sentence at home, recording myself over and over on a cassette tape. Replaying it so I could regulate the speed of my words. The cadence of my voice. I was aiming for a seductive Burt Reynolds vibe.

But as I stepped in front of her, my shaking tray outstretched, her head remained bent. Stray hairs sticking out of the brown net. Then the squelch of soft food hitting my plate. Was that a gold band on her left hand? She certainly hadn't been wearing one before. I'd have noticed that.

"Next," she yelled at nobody. "Come on. Move it along."

My heart sank, and I shuffled forward, found my seat at a table. She hadn't even noticed me. I pushed the meatloaf around, but I couldn't eat. Did girls her age wear rings on any old finger? Or had she gone and made a terrible mistake?

That evening, in bed, blinds closed, lights out, I imagined myself back in that ditch. Crouching in the icy water. Rain gliding down the back of my neck, into my crying mouth. I mulled over the threats of the situation. Hypothermia. Rabid animals with foaming mouths. A horny hermit stomping closer, wanting to drag me back to his drafty shack.

Then the crunch of cold gravel. Her warm, wide smile through an open door, and she whispered, "Can I give you a lift, handsome?"

That sweet ripple of relief.

"Sure can." I swaggered up the incline. Jumped inside. "Appreciate it."

She opened the heating vent, and I felt the warm breeze on my skin. "All better now," she said.

I turned in my seat. Before we could proceed with any conversation, any banter, I had to understand the ring. "I need you to be honest with me. Did you get married?"

She lowered her gaze. "Yeah. I did."

"But how could you do that?"

"It's hard to explain," she said. "It doesn't matter, and I don't want to talk about it."

I didn't press. My mother often told me that life got messier, more complicated, as a person grew older. The lunch lady was several years my senior, and though I didn't fully understand, I decided to trust what she said. If she said it didn't matter, then it didn't matter.

"Well then, we won't talk about it. Will we?" I assumed that was the mature statement I needed to make.

She sighed, reached across the gear shift, and tapped my leg. "Straight home to your mom? Or should we take a little spin?"

I pulled the blankets up over my head and slid further down the mattress. The pocket of air in front of my face was damp and sweet from my breath. "A spin sounds good," I said quietly.

Really good. I was already dizzy.

•

I kept our outings to a minimum so they wouldn't lose their special-ness. Only allowing her to coax me out of that ditch once a week at most. Other than hanging out with my buddies, it was the only part of my existence I looked forward to.

On each drive, we spoke of different things. I told her I still hadn't figured out slope and y-intercept. She said my new haircut was super snazzy. I complimented her mini-skirt, and she encouraged me to try out for track and field.

"You in any rush to get home?" she asked one evening.

I pressed the button on the side of my watch. The time glowed, showing it was nearly midnight. "No. Mom's gone to bed, and tomorrow's the weekend."

"Good. Because I'm not ready to say goodbye."

I rolled onto my side beneath the sheet and closed my eyes. My breathing slowed as we cruised around Aymes. The sidewalks were dark, vacant, but the sign in the window of the ice cream shop gleamed "Open!" It was her suggestion to stop for a vanilla soft serve, chocolate dipped. We sat at a table for two out front. She laced her slender fingers through mine. I couldn't help but stare as her tongue stroked the sides of her cone. Catching all the drips.

Late one night during the winter, I was feeling particularly brave inside my mind. I told her I'd never done it. Never even kissed a girl. She tilted her head, and her wavy hair tumbled over her shoulder. "That's so wild," she said. "Passing up a decent guy like you?" She kept one hand on the wheel, and the other reached over. Grazed my knee, then crawled up the inside of my thigh. The innocent *tick-tick* of the car's blinker as she turned onto a dirt road. She drove up the incline, wheels slipping on the ice, and parked in a clearing that everyone called the overhang. She kept the engine running, cranked up the heat. Then moved her hand between my legs. Clutching at me through my pajama bottoms.

I gasped. "What are we doing?"

Her sultry smile sent a hot shiver down my spine. "What do you say? Should we fix things?"

•

For months and months, I'd been approaching the front of the cafeteria lineup with fidgety insides. Mouth bone-dry. I kept wondering when she'd finally lift her head, meet my eager eyes. Would she take one glimpse and understand on some otherworldly level how much we'd shared? Or how vulnerable we'd been? Would she remember how her body fit so securely onto mine, as though we'd been designed for each other?

Or would I spend yet another lunch hour being invisible? Blending into the blur of bell-bottoms and sweaty T-shirts and shaggy hair and tables and olive walls and scratched orange trays.

At some point, I stopped waiting for an obvious sign. I'd already noticed her silver scoop sneaking me an extra meatball. And those metal tongs clutching the larger slice of pepperoni pizza. That had to be her subtle way of communicating. She clearly did not want to make our connection obvious. She was married after all.

·

One Sunday evening in late spring, I was sitting beside my mom and watching a television program about a man with mysterious powers. He'd sneak up behind people on the street and then match their gait. Mimicking the steps, the breathing, the way their hands swung through the air. After a few moments of this, he'd claim his body was now in tune with the apparent stranger's. They'd established a deep and intense connection, creating a oneness between them. For proof, he would then dramatically collapse onto the sidewalk, convulsing. And the stranger he'd been following would suddenly do the exact same thing.

"Who'd believe the silliness?" my mother sneered, but I could barely blink as I witnessed his powers. The concept was immensely appealing to me. If I could hone such a skill, perhaps I could use it with the lunch lady. Not just inside my mind, but for real. Even though we'd met over a year now, she barely glanced at me when she filled my tray. This trick could change that. Maybe she'd even greet me as she strolled across the parking lot after work. Or if we happened to meet outside after dark, I could guide her down a hidden path. I wondered, too, if I made her body align with mine, could I also do that with her emotions?

It was exciting new territory, and over the next couple of weeks, I practiced frequently. In the hallways of school, on the bus, moving along the aisles of the grocery store. Easing closer and closer to various teen-aged girls I cared nothing about. I made note of every nuance. Shoulder lifts and hair flicks. The way they'd sway their narrow hips. But it didn't work a single time. A complete and utter fail. I was the only one who tripped, who slid from my seat, who tumbled down the stairs.

My mother's reaction was swift and over the top. She'd forgotten the program, of course, and was convinced there was something wrong with me. A degenerative neurological ailment that caused my whole body to turn to jelly. I was not about to tell her the truth, and my silence prompted several trips to the family doctor. When he found nothing of note, my mother marched me off to a specialist at the hospital in the city. The specialist proclaimed me a physically fit young man, free of pathology, but likely suffering from an anxiety disorder. "The mind can have a profound impact on the body." Which I thought was funny, as the man on television said that, too.

From there, my mother sent me to see Mrs. Fischer. She taught health at the high school, but she also saw clients in her home. An economical alternative to therapy, she called it.

"It's important to get in touch with your body," Mrs. Fischer said during my first appointment. Her home office was painted a bright lime. On the wall behind her head was some velvet art, a button-chinned girl with watery blue eyes. "And in touch with your inner self, of course."

I shifted in my seat. I'd spent considerable time "getting in touch." So much, in fact, some parts had gotten a little raw.

"Panic can start with a quiver," she continued. "Kind of like a small bird inside your ribcage."

I had no idea what she meant, but if I had to have a bird in my chest, it would probably be a thrush. Or a junco. Something sturdy but unremarkable.

"Those physical changes are tiny signals that you can catch. Reminding you to slow down. To breathe. To release that bird from its cage."

"Cool. I didn't know that." I pretended to be interested, but the whole thing was lame. I'd made a dumb mistake. Believed some asinine garbage I saw on the boob tube.

"You look unimpressed," she said, leaning forward in her seat. Her hair was perfectly smooth, minus the ends, which flipped upward, "But trust me, we will navigate through your challenges, and you'll come out stronger on the other side. These are skills you can use throughout your lifetime."

I nodded.

She smiled at me and lifted her eyebrows. "So. What does it feel like for you?"

"What does what feel like?"

"In those moments. Just before you crumple onto the floor."

"Like nothing," I said.

"Oh, come now. You're a smart boy. You can do better than that. How about you describe it? Sure, give it a go."

I hesitated.

"Does your heart race? Do you feel disoriented? Your palms sweat?"

Yes. Yes. And yes. But it came from the sight of a pink bra strap. The hint of unwashed sweat beneath baby powder deodorant. The startle in a girl's eyes when she realized how close I could get without our skin touching.

Then the words bursting from their mouths. And sinking into me.

Creep.

Asshole.

Freak.

But I played along, until Mrs. Fischer said cheerfully, "I think we've done quite well today." She took the damp roll of bills I'd kept in my fist. "You'll see. We'll get this sorted."

I nodded again, even though I wasn't sure I even wanted it sorted. I quite liked the feeling of falling. An instant of weightlessness before that sharp and sudden pain when I struck the ground. It was something I'd done for the lunch lady, in an effort to discover the string that surely connected the two of us. It seemed right that a meaningful endeavor would require suffering. Wasn't love a seesaw of heavy and light, bright and dark, hot and cold, sick and healthy? That's what Shakespeare said, anyway.

"Next week?"

"Yup," I mumbled. "Next week."

After I climbed the concrete stairs from her lower-level office, I took a deep breath. The air was fresh and sweet, as though a sense of newness permeated it. I decided to take a shortcut home and cut through the backyard of Mrs. Fischer's neighbor. The house was aglow, curtains wide open.

As I gazed in through a pair of sliding glass doors, I finally understood the reason why I'd twisted the television dial at that moment. Why I'd paused to watch that magic man. Why I'd wound up talking to dippy Mrs. Fischer in her basement. It was Fate at work once again. Taking me on a roller-coaster ride. Careening down and down, before the stomach lurch and the thrilling loop upward.

On that warm spring evening, I saw her through the windows. The lunch lady lived inside.

NOW

.

CHAPTER FIFTEEN

Molly

THE DESK IN her father's home office was so old it could once again be considered trendy. Heavy blond wood, two sets of drawers on either side, black lacquered handles, and angular silver legs.

Molly had sat at this desk as a child, drawing pictures or practicing her cursive. Back then, she'd thought it was enormous. Her father would pile pillows on the chair to lift her up, or he'd balance her on his knee so they could "work" together; she'd complete her "papers" on the left side of the desk, while he'd complete his on the right.

Just recently, she'd come to realize that every crevice, every surface of that house was associated with her childhood. Things long forgotten were now pushing their way to the forefront. She'd spent the entire morning sitting beside her father, chattering about the past. Their Boggle competitions on the coffee table. The apple cider he mulled each fall inside a huge pot. That time he'd forbidden her to bleach her hair, and after Molly did anyway, he'd taken her to a salon for a "snazzy pixie cut." Once, when he had the flu, she'd

tried to make chicken soup. "Best ever," he'd said, even though the
noodles had dissolved into glue.

She pulled out the old bankers chair and sat down. With a shift
of her body, the squeaky wheels rolled over the piece of heavy plastic protecting the carpet. Tugging open the drawer to her left, she
made note of the banking statements, property tax documents,
utilities bills. Everything was meticulously sorted in labeled folders.
Arranged by date, some stamped "Paid" in indigo ink. A "Personal"
folder contained only a few receipts for dry cleaning.

In the drawer below, there was a bottle of scotch, some shoe polish.
Tucked into the back corner, she found an ornate tin, its hinges broken. In it, she discovered a handful of unfamiliar photographs. As she
shifted through them, she realized they were snapshots of her mother's
family. The Paltrys. She recognized her mother as a teenager, perched
in the branches of a tree with two other kids. The boy on the higher
branch had to be Molly's uncle, and the girl with the mushroom haircut had to by Molly's aunt. She could not recall either of their names.
Other photos showed her grandparents, who'd died before Molly was
born, beaming at the camera. She couldn't understand why her father
hadn't shown her those before. Or had she seen them and forgotten?

At the very bottom of the pile was a picture of Molly and her
mother. In the image, Molly was around two or two and a half, standing on a grassy patch near a body of water. No doubt Rabey Lake.
Her chubby arms were extended toward her mother, who appeared
to have her hands raised in playful protest. Molly could imagine the
moment her mother bent to lift her up. Comforting her.

The other drawers held more of the same. Cable bills. A packet
secured with an elastic band that contained the details of the sale of
the pharmacy. Even original paperwork from when the home was
bought in the 1970s.

She leaned forward into a rectangle of sunlight, spread her palms over the wood. Relaxing her shoulders, she lowered her head onto the desk and inhaled the smell. She was drained, sleepy, but at least sorting her father's affairs would not be too challenging. While the quantity of his belongings was overwhelming, it seemed his careful organization would keep the legal paperwork straightforward.

Her eyelids closed, and gradually her breathing slowed. After a moment, she realized someone was standing behind her. Molly felt a flash of confusion, but then she heard a woman say, "Be good and stay right here."

Slender fingers appeared in her peripheral vision. Picking at the flap on a green and yellow box. The sound of cardboard tearing, and with a quick shake, crayons clinked on the desk in front of her. "And don't let them melt," the lady said.

Molly stared at the damaged box, then at the marked-up piece of looseleaf that had appeared beside the crayons. "What is it?"

"A pumpkin, silly. Of course it's a pumpkin."

A wisp of perfume. Or cherry lip balm. The door clicking shut. The woman evaporating.

Now alone, Molly whispered to herself, "A pumpkin, silly. A silly pumpkin." Crouching, she picked up orange in her fist and began coloring. For several minutes, she filled in the hastily drawn circle, the squiggling line sprouting from the top.

A flurry of movement in the street caught her eye. She stood up on the chair to peer through the window over her father's desk. A man with messy black hair tumbled out of a car. He stopped on the sidewalk just in front of their house. Then slowly he walked up the driveway. He was coming closer.

"And what did you see, Molly?"

She was sitting again. Her legs swinging back and forth. There
was a hitch in her navy tights, and as she picked at the hole, more
and more people were watching her.

"The bad man," she finally said. He was looking at their house.
She thought she'd seen him before. In the backyard. Or sitting in
a tree. That day he tried to sneak inside.

"The bell went ring, ring, ring. And the door went bang, bang,
bang!"

A sudden scream sent a spark of fear up Molly's spine. Her eyes
sprang open, and she sat upright. For a moment she was disoriented,
couldn't quite grasp the contents of her dream. Then she realized the
noise had come from outside; a handful of young kids strolling along
the sidewalk. Yelling and laughing.

As the teenagers disappeared into various homes, she took a
moment to calm herself. Her poor sleep was getting the better of her.
Dozing off like that, obviously exhaustion had set in. She rubbed her
eyelids, then leaned back in the chair and tugged open the middle
desk drawer. The only item in there was a worn leather folder, where
her father kept items that needed to be addressed in the immediate
future. When she opened it, she found a cashier's check, issued by
his bank for the hefty sum of $10,000. The "Pay to the Order of"
line was blank. She picked it up and turned it over, and over again.
She could think of no explanation for a check that size. Unless he'd
been planning a renovation. A gardening project. Or there was some
issue with the house? Perhaps that was what he wanted to talk to her
about on their last call.

"Molly?"

Through the open door, she could see Glenn, from the waist up.
He was standing on the stairs.

"Dad okay?"

"Yeah, he's fine, it's just your phone." He held it aloft. "You left it downstairs."

"Oh?" She yawned as she patted the front pocket of her cardigan. "I hadn't realized."

"It's just been ringing and beeping nonstop. Didn't mean to pry, but it's your son."

Molly rushed from the office then, and tore the phone from Glenn's outstretched hand. Sure enough, there were six missed calls from Alex. And a flurry of texts.

"mom"

"mom!"

"where r u"

"mommmmmm"

"cmb"

"srsly?"

"MOM"

It began ringing in her hand. She swiped up. "Alex? Are you okay?"

"What the hell, Mom. Seriously, what the hell. Where are you?" He was breathless.

"At your grandad's."

"Why? Why are you there? You need to be here."

Molly scrunched her brow. Was he injured? Or was he just being self-absorbed? "Where's here, Alex? What's going on?"

"I mean, I forgot my keys, Mom. Like, I don't even know where they are. I'm totally locked out." He was stumbling over his words.

"It happens to all of us," she said, trying to calm him down. "Is Russell at home? Or you can wait for me. I'm near finished up here anyway, so just enjoy the fresh air un—"

"And I checked all my pockets. And I don't have any candy. I dumped out my whole book bag. My homework is all blown away. There's nothing, Mom. And I feel really—I really don't."

"Alex?"

"Where are you? How far away?"

"I told you. I'm at Grandad's." She stood and headed for the stairs. "And I'm getting my shoes on. I'll be there in five." She was in the car, foot heavy on the gas as she backed out of the driveway.

"That's too long. I don't have any."

"Alex. Listen to me. Go bang on a door. Tell them you need juice. Show them your medic alert necklace."

"No way. I'm not doing that. I won't."

"You have to, Alex."

"I can't. I don't know them."

What was wrong with asking a neighbor for help? Hypoglycemia was impairing his reasoning, his thinking. "Then shove the door in."

"Mr. Farrell'll shit his pants, Mom. Like, literally."

"So what? We'll deal with it later." She pressed down harder on the gas. Whizzing past the sprawling homes, then down streets with smaller two-stories, shallow lawns. She barely slowed at stop signs.

"How far are you, Mom?" His words were slurred, quivery. "I'm serious. I'm not joking. You need to get here. Now."

"Do what I said, Alex. Do what I—"

Then silence. She could picture him in her mind. Slumped against the side of the house, body shaking, his damp face a sickly shade of gray. Refusing to do what he needed to do. Plummeting blood sugar could happen quickly, and there was a fine line between jitteriness and coma.

She sped along the road. Cursed the afternoon traffic, red lights. The school bus with its constantly swinging sign and frequent stops. Twelve whole minutes later, she tore up the driveway. Leapt out of the car and dashed around the back of the house. She expected to see him lying on the ground, but there was nobody there.

Yanking open the screen door, the main door was intact, still locked. She searched the backyard, under the table, along the side of the shed. She even ran up as far as the border of fir trees. He was gone.

Panting, she rushed to the stone patio. He had to be somewhere. "Alex?" she called. "Alex?" A second time. Even louder.

Then Russell strolled around the side of the house.

"Russ," she stammered. "Have you seen—" Her son was right behind him. "Alex!"

"I'm fine, Mom." He shrugged. "You don't need to freak out. My phone just died."

"Yes, he's okay, Molly."

Molly bent slightly at the waist, clutched her chest. "I was so worried. I couldn't find you."

"We've got it all under control," Russell said. "Don't we, Alexander?"

"Yup. All good, Mr. Farrell."

Molly exhaled loudly. "He came and got you, then?"

"No, I heard the scuffling. Figured that family of possums was back. Last year they got up under the roof"—Russell pointed at the eaves of the house—"and settled right in." Then he smiled. "Rent free, too."

"Hey, Mom, can you open the door? I need to change my shirt. It's drenched." Though Alex's face was pale, there was faint pink in the center of his cheeks.

Molly unlocked the door and he was already peeling off his T-shirt before he disappeared inside.

"Thank you," she said to Russell.

"No need. Nothing a glass of orange juice couldn't fix."

"I'm just glad you were home. I don't know what he's doing these days. He used to be so meticulous, checking his sugar, carrying sweets."

"I get it. My mom has diabetes too. Not the young kind, but the one you get when you're older and rounder." He patted his stomach. "When it drops, she becomes near impossible."

"Alex is the same way. You mentioned she's in a nursing home?"

"For a few years now," he said as he flipped up the cuffs on his shirt. "So everything's monitored, I'm sure. I don't need to worry."

"I guess I've got Glenn for that with my dad."

"Glenn." He cleared his throat. "I suppose he'll do for now, Molly."

Was Russell frowning? Though he was right. It would do for now, but employing a live-in nurse for her father was not a long-term solution. At some point soon, Molly would have to explore other options.

"Well," she said, "I really appreciate you swooping in to save the day."

When Molly went into the kitchen, Alex's clothes were piled on the floor.

"I'm glad you're okay," she said as he came out of the bathroom, wearing clean track pants and a hoodie.

"Why wouldn't I be?"

She stared at him. Barely twenty minutes ago, he'd been on the verge of collapse, and now he was tall and strong and certain again. "I don't know. You sounded in rough shape on the phone."

"And you overreacted, like usual." At the sink, he filled a large glass with water. Took it to the table and sat down. "Guess what I learned today."

"That you should always check your book bag before you leave the house?" She plucked up the ball of clothes.

"No. Related to the case."

Her fingers tightened on the damp cotton. "Your assignment about my mother?" She'd pushed that out of her mind.

"How'd you know?"

"I was alerted. To make sure I was okay with it."

"Whatever. Cool." He slumped in his seat, knees spread. "Well, did you know Mr. Farrell testified?"

For a split second, Molly had vertigo. As though the tile floor was not completely level. She wobbled toward the closet that hid the washer and dryer. Tossed the laundry into the basket. "Mr. Farrell, like our landlord Mr. Farrell?"

"Yeah. He told me about it. He was with the guy before he went to find your mother. He also said Terry Kage was kind of delusional about her."

She was definitely dizzy and brought a hand to her forehead. The stress of the afternoon had clearly gotten to her.

"He said a group of them were hanging out. Bunch of guys from high school. Grandad's nurse was there, too. And the neighbor's kid. Plus, Officer Kage."

She scanned the kitchen. She needed to keep her hands moving. "If he says so, Alex. I don't recall everything." From the fridge, she pulled roasted chicken and a plastic bag of baby carrots. Tubs of store-bought salad, potato and creamy coleslaw. She collected plates and cutlery and napkins. Then joined Alex at the table.

"And did you know the school is haunted?"

"Alex. That's absurd. Did he say that, too?"

"No, kids in my class." Alex tore off a drumstick. Chewed and talked. "Your mother and that guy wander around the cafeteria, apparently. Like they were Romeo and Juliet."

She forced a thin laugh. "My mother was young, but she was happily married to your grandad. And besides, Romeo didn't kill Juliet and then dump her in Rabey Lake."

"You score a point for that, Mom. Too bad I can't use it in my presentation. No comedy allowed."

"Good. Fine. Can we talk about something else?"

A piece of chicken was hanging from Alex's chin. With a greasy finger, he picked it off and ate it. "How come you never told me he hanged himself?"

"What?"

"Not like it's a secret or anything," he said, shrugging.

She pushed her chair back a couple of inches. "I never told you because . . . because it was a lifetime ago, and it's upsetting and unfortunate." And any time she imagined Terry Kage swinging from that light post, a seam of worry split open inside of her. Wondering if she'd gotten her testimony exactly right, or if she'd misunderstood. Or misspoke. Or just missed . . . something. And a part of his death was actually her fault.

After Alex had gone to his bedroom, Molly lay down on the couch. She considered calling Casey or logging into the support line but couldn't muster the energy. When she closed her eyes, she could see the boy standing in the driveway. Studying everything, as though he'd taken a wrong turn and was unfamiliar with his surroundings. Then he was banging on their door. Ringing the bell.

She'd finished coloring her picture and then crept downstairs. Following the voices, she found him with her mother in the garage. "You can't do this to me," he'd wailed. "You can't do this." Perhaps

Terry Kage *had* been in love with her mother. And his feelings had morphed into something dangerous. A teenage obsession, like Russell had told Alex. Molly could hear that desperate urgency in her memory of his tone.

After that, it was like watching a high-res movie in a theater. The violent push, the fall, the blood. Though as she rewound or skipped forward through the scenes, she always sensed something unwanted buzzing around her head. A bottle fly, or a flick of ash. But no matter how hard she tried to grasp it, her hand always met with nothing.

CHAPTER SIXTEEN

"I THOUGHT YOU'D ditched me."

As Molly approached the table, Bradley Fischer stood up. "Sorry I'm late," she said. "I didn't want to rush off the moment your mom stopped by."

Just as she'd been about to leave her father's house, Mrs. Fischer had appeared on the doorstep. Molly had shown her into the living room and then waited in the kitchen to give them privacy. She could hear Mrs. Fischer talking at first, then softly weeping. Telling Molly's father how much she thought of him and that she wasn't sure what she'd do without him. How she worried she'd brought too much stress into his life. Molly realized she really didn't know the details of the relationship during those years. Had they argued? Had her father wanted them to be together in some way that Mrs. Fischer didn't? Or vice versa?

Bradley threw up his hands. "My mother? Trying to keep my date to herself, was she?"

"Hardly. And this is certainly not a date." Molly shook off her coat, hung it on the back of the stool. The bar had an intimate atmosphere with low lighting, rich mahogany, every edge softened to a curve. In the middle of the table, a single white rose floated in a flattened glass globe.

When the waiter appeared, Molly ordered a green apple gimlet.

"So, I couldn't find a boozy dive, like I promised, but as for the charm factor"—he pointed both his thumbs at himself—"I've got it totally covered."

She grinned and shook her head. Absurdity was attached to every word he spoke, and she could see why multiple marriages had imploded. While that jocularity might appeal at the onset, it wouldn't get the electricity bill paid or the garbage to the curb.

"So, this is nice, hey?" he said. "Neighbors being neighborly."

"It is," she agreed. A single drink to be sociable with the boy next door. Something to amuse Casey the next time they spoke.

"You're vibing on being back in town?"

Molly grimaced. "I'd hardly use the term *vibing*."

"Other than your dad and all, I meant." His glass of amber-colored beer was nearly empty. "But I get it. Taking care of my mother gets heavy. She expects a lot."

"Really?" Molly remembered Mrs. Fischer as being extremely independent.

"Oh yeah. Just yesterday she forgot she'd already added salt to the soup. Completely ruined it."

"I hardly think—"

"Tip of the iceberg, Moll. She'd be embarrassed if I shared. Girl's gone downhill."

"Understood," she said. She wasn't going to press for details.

Her drink arrived. Spring-green liquid in a coupe, paper-thin slice of apple floating on the top. It tasted sweet and sharp.

"Can you believe it's been nearly forty years?"

"Since?" she said, even though she knew exactly what he meant.

"All that with Mrs. Wynters. Your mom."

She took another sip. "I'm surprised you'd remember." And surprised he would broach such a delicate topic after only ten minutes across from each other.

"It's still a big deal around here, you know. I'd say the local paper'll likely do a piece. Probably ask you for a comment."

"I certainly hope not." Even the thought made her feel queasy.

"Well, if anyone approaches you, just tell them to fly to fuck."

"Perfect," she said. "That'll read well in print."

"You better believe it. I had to do just that again today. Another group of loser kids outside your dad's house. Right up on the lawn. Taking selfies."

"You can't be serious. Why would they do that?" She was reminded of the cluster of teenagers a few days ago. She was certain she'd seen one of them pointing at her father's home, but then dismissed it.

"Apparently, that's a thing for some people. Murder anniversaries. These assholes get photos and post trash online."

"That's disgusting," Molly said.

"Human nature, I suppose. Everyone wants their likes or follows, right? But I'll keep an eye out. And I'll get Lyle Kage to patrol the street. Me and him have always been cool."

Molly folded the napkin into halves, then quarters. "I appreciate that, Bradley. Not sure it needs police presence, though. I'll just mention it to Glenn."

"That drip? He'd probably offer them snacks."

"You're awful," she said, shaking her head. "I don't know what you've got against him."

The waiter passed their table, removed Bradley's empty glass, and replaced it with a full one.

"So, do you miss it?" he said, wiping foam from his mouth with the back of his hand. "Being in Aymes, I mean?"

"Not really." Not at all. If it wasn't for her father, she would never set foot in the town again. Though no label had been used at the time, she now recognized the childhood bullying she'd experienced. The sideways glances. The half-joking jabs about her mother. The lurid innuendo about Terry Kage. For years, she'd tried to reinvent herself, tried to find her place. She was so desperate to belong, she'd even lost her virginity to a football player in a bathroom stall. After which he promptly told anyone who would listen. The day her father dropped her at college was one of the best of her life.

"Yeah, a lot of it totally sucks. Sure, I wouldn't be here but for 'family responsibilities.'" With his fingers, he made air quotes.

"Same," Molly said.

"Not that I want to bring it up again, but I'm still shocked forty years have passed, aren't you? Just guts me what happened to Terry. He was shy. Bit of a fucker, too. But man, I loved him."

Molly did not want to talk about any of that. Terry Kage might have been shy, or a "bit of a fucker," but he'd also murdered her mother. Had that slipped Bradley's mind? She gulped her drink. Was grateful the mix was gin heavy, simple syrup light.

"You knew he was one of my buddies, right?"

"I didn't," she said. She glanced at the other patrons. Hoping he'd detect her discomfort. Her lack of interest.

"Yeah, we used to run as a pack. Wild as wolves. Me and Terry. Sometimes Lyle. A couple of other fellows, too. Plus Rusty Nail. Oh, and Mother Hen Glenn."

She tried to shift the topic, asked Bradley what sort of work he'd been doing.

"Got my fingers in a dozen pots. Business deals and such."

"Anything in particular?"

"Considering franchises. Bit of real estate. Was thinking of doing a house flip, actually."

They chatted about Mrs. Fischer's retro furnishings. "It's like living in a museum." The styles he'd choose for a modern kitchen. "Calacatta marble all the way." The monotony of Aymes. "Booring." The drunken lady out near Rabey Lake who'd sold them both liquor underage, but fifteen years apart.

"She's probably still there," Bradley said. "If your son's looking for a source."

Molly laughed. "Yeah. Not something I'm about to mention."

As she stood up and made her way to the washroom, her legs were slightly unsteady from the cocktail. She sensed Bradley watching her, and she became aware of her footsteps. The curve of her spine. She wondered on what part of her body his gaze had settled.

When she returned, he was working on his third glass of dark beer. A fresh gimlet had appeared in her spot.

"I really shouldn't," she said. She hadn't eaten dinner, and she'd barely had a casual glass of wine in weeks. She was already feeling woozy.

"My mother's treat, you know. She wanted to pay. And you know she's stingier than a fat kid on his last Milk Dud."

Molly laughed again. "That's so untrue, and you know it. Your mother's selfless to a fault."

"Not if you're her son, she isn't." Leaning forward, he said, "Can I confess something terrible, Molly?" His eyes glowing.

She put her elbows on the table, base of her palms under her chin. "Sure, tell me your dark secret."

"In your dad's family room, you know those huge windows?"

"The ones on either side of the fireplace?"

"Exactly. I used to see your mother and father through them."

"That's no surprise. The windows face your house."

"No, I mean *saw* them. Going at it. Right on the couch. Lights full blast."

"What?"

"Yeah. Perfect view from the top of our stairs. Sometimes I'd even take popcorn."

Molly started coughing. She'd inhaled a sip of the gimlet. "I'm absolutely going to pretend you didn't say that," she blurted the moment she could breathe again. "And I didn't hear it."

"Open mouth. Insert foot, huh?" He grinned and smacked the table. "And that's me we're talking about now. Not what I saw your folks doing."

The banter lightened between them, but as the hour passed, Molly found herself increasingly unable to follow the threads. While Bradley had moved on to induction versus gas cooktops, she was still explaining how badly the town sign needed new paint. She yawned wide before she lifted her hand.

"Am I that lame?" he asked. He twitched his fingers toward the waiter.

"I'm sorry. These past days. Knocking me sideways." She pointed at her drink. It had been nearly finished, but was now completely full. Was that the third? Or fourth? Hands lifted, she said, "Not a chance. I've got to get back. You know, to Rusty Nail's." The watch on her wrist was farther away than it should be. "Alex is home by now. Homework, I hope."

"Now there's a waste of time."

"I disagree," she slurred. The glass globe in the center of the table was empty. A heap of white petals sat beside her purse. Had she fished the flower out, plucked them off? "What's the alternative?"

"Like enjoying your friends? Enjoying your life? That's what we did. Mostly in that alleyway next to the drugstore. Made your dad wild. Hell, those were good times."

"Sure, some good times. But not constant good times. That's shortsighted. Won't get him anywhere."

Bradley slapped the table again. "That's what happened to me, I guess. Too much fun."

"Not what I meant."

His head moved in jagged spurts, as though milliseconds of time were dissolving. "You've been amazing company, Molly Wynters."

She yawned a second time. "You're such a liar." When she turned, the lights had long tails. "I'd better be—" She slid off her chair. Removed her coat from the stool. Top or bottom. Front or back. The armholes were confusing.

"Here. Let me help."

"I got—"

She squeezed her eyes together. A hundred-dollar bill drifted down among the rose petals.

"No rush to end things, you know . . . separate entrance. Like your father's place."

"Huh?"

"Private . . . any the wiser." He bit his bottom lip, and his upper front teeth were perfectly even.

"You think I want—" She turned his suggestion over in her mind. He was a pompous man, with grandiose ideas, but she'd adored him when she was little. With his wavy hair and his worn jean jacket. The brooding slump of his shoulders. Her five-year-old self had terrible taste.

"I'll just be . . . and then we can get going."

And she imagined floating home with him, sneaking down the basement steps. His bedroom. Would it be decorated the same as when he was a teen? Nubby flannel sheets. Posters of Pink Floyd or Led Zeppelin. Record player. Box of tissues on a veneer night table.

Then she was gazing up at the sky. A million points of light miles above her head, but so close to her face. Like a sheet she couldn't touch. The faint smell of trash in her nostrils. Bins lined up on the sidewalk beside her. She must have wandered outside. Found her way to a wooden bench.

The air was cool. Pressing in on her skin. She would wait for him. Did she bring a scarf? Her car was steps away. License plate a blur. But no to driving. Big no. He'd only be a minute. The wooden slats against her spine were becoming soft. Agreeable. She laughed silently. She and the bench were supporting each other. Getting friendly.

"Molly Wyn—?"

She bumped her knee. Or her knee bumped someone.

"Yes?"

"What a surprise. We haven't met, but I'm—"

Her own voice in her ears. "I'm supposed to tell you . . . fly to fuck."

As she leaned away from him, the bench pressed into her back. The man's hands shot into the air. A phone? She pushed her face into the bend of her elbow. Blinded by flashes of light.

"Still being an asshole, I see." A man speaking. To her? A wide hand squeezing her shoulder.

"Watch it, buddy." Maybe that was Bradley.

"I'm just a woozy touch," Molly whispered into the darkness. "A little touch."

She was gliding through a tunnel of air. One wiggly step, then the next. Inside a car, too many buttons on the dashboard. She wasn't sure where she was going, but she wasn't all that worried either.

CHAPTER SEVENTEEN

A CLICK. SHARP and metallic.

Again. And again.

Molly sat up in the bed. Her head throbbed and she was disoriented. Where was she? What was this place? Through narrowed eyes, she scanned the gray walls and the gray ceiling and the gray patterned curtains. Shadows wobbling over the floorboards. Several seconds passed before she recognized Russell's house. She'd woken up in the bedroom of her rental. Still wearing the blouse and pants she'd had on last night.

She could barely recall getting home. Surely, given her state, she'd left her car on Main Street. Bradley must have driven her, or she'd taken a taxi. Had Alex seen her when she arrived? She gripped her throbbing forehead, felt the warmth of embarrassment spreading over her face. How had two or three drinks knocked her sideways? After the first one, much of the evening was an absolute haze. Was that odd? Or should she have expected it? Nights of poor sleep, poor appetite. She hadn't eaten dinner, and she'd also refused the tomato and cheese sandwich Glenn offered at lunchtime. One thing she knew for certain. She would never touch another green apple gimlet.

When she was about to lay down again, she became aware of the clicking. The repetitive noise that had appeared in her dream and then seeped into reality. She held her breath and listened. It was coming from outside her bedroom. Perhaps closer to the front of the house?

She should ignore it, try to sleep away her dry mouth and pulsing head. But there it was again. *Click. Click. Click.* Was it mechanical? Like a person snapping open an old-fashioned lighter? Was someone wiggling the handle on the screen door? Or could it be a footstep? Hard-soled slippers inching closer.

She checked the clock. It was 4:15 a.m., and her mind was having ludicrous thoughts. She'd been that way when Leo traveled after Alex was born. Her muscles, her skin, her eyes, her nerves, all in a continual state of high alert. At night, she'd remain wide awake until the dingy light of predawn. By the time Leo returned home on Friday evenings, she was a jumpy mess.

She pushed off the floral comforter, put her feet on the floor. A cold draft snaked around her ankles. Creeping into the hallway, she paused outside Alex's door, heard nothing, and then inched toward the kitchen. She stopped in front of the door beside the refrigerator. Reached out and touched the doorknob. It was icy cold. When she twisted, it was locked. Just as she'd left it.

Then she tiptoed to the vent in the living room. Kneeling down, she laid her ear to the floor. Only silence from below.

Of course it's quiet. Because normal people are asleep.

As she stood, the echo of her knees cracking made her freeze. She forced herself to exhale. What if Alex came out of his room and discovered her attempts to eavesdrop on their landlord? He'd surely think she was unhinged.

Another *click*. From behind her this time.

She twisted around. The curtain over the kitchen sink was moving. A soft billowing. She moved toward it and pulled it aside. Someone had left the window open a crack and a breeze had been driving the fabric forward. When she gripped the hem, she felt a hard round disk, like a steel washer, hidden inside the seam. Likely to weigh it down.

She let out a groan. Full-on alarm over a fluttering curtain. Enough fear to wake her from an alcohol-induced stupor when it was still pitch-dark outside. Why would Alex leave a window open? It had to have been him. But it was cold outside. Maybe he'd had friends over? Maybe they were smoking? That sort of scenario would make sense. With the tips of her fingers, she slid it closed.

After swallowing two pain relievers, she made herself a black coffee and brought it to the couch. As she sipped the hot liquid, she tried to piece together her evening. The wrinkles around Bradley's eyes when he grinned. His mention of the upcoming anniversary of her mother's death. Trespassers on her father's property. Her index finger playfully swirling the thin apple in her glass. Snippets of disconnected memories. She was ashamed of her behavior.

She reached for her laptop then, flipped it open, and logged into the peer support website. No one was going to call at this hour, of course, but perhaps doing something positive would temper her remorse. The glow from the screen lit up her face.

Sinking into the couch, she focused on the telephone icon and drank coffee until her mug was empty. She was surprised when the receiver lifted and shook. "Hi?" a young girl said. "I need help. I really need help. My mom's going to murder me." Her nose was either pinched or stuffed up, as though she'd been crying.

"Can you tell me what's worrying you?"

"I totally fell asleep and I've got this huge geography assignment due today and I'm not even finished and I'm totally going to fail and my mother's going to kill me when she finds out."

Molly leaned forward. While some teens brushed off grades, others felt intense devastation if they slipped. "I need you to listen carefully to me."

"Alright," she murmured.

"I'm going to ask you to take a few slow breaths, okay?" She waited while the girl inhaled and exhaled, and then she said, "Everything is going to be fine." She talked to the girl about asking for an extension. Getting help from her school counselor on organizational strategies. Methods to share her struggles with her mother.

"Okay," the girl said, sounding calmer. "Okay."

Molly clicked "End Call" and waited. But the receiver never rose again, never shuddered. As she gazed at the screen, the pressure inside her skull began to recede and her head dipped down, down. Sleep rinsing over her.

When she opened her eyes again, the light in the room had changed. Through the front window, she could see the faintest hint of orange eating away at the black. She stretched and went to the coffee carafe. Poured herself a second cup.

The *brrring* startled her, and as she rushed back to her laptop, scalding liquid sloshed onto her hand and wrist. "Shit!" she stammered. "I mean, Peer Support Line. Molly speaking."

"A little frustrated this morning?"

It was him. Or her. That voice, almost automated. The fine hair on the back of Molly's neck stood up.

"Just a small mishap," she whispered, pressing the red blotch of skin to her blouse.

"Or has your conscience been bothering you?"

Molly swallowed. "If you're having a problem, I can try to direct you to the right support. Otherwise—"

"I don't blame you, Molly."

"I'm sorry?"

"And I'm not angry. You were only a child then. You didn't know what was going on. All those complications behind the scenes, so to speak."

She suddenly felt nauseous, her mouth filling with saliva. "Why are you doing this? Is it some type of stupid game?"

"No, it's not a game. It's time you remember, don't you think?"

A flash of anger, then. At the caller. At herself. She was allowing a sick person to use her for entertainment. "Obviously you've got nothing to actually say. So you can keep your advice. Everything is crystal clear, thank you very much."

"Is it really, though? I'm impressed by your self-deception."

"This stops here. You got that? Whoever you are! I'm sure you think it's—"

"Figure it out, Molly. The time has come to pay your dues."

Her fingers shot out, striking the trackpad. The call disconnected. She closed the lid of her laptop, smoothing her hands over the warm aluminum cover. Shawna would have to remove her photo from the website immediately. Being featured like that had turned her into bait. Chum in the water. An easy target for any disturbed person who recognized her face. Remembered her family's history.

She stood up, began pacing back and forth. Brought her thumb to her mouth and chewed on the nail. *Figure it out, Molly.* What was there to figure out? Her memory of that afternoon was not muddy. She hadn't been deceiving herself for forty years. The only uncertainty involved the relationship between her mother and Terry Kage. When she was young, she'd heard the raunchy jokes. That the murder was motivated by young lust. That her father had "robbed the cradle" when he married a girl half his age. Could not keep up with the "demand." All of it was the mindless gossip of a small town, and while it certainly made Molly feel even more ostracized, it did not alter the truth.

"What happened to you last night?"

Molly looked up. Alex had shuffled into the kitchen, and she hadn't even noticed. He dropped his backpack onto the floor, poured a bowl of cereal.

"What do you mean?"

"I never heard you come in. Way past curfew, you know."

She unfolded her arms, tried to shake away the stress. "Was it?"

"Hell yeah, Mom. You're usually crashed by nine."

"I'm sorry. I should've let you know I was running late. Time got away from me."

"More than time, Mom," he said as he shoveled cereal with a soup spoon. "Seriously. I heard some guy walking you right to the door."

She blushed, handed him a paper towel. "It was only your grandad's neighbor. We had a drink." He must have driven her home. Or perhaps it was the cab driver. She sensed another fresh flush of red crawling up her neck.

"And here I was thinking I'd have a new stepdad here this morning."

"Hardly," she said, clenching her jaw. "I'm not finding this particularly amusing, Alex."

"But I am, though." He dropped the half-finished bowl in the sink. "Finding it hilarious, actually."

Molly followed him outside, and in the soft morning light, she watched him traipse across the front of the house and then along the road. She stayed there until he disappeared.

"Please remind him, Molly, my lawn is not a shortcut."

She startled and turned toward the voice. Discovered Russell kneeling near the top of the driveway. He was wearing forest-green rubber boots and had sheets of newsprint spread on the ground around him. Three lean brown rabbits lay on their sides, legs outstretched as though they'd been caught mid-hop.

"Sorry, Russ. I'll tell him as soon as I see him."

"That would be appreciated." Then he gestured toward the backyard with the knife he was gripping. "Beautiful, isn't it?"

Molly followed the direction of the blade's tip. Saw that every surface, every branch and blade of grass was coated in an iridescent frost.

She nodded. "Almost expect a gnome to leap out, don't you think?"

"No," he said, glancing at her over the top rim of his glasses. "I certainly wouldn't expect that." He peeled fur away from the rabbit's body. Sound of packing tape being yanked.

"Well, I hope I didn't disturb you with all my pacing around early this morning."

"Not at all. I heard mumbling. Were you talking to someone?"

"Oh, yes. Shawna's peer support line."

"Was anyone in need of help?"

When the rank odor of his task reached her nose, she stepped back so as not to gag. "I'm not sure, Russ. Just a lonely soul, I suppose. With nothing better to do." She shuffled her feet. "Can I ask—is it actually anonymous?"

"The support line?"

"Yes."

"Completely. You couldn't have it any other way, of course. It's necessary to gain the community's trust."

"Even, you know, if you peek under the hood." She was uncertain how any of that worked, but perhaps there was something in the program. In the coding.

"Nope. Not even. Each telephone number gets converted to a random string of digits and letters." He slid a cleaned headless rabbit to the side, then took his knife to number two. "Has a person been bothersome? There are ways of blocking a caller if they're abusing the resource."

"No, just someone this morning who was a little odd. Nothing I can't handle, though."

THEN

·

CHAPTER EIGHTEEN

Gil

WHEN GIL PULLED in to pick up his mother-in-law, Mrs. Paltry was already waiting on her stoop. Same as she always was. As she made her way down the concrete steps, she was already apologizing. Concerned that she'd been a bother. That he'd troubled himself.

Most Sundays, his wife invited her mother for dinner. Nothing fancy, as Gil soon discovered Edie's abilities in the kitchen were limited. And his were practically nil. Today he was going to toss pork sausages onto the hibachi grill, and Edie would rip lettuce and slice tomatoes. From the supermarket, she'd purchased a premade loaf of buttery garlic bread already wrapped in foil. "Easy-peasy," she'd said.

Mrs. Paltry was wearing a belted floral dress. The sleeves were short, and the thickened sores that previously marked her arms, elbows, had diminished. In her hands, she carried a pale green cake on a platter.

"I do believe that dessert will be the highlight of the meal."

"Nonsense. It's just angel food cake with lime gelatin." She shifted in her seat. "Cal's favorite."

"Oh?" He and Edie had not revisited the topic of her brother. Gil suspected there were painful memories there, and he didn't want to press. "Well then, it's too bad he'll miss it."

"Probably for the best," Mrs. Paltry said, laughing lightly. "I doubt he'd leave you a bite."

They drove along the worn roads. Cracked pavement, no sidewalks. In the bungalows, Gil noticed grimy windows with broken panes, tattered curtains on the inside. Most of the homes were constructed of wood planks. Some were peeling, but others were painted in garish tones of frothy pink or ocean teal. The rooves dipped.

Though Mrs. Paltry's home was not among the worst of them, it desperately needed work. But as often as Gil had told Edie they should help, Edie had been adamant. "She won't accept your money. You'll insult her if you offer."

"Everyone's outside on such a fine day," Mrs. Paltry said.

In Gil's view, her cheerful tone was out of sync with reality. A man was dozing on a front step, a cluster of brown bottles beside him. And muck-spattered children were chasing each other over patchy lawns. A red-haired boy scampered onto the hood of a rusted car, stomping his boots on the metal. Gil winced when he disappeared through the smashed-out windshield.

He'd once asked Edie, "Isn't it dangerous to leave all that trash sitting there? Couldn't a child get tetanus?" She told him he didn't understand. People never fretted over a scrape or a scratch. They were only concerned whether or not they could repair something or remove a spare part to sell.

"So," he said as he bumped over the railroad tracks. "When will I ever get to meet this Cal fellow?"

"Soon," she said. "He's working on a project, but when it's over, he'll visit, I'm sure."

"Must be intense."

Mrs. Paltry tugged the hem of her dress over her knees. "That's the way he is. Always been. Once he starts in, he doesn't let up 'til the job's done."

"I get that," Gil said. Nothing wrong with being tenacious. "What sort of project is it?"

"It's not glamorous. Clearing an area of land, is all."

"I bet it's exhausting. But rewarding."

"He prefers to work with his hands. My Cal never went in for books or such."

They were heading down Main Street now. They passed Wynters Even Drugs, which was closed on Sundays and Mondays. He straightened a little in his seat. The sign always made him feel a glimmer of pride. He said, "Not everyone's meant for academia."

"That's good of you to say."

"If we all had our noses jammed in the books, nothing would get done in the real world, now would it?" Though he was certain his and Edie's children would attend college. Establish professional careers.

Mrs. Paltry smiled.

Gil was relieved to turn down his street. Two-storied homes, manicured lawns, a grassy median dividing the two lanes of the road. The trees and shrubs were covered in a fresh green mist, as buds were beginning to open. More than once, Edie had told him his reactions were snobbish. But that was not the case. Gil made no judgment on the people who resided on the other side of the tracks. Instead, it was the weight he felt whenever he was there. As though hopelessness had bound to the oxygen molecules in the air. The feeling made him want to hide his eyes. Or flee.

As they approached the house, Gil noticed the flash of red and blue lights in his rearview mirror. A police car gliding up behind.

Mrs. Paltry clutched the collar of her dress. "Did you miss a sign, Dr. Wynters?"

"I don't believe so." Gil was meticulous about the rules of the road. He put on his indicator and allowed the vehicle to pass. It continued beyond his driveway and pulled into his neighbor's. Two officers stepped out.

"That's Mrs. Fischer's," Gil said as he parked, shut off the engine. "Lovely lady. Kid's a bit of a handful."

As they watched, an officer opened the back door of the police cruiser. Bradley Fischer emerged, his long hair curling down over the collar of his undersized jean jacket.

"Oh, that poor boy's like a wet dog, isn't he?" Mrs. Paltry said. "I have a feeling his mother's about to be very upset. I hope the father doesn't take him to task."

"There is no father. She's a widow."

"Even worse. Handling that on her own."

Gil got out, walked around to the passenger side, and opened the car door for Mrs. Paltry. "I'll just pop over," he said as she hoisted herself from her seat. "Check in with June." Since he and Edie moved in, their neighbor had been extraordinarily generous. Bringing over casseroles, fresh vegetables from her garden, plant clippings. Never asking for anything. Maybe he could offer her a little support. Return the favor.

Mrs. Paltry said she'd let Edie know, and Gil made his way across the grass, gently tapping on his neighbor's door. June answered, her face flushed.

"Oh, Gil," she said. "Is everything okay?"

"With me? I came to ask you the same question." He angled his head his toward the police car.

"It's Bradley. They've brought him home."

"Was he hurt?"

She pulled the front panels of her cardigan around her. "Not hurt. Could you come in? I'm so flustered right now, I can't keep a thought straight. They're asking me questions."

After wiping his shoes on the welcome mat, Gil stepped inside, followed June. Bradley was slouched on the sofa in the living room, lower jaw jutting out, sneakered foot hoisted on the table.

The officers were in chairs opposite him.

"And did you buy him the paint, Mrs. Fischer?"

"I did. He said it was for art."

"Art, huh?"

"Yes, a project for school."

"And you accepted that explanation?"

Her voice shook as she said, "Why wouldn't I?"

Gil cleared his throat. "What's going on here, gentlemen? This is a young boy you're intimidating." Though Bradley's demeanor did not suggest nervousness.

The officer closer to Gil stood up. "Just trying to get the facts straight, Mr.—"

"Wynters," Gil said. "Dr. Wynters. I live next door. Mrs. Fischer asked me to join the conversation."

"You can join if you want; that won't change what the kid's done."

"And what exactly do you think he's done, sir?"

"Why don't you tell the good doctor, Bradley?"

Bradley shrugged. "Nothing," he said. "I was chasing a dumb cat."

"What cat?" Gil said.

Bradley brought his foot down and leaned forward. Elbows on his knees. "There was this poster stapled to a telephone pole. Reward was five whole bucks for a missing cat."

"And you saw it?" Gil asked.

"Yup. Exact one. I took off after it."

"So, a good deed, then," the officer said. "Is that your argument, son? That's why you were down in that alleyway?"

"Sure was."

"I expect it's all a simple misunderstanding," Gil said. "The boy was trying to earn a few dollars."

"Sure, sure. And when the cat escapes, he decides to vandalize a building."

Bradley shoved his hair back. His forehead, a spray of acne. "That was an accident. I swear."

"An accident, huh?" The other officer flipped his notebook closed. "That's a new one." He stood up as well. "Here's what's going to happen, chum. Tomorrow morning, you're going down there with a bucket, some suds, and a brush bigger than your attitude. You hear me?"

Bradley's mouth was tight.

"I said, Do you hear me?" the officer repeated.

"I'll do it." June stepped forward. "It's my fault. I should never have bought the paint."

The officer scratched his head with the back of his pen. "All due respect, ma'am. It's not my business to tell you how to parent, but if he doesn't clean up his own mess now, he'll only make a bigger mess later."

June nodded as though she understood, but Gil knew what would happen. Not once had he seen Bradley mow the lawn or pull a weed. Carry in a bag of groceries or haul out a bag of garbage.

Then the officer pointed his finger at Bradley. "And if you get caught stealing so much as a penny candy in the future, we'll drop on you like a ton of bricks."

Gil followed them to the front door. When they reached the car, the same officer slowed and said, "You might consider having a talk with him. Sometimes boys respond better to a man's advice, rather than some lady chirping in their ear."

"I'll try," he said.

"Good. He's headed down a bad road if he doesn't curb it."

"What did he write, anyway?"

"That was a funny one. Huge letters. *Bradley Fischer loves Jenny Dawson.* If he'd had more time, he'd probably have spray-painted his own address."

Love, then, Gil thought as he closed the door. He smiled to himself. The boy did something foolish and illegal for love.

When Gil returned to the living room, Bradley was still on the couch, legs sprawled, hand resting beside his crotch. June was gone, and Gil assumed she'd given them a moment to talk. Man-to-man.

Perching on the edge of a chair, Gil tried to choose his words carefully. He mentioned the necessity of making responsible choices. How such poor judgment could seriously affect his future. His opportunities. That it was crucial he clean up after himself, and not permit his mother to do so.

"Did you mean it?" Gil said softly.

"Mean what?"

"Your declaration—" His voice hitched and he paused to clear his throat. "Your declaration of love."

"For Jenny Dawson?" Bradley slapped his stomach with a paint-stained hand. "Hell, no. She's the ugliest girl in my class. That's why it's hilarious."

CHAPTER NINETEEN

"I DON'T SEE why you're making such a fuss."

Edie leaned against the doorway of the garage as Gil held a metal bracket against the wall. Whirl of the drill as he drove in a screw.

"A man wants to have his belongings organized, right?" He was building much-needed shelving. For his toolbox, tools, paints. Up high for when there were little hands in their house, exploring, reaching.

"My father never did."

"Well, I'm not your father."

"No," she said as she turned around. "You're not even close."

Through his plastic safety glasses, Gil stared at her back. That raggedy cardigan she refused to replace. Her cottony dress, too thin for the cooler months. Feet bare on the linoleum.

Without replying, he returned to his task. Used an anchor to drill the next screw, securing the bracket to the wall. Surely, he'd misheard Edie. He'd spent his entire Sunday trying to make a home for them. A place that was clean. Functional. After all the terrible things she'd told him about her father, the instability of her life growing up, he had to be imagining that puff of disappointment in her voice.

•

"Put this on," Edie said, pressing a soft clump of fabric into his hand.

Gil shook it out. A black and white checkered bandana. "On where?"

"Over your eyes, silly. I'm taking you out."

Excitement rippled through Gil, as it had so many times since they'd been married. But he always noticed another sensation lurking beneath it. A lump of apprehension. Reminding him of those jawbreakers he'd loved as a child. Swaths and swaths of flavored sweetness, only to discover that awful anise seed in the center.

Reluctantly, he covered his eyes with the cloth, and Edie came behind him, pulling it tight and knotting it. Pressure against the bridge of his nose. Then he felt her warm fingers slide into his and she led him out of the house and into the car. Within moments, the engine was growling.

"Can you give me a hint?"

"Uh-uh," she said. He heard a sigh. "I mean, it's no big deal. Just somewhere I go to catch my breath."

They drove for maybe ten minutes. Or perhaps much longer, as he found it impossible to gauge time. At first, he tried to keep track of their direction, the stop signs, the way his body leaned left and right. But soon he was befuddled and slightly nauseated. He imagined being a kidnapping victim. Blinded, immobilized, tossed into the cold trunk of a car.

Edie braked suddenly and shut off the car. He felt a gush of air as his door opened, and she guided him onto a flat surface. Through the slender gap at the base of the cloth, he detected a yellow glow, could see painted divider lines on the pavement.

"Where are we, Edie?"

"Eyes closed!"

They moved forward, Gil lifting and lowering his feet. "Bend a bit," she said. "Or you'll scratch your head on the wire."

He did as he was told. They paused then, and he heard metal. Like a latch. Squeal of wood, as though a door did not properly fit its frame.

When Gil hesitated, she said, "If you really trusted me, you'd be fine."

He did trust Edie. Didn't he? Then why did he always feel on edge when she went for solo drives in the evenings. Or when she hurried off the telephone the instant he arrived home. Or when she took long baths, and he could hear water lapping, soft moaning behind the locked door.

When he had talked to Seth about it, his friend said, "Any solid marriage has its share of secrets, buddy." But Gil didn't want that. He wanted to know every single thing about his wife. Where she went. To whom she spoke. What she did to her own body that caused such guttural noises of pleasure.

Those were issues of concern. Safety, even. Rooted in adoration, not mistrust.

When Edie stopped walking, Gil's palms began to sweat. He sensed a hollowness around him, as though he was trapped in the middle of a bone-dry chasm, walls of stone.

"When nobody's here, it's so calm."

"Really?" He did not feel calm at all.

Then the monstrous racket of paper tearing. "Taste this," Edie whispered.

Gil paused. Just last week, she'd told him to close his eyes and then fed him a warm spoonful of dinner. Throat seizing, he opened his eyes to a glass baking dish filled with six warm bananas wrapped in sliced ham, covered in a salty orange sauce. "It's from a magazine," she'd said. "I followed the recipe." He lied and told her it was delicious. Apologized for eating a pastrami and cheese right after work.

Now there was iciness on his lips. He licked. Chocolate and vanilla. This was much better.

"Okay, you can take it off now."

Gil tugged the bandana off his head and looked around. Moonlight streamed through the high windows, casting an eerie paleness over the room. A cash register. A long metallic counter. On the opposite side of the counter, a vast space filled with neatly arranged rectangular tables. Dozens of chairs flipped upside down, all those legs like bristles on a brush.

Gil was not sure what he'd expected. Where he thought Edie would take him. But this was certainly not it. They were inside the darkened cafeteria of the high school.

He resisted the instinct to squat down, hide himself.

"Edie, we can't be in here."

"Why not? This is where I work."

"Yes, but in the daytime. Not when it's locked up. That makes it breaking and entering."

She sniffed. "It's no such thing. The back door doesn't even lock properly. We just walked in."

"Do you think there's a difference, Edie? And where did you get this?" The ice cream sandwich was now in his fist.

"From the freezers. There's tons of them."

"I don't want it," he said, dropping it on the counter. "We need to leave."

Leaning her lower back against a freezer, she slowly bit into the ice cream with her front teeth. After she'd swallowed, she said, "Why do you got to be like that?"

"Like what?"

"So uptight?"

"I'm not uptight. I just don't want to get caught. How do you think that'd look?" Maybe nobody where Edie came from would care. East Aymes had different ideas of what was acceptable and what was not. But his neighbors, his customers would certainly take note. *Local pharmacist stealing snacks from students.* He'd be a farce.

She grabbed his ice cream and slammed it, along with hers, into the oversized sink. "You are really ridiculous. Nobody cares." Without waiting, she stomped down the hallway, out the broken door, through the hole in the chain link, and back to the car.

"Happy now?" she said once they'd exited the darkened parking lot. Gil was driving this time. Blindfold tossed onto the backseat. "You just suck all the fun out of everything."

"Have you done that before?"

"Yup. Tons of times."

"With other people?"

In his peripheral vision, he could see her chest rising and falling. "Sure. I meet the lunch girls and we swipe Creamsicles and smoke cigarettes and have a riot."

"Well, that's the last time. I forbid it."

She chuckled. "You forbid it."

"I do. You're a married woman, Edie. With a husband and a home." This was hardly different from what Bradley Fischer had done. Taking childish risks. Being an imbecile. "You have to stop acting like a teenager."

When he glanced over, he expected her still to be looking out the window. Or have her eyes fixed forward. But instead, she was staring straight at him. Mouth turned slightly down. An expression of disappointment or disgust on her face.

CHAPTER TWENTY

GIL TIGHTENED THE cap of the bottle and smoothed the label onto the front. "There you go, Mrs. Harris." He handed her the prescription. *Bendectin 5 mg.* "Two tablets before bed, and you'll feel better in no time."

The woman caressed the slight swelling on her lower stomach. "I hope so, Dr. Wynters. I thought it was supposed to fade, but I can barely keep a cracker down."

Gil watched Mrs. Harris exit the store, gripping the paper bag of morning sickness pills. How miserable must it be to experience nausea all day long? To gag from a wisp of cigarette smoke, or vomit from a bite of red pepper? He wondered, when it eventually happened, if Edie would suffer in similar ways. Or if she'd take to pregnancy like Seth's wife, Andrea. Producing son after son, with never a murmur of discomfort.

Seth strode into the shop. Tossed an apple core into the garbage and disappeared into the storeroom.

"You're early," Gil said, when his partner reappeared wearing his white lab coat. "Can't handle the sunny days?"

Seth leaned against the counter, chewed the skin on the side of his fingernail. "Put me on a beach with a tequila sunrise and I'd manage just fine."

"What's going on, pal?"

"Go ahead," he said. "Ask me when I last ate a peaceful meal. Or saw the carpet through the piles of blocks and cars. And the screeching and squealing? It never, never stops."

Gil listened and nodded. He was used to this conversation. Every so often, Seth had an explosive rant about the chaos inside his home. While Gil was an only child, Seth had grown up in a large household with five brothers. He'd fooled himself, he'd said, thinking he could do a better job. And now he'd recreated his own childhood hell.

"What do you expect with so many youngsters?"

"And she's on about another one. Still wants a daughter. All I got to do is look at her sideways, but I swear I'll snip myself with a pair of rusty nail clippers before she gets a—" Seth stopped himself, sighed, then said, "Sorry about that, buddy. Me and my problems, huh? Still no luck for you two?"

Gil shook his head. "It's fine. It's going to be fine." At least he hoped it would be. He and Edie had been married for over a year. They'd both anticipated an instant pregnancy, not this recurring sense of failure.

"But you're trying though, right?"

Gil smirked. "Yup. Often as we can." Two months ago, he'd urged Edie to make an appointment at her clinic for an examination. After she went, she told Gil the doctor said nothing illuminating. "I'm in good shape. Sometimes it's just down to timing."

"And she's as keen as you are?" Seth asked.

Gil blinked. He found it irksome when he sensed Seth probing for issues between him and Edie. Not that his friend would gloat exactly, but if he detected any hint of disconnect, he wouldn't hesitate to bring it up again and again. "Of course she is," Gil said. "My wife talks of nothing else."

"Well, then, careful what you wish for." Seth buttoned up his coat, flipped out the collar. "What I wouldn't trade for an hour of quiet."

Gil was grateful when the bell tinkled and a customer walked into the shop. Seth waved his hand at the man, smiled wide. "Good afternoon, Mr. Landry. How have those sleeping pills been working for you?"

Turning his back to them, Gil tapped his fingernail against his front teeth. There was a sourness in his stomach that hadn't been there fifteen minutes before. *She's as keen as you are?* He had no doubt. Zero. Each month when she realized their efforts were in vain, her face would contort. Tears would spill.

Behind him, Seth was still talking to Mr. Landry. "Now you know you're not supposed to share medication with your sister. Or anyone else for that matter."

"But if I could only grab a couple dozen more, Dr. Even. I'd be set."

Without thinking, Gil stepped toward the cabinet, tugged open the door. Looked under *Wynters*, but Edie was not there. He found her still under *Paltry*, and when he flipped open the cover of her file, he noted there was nothing new since the month they'd met. She'd been prescribed penicillin last winter for a respiratory tract infection, and though Gil had offered, she said she'd collect the pills herself. "The fresh air'll do me good."

No doubt Seth had been working when she'd stopped by the drugstore. Why was there no note of that? Seth was meticulous about updating patient records. Had she not bothered to fill it?

"I'll reach out to your physician," he heard Seth say. "But in the meantime, try warm milk. Or a dull book."

Gil slipped Edie's file in behind Mrs. Paltry's, then nudged the metal door closed with his knee.

"You still here, pal?" Seth said, hand slapping his shoulder. "Why don't you head out? Enjoy the rest of the day."

"Sure, sure." Tension was building between Gil's eyebrows. "Sounds good. Appreciate it."

On the drive home, that niggling feeling began to spread out from his center and into his lungs. He was breathing a little too quickly, and his arms tingled. Was Edie actually as keen as he was? Did Gil really have zero doubt? He couldn't quite identify it, but something was not right. Then he told himself he was being absurd. How could he deny the sight of her weeping? That despair arriving every twenty-eight days. Like clockwork.

When he pulled into the driveway, Edie's car was gone. He went inside and, without taking off his shoes, walked straight up the stairs and into their bedroom. After they'd returned from their honeymoon, he'd asked Edie to decorate it exactly as she wished. Wanting her to feel at home. She'd ordered new red and orange shag carpeting and bought a textured comforter printed with yellow poppies. Bulbous ceramic lamps. The wooden headboard had built-in cubbyholes on either end.

Gil slid open the thin door that covered her compartment. It was mostly empty, besides a box of Red Hots cinnamon candy and a paperback copy of *Expectant Motherhood* he'd bought for her. Picking it up, he examined the spine. She had not cracked the cover.

He tossed the book back in and flicked the panel shut.

Gil took a couple of steps and then turned a full circle in the middle of the room. The bed was made, furniture dusted, laundry folded, throw pillows plumped. It was like a snapshot out of a lady's magazine. Picture perfect. But why, then, was he convinced there was something obscured in the design? And that if he searched, he was going to find it.

He tore open the drawers of her night table, rifled through papers, receipts, old bills. Slipped his hands in between the sweaters on the shelf and dipped his fingers into the pocket of every shirt hanging in the closet. Lifted her side of the mattress. Snapped through the pages of several books. He went to the dresser and, one by one, pulled open the drawers. Cotton T-shirts, shorts, jeans. Ankle socks. Scented paper liners. Nothing unexpected. Nothing that raised an alarm.

He gripped the handle of the final drawer and slid it open. It contained Edie's undergarments. Bras and panties, all arranged by color: pinks, light blues, beige, and white. A black set of lace and silk that was Gil's favorite.

In the same drawer, neatly arranged on the right side, was a woolen vest. Garish blue and gray in a zigzagging pattern. He tilted his head and stared at it for a moment. It was something a young boy might wear, out of place with all those feminine items. It had to be sentimental for some reason she hadn't shared. Perhaps it had belonged to father. Or her brother, Cal.

Slowly, he eased his hand inside the V-neck, and then his fingers bumped an object that had been tucked inside. Flat and hard, he covered it with his palm. When he withdrew it, he recognized it immediately. The circular blue base on the bottom, cold clear plastic dome covering the top. He clicked the dial and it moved around, day to day to day to day.

"Like clockwork," he whispered to himself.

There it was. Inside his fist. The reason behind the regularity of her cycles. She'd never stopped taking hormones to keep them that way.

Gil was light-headed as he carried the disc down the stairs and into the living room. The label was stuck to the back of the container. It had not come from Wynters Even Drugs but from Lottie's Pharmacy. He knew where that was located. A solid twenty-to-thirty-minute drive out of town. So out of the way that no one in Aymes ever went there for prescriptions. Why would they?

He picked up the telephone and dialed. All sevens and eights and nines, it was taking forever for the rotary to reset. Then a man answered.

"I'm calling about a prescription," Gil said. "For my—for Mrs. Edie Wynters. W-Y-N."

"Wynters? Give me a couple of minutes, sir, to take a look."

Gil waited on the line.

"Do you have the number handy?" the man asked.

Gil brought the label closer to his face, read out, "B-798871."

"Gotcha." The man cleared his throat. "Seems she's due for a refill soon. We'll get it ready for pick up."

"Okay." Gil's voice was faint.

The pharmacist mumbled something to himself, then said, "Should we charge it to your account again, Doctor?"

Doctor?

His account?

Why on earth would her family physician be paying for her medication? Though he'd helped people in need at the pharmacy, Edie was not in that situation.

Gil put the phone down without responding. He clutched the disc and paced back and forth around the furniture in the room. He stopped in front of the sliding glass doors, could see his neighbor, June Fischer, in her backyard. Humming a song and clipping roses from a bush. She was wearing a one-piece bathing suit beneath a pair of white shorts. Bradley was sitting on the deck, sipping a drink through a straw.

Last summer, Edie had claimed to love gardening. Said she couldn't wait to wriggle her fingers into the dirt. But not once could he recall her lifting a trowel, nurturing a seedling. A small unimportant lie, that was. But Gil should have been paying attention. Maybe he'd have noticed she'd been lying about other things, too. More significant things. Pretending that they shared the same desire for a child. Had she even gone for that checkup? He squeezed his eyes closed, and there she was, right behind his lids. Pushing the words from her throat, eyes welling up, asking him to pick up another box of tampons, another box of sanitary pads.

As he moved about the living room, his dismay began to crumble under the leaden weight of something else. Something easier to digest. Anger.

He went to the kitchen and reached above the fridge. In that cupboard, they kept aspirin and bandages, Mercurochrome and Kaopectate. Tucked in behind it all was the container of vitamins Gil had given Edie. *Folate 1 mg.* Months ago, he'd offered it up to her in his cupped palms, as though it were a gift. "What's this?" she'd asked. Gil explained that early research had shown folic acid was important for a developing baby. She'd taken the bottle, then smiled at him. Gil had barely been able to glance at her beautiful face, his eyes stinging as though she were radiating summer sunshine.

The cotton stuffing in the neck of the container was undisturbed. Gil removed it, tipped several vitamins out onto the counter beside the sink. Compared them to the pills Edie was consuming each and every night. They were the same color. Nearly identical in size. With his fingertip, he counted the correct number. Then clicked the dial to each of the remaining days, replacing one white tablet for the other.

Him

EVEN THOUGH I'D spent my summer vacation planning it, in the end, it was a spur-of-the-moment decision. I left school before last class. Told Mrs. Even, the secretary in the front office, that I was overwhelmed.

"Forgot to do my English essay," I explained, my fist jammed into my stomach. "*Pygmalion*'s really tough." She knew about my faux disposition, how my brain could apparently short-circuit from so-called anxiety, and she waved her hand at me. "Dart home and finish up, love," she said gently. "I'll sign you out."

I didn't intend to go home, though. I'd already handed in my essay. Even though I was supremely skilled, I usually hated language arts. But I'd actually enjoyed that particular assignment. Especially the part where I had to research the inspiration behind the story. How a sculptor had fallen head over heels for his own creation. I recognized myself in that scenario. Hadn't I carved the lunch lady from a cold stone of nothingness? A scrape or two each evening, but over time I'd discovered every crevice of her body, every corner of her mind. Whenever I saw her, real or imagined, my nerves stretched and twitched. I was in love with her, as deeply as that sculptor was in love with a hunk of ivory.

As I strode along the sidewalk, I invited her along. Same as I usually did. This was the start of her favorite season, where she could kick up leaves and watch the animals gathering acorns. There was a softening, a sleepiness happening in the world. I could feel it in me, too. That desire to begin settling in. With her.

"Much better here," she said, grabbing my hand. "I hate being cooped up in the cafeteria."

"Figured as much. Wasn't hard to lure you away."

We roamed the streets, our fingers knotted together. Her upper arm was pressed into my upper arm, and she skipped once so that her steps were in tune with mine. A breeze made her corduroy skirt puff up. I tried to catch a glimpse of the lacy trim on her panties, but the fabric was too heavy. Or the wind too weak.

"You've got goose bumps," I said. "Want my sweater?"

"Nah. I'm okay." She was like that. Never one to complain.

As we wandered around, I found the tiniest fragment of sidewalk chalk on the ground. A child's lost possession. I bent down and drew a pink heart, pierced by a lopsided arrow. Her laughter filled my ears.

"Where'd you learn to charm a girl?"

"I don't know. Comes natural, I suppose."

Our meandering took us to her street. The same street where Mrs. Fischer lived. At first, I'd had weekly sessions with her, then every two weeks. Apparently I was a quick learner, as we'd begun to discuss taking the visits down to once a month. A check-in. To evaluate my progress. Make sure I had my pretend nervousness under control.

"Can we stop on that bench there?" she asked, pointing at the expanse of grass that divided the two lanes of traffic. "So you can brush my hair?"

When I glanced at her, dozens of tiny tangles were forming in the strands.

Of course, I agreed to her request. We sat together, and I removed the hairbrush that had appeared in my knapsack. I leaned my back against the wooden slats. Closed my eyes. Warmth from the sunlight washing over my face.

She slid down onto the ground in front of me, and as I pulled the brush through her hair, I noticed pink creeping up the skin of her neck.

"Why are you blushing?"

She looked up at me. "I'm a bit embarrassed to say."

"C'mon, now. You know you can tell me anything."

"It's about last night. What you did with your pinkie."

"Oh, that." I grinned, rolling my eyes. "I was just horsing around."

"I never had that experience before. I thought I was going to go crazy."

She was whispering the most exciting words when someone else coughed. I opened my eyes, and a man was standing too close to me. He was wearing a torn field jacket and a grimy ball cap. "Ducks Unlimited" across the front panel. His eyes were hidden behind glasses with mirrored lenses.

"Why'd you blow off school, kid?"

"Sorry?"

"You on something?"

"What? No!"

"Yeah, right. I just saw you talking to yourself."

"I wasn't," I said. A quick glance at the grass to confirm the lunch lady was gone.

"I could get you in heaps of trouble, you know. Being truant."

"I didn't do anything."

He took off his glasses, put the end of one arm into his mouth. "Don't worry, kid. I'll keep your little secret between the two of us. But you got to give me some motivation."

His lips were parted, and his eyes moving down over my body. When I followed his gaze, I saw the front of my joggers were lifted to a peak.

"Leave me alone," I yelled. I jumped up. Held my knapsack in front of my hips. Hurried away.

"He was awful," she said when she caught up to me. She threaded her arm through mine.

I grabbed her hand and squeezed it. "Don't worry. I won't let anything happen to you. Not ever. You've got my solemn word."

And I meant it, too. I would do whatever it took to make sure she was okay.

When we reached her backyard, I tried to act surprised. As though it was pure coincidence, a happy fluke. After all the months we'd been together, I wanted her to show me the world where she existed without me. The parts that were out of my reach. Places I couldn't create in my mind. I decided it was time for her to invite me inside her house.

But she didn't stride forward, swing open the door. Instead, an uncertainty spread across her face. A vagueness I couldn't pin down. I had the sudden cutting fear she was trying to hide something from me.

"Well?"

"You go on," she said, glancing over her shoulder. "I'll wait here."

"Fine, then."

I was irritated. This wasn't how I'd imagined things playing out.

Staying close to the brick, I moved around to the side of the house. I found a door there with peeling paint, a single brass knob, no dead bolt. From my backpack, I withdrew a screwdriver. Pressed the flat metal tip into the wood frame. A tiny twist and the door came open.

I was inside her garage. Oil stains on the concrete floor. Shiny power tools that looked like they'd never been used. High shelving with paint cans, a scuffed yellow toolbox. A set of winter tires stored in the corner.

When I opened the door to the main house, I wasn't afraid like I was when I stole the grenadine from that lady's house. I was younger then. Less worldly. Besides, who was to say I didn't have the right to be there? At least, that was my perspective.

The living room was not what I'd envisioned. Nothing soft and feminine. No pinks. No flowers. No romance novel on the side table. Instead, it was all dark wood furniture and heavy curtains. Masculine-colored fabrics, a blue and beige rug. The sight of it agitated me, and I wondered where she belonged in all of that. If she belonged at all.

As I wandered about, I touched everything that I knew she'd touched. I went down the narrow stairs into a low-ceilinged basement. The washer and dryer were in the farthest corner, and inside the washing machine, damp sheets clung to the sides of the drum. When I pulled down the metal door on the front of the dryer, it was empty.

Back up the stairs to the main floor, and then up another flight. In the bathroom off the upper hallway, two toothbrushes hung from the holder screwed to the wall. I lifted the blue one, discarded it into the bin full of used pieces of tissue. Then I brought the pink one to my nose. In addition to the toothpaste, I found the scent of her mouth on the bristles. A sweetness, like bread soaked in condensed milk. For a single moment, I pressed it to my lips.

The shower curtain had loud brown and orange octagons. Someone less articulate than myself might have called the geometric pattern "groovy." Pulling it aside, I found a bar of soap on the rim of the tub. I lifted it up, turned it over, plucked away a coarse dark hair. She'd used this soap in the shower. Water pinging off her bare skin, the lather gliding over every inch of her body. I could not resist tucking it into my pocket.

In her room, the bed was neatly made. I slipped my hand beneath her pillow, and as expected, I discovered her nightdress folded there. A sheaf of slippery fabric. I rolled it into a ball, pushed it down the sleeve of my jean jacket.

Next I slid open a drawer to her dresser. Moved my fingers slowly through a mound of silkiness. My mother always called those items "unmentionables" and said no one should ever see them. While I could apply that reasoning to her stretched-out panties and tattered bras, the lunch lady's delicates were in a different category. Those pieces were meant to be appreciated.

I was about to choose a single item as a keepsake when I froze. A noise was rumbling through the house. Mechanical whirring. Was a car entering the garage? Then the whirring again as the door lowered. A slam. A second slam. Voices. Laughter. They were in the kitchen now.

I was no longer alone.

"You're absolutely wild."

"Really? Like what?" That was her speaking.

"Oh, I don't know. A hungry crocodile. With a mouthful of sexy teeth."

What a moronic thing to utter. The voice obviously belonged to a grown man, but he sounded as mature as a twelve-year-old. But my lunch lady was laughing. She was actually laughing.

Tearing then. Paper or cardboard packaging?

"I told you already," she said. "You don't need those things."

"I know, I know. But still."

Hurrying out of her bedroom, I rushed into the empty room across the hall. Closed the door, but not quite all the way. I pressed my eye to the crack and tried to slow my breathing, calm my pounding heart. They were skipping up the stairs. The top of her head arrived first. She was leading the way up, pulling him.

Then I squeezed my eyes closed. I did not want to see the two of them. I did not want that snapshot inside my mind. Husband and wife, side by side. It would be too difficult to erase. Her playfulness. Her betrayal.

When I opened my eyes again, I knew they were in the bedroom. Hadn't even bothered to close the door. I could have stayed to watch them if I wanted to. Based on the moaning and the steady wet smacking, I doubt if they'd have noticed my presence. But I felt as though I might vomit, and I only wanted to leave.

As I tiptoed down the stairs, I saw an opened box of condoms dropped on the landing. That was what they were using. I would never insist on cheap rubbers. When she and I had our private moments together, there was never anything between us.

Once outside, I felt a horrible discomfort inside my head. As though a beetle with a broken shell was buzzing there. Spinning in frenetic circles. It had been a mistake, sneaking into her home. Trying to gather authentic tidbits to flesh out our illusionary world. I should have left well enough alone. Been satisfied with what we had. Instead, I'd risked tainting everything.

I needed to find a way to make things better. My mind began to churn at high speed, developing a scenario for me to ingest and process. The lady rushing up those stairs was somebody else. A sister or a cousin? I hadn't gotten a clear look at her face, and though the voices were similar, they weren't exactly the same. My lunch lady had lent her relative a key. In a simple good deed. A kindness offered to support forbidden attraction.

I sighed. Some of the distress beginning to melt away.

"That was nice of you," I said, as she caught up to me on the sidewalk. "To do that for your friend."

She tried, then. Begged, even. But I wasn't quite ready and refused to ask her along as I made my way home.

●

Several friends were sitting on the worn plaid couch. The one in the middle had his elbows on his knees and was twisting a rolling paper into a tight slender tube.

"Where'd you get the stuff?" I asked.

"Never you mind. All you got to know is it's real good."

I didn't want to say anything, but I was worried my mother would come home. She was out shopping at the mall, and I'd made the mistake of offering up my basement when the rain began to peck.

He sparked up the joint, handed it to me. I brought it to my lips, squinting as the ribbon of smoke burned my eyes. I pretended to puff, then pretended to cough before passing it along.

"You got anything to eat or what?"

"Cookies or shit?"

"I'd kill for some barbecue chips."

"Fuck that. Salt 'n' vinegar's where it's at."

"I don't have any of that stuff," I explained. "My mother doesn't buy junk food." Which wasn't entirely true, though she did monitor the groceries. Knew what she ate, what I ate. How much of every-thing was left. If an entire bag or container disappeared, it would spark a conversation.

"Check that one out."

He was pointing at the television set that was pushed into the corner. *American Bandstand* was on, and the camera was panning around all the girls. Tiny dresses and short shorts. Flared pants and pointed collars.

"Yeah, I'd jump her bones."

"Look at the guy next to her. How does a dork like that even make it on there?"

Then someone mentioned that one of the girls on the screen looked exactly like the lady who worked in the cafeteria. "I'd bet ten bucks it's her."

I sat up, held my breath. The camera zoomed in on a dancer swaying on a raised platform. Head swiveling, high ponytail twirling. White booties and a backless floral dress with a knot behind her neck. I could count the pointy bumps of her spine.

When her face was revealed, I knew immediately it wasn't her. The angle of the jaw was harder. The shape of the eyes less almond-like. "Nope," I said loudly. "Not even close." But I didn't like seeing so much of her almost-twin exposed.

"And who made you the authority, huh?"

"Yeah. Like she's ever gawked at you sideways."

I shrugged. I had no plans to share the depth of the relationship we'd established. Months and months of secret interactions. Confidences. Intimacies. Aside from that moment of awkwardness outside her house last week, we'd never had an argument.

With their cottony mouths, they began discussing her. How small her tits were. What she'd look like bent over the back of a chair. Which one of them she'd want to screw first.

"Me," I blurted. I hadn't meant to speak, but I had to admit I felt a quiet confidence brewing. My mother would say I was developing some "pluck."

Snickering, then. "You seriously think so?"

"Come on, she might do him, guys. If he put a gun to her head."

I tried to maintain a casual exterior. Giving away nothin, even though she and I had already done the dirty deed a ton of times. My friends were all stoned, anyway. Would never be able to grasp the beauty of such a grown-up union. And besides, a gentleman would never spill those kinds of sordid details. "Forget it," I said and folded my arms across my chest.

"Okay, so listen up. If you had to pick who you'd bang, which would it be?"

"You mean out of the lunch ladies?"

"Yeah. Between the three."

There was an older woman with jowls who worked the cash register. She kept her hairnet so low, the elastic band bit into her eyebrows. Then there was the one who refilled the trays. Her teeth were yellow, and she had deep wrinkles around her mouth, like she smoked two packs a day. Finally, my lunch lady. She always served the food and was the only one who would ever stand a chance on *American Bandstand*.

"I'd take the old bag. I bet her cooch is all worked in, could handle what I got down here." He grabbed at his crotch and shook.

Dopey laughter. "Anything could handle a gherkin, you loser. I'd take Horse Teeth." A whinny.

"You're messed up."

"No, seriously. Think about it. Mug like that, she'd be real grateful, right? I'd probably get free lunches all year. Win-win!"

"You'd have to screw the old lady for free lunches, idiot. She takes the cash."

"I'd need way more than a free lunch for that. But I'd take a run at the other one. She lives right next door to me. Always out back, too, in her bathing suit. Showing off her ass."

"You're shitting me."

"Nope. During the summer, I heard them at night. She's married to that geezer who owns the pharmacy. Like dogs in heat, man."

I swallowed. I did not appreciate this line of conversation. They shouldn't be talking about her like that. Or the man she married, who meant nothing to her. She and I had already discussed it multiple times, and I was doing my best to be patient and understanding. I'd accepted that he provided a home and a decent life for her. Something I was unable to do just yet. But in time, yes.

"Like, how could you hear?" I asked.

"What? Them going at it? It's not rocket science, buddy boy. Windows wide open. All kinds of stuff just floats through the air."

"But it's so far away. Their house from yours."

He glared at me, scratched his armpit with his thumb. "That's right. You've been coming to my place. Yakking it up with my mother."

"So?" I asked. "I got no choice. My mom makes me go."

"My maawwwmm makes me go," he mocked.

I blew out a lungful of air. Straightened my back. "You're just talking bullshit, is all. Her bedroom's all the way on the other side. They'd have to have a megaphone for you to—"

His eyebrows lifted. "How'd you know where her bedroom's at?"

"I-I'm just guessing."

"You ever been in there?"

"Hardly," I sputtered. My hands and armpits were suddenly sweaty. I needed to slow down. To release the caged bird, as Mrs. Fischer always said. "I just figured from how it looks on the outside."

He grinned then, lurched toward me, and gripped my nipple through my T-shirt. Twisted. I tried to shove him away, cried, "Stop that! You're hurting me!"

When he released my chest, he said, "You're a shifty dude, you know. I've seen you on their property. Like some sort of Peeping Tom freak."

Heavy footsteps clomped across the ceiling, interrupting us. My mother's reedy voice then, seeping through the floorboards. "Are you down there, love? Come see my new fall coat. I caught a wonderful sale."

More chuckling from the boys, and heat pulsed into my cheeks. "In a minute, Mom." I tried to sound gruff, but my words were wobbly. He'd seen me skulking around their backyard? I thought I'd been concealed by shadows. "I'm not a Peeping Tom. I used it as a shortcut is all."

"Yeah totally." A wink. "Shortcut with perks, huh? Me, too. Some nights, there's quite a show."

A few more footsteps above us, and she said, "Have you got guests, sweetheart?"

"Yeah, I do, Mom," I yelled upward. "We're hanging out."

"Well, now's not the time. Kindly ask them to leave. I'm not set for company."

Then they all burst out laughing. Rolling backward, gripping their ribs.

"Not set, she says. Like she's watery fucking Jell-O."

I stood up. "Guys, she's in a mood. I think you ought to head out."

They nodded and mumbled, grabbed their jackets, followed me to the door. The rain had stopped, and the new leaves were glistening. So bright, it pained my eyes.

"Catch you later."

"Next time, get some snacks, yeah?"

Once they'd left, I sprayed lilac-scented bathroom freshener around the room. But it was too late. My mother was talking again. Not loudly, as she never needed to. Her voice had a razor's edge that could slit through linoleum, wood, wires. Fiberglass. Galvanized nails. "Are you trying to disguise something, dear?"

"No, Mom."

Her footsteps stopped. "We'll need to have a chitchat about what's been going on."

My throat tightened. Another chitchat. I hated those. Usually, it was because some aspect of my existence had unsettled her. It might be worth a mention, like a poor grade in chemistry, or pointless, like a bone-dry toothbrush after I swore I'd cleaned my teeth.

"Just a minute," I called.

On the television screen, she was in front of the camera again. My lunch lady doppelgänger. Bending her knee, lifting a skinny leg, shaking a glossy white boot. I was certain she was gazing into the lens directly at me. I smiled, but she didn't smile back.

"Why'd you do that?"

"Do what?"

"Let them insult me. They were saying mean things."

I knelt down, placed my hands on top of the box. "I didn't think. Look, I'm really sorry." Part of me wanted to tell her to close the curtains of her house. Someone had been spying on her. Someone besides me. But I bit my tongue. While I didn't want him peering in, I also didn't want my view blocked.

Then her image became distorted, hazy, and I tried to adjust the antennae. To find her again. For only a second, I saw her way back in a corner. She was glaring at me over her shoulder. Seeing her face, so disenchanted, gave me one of the worst feelings in the world.

"Sweetheart? I'm still waiting." My mother again.

"I said I'm coming!"

A twist of the brown knob, and the girls and guys collapsed into a white circle. A soft pop, and the screen was black.

NOW

•

CHAPTER TWENTY-ONE

Molly

"BUT IT GAVE me chills." Molly held her cellphone to her ear as she stepped into her father's backyard. "The person knew exactly who I was."

"You did say you were featured on the website," Casey replied.

"Not anymore." Through her sweater, Molly pressed at the area of skin in the crook of her elbow. The patch was sore and raw from scratching. "It's eerie. Who ever said small towns were nice?"

Casey snorted. "One thing I've learned, deviance doesn't have a preferred address."

"You can say that again." Over the years, Molly had worked with enough traumatized children to know perversion or cruelty was not constrained by neighborhoods or socioeconomic boundaries.

"Listen, I just want you to look after yourself. Not get sucked into some asshole's game."

Even though she rarely smoked, Molly had an intense craving for a cigarette. The vacuous calmness it brought. Next door, the lights flicked on. Mrs. Fischer was inside, going from window to window dragging across the curtains. Then the bulb over their basement entrance began to glow.

"Fair point, Case. But what—what if it's possible I made a mistake?"

Is it really, though? That asinine question from the caller had stuck in her mind. Had she somehow deceived herself? Even the thought seemed outlandish, but she couldn't deny that since returning home, she'd felt like she was on the edge of a dark hole. And the border on which she was balancing was growing thinner and thinner.

"Of course you didn't make a mistake. How could you? You were practically a toddler. How much more innocent can you get?"

Her friend was right. As a child, Molly could never have grasped the gravity of it. She'd simply relayed the truth. As she saw it.

"Listen, if those calls are causing you stress, just stop the whole thing. You're not there to volunteer."

"I don't want to quit. I do actually help on occasion." And no matter how miniscule the issue, that felt good. Why let some bored and twisted loser ruin a positive? "Plus, it gives me something to think about at night besides my father."

"Then have the landlord guy do his techie magic so that caller can't get through. Obviously, that person doesn't need support. Is just looking for a sick thrill."

"Good idea," she said. Though she didn't want to do that either. Asking for help had never been her strong suit. She'd always prided herself on solving her own problems. Whether that was tuning out the childhood taunters or leaving Aymes as soon as she was old enough. Besides, she was capable of disconnecting if it happened again.

Molly had finished her call and was about to go in when she heard scraping. Heavy feet dragging over pavement. In the gloomy light of the streetlamp, she made out the shape of Bradley Fischer. Limping up his driveway. One of his arms was hugging his body, and his left shoulder was cricked up higher than the right.

Leaning back against the house, she attempted to hide behind an overgrown euonymus bush. She hadn't seen or spoken to Bradley since the drinks a few nights ago. When she'd gotten sloshed. It pained her to remember those awkward moments of conversation. How she'd likely stumbled out the door.

"Well, hello, you," he called, turning in her direction.

As he approached, she was about to apologize. But then she saw his face. Split lip, a strip of raw skin on his cheekbone. His left eye was framed in mottled purple.

"What happened?"

He drove his hands into the pockets of a shiny oversized bomber jacket. "Went hiking with my buddy. Wrong shoes." He pointed at his basketball sneakers. "Slipped down over an embankment."

"That's terrible."

"And now I can ask the same. What happened to you? You left me high and dry."

"Oh. That," she said. A random taxi driver must have driven her home. Escorted her to her door.

"Yeah. I came outside and you'd vanished. Yours truly was totally ditched." He grinned, then winced and touched the butterfly bandage above his eyebrow.

Molly scratched her neck. "I was wiped. I headed home."

"Figured. We'll do it again, though, yeah?"

"Sure." She wouldn't do it again.

As Bradley lumbered away, she opened the sliding door and stepped inside. The air was weighted with the earthy scent of vegetables. Through the dining room door, she saw Alex kneeling in front of the coffee table. With a serving spoon, he was scraping a large pumpkin. Tugging out strands of membrane, clumps of seeds. Her father was leaning against the side of his chair, his hands resting in his lap.

"Molly? Quick word?"

Glenn gestured to her from the kitchen. He was wearing a new apron today. Mint green, covered in white coffee cups.

"Everything okay?"

She was expecting an update on her father, but instead he stepped closer, lowered his voice. "Did you hear what happened to Brad?"

"I just saw him outside. Poor guy slipped on a hike."

Glenn shook his head. "Is that his story? He slipped?"

"I mean, that's what he told me."

"He got jumped, Molly. Couple of nights ago. After you two were out together."

Out, sure. Not quite *together.* "What do you mean *jumped*?"

"Not to spread rumors, but it seems later that night he was cavorting around in the village green near Main Street. And let me tell you, nothing respectable's going on there after dark."

"Come on. How bad can it be?"

"All kinds of drugs. Folks doing who knows what under the trees. One of those vagrants caught Brad off guard, apparently. He turned up at emergency, thinking he had permanent damage to his—" Glenn gestured toward the lower half of his apron.

Was a nurse permitted to share that sort of personal information? "That sounds awful."

"I wouldn't go for drinks again if I was you. I've known Bradley Fischer for years, and he's about as greasy as a refried corn dog."

"You can't be serious." She was reminded of the nickname Bradley had used. *Mother Hen Glenn.* He was living up to it. "It was just old neighbors catching up."

He nodded vigorously. "And you and Alex should be careful if you're out at night. There's been a rise in incidents lately."

"I'll certainly share that. To be extra cautious."

"That's best. I wouldn't want to alarm him."

"Hard to alarm a teenager, Glenn. Not when they're invincible."

"Yeah, we were all invincible then, weren't we?" Then a sudden flush filled his cheeks, and he cleared his throat. "Until we weren't."

Molly was certain that in that moment, Glenn had been reminded of Terry Kage. As she had. Terry must have thought nothing could harm him; no circumstance could possibly alter the joyful maddening ride of adolescence. Until a single moment in a single afternoon had done exactly that. Destroyed his entire existence. Altered his family's world, too. As well as her father's. And hers. Death was impossible to repair.

She turned away, brought her focus back to the dining room. Alex had the huge pumpkin balanced on his lap now, and he was using a miniature saw to cut out a face.

"He needs some decent sharp teeth. Hey, Grandad?"

At first, Alex had been reluctant to visit. He said it was stupid to just sit there, pretending nothing was wrong. "Who needs to pretend?" she'd replied. "Why don't you assume he's listening really intently?"

"That's probably bullshit, Mom."

"Maybe, Alex. But also, maybe not."

"I'm going to do fangs," he said then. "But missing a couple, too. Like he didn't go to the dentist."

As her father stared ahead, Alex worked the saw in and out around the lines of his design. Though they'd never visited all that often, a certain comfort had always existed between grandfather and grandson. An easy banter. That feeling still seemed to be there.

In a lowered voice, Alex said then, "She never asked once, you know. Why I did it."

Molly froze. *She?* Was he talking about her?

He put down the saw. Flicked away the orange pulp collecting in the grooves. "That's the thing, though," he said quietly. "It wasn't even me, Grandad. It was my buddy. Grabbed my phone and shared stuff. He was sticking up for me because she did it first. Blasted my photos. And nobody even cared."

More sawing. Eyes like crescent moons.

"But his father's this total maniac who'd freak out and rip him apart. I mean, like literally." He tapped on the cut pieces, and they fell inside the pumpkin with a faint *thunk*. "My friend feels like shit about my community service, but it's not a big deal. I'm cool with it."

Molly pressed her hand beneath her ribs. A dull pain was forming. She'd been so angry with Alex when the whole thing happened. So deeply disappointed. And even though it was completely out of character, not once had she set aside her emotions to press him for details. Or try to find out what happened.

And here was her father, in his absolute silence, providing the security needed to gently peel away those sandpapery layers. Alex exposing his soft underbelly. Willingly. That was because he knew there would never be a judgment or negative reaction. Always acceptance. A pure openness to understand.

She realized then that when her father died, it was going to hurt her son. Hurt him badly.

Molly took a step into the room, and Alex glanced toward her, met her eyes.

"Hey," she said.

"What?" A small punch beneath the word.

"Can we talk for a minute?"

His jaw opened, and he glared at her. "Seriously, Mom? You were spying?"

"I overheard." Her hand hovered in the air over his arm. "I should have asked you."

"So? Okay?"

"And I am—I was wrong to assume."

"No matter what you say, I'm not ratting. I'm not messing up his life."

"We can talk about that later, but first you need to know that I'm sorry, Alex."

"Okay," he repeated and lowered his angry gaze. She could have imagined it, but his second "okay" seemed slightly softer.

"Molly?" Glenn called, leaning around the doorframe of the kitchen. "Can you come here for another quick sec? Someone tucked this into the mailbox." He held up a folded newspaper.

Molly sighed as Alex pinched the pumpkin carving knife, continued to saw away at the mouth. She left the dining room and crossed the hallway. "Who?" she said. "A delivery boy?"

"Nope. Your father doesn't subscribe. But you might want to have a gander at page three. It's a bit odd."

She took the *Aymes Gazette*. Flipped through the first pages. Glenn stood there waiting, a look of concern on his face.

A half-page article. The first paragraph in bolded font. *Forty years later, the murder of Edie Wynters and subsequent suicide of her once-convicted killer Terry Kage continues to capture the interest of the local community.*

"Weird, hey?" Glenn pointed at the page with his index finger.

There was a blurred photograph of Molly sitting on a bench out-side the bar where she'd had drinks with Bradley. Her arm was in the process of being lifted, and her mouth was open. Though the image of herself and the rude quote she'd apparently offered was appalling, that was not what Glenn was referring to.

In red Sharpie, scratched across her gray face, was the word *LIAR*.

CHAPTER TWENTY-TWO

AFTER MANAGING THE trick-or-treaters at her father's house, Molly headed back to her rental. She discovered the bucket of candy she'd left out front emptied and upturned. Her note asking children to "Please take one!" was crumpled, stuck to the glass in the door. As though a small goblin or a fairy had chewed it up, shot it out like a spitball.

When she went inside, she expected to find Alex there. Face hidden in his laptop. Watching some sort of holiday-appropriate slasher film. But in the kitchen, she heard no screaming teenagers, no stabs of music from a violin, no flattened tone of a psychopath. Just an emptiness. He wasn't home.

Molly wandered from room to room inside the bungalow. After Alex finished his pumpkin, he'd taken a bus to the community center to complete some hours. She'd offered to pick him up later, but he insisted he could find his own way. And now, she wondered if the buses were still running.

After an hour passed, she sent a simple text: "Check in, plz." He didn't reply. Another hour went by, and she tried calling. He didn't pick up. From the front window, she scanned the length of the road. A few teenagers wandered past, blasting metal music from a speaker, but none of them branched off, strolled up the driveway. She went to the back of the house then, and stared at the thick woods through the window over the sink. As though he might emerge from the black spaces between the trees.

Ever since she was a child, she'd hated Halloween night. She'd always sensed something sinister beneath the playfulness of it. As she stared into the darkness, she had that same awareness now. That bad things were happening. The newspaper Glenn had handed her had not helped. *Liar.*

While she guessed older residents might recall the murder, Molly had not been prepared for this piqued interest. Was it a single person who had a bone to pick, or a group of random individuals? Maybe those teens who were trespassing for a selfie. Having a laugh at her expense. Twice, she'd also seen a navy car idling in the road right in front of her father's house. Indicator on, as though whoever was behind the wheel intended to turn into the driveway.

Molly silently chastised herself. She was being silly. Everything was not connected to her. Her father. Their past.

She went outside, stood beneath the streetlamp at the bottom of the driveway. All the little trick-or-treaters had long gone home, but the air still felt charged. A jack-o'-lantern had been smashed on the sidewalk. The house across the street had a life-sized animatronic witch on the front step that was still lifting its cloaked arm and cackling. Streaks of egg marked the siding, and toilet paper flapped from the branches of a nearby tree.

It was nearly eleven thirty before a wispy shadow drifted up the road. By the loping sound of his footsteps, she immediately knew it was Alex, and he startled as she rushed toward him, wrapped her arms around his chest. "Where have you been?" she asked, her face buried in his coat.

"What the hell? Let me go!" He twisted, breaking free from her embrace. "Stop being a freak, Mom."

"I was worried, Alex."

"I forgot my knapsack. So I couldn't call you." He took long strides toward the house.

She hurried behind him. "No one would lend you a phone?"

"What difference would that make? I don't have your number."

"Of course you do."

"You're in my contacts. I tap your name. No one memorizes numbers."

"Well, you'll be memorizing mine tomorrow. I don't care if you have to sit at the table and copy it out a hundred times."

He chuckled at that. "Yup, writing lines at fifteen. Cool." In the kitchen, he went to the fridge. Poured himself a tall glass of apple juice. His face was ashen. "I don't get why you're flipping out."

She didn't either. All he'd done was make an innocent mistake. Leaving his knapsack behind at community service. He wasn't staggering, reeking of alcohol or weed. It wasn't even that late. But whenever she blinked, she saw images, a disturbing fusion of her own memories and make-believe. Alex lying on the ground. Back cricked, face contorted, bright red foam burbling out between his lips. And leaning over him, several unfamiliar boys, faces skeletonized with gray makeup, bloodied dresses, wigs of wet stringy hair. "Who are you," she'd asked all those years ago. "Dead lunch lady," they'd replied.

Alex turned to face her. In the low light of the kitchen, she noticed a tiny rip in the sleeve of his jacket.

"How did—"

"Some piece of shit."

A bead of sweat trickled down the inside of her upper arm. "Alex. Tell me where you were."

After several gulps of juice, he said, "Promise you won't get more pissed off."

"Fine. Promise."

"I was at that place. You know. They call it the overhang."

"What?"

"You know, Mom. That cliff. Above the lake. Where Terry Kage was, um, with your mother."

"Why on earth would you be there?" She tried to hide the quiver in her voice.

"Some kids from the community center. Said they were hanging out and asked me to come along. I didn't know."

Molly put her palm on the counter, spread her fingers. "And what were they doing?"

"Stupid stuff. Playing music. Joking around. They thought it was cool or creepy or whatever because of what happened there. Like it's haunted."

"You've got to be kidding me. She was the ghost in the cafeteria last week. Now she's back up in the woods?" Though Molly pretended to sound surprised, this was not new to her. Teenagers were saying the same idiotic stuff when she was young. She was mortified to recall how often she'd prayed someone else's mother would die in a horrible way. Then the focus would shift away from her family.

"I guess ghosts can float around wherever they want."

"Well, that's still stupid."

"Look, they just want to talk shit, okay?" He sat down on a kitchen chair. Finished the rest of his juice. "Nobody cares about the physics of it."

His joke hit the target, and Molly couldn't help but smile slightly. Muscles in her shoulders and neck loosening. "So, what happened to your jacket?"

"It got torn."

"I mean, I can see that, Alex. I'm asking how it got torn."

"One of the guys was daring a girl. To go to the edge. And call out."

"Call out to whom exactly?" Though she already knew the answer to her question.

"It's dumb, Mom. Summon up your mother. And the girl was kind of drunk and she could've fallen, and I told the guy to leave her alone and called him a loser, and he grabbed my sleeve. Tried to punch me in the face. But he missed. And that's it."

Her smile quickly faded, and a fresh wave of irritation rolled through her. But she kept her tone calm, steady. "That's it?"

"Pretty much, but I punched him back. Knocked the wind right out of him."

Molly swallowed. Waited a few seconds, then said, "It's incredibly dangerous, you know. Lurking around up there in the dark. That place is blocked off. There's a sign posted."

Alex rolled his eyes. "Yeah. Which seems like an invitation to me."

He stood up then and went to his room. Molly waited five minutes before scooping up her purse and striding out the door.

•

Using the flashlight from her phone, Molly illuminated the path that sloped upward. Her shoes slipped on the layer of rotting leaves and pine needles, bushes scraping against her skin. The air smelled of woodsmoke and organic decay, and she heard raucous laughter in the darkness ahead. She knew she should turn around, but her legs kept marching forward.

When she reached the clearing, she came upon two teenage boys sitting on the damp ground beside a dying fire. She shone the light into their faces.

One of the boys held up his hands, protecting his watery pink eyes. "Holy shit, man," he slurred.

"Woah," the other one said. He blinked slowly. "Like, are you her?"

Molly's heart was thumping as she planted her feet farther apart. "No, I'm not her. But you get she was a real person, right?"

"Like, duh." Chuckling.

"And she lost her life here."

"Double duh. That's why we're paying our respects."

Stepping closer, she kept the cone of light directed at their eyes. "Well, this area is blocked from the public."

"Yeah, so?"

Molly had the urge to shriek at them. So loud and shrill that fear would knock their heads backward. But as she looked more closely, she realized the boys were younger than Alex. Thirteen at most. She took a chance. "I've called both your mothers."

"No way," they exclaimed in unison.

"Yes, way. They'll be here any second."

The boys clambered to their feet, then tumbled down the slope, shoving at each other. Their juvenile banter fading. "Fuck off." "No way, you fuck off." "I'm, like, not fucking off."

Molly moved closer to the firepit and, with a stick, prodded at the ashes. On the ground was a litter of broken bottles, candy wrappers, chip bags. She found a full can of ginger ale, cracked it open, and poured the contents onto the last embers.

The rock edge was only a few feet away. Beyond that, the lake was not visible. All she could see was a dull nothingness. Like the starless sky and the water were one and the same.

She'd only been seven when a female's skull washed up on the shore of Rabey Lake. No one told her, of course, and she hadn't heard about it until she was much older. All she understood as a child was that her mother lived beneath the water's surface. She used to imagine a woman's body gliding through the water and weeds. A sheer white ribbon. Molly had a plan, that one day she was going to dive down among all the trash and grab the tail of her mother. Spool her up and bring her home.

As she turned away from the lake and stepped around the dead fire, she tripped over an exposed root. Her phone shot from her grasp. The glow from the flashlight vanished when it struck the ground. She was suddenly enveloped in darkness. Thick and pressing into her face.

"Shit," she said as she bent, felt around the ground. But she couldn't locate it.

She was disoriented. Turned in a circle. Felt a little woozy. Clouds hid the moon, and a fine mist was beginning to fall through the branches. Coating the back of her neck. She could barely see her hand in front of her face. Two steps in the wrong direction and her foot would meet nothing but air. She'd plunge into the lake below, in the same spot as her mother had, with barely time to scream.

Why hadn't she learned? It was never smart to act on emotion. She crouched, pressed her fingertips into the wet dirt. Squinted into the thick black until she felt a dull ache behind her forehead. Given enough time, maybe her eyes would adjust. She'd know which way was disaster, and which way was safe. She hoped Alex had gone straight to sleep and hadn't heard her leaving.

The mist was becoming thicker. Clinging to her. She was well versed in making stupid choices. Her ex-husband was a solid example. Initially, she'd been overwhelmed by love for him, but as soon as they were married, his shine quickly turned to tarnish. He was uninterested in her and, eventually, Alex as well, but he did not want to divorce. She was certain he'd had affairs while traveling, and at some point, she had one as well. With a new teller from their bank, no less. A man in his mid-twenties, bleached smile, tight stomach, and overpriced clothing. She'd bumped into him at a coffee shop, and somehow that led to nearly a dozen lunchtime meetups. Fumbling sex in a cheap motel room or the backseat of his secondhand car. Then she'd return to work, distracted and twitchy, the scent of him still lingering on her skin.

Leo eventually found out. Through nosy colleagues. Likely he wouldn't have cared, but as his business associates were aware, he'd railed against her indiscretions. It was a relief when he finally left. The end of monotony. The end of the ruse.

Molly inched forward. She could sense someone close by. The subtlest sound of fabric shifting. A breath in. A breath out. Was she imagining the odor of onions?

"Who's there?"

Silence.

"I said, Who's there? If it's one of you kids, I'll be—your mother will hear about this!"

Footsteps. Solid and certain, growing louder. The soft crunching sound bouncing off the trees making it impossible to tell the direction. Was it coming from in front of her or behind? A circular light, then, swinging left and right across the ground. Blinding her.

"Sorry." A man's voice. When he lowered the beam, Molly caught sight of her phone. Reached out and grabbed it.

"It's fine," Molly said, though fear was still zapping through her nerves.

In the glow, she recognized Lyle Kage. His hair was combed back, and instead of a uniform, he was wearing a thin puffer, blue jeans.

"I saw your car on the shoulder. Came up to check on things."

He'd recognized her car? Had he made specific note of it when dropping off Alex? "There was a group of teens," she said. "But as you can see, the party's over."

With the toe of his boot, he kicked a broken beer bottle. A shard flew over the edge of the overhang. Quiet splash from below. "It's treacherous up here," he said. "In the dark or otherwise."

Molly swallowed. "That's why I came. Alex told me—" She got to her feet and turned on her phone flashlight again. The path to the road was right behind Lyle. "Though, if I'm honest, knowing kids were up here irked me." In senior year, Molly had been invited to multiple gatherings at the overhang. Perhaps those kids were actually reaching out in friendship, but she'd never allowed herself to trust anyone. Had always assumed the goal was to use her for some twisted entertainment, and she'd avoided the place if she knew anyone was there.

"I've petitioned the town for fencing multiple times, but it seems the council needs a tragedy first."

Another tragedy, she thought, silently correcting him.

With Alex's community service, she knew she'd eventually cross paths with Lyle Kage. In many ways, it was surprising that over the years she already hadn't. She always assumed that if they ever spoke, Lyle would be gruff or angry. Perhaps even accusatory. But instead, his tone was even. She could not determine if he was concerned or keeping himself under control.

"Well," he said, as he scanned the ground one last time. "Perhaps we should head out together. Unless you're not finished here?"

"Nope. All good."

As they walked down the path side by side, he said, "He's a solid kid, your son. Works hard. Not a single complaint, no matter the task."

Molly's shoulders relaxed. "That's nice to hear. Just because someone missteps doesn't mean they're tarred for life." In that moment, she was thinking of Alex's friend. Not Alex.

Though he hadn't mentioned a name, she was certain she knew the identity of the boy who'd shared the photos. He'd been at their house most afternoons, slept over constantly. A few weeks before she and Alex came to Aymes, the boy had moved in with an aunt due to problems with his violent father.

When Alex left for community service that day, Molly had immediately called Casey. Her husband was a lawyer and confirmed what Molly suspected. It would be a tremendous uphill battle even if Alex did choose to recant his admission. Best bet was to scrub a few toilets, and when the time was right, ensure his record was wiped clean of any trace of his "good deed."

"Yeah," Officer Kage said. "People make mistakes, but they can do better. Just look at me."

She glanced at him out of the corner of her eye. Rod-straight spine. Serious jaw. She could not fathom him making an error with anything.

Near the road, his car was parked right behind hers. Blocking her exit. He pulled a fob from his pocket, but then stopped. Turned toward her. Cleared his throat. "This might come across as weird, but . . ." He hesitated. "Over the years, I've often thought about calling you."

Molly's breath moved to the very top of her lungs. He was going to speak his mind now. Tell her what he thought of her. The same stuff she'd heard before. From a teacher once. Another time a woman in a grocery store when she was picking up milk. Telling her she'd done so much damage. Was spoiled and entitled and had ruined countless lives. Especially those "decent folks" who lived on the other side of the tracks. Terry Kage's parents and neighbors. It was as though that literal border split the town not only between affluent and impoverished, but also between Molly supporters and Molly haters.

"I left, you know, after everything that happened. But I knew you took a lot when you were younger. I heard the stories."

"I mean. I suppose." As a child, she could not process the animosity toward her. Had those people forgotten her mother had grown up in East Aymes? In one of those dilapidated bungalows with a sagging roof and nonexistent insulation? A family life riddled with apparent hardship. Though her father never spoke of it, Molly believed she had no surviving maternal relatives.

"I'll never be able to wrap my mind around it all, what really happened, but I know your mother was a decent person and didn't deserve that." He scuffed his feet. "We lived on the same street. The Paltrys were a few houses down."

Molly was standing on a mound of spongy moss, and she placed her hand on the car to steady herself. "I-I hadn't realized." That the homes were quite so close.

"I was often gone when Terry was a kid. But when I came back, she gave me a chance. Your mom did. Got me a job in your father's pharmacy."

"I never knew that," she admitted. "Until Alex told me."

"And . . ." He clicked his Maglite off. Only the outline of him visible, now. A tall gray stone. His next words were quieter. "I wasn't necessarily a reliable employee, I should say. Sometimes your dad would step out, and I'd take a few things. And so did my friends."

Molly stood a few feet in front of him, remaining silent. Likely he meant some harmless pilfering. Surely that wasn't uncommon for teenage employees, especially before video cameras were installed in every corner.

He cleared his throat. A hard rasp. "This probably sounds like it's coming out of left field. Me unloading."

It did. Certainly wasn't what she'd expected, but she said, "Not at all. Who didn't pocket a chocolate bar at some point?" She recognized that the tiniest moments sometimes lingered in the mind. Wispy threads of guilt.

"Well, it was a bit worse than that. The pills my brother took that day came from your dad's pharmacy. They were delivered by mistake and were supposed to go to the vet next door."

Molly leaned her weight against her car. She didn't quite understand. She knew Terry Kage had consumed drugs, but not that. "He ingested medication for animals? For pets?"

"That about sums it up. It won't help to point any fingers now. Who took them from the store. Who passed them around. Let's just say I didn't put a stop to it."

Molly slid her hand into her purse. Felt for her keys. She heard a sudden hardness in his tone. Was it him? Had he drugged his own brother? She was again aware of the isolation of their location. No streetlamps or moonlight. Not a single car on the road. Barren fields to the left. Wall of trees behind them, shifting with the wind and light rain. As though the very branches were inhaling the darkness.

"I wanted you to know. The kid they arrested on the over-hang wasn't Terry. It was a messed-up version of him. My brother was never violent. He was a gentle dreamer. That's a good way to describe him. None of us had any idea what was going to happen. Like it was funny to swallow whatever was dropped in your palm. We thought we were untouchable. I blame myself. I should have protected him better."

Her mouth was dry. She wasn't sure what to do. Or say. "Officer Kage, I'm—"

Her phone began ringing. She glanced at the screen. Alex. With her thumb, she slid on "Answer." "Hi," she whispered.

"Mom, where are you?"

"I'm—I'm at the overhang."

"Seriously? What the hell? Why would you go there?"

Alex's voice was booming, and she pressed the phone into her ear to muffle it. How could she explain it? When growing up in Aymes, she'd been incapable of defending her mother. But she could surely do it now.

"Listen, I'm okay. Really, darling. I'm on my way back." She glanced at Lyle, mouthed "it's Alex," and then unlocked her car, slipped inside. Lifted a hand to offer a goodbye. "I'm not far."

Alex grunted. "You know what, Mom? Can't you just chill? You've been weird since we got here."

CHAPTER TWENTY-THREE

MOLLY HAD A headache. As she wandered the farmers' market, the sound of squealing youngsters grated on her. They were zipping about, spinning and leaping among the vegetable booths. Kicking at the massive rolls of hay that were painted on the flat side. A bumble-bee. A halved watermelon. The head of a grinning clown.

She saw people who were familiar. Former peers from high school. Her old history teacher was pulling a grocery trolley over the lumpy ground. Plus Shawna and a man, presumably her spouse. Two sullen preteens trailing behind then. Molly adjusted the visor of her ball cap, hoping her face was obscured. The last thing she could handle now was a fake reunion. Smiles, offers of catching up, acting as though Molly wasn't an outsider her entire childhood.

She found Alex standing behind Russell Farrell's stall. Taking a vacuum-sealed package of rabbit sliders from a cooler and handing it to a customer. Russell had asked if he'd like to "man the ship" as he had an appointment, and Alex agreed. Even seemed somewhat eager. Much to Molly's surprise, the two had been spending time together. Ever since the hypoglycemic episode, a camaraderie had formed between them. Alex had been helping to prepare the sliders, and in exchange, Russell had been tutoring him in trigonometry.

"There you go," Alex said. "That'll be twelve dollars."

Once he'd finished with the customer, Molly stepped forward. "You ready?"

"Not quite." He lifted the lid of the cooler and then let it snap closed. "Only a couple left and then I'm sold out. People are buying this stuff up. Mr. Farrell should raise his prices."

"I'll take those last two. And then we can get out of here." She didn't want to stay any longer.

"Sure," he said, as he took her cash. "But I'm not giving a discount."

"Didn't expect it." She laughed lightly. Imagined the corners of Russell's mouth flickering with consternation if Molly did not pay full price.

After packing the cooler and signage into her trunk, Molly drove straight to her father's house. Pulling into the driveway, she noticed that same dark blue car parked in the street. A driver was sitting inside. With the tinted windows, it was difficult to make out the person's face. The first couple of times she'd assumed it was just a coincidence, or a teenager looking for social media content. But how often was it now? And besides, the vehicle was too expensive. Too clean.

"Go on in, Alex. I'm going to see what that's about."

As she got closer, the driver lifted his head. She recognized him. Her father's friend. The older man she'd met outside the pharmacy the week after she and Alex had arrived.

When she tapped on his window, he fumbled with his keys, started the ignition. Pressed a button and the window slid down.

"Hi there," she said. "Mr.—"

"Dr. Even."

"Yes, that's right. Have you been sitting here long?"

"I'm not sure. A few minutes, I suppose."

His lips had a blue tinge. She knew he'd spent much longer in a cold car than he was admitting. He appeared disoriented, too, and she wondered if perhaps he had some degree of dementia.

"If you've come for a visit, I doubt Dad's up for guests this afternoon. Unfortunately."

"Yes, yes. Of course. I don't want to trouble anyone." His tugged up his coat sleeve and checked his watch. "Time's gotten away from me. My wife is waiting."

"Best to call first, Dr. Even, if you plan to drop by again." Though she hoped he wouldn't bother. She would not allow him to go inside. "Old friend," as he initially called himself, did not fully encapsulate their relationship. Intially, she'd had no memory of him, but hours later she recalled something. When she was in her early twenties, she'd come across a photo of the pharmacy from opening day. The sign read "Wynters Even Drugs." At the time, she'd questioned her father about the *Even*, and her father explained he'd once had a business partner. A man with too many children. Too much pressure. While the exact details were hazy, she was fairly certain he'd insinuated that Dr. Even was a sly man who was creative with the accounting. Funneled cash from the business? Or purposefully botched the inventory of drugs? Something like that.

"I-I don't know," he stammered. "I don't know why I came. I shouldn't be here."

"Well," she said, stepping backward. "It was nice to see you again, sir."

With a leather glove, he touched the brim of his hat. Window closed, he started the engine. Molly felt a twinge of irritation fade as he drove away.

•

Lifting the miniature bun, Glenn squirted ketchup onto a patty. "I really don't get the deal with tiny hamburgers."

"They're cute," Molly said as she took a bite. "And people like cute."

Alex had grilled the two packages from the market, and the three of them were eating an early dinner around the kitchen island. A platter heaped with too many rabbit sliders.

"Still dumb." Glenn pushed an entire one into his mouth. Then he mumbled, "But good. They do taste good."

"Decent product," Alex said as he layered up his toppings. Cheese, tomato, onion, lettuce. Chipotle mayo. "But expert barbecuing. Might be my calling."

"Maybe," Molly said. "But I wouldn't ditch school quite yet."

"How's that going, anyway?" Glenn asked.

"Mostly boring," Alex said. "But I like law class. Mrs. Eliason's cool."

"That old crone's still there?" Glenn said. "Heck, I had her when I was your age. Can't remember a thing, except the classroom was an icebox. Did you have her, Molly?"

"Nope," she replied. "Never took law."

"Huh," Glenn said.

Molly took a large bite. Wondered for a moment what the *huh* meant. That he assumed she'd be interested in law? Simply because she'd testified in court? Or did it mean absolutely nothing? An absentminded *huh*, and she was seeking out negatives. Reasons to be aggravated with her father's caretaker, for whom she held a sliver of resentment. Even though she'd hired him, and he was doing a stellar job. She should be caring for her father. And would be, if she had more fortitude.

"Yeah, she still keeps it freezing. No chance of dozing off." Alex balanced the buns on top, pressed them down. "I have a question, though."

"For me?" Molly asked.

"No, Nurse Glenn."

"Shoot," he said. "I'm all ears."

"Were you there, too? Like Mr. Farrell was? When Terry Kage took those drugs?"

A lump of bread and meat stuck in Molly's throat. "Alex," she managed. "We're having a pleasant dinner. I don't think Nurse Glenn wants to discuss—"

"I'm just asking, Mom." Then to Glenn, "It's for school. An assignment."

An assignment. Sounded so basic, but he'd never given this much attention to a classroom project before. He'd been researching online, poring over newspaper clippings, reading police documents with an astounding attention to detail.

Glenn plucked another burger from the platter. "And the curriculum includes local crime now?"

"Not exactly," Alex said. "I could choose any case for my report. And Mom never talks about it, so I've been looking at the trial transcripts and stuff."

"Really going deep," he said. Then to Molly, "Okay if I answer?"

She nodded. "If I say no, he'll just squeeze it out of you later."

Glenn put his elbows on the counter. "Well then, yeah. I was with Terry. Same as everybody else. We weren't being responsible; I can say that for sure. A lot of the crap we did back then wasn't safe. Or healthy." He shrugged. "That stuff was a head trip. And I don't mean that in a positive way. It was nasty, and I barely even remember. I know Terry left. Most of them stayed, I think? There wasn't more to it than that."

"Can I quote you?" Alex asked.

"I suppose. If you want."

"Cool, thanks. I'm writing about why it was an important case."

"And do you . . ." Glenn leaned forward. "Do you think it was an important case?"

Molly chewed her lip, listening to every word as conversation bounced between them.

"I mean, obviously it was important to Mom. And Grandad. Because she was somebody they loved. But it's important for other reasons too."

"Sweetheart," Molly said. "Burgers are getting cold."

But Alex continued. "You had a teenager convicted based on what a three-year-old said. No offense, Mom, but wouldn't a kid lie for an ice cream? And people at school are still talking about it. Saying Terry Kage wasn't some random guy; he was actually hooking up with—"

"I'm going to stop you right there," Glenn said, cutting the air with the side of his hand. "Absolutely not true."

"But what if—"

"Nope. You can't spin it. Every dude in high school had a crush on Mrs. Wynters. She was a pretty lady. Looked exactly like your mom. She worked in that cafeteria, and no one ever went hungry when she was serving the line." Alex opened his mouth to interrupt, but Glenn lifted his hand a second time. "We all might've wished or dreamed, mooned over her, but that's because we were lame teenagers. Nothing ever happened with anyone, or sure as hell everyone would've known." Glenn's nostrils flared. "And you can quote me on that, too."

Molly scraped back her chair. "I think I've had enough now, Alex." She went to the trash container, tugged up the plastic bag, and pushed it toward him. "Didn't I ask you to carry this out?"

"I'll do it after I'm finished."

"Now," she said. "And haul the bins to the curb."

He snatched the bag. "Chill out, okay? I got it."

"I'm sorry," Glenn said, after Alex closed the front door. "That was insensitive of me. I shouldn't have encouraged him."

"It's not your fault." She brought her plate to the sink. "He doesn't understand. For him, she's mostly a name on paper."

Before Glenn could continue, she picked up the box of Halloween decorations and left the kitchen. It was disconcerting to hear him compare her and her mother's appearance. And describe her mother's character with such authority. Dismissing salacious chatter and setting the record straight. Molly never had that same confidence. Even though her father had told endless stories of warmth and affection, and she tried to believe every single one, there were moments when she detected a barrenness there. As though the stories were too perfect. Her mother, that version, was a figment. A construction. Though this was painful to admit, she occasionally wondered if the woman he'd described was real.

Molly carried the box down to the basement for storage. When she yanked the string, she surveyed the floor. Was it possible that the area was even messier than it was before? Had Glenn lied about digging through her father's belongings. No, it had to be Alex.

Hunting around for anything related to his project. There was no point nagging him about it. He would just sneak down later and continue snooping.

She shoved the Halloween box into the crawl space and began cleaning up. Dumping papers back into containers, folding over the lids. At some point she'd have to sort through everything, but that daunting chore could wait for another day.

As she gathered up a pile of file folders, a label caught her eye. On the upper flap, a single typed word: *BirdSong.* Her brow scrunched. She was aware of a private treatment facility by that exact name. A long-term in-patient psychiatric clinic that had been in existence for more than fifty years, located about an hour outside the nearest city. For women only.

She opened the file. A single moldy page was inside, and that appeared to be a receipt of payment. Her mother's full name and address was in the top left corner. A few handwritten notes, but the ink had faded. Was illegible.

Bizarre that her father had never mentioned her mother's connection to such a place. And Molly had no memory of being separated from her for an extended duration. Though she was only three when her mother died, so there were certainly events to which Molly was not privy.

She tugged out her cellphone, searched up the clinic, and clicked the string of digits to automatically dial.

"BirdSong Wellness. How might I help you today?"

The woman's voice had the crackle of old age, and Molly imagined a thin face, lipstick bleeding into wrinkles.

"Hi there," she said brightly. "This is Dr. Molly Wynters calling. I'd like to inquire about a former patient."

"One of your clients, Dr. Wynters?"

Molly cleared her throat. "Close connection, yes. She would have been there in the 1970s. Edie Wynters."

The line was quiet for a moment. Then the woman said, "I'm sure you'll understand that patient files are strictly confidential. Are you a designated family member?"

"I'm her daughter."

"That doesn't necessarily make you designated."

"No?"

Another pause. "And did I hear you say 1970s?"

"Yes. Earlier in the decade."

"Oh dear. Any files from that timeframe have been destroyed. Quite a while ago, in fact."

"So you'd have no records?"

"Nary a one, dear. We simply didn't have the space back then with all that paper. I'm afraid your only option is to discuss this with your mother."

Molly's fingers tightened around her phone. "That's not an option at all."

"I'm sorry, but there's nothing more I can offer."

Molly tap-tap-tapped the red circle on her screen, heard the soft and unsatisfying click as the call disconnected. Sometimes she missed slamming down a phone.

THEN

.

CHAPTER TWENTY-FOUR

Gil

"I'M LATE," EDIE said, her hand grasping the bathroom doorframe. "With . . . you know."

The floor beneath Gil tilted. "Late? How long?"

"Six days."

He had to sit down. "And you think that's significant?"

He already knew the answer to that question. Edie was still using contraceptive pills. Once Gil's anger had subsided that afternoon a few months ago, he'd switched them back. Dumping the vitamins and returning her prescription to the carousel. Then he'd tucked the disk inside the gaudy vest where he'd found it. He could not do that. Lay down a barbed hook and wait for her to step on it.

Instead, gastroenteritis was what had caused the gap in protection. An outbreak of a stomach virus had ripped through the high school, and Edie picked it up. For several days, she stayed in bed with a moderate fever, vomiting, and diarrhea. Managing only ginger ale and saltine crackers.

"I mean, sure. Yeah, I think it's significant. It's always sort of regular?"

"Oh," he said, taking slow sips of air. "Okay." He brought his hand to the side of his neck, could feel his blood pumping beneath his fingers. He looked at Edie, but it was not just his wife standing in front of him now. There was a grouping of new cells concealed somewhere in the warm folds of her insides. A cluster that would turn into a baby.

A hard cramp began to build inside his chest. He slid his hand from his neck to his forehead. *This is joy,* he thought. *This is the most painful joy.*

"Give me one sec," he said as he stood up on wobbly knees, made his way past her and into the bathroom. He could hear his own laughter, downy soft, hanging in the air behind him. Closing the door, he opened the medicine cabinet. Sorted through the bottles. The one containing Valium was empty, so he swallowed a Librium with a scoop of water from the tap.

Several minutes passed, and she rapped on the door. "Gil?"

"Sorry," he called out. "It's nothing. Had to rush."

"Is it the same stomach flu like I had?"

"I—maybe. Probably not." He knelt on the floor of the bathroom, waiting for the vibration in his body to shrink. Down to a singular germ of happiness that did not threaten to split him in two.

When he emerged moments later, he clutched Edie's hand, then put his arms around her. "I'll be damned," he said. "You're feeling well?"

"I suppose so."

"After all these months of waiting. This is the best news. You'll have to go for a blood test. Straight away."

"Yeah. I know."

He sat back on the bed, tugged her toward him. Wisps of her feathered hair tickled his face. "They used to use a rabbit, if you can believe it."

"For a blood test?" She was sitting on his thighs, her back to him. He slipped his hands around her waist. Felt her hip bones, the flatness between them. No swelling yet, but soon enough. Soon enough.

"No. To confirm things. Inject them with a woman's urine, and then they check to see if the ovaries enlarge."

"Check how? Push on its stomach?"

"They open it up."

"So the rabbit died?"

"Exactly. That phrase, *the rabbit died*, used to be synonymous with pregnancy. Twenty-plus years ago. Isn't that peculiar? You've never heard it?"

Edie placed her palms on her lower abdomen, then she edged her hands up her ribs and cupped her breasts. Wincing slightly. "Why would you tell me that? Why would you ever think I'd want to hear that?"

He hadn't meant to say anything sinister. It was a curious scientific fact from a bygone era. He wasn't sure why it had even come to mind. "Forgive me," he said. "That was insensitive."

She started crying then, got up, and moved away from him. "It's awful," she said. "It's just awful."

"Forgive me," he said again. Calmly. Quietly. "That was a thoughtless thing to say."

From the bed, Gil watched through drooping eyes as she paced about the room. Snapping on the bedside lamps. Putting away laundry. A stillness had taken over inside of him, replacing the agitation. He knew the sedative had been absorbed into his brain, and he was grateful for it. It allowed him to hover at a safe distance above the tension in the room. He was no longer anxious and could resist the urge to ask his wife what she thought was awful. The dead rabbit. Or their baby.

•

For the first few months, Gil's feet barely grazed the ground. Edie, though, carried on as if nothing had changed. She never mentioned the pregnancy to anyone besides her mother. Whenever Gil wanted to join her at the obstetrician, she insisted she did not need hand-holding. If he asked how an appointment had gone, she became annoyed at his probing. Day after day, she kept working at the school cafeteria, and only shared the news once she was large enough that an announcement was no longer necessary.

When Edie was six months along, Gil came home to an empty house. He called to her, searched the rooms, but she was nowhere to be found. In the garage, he discovered her car was missing. They'd spoken about these occasional vanishing acts. Or he'd spoken to her, and she'd gaped at him blankly, as though his concerns were pinging off her body. Never absorbed into her skin.

He waited throughout the evening, as he always did. To hear the rumble of her engine as it approached. Her dragging footsteps. At dinner, he ate a meal of bran cereal and milk. Washed his bowl and dried it. Flicked through the newspaper. Turned on the television and watched the news. As Walter Cronkite was wrapping up his report, Gil received a call from Mrs. Paltry. She was whispering. Edie was there, already fast asleep. She was fine for the night and did not want Gil to be concerned.

Gil insisted on driving over. Inside his mother-in-law's house, the air was chilly and damp. As it always was, with an odor of wet wool and overboiled vegetables. He'd offered to pay her heating bill. Have her insulation replaced. Repair her chimney so she could enjoy a crackling fire. As Edie had warned, she'd flatly refused every overture, and he could not understand why. Unless she simply did not want to erase the sights, the smells of the past. Took some comfort in suffering.

He made his way down the narrow hallway. Found his wife inside the childhood bedroom she'd once shared with her sister. The space not much larger than a storage closet. Discolored wallpaper. Threadbare carpet. Fingers of what appeared to be mold on the ceiling. She was curled up on the sagging bottom bunk. Facing the wall.

"She's alright," Mrs. Paltry said as she slipped in around him. She unfolded a patchwork quilt and covered her daughter. "Just needed to be home, I suppose."

Though Gil knew it was an innocent comment, it chafed at him. That was not his wife's home. She had her own. One he happily provided.

He said nothing, though. Kept his mouth shut the next night, too. And for the rest of the week. But when Edie's visits to her mother's became a habit, he had to put his foot down. Explain to Mrs. Paltry that her daughter was a married woman, and they would soon be a family of three. Besides, no man could survive on cereal for dinner.

That night, Edie stormed into the house. Slammed the front door. "What did you say to my mother? What did you say?"

•

Gil was the one who selected the bedroom right across the hallway from their own. Easy to hear the baby during the night. He ordered a crib and a six-drawer dresser in light wood. Tore up the olive shag and replaced it with a spongy white plush. On the walls, he pasted strips of paper. A print of playful forest animals, possums and foxes, chipmunks and raccoons.

After work, he visited the new baby boutique that had opened four doors down from the pharmacy. Thirty minutes later, he emerged with a dozen miniature sleepers in cream and lemon and mossy green. Washed them and hung them in the closet on tiny plastic hangers. He installed shelving and selected a book of nursery rhymes. Bought an enormous macrame owl with outstretched wings and hung it on the wall. A Raggedy Ann. A Raggedy Andy. And a tiny silver cup and bowl that he stored in a kitchen cupboard.

"Only rich people choose white carpet," Edie said, as she tapped at it with her toes. The front panel of her overalls was stretched tight. "Or ridiculous people."

"We'll just have to be careful."

She frowned as she examined the wallpaper, her fingertips gliding over the animals.

"What's wrong?" Gil said. "You don't like the pattern?"

"It's okay," she said, shrugging. "Eventually they all end up together anyway. Predators and their prey."

•

In the spring, Mrs. Paltry suggested a surprise baby shower for Edie. Tea and finger snacks. Some silly games with toilet paper and a frilly bonnet. June Fischer had graciously offered to host it in her backyard, and they invited about a dozen young women to attend. Including Edie's lunchroom co-workers from the high school. And Seth's wife, Andrea. It would be a small gathering of people who loved Edie. People Edie loved.

On the afternoon of the event, Gil pulled into Mrs. Paltry's drive-way to pick her up. For the first time ever, his mother-in-law was not waiting on the concrete stoop with her purse clutched in her hands. He parked and turned off the car. Did not want her to feel rushed. As he waited, he poked through the pile of 8-tracks on the seat beside him. Merle Haggard. Slim Whitman. Loretta Lynn.

Over the past months, whenever he saw Mrs. Paltry, she was wearing a continuous smile. Her spine was straighter. She moved about more easily. The patches of psoriasis, once so raw, were now pale shapes in the crook of her arms. "Our family has had too much hardship," she'd said last week at their Sunday dinner. "That little one's our spark of light."

Edie had shaken her head and rubbed her stomach. "Can a spark punch like a boxer?"

But Gil understood what his mother-in-law had meant. He'd learned enough about the Paltrys to grasp the turmoil they'd experienced over the years. A new baby was an opportunity to alter the balance. Up the goodness. Dim the shade.

Gil watched the doorway of her bungalow and checked the windows. He'd expected to see a curtain pulled across, her face appear. A shy wave. This was unlike her. After several more minutes passed, he climbed out of his car.

The screen door opened with a creak. He stepped inside.

"Mrs. Paltry? I'm here."

The instant he entered the house, he knew something was off. There was an alarming emptiness to the air, as though one of the walls of the structure was missing. Yet the warmth of the day was absent, and instead, a film of coldness surrounded him.

He tried to tell himself she simply wasn't home. She'd forgotten an item at the store. A loaf of bread. Stick of butter. But there was an intense reek of burnt starch. She'd never have gone out and left the stove on.

"Mrs. Paltry?" he called again. "Are you ready?" He stood still in the front hall. There was no reply, just a cracking and popping from deeper within the house.

He found her there. Seated in a wooden chair in the kitchen, her back to the door. Her head was sharply lowered, as though she were examining a stain on the front of her floral dress. Gray hairs ran down the nape of her neck. Spread out on the table before her were ingredients for a dessert. Marshmallows. Boxed pistachio pudding. An opened tin of pineapple had been spilled on the floor beside her feet.

He moved around her. The floor tacky from the drying fruit juice. With the tips of his fingers, he reached out and tapped her arm. She never budged.

"Mrs. Paltry?" he said, though he knew she would not answer. He just needed to hear a human voice. And his own was the only option available. "Let's get this turned off, shall we?" He reached to twist the knob on the stove. With a dishcloth, he grabbed the handle and slid the smoking pot to the side. Chunks of blackened potatoes, all the water evaporated.

"Well, that's all sorted."

Gil called for an ambulance. As he waited, he slipped into the chair beside her, placed a gentle hand on her stiff shoulder. Continued to chatter. Saying whatever words appeared inside his chest. "The blanket you made is already folded in the crib, Mrs. Paltry. You didn't see the wallpaper yet, did you? Edie's not so sure about it, but the seams are lined up perfectly."

The ambulance arrived. Heart attack, they suspected. As they rolled her out on a stretcher, one of the paramedics said, "Best way to go, if you ask me. Lady never had a clue."

When Gil arrived home, he stood beside his car for a moment. Watched the women sneaking into June's front door. They were all dressed in bright colors and carrying gifts. He considered keeping the news from Edie. Letting her have the afternoon. But once she discovered the truth about her mother's unexplained absence, she would never trust him again.

As he went into the front hallway, Edie was emerging from the basement. A pile of folded towels balanced on top of her round stomach. She stopped when she saw him, her jaw going slack. He wanted to dash to the cabinet, swallow a pill to numb the sadness. But she was suddenly standing right in front of him.

"What is it?" she said. "Tell me. Who's died?"

As the words left his mouth, she dropped the towels. She began searching his face, frantically. "It's not true. What a cruel lie. Why would you do that to me?"

She bent at the waist. Keening. An animal who'd just been caught, teeth sunk into its middle.

Lowering his head, Gil gazed at the creases in his pant legs. The ferocity of her grief was making his legs unsteady. For an instant, he had the desperate notion to strike her face. To shock away her tears. But he could not touch her that way. Instead, he remained beside her, catching her as she crumpled to the floor. She held the smooth ball beneath her dress and cried, "I can't do this. I can't do this alone."

As he waited for her to exhaust herself, he thought back to those moments he'd spent with dead Mrs. Paltry in her smoky kitchen. The favor he'd asked of her. To watch over the baby when it was born. While it grew up. And at once, he had this sinking feeling that he should have mentioned Edie. He should have asked his mother-in-law to keep a hand on his wife as well. She was coming apart, and he had no idea how to fix her.

•

After the funeral, Edie went upstairs to their room. She closed the curtains and climbed into bed. For days, she would not get up. Gil tried to coax her to take a walk, let in some fresh air, sip a cup of honeyed tea, but she would not budge.

He went over to Mrs. Paltry's home and packed up her belongings on his own. Filling cardboard boxes, black garbage bags. He donated what was usable to the neighbors, the church. The front hall closet still contained men's clothing. Two sizes of coats, shoes. Likely belonging to Edie's late father and her absent brother. Gil packed up every thread. Edie had insisted he discard it all, but he couldn't help but keep a few pieces of Mrs. Paltry's jewelry. Modest gold earrings. A chain with a pendant that he guessed was a daisy.

In a drawer, he found a metal tin full of photographs. Gil spent the better part of an hour sitting on the floor of Mrs. Paltry's bedroom examining them. Edie and her two siblings wearing matching striped shorts and T-shirts, sitting in the branches of a tree. Edie's father proudly holding a rifle over his head, an inch of his hairy stomach exposed. Edie's sister, cross-legged on some grass, making macrame. A black-and-white of a young Mrs. Paltry in the very kitchen where she died. Her head arced back in laughter as she washed what appeared to be a raw chicken.

He knew bits and pieces of the Paltry's history, but there was more to them than their dysfunction. All those photographs were proof. There was goodness there. There was glee. Captured and exposed. A happy family of five.

When he brought the tin home to Edie, she said, "I told you to throw it all away."

"But they're wonderful memories," he said.

She rolled toward the wall, mumbled into her pillow. "That only makes things worse."

Two weeks passed, and still, she did not move from the bed. He could not grasp how a person could remain that way. Gaping at nothingness. Oxygen passively easing in and out of the lungs. Face and legs growing thinner while her stomach appeared ready to burst.

"This can't be good for you," he said.

"I don't care."

"Or the baby, Edie."

"Still don't care."

•

On the due date, Edie was getting up from the toilet when her water broke. Gil heard the splatter of amniotic fluid, the desperate yelp. When he rushed to her side, the toilet seat and floor was covered with liquid, flecks of white.

"I won't do this," she yelled at him. "I refuse."

Sixteen hours later, Gil peered through a smudged wall of glass. Into the hospital nursery. Two rows of white metal carts. Each containing a minuscule bundle, wrapped tightly.

"That one there," the nurse pointed. And a second nurse, on the inside, picked up a baby and brought it to the window. A six-pound parcel. Blanket the color of a blushing cheek. A tuft of ebony hair was sticking out around the doll-sized hat.

He closed his eyes, leaned his forehead against the cool glass. He could not take it all in. The sight of his newborn daughter. Her swollen face a deep pink, wrinkled like an angry old man.

"And Molly's such a pretty name," the nurse said. Edie had chosen it. Named after her mother, who had been Mary.

Breath quivered at the very top of Gil's lungs. Then he gulped and the tears came. He turned away, covering his face with a hand. For an instant or two, his chest convulsed as he tried to swallow the sobs.

"I'm sorry," he said. But he could not control himself. This time, there was nothing available for him to take. He could not press down the softness. "I'm so sorry for this."

"For what?" the nurse said, handing him a tissue. "You think you're the first man who's bawled at these windows?"

He blew his nose. Folded the damp tissue and put it into his pocket.

"Just means that baby girl's going to be blessed," she continued. "Blessed with a father who loves her."

CHAPTER TWENTY-FIVE

WHEN GIL ARRIVED at the hospital to bring his new family home, the head nurse of the maternity ward pulled him aside. "And you're the—?"

"Um, husband?" He hadn't meant to sound uncertain.

"Well, you'll need to keep an eye on Mom. She hasn't gotten a wink."

Gil assumed the nurse was exaggerating. Surely Edie had been resting, and once they arrived home, she would continue to do so. But instead, she seemed energized. After laying Molly in the wicker bassinet, she slipped into a loose dress and began cleaning. Wiping away messes that were invisible to Gil. A magazine out of place. A sticky ring on the table where he'd left a juice glass. Shiny fingerprints on the cupboard knobs.

When he noticed a line of blood trickling down the inside of her leg, he tugged the damp cloth from her hand. "You need to slow down. None of this matters. How about a sitz bath?"

She shook her head, then went to the kitchen drawer and pulled out another cloth. Other than nursing the baby, she did not sit, or nap, or ease into a tub of warm water. For hours, she wandered from room to room, hunting for specks of dust, flattened pillows that needed plumping.

At dinnertime, June Fischer brought over a casserole dish. Shepherd's pie. "Warm oven for twenty minutes, Gil, and you're all set."

He thanked her and asked if she'd like to see the baby. "A girl," he said, and swallowed to release the emotion that was constantly tightening his throat.

"Oh, how lucky. But another time. I don't want to impose when · everyone's exhausted."

He stepped outside and closed the door behind him. "She's not, though. Not in the least."

"The baby?"

"No, Edie. She cleans nonstop."

June nodded. "It's an adjustment. I did the same when Bradley was born. Bleached every single towel and sheet. Curtains, too."

"So it's okay?"

"Of course it's okay. She's finding her footing. Plus after losing her mother. Poor girl." As June strolled across the grass, she called over her shoulder, "Enjoy the dinner. Mrs. Wynters must be ravenous."

He thought back over the day. His wife hadn't eaten anything either.

At dinner, Edie pushed the food around her plate. Made train tracks through the mashed potatoes with the tines of her fork.

"No appetite?" he asked.

"It has a weird taste."

"Do you find?" He thought it was delicious.

"What kind of meat is it?"

"Ground beef, I suppose?"

"No, it's not." She lifted the corner of the tablecloth, glanced at the floor beneath. Then she said, "A cat can't catch a cow."

He was about to ask what she meant, but the baby was mewling again. Edie stood instantly and went to the couch. Balancing on the very edge of the cushion, she unbuttoned the top part of her dress and peeled it down over both shoulders. Gil carried Molly, his hands shaking as he navigated every trip hazard, the table legs, the edge of the rug. When Edie latched her onto a breast, she pressed two fingertips into the nipple of the other and groaned.

"Does it hurt?"

"Prickles," she said. "Like when my foot's dead and it's waking up."

He smiled at her, said, "Not so bad, then."

As he watched his wife, so responsive to his daughter's needs, a pleasant warmth pulsed through his entire body. It was all an adjustment, like June had said. Soon Edie would settle into motherhood. She'd fall in love with the closeness of their perfect tiny family. The three of them. Together in their home.

The baby began to sputter and choke on the rush of milk, and Gil lifted her from Edie's arms. "It's okay, it's okay," he whispered, and gently bounced her up and down. He pretended not to notice that Edie hadn't budged. Her arms did not move from that baby-cradling position. And she was transfixed by the empty fireplace. The gray ashes, the dirty grill.

•

Eventually, as Gil had hoped, his wife's struggles faded. He attributed that success to June Fischer, who flitted back and forth between their homes for the entirety of summer. Edie was alleviated of nearly all childcare responsibilities and forced to recuperate. Molly transitioned to formula, which June prepared daily. Ready and labeled in the refrigerator. Gil managed late-night feedings, and when he left for the pharmacy in the mornings, June was already bustling about the kitchen, Molly changed and fed and cooing in her bassinet. Edie passed her days sleeping, reading, snacking, watching television. Sometimes she would take long drives to clear her head. The obsessive cleaning faded. The jumpiness disappeared.

"I don't know how I can possibly thank you," Gil said to June.

"What for?" She placed her hand on Gil's forearm. "That baby's an absolute dream."

"She is, isn't she?"

"And though she looks like Mrs. Wynters, her personality's all you, Gil. One hundred percent. It's uncanny."

"Oh, I wouldn't say that." He grinned, brushed Molly's cheek with a finger. "Surely my wife's in there somewhere."

A cough. Edie was standing on the stairs behind them, her open hand bouncing up and down on the railing. "I'm going out," she said.

"This early?"

"Yeah."

"Don't you want to come say good morning to Molly?"

She did not answer him. Hurried down the stairs. The front door opened and closed.

"I guess she's in a rush," Gil said.

"Mm. I guess so."

An argument ended the arrangement with June later that evening. When Edie strolled into the kitchen, she noticed Molly had been changed into a new pink sleeper.

"Isn't it sweet?" June said. "I picked it up yesterday. I love the little frill around the neck."

Edie leaned over, pinched the cotton fabric between her fingers. "Take it off."

"What?"

"You heard me," she said to June. "Take it off."

"But she's sleeping. I don't want to disturb her."

Gil stood up from the table. Put his spoon down beside his bowl. "Edie?"

She went to the stove, then. Plucked the stockpot off the back burner and carried it to the kitchen sink. With a twist of her wrists, she began pouring out the contents. A cloud of steam rising up as the broth and cubes of chicken, the diced carrots and celery tumbled from the pot. Scalding liquid spattered her arms, her abdomen, but she did not flinch.

Gil kept his voice calm, low. "What are you doing? That was perfectly fine food."

Beneath the sink, she dug out a black garbage bag. Dropped the pot and lid inside. The hot bottom instantly melting through the plastic, the pot tumbling back into the sink with a loud clunk. "Oh, hell," she said, as she pulled out another bag.

"I think I'd better go," June said, as she moved toward the door. "Bradley's probably wondering where I am."

"I'm so sorry," Gil said. "I don't know what's gotten into her."

Once June was outside, door closed, Edie hissed at Gil, "What's gotten into me?"

"Yes, exactly." Gil threw his hands up in the air. "You were rude to a woman who's given us—given *you*—an extraordinary amount of support."

Edie snorted. "Do you think I didn't notice?"

"Notice what? She changed the baby's outfit after a spit-up?"

Edie made a face then. Her eyes rolled upward, tongue hanging out. A loud groan, "I'm June, I'm June." Lunging at Gil as though she were starving, and he was a savory meal.

"Quit it," he said, stepping backward. "You're acting crazy."

Edie straightened her back then. "You think I'm bothered by a snake in the grass?"

"Come on. You're being completely unfair."

"Am I? I thought I kept my cool, actually. Considering that bitch just used my mother's soup pot."

•

When Molly was ten months old, Gil awoke in the darkness. Voices were drifting up over the stairs and in through the open bedroom door. Edie was having a conversation with someone in the living room. He checked the clock on his night table. The hands said 4:07 a.m.

They'd been managing overall. Though he'd wanted Edie to simply stay home with Molly, Gil agreed to enroll the baby in a Tiny Tots daycare near the pharmacy. Edie then went back to work in the school cafeteria. Their routine had been steady and predicable. That was until the past few weeks. Molly had begun teething, her gums swollen and her cheeks brilliant red. She was pleasant when the sun was up, but whining, fussing, wanting to be carried for long hours through the night. At the start, Gil brought home a remedy from the pharmacy. *Paregoric 3 ml.* But Edie refused to administer it.

"It's harmless," Gil had explained. Minutest dose of opium dissolved in alcohol. "New mothers are grabbing it off the shelves."

"No," Edie said, arms folded. "She needs to get used to it."

"Used to what?"

"Misery."

Night after restless night, Gil began to detect shifts in his wife. Similar things as when Molly was born, as though they'd always been lingering beneath the surface. Edie was watchful. Fidgety. Refusing to go down into the basement. She misplaced things. The electric bill inside the dishwasher. A pair of scissors in the top drawer of Molly's dresser. Twice he had to go to her childhood home in East Aymes after the new owners called. Edie was banging on the door, insisting she be allowed in.

"My whole everything is in there," she cried.

"You're not making sense, Edie. What whole everything? I emptied the place out."

She would not explain what she meant.

Pushing back the sheets, Gil got out of bed. Flicked on the lamp, but it did not work. He'd forgotten Edie had been unplugging things. The stereo, the electric kettle, the television set. She'd said the buzz in the wires was aggravating her.

He went down the hallway and into the nursery. Checking the crib, he noted that Molly was there, her tiny body still beneath a blanket. It was not teething that was keeping Edie awake this time.

His wife's laughter crinkled the air. "Yes, the sink fell off the wall," she said. "We brushed our teeth in a bucket for weeks."

Had someone stopped by during the night? Did they have a visitor?

"Edie?" Gil called softly as he came down the stairs. "Who's here?"

"Painted all those eggs, then tossed them at the train."

"Edie?"

"He was boiling. But he couldn't stop. He couldn't stop!"

Gil found her kneeling on the floor in the corner beside the brick fireplace. She was wearing a pair of his striped pajama bottoms, and nothing on top. In the hazy moonlight, everything was gray. Except her back, which appeared to glow. Her spine was jutting out, and he realized she'd lost weight again.

He walked closer. She was holding a white square of paper in her hand. A notepad and pencil lay on the brick hearth.

Crouching down beside her, he said, "You must be cold. Can I bring a blanket?"

"She's blinking."

"Who's blinking?"

Edie turned the paper around. A worn snapshot of Mrs. Paltry. Creased down the middle, as though it had been folded in two.

"Is that a photo from your wallet?"

"She's blinking out a message."

Edie focused intensely on the image, and with her other hand, she plucked up the pencil. Scratched out a series of dots and dashes and hollow circles and squiggly lines. Some large, some minuscule. Some on the line, some off.

Gil began to shiver. "Edie, please."

She stared at him, mouth open, her eyes dark and sunken. "All you do is squeak," she growled. "It's disgusting."

"Listen to me."

How had they gotten here? She'd been fine. Or almost fine. Well enough that Gil's worry had begun to recede. And now, a few sleepless nights had triggered a downward spiral.

"I told you to quit bugging me." Her fist circled around the shaft of the pencil. "I'll mess up her message."

"Talk to me, Edie. Try."

He reached out and touched her knee. It jerked upright, and she scuttled backward, pushing her shoulder blades deep into the corner near the fireplace. Her toes were curled under her soles.

"Why you?" she said.

"Because I can help better than a photograph."

She looked down at her mother in her palm. "But you don't know me."

"Of course I do. I'm your husband."

"My husband?" She sneered then. "I see you now. You scrambled up my leg."

Gil sighed. "Okay, Edie. Just listen to yourself. You're not making any sense."

"I only want to make her happy." With a finger, Edie smeared the graphite on the page, then scratched her scalp with the sharp end of the lead. "I was going to stomp on you, but see what she says?"

He stared at the scribblings. A code only Edie could decipher.

Gil went to the kitchen and dropped two tranquilizers in a cup of breakfast tea. Stirred until they disappeared. Took a generous gulp himself, then brought what remained to Edie. She drank it. He expected her to doze off in minutes, but while she appeared drowsy, sedate, her eyes did not close. She lay her head against the cool brick, photograph pinched in her fingers. "I was going to stomp," she murmured.

When the sun crawled up through the sky, Gil began making phone calls. Before mid-morning, he'd found a place that could help her.

He put some essential items into a small suitcase. Carried Molly over to June's house. He opened his mouth to explain, but nothing came out. "Whatever you need," she said, as she took the baby into her arms. Along with the bag containing diapers, gripe water, several bottles of formula.

Edie followed Gil to the car, tiptoeing over the pavement with bare feet. She was still wearing the striped pajama bottoms, and he'd forced a cotton sweater on over her head. They drove for several hours, all the way to the city and then another fifty minutes on. He could tell when the sedative wore off, as her knees started twitching, her eyes darting left and right. She reached down and lifted the floor mat. Pulled her feet up onto the seat.

"And here we are," Gil said, as he drove past the open gates. Ornate metal painted steely blue. "We're going to get you fixed up. Good as new."

The main building of BirdSong Wellness was lemon-yellow stucco, and two nurses were waiting on the front steps. Robin's egg uniforms, folded hats pinned to their hair. As they tried to coax Edie from her seat, Gil went inside, spoke with the attending physician.

"Based on our conversation, I suspect she's been suffering from a nervous condition since giving birth," the doctor said.

"Since birth? It was a bumpy start, but she's been doing so well."

"Has she really?"

As the doctor listed signs Gil had missed, he leaned back in his chair. It was hot inside the office. Even though the weather was warm enough to open windows, two radiators were pumping out heat. He wanted to close his eyes. To doze.

"These issues likely started out as maternity blues, as we call it. But I suspect she hasn't been herself since your child was born. And with the chronic insomnia, it has transformed into something more severe."

"More severe?"

"A breakdown can happen shortly after Baby arrives. Less commonly, it occurs some months later. A delayed psychotic episode."

Gil slowly shook his head. "She's hardly psychotic. Not like she . . ."

"Here at BirdSong, we understand," the doctor said. "Your wife needs help, some treatment, and she'll be back to herself in no time."

The doctor guided Gil to the reception area and handed him a clipboard. Gil completed the dozen pages and wrote a hefty check that made his mouth go dry. Over the phone, they'd recommended twelve weeks of in-patient treatment.

"Will three whole months actually be necessary?" he asked the nurse behind the front desk. That would mean Edie missing Molly's first birthday as well as their third wedding anniversary.

"At a bare minimum, dear." She smiled. "Depending on the severity, some women stay with us for an entire year."

"What? I don't think that's—"

"Your wife didn't get where she is overnight, now did she?"

Gil nodded, though he disagreed. It certainly seemed like it had happened overnight. He strode over to the front desk and handed the clipboard to the nurse.

As he was saying goodbye, Edie reached out and held his wrist. A feeble grip.

"Everything's going to be okay," he said, as he patted her fingers.

"You have to cut them." Those were the first words she'd spoken since before they'd left the house.

"Cut what?"

"Her whiskers," she said. "You can't trust something wild."

Him

THE BABY NEWS was like an electric shock. Jostling me sideways. She was quivering when she made the announcement, her head tilted, eyes gazing upward. I was too much of a temptation, she'd said. We should have used rubbers. I hadn't pulled out like I'd promised. And now here we were. With this not-so-surprising result.

For days I was beside myself. To even contemplate it! From our love, our connection, we'd created an actual person that was breathing and crying. Whenever I approached the front of the lineup for lunch, I wanted to grab her hand. Tell her that I was so happy she was finally back at work. That I was elated about the development, and I was going to step up. No matter how hard, I'd find a way to juggle schoolwork and our child. I'd even get a job so I could provide. Nothing else mattered to me.

In the months that followed, our relationship grew even deeper. As we were officially a family, I told the lunch lady every single thing about myself. Even the parts I was mortified to mention. She never once mocked me. Instead, she listened intently, patiently. Without judgment.

"That's natural, I'm sure."

"It must have been so draining for you."

"Things will totally get better. You'll see!"

I explained about my father. How when I was four, I discovered him at the bottom of a flight of stairs with a broken neck. I couldn't recall much about him, other than he'd always smelled sickly sweet. And that his arms and legs were stick-thin, but his middle was bulbous. Cinched in with a thick leather belt. I told her how often I thought of that belt. His pink puffy hand unbuckling, gripping the silver oval, a harsh tug, and it was released from the fabric loops. Snapping in the air, ready to do its job.

I also shared the problems I had with my mother. How a hefty insurance settlement allowed her the luxury of never working again. But with so much free time, she turned all her attention to me. She was mostly indifferent to my older sibling, so I'd dare to say I was her favorite child. And that had its perks, of course. If an assignment was late, she'd craft an essay, write it with her left hand. If I wanted steak Diane and fried potatoes, that would be our next meal. If I snuck money from her wallet, she'd chastise herself for leaving her purse out on the counter.

There were plenty of drawbacks, though. She knew about every aspect of my existence. When I was backed up, bran muffins would appear on the counter. A wet dream, and my sheets would be freshly laundered before I got home. If my hidden container of Vaseline was empty, it would be quietly replaced with a full one.

I did not reveal that the entire school year, my mother had been peppering me with questions. And I'd been sidestepping with evasive replies. I suspect she sensed I'd been keeping some parts of my life secret. Places where her poking fingers couldn't reach. But what else was I supposed to do? How could I explain the complicated situation I found myself in. A married girlfriend. A growing baby.

My mother could never grasp the depth of the bond I shared with the lunch lady. While not traditional, it was still profound. That supportive, amazing, gorgeous, hungry person was always there, waiting inside my head. It wasn't only about the dirty stuff, either. Our mouths, our hands, our warm private parts. She heard me. Actually listened, in a way nobody had ever done before. Not even Mrs. Fischer.

I knew my mother cared, but her unwanted attention was beginning to weigh on me. I felt as though I was wrapped in layers of padding. But I realized there was no room for anyone else inside our insulated existence. Not a friend. And certainly not the single person who filled my dreams, my every waking thought.

I told my lunch lady that I was reaching my limit. I needed to slough those layers off.

•

"Sweetheart, someone is calling on you."

"Who is it?"

My mother appeared in my bedroom doorway. "A boy. In a highly inappropriate T-shirt, if you ask me. I've left him standing outside."

I sat up on my bed. "You didn't invite him in?"

"Not with what he's wearing. No, I didn't."

"Mom. Really."

I hurried to the door. My friend was waiting on the stoop. "Hey," I said.

"What the hell? She slammed the door in my fucking face."

"Um, sorry." I looked down at his T-shirt. Clean white cotton. "Stoned agin" in wavy letters across his chest. "She's just like that."

"We're all hiking over to Rabey Lake. Hanging out. You in?"

"I—"

But before I could finish my reply, my mother was behind me. Her fingertips tickling my back. "You've got things to do, dear. Some garden cleanup. No time for socializing."

I scuffed my feet. "I can't, I guess."

"Your loss." He tapped his forehead and then jogged away. Toward a good time that I was not going to have.

At dinner that night, as I was scraping the skin of my baked potato, my mother said, "I didn't like that young man. Did you see the cartoon?"

She was still talking about his stupid T-shirt. Several frames beneath the words. A face balanced on two hands, normal at first, then drooping, then finally oozing right through the fingers.

"It's nothing, Mom."

"It's not nothing, dear." She reached over and wiped my lips with her already crumpled serviette. "It's a reflection of who he is. Who he's going to become."

I swatted her hand away. "Can't you just let it go? I'm not a kid anymore. I need to make my own choices."

Her face went white, as though she were stricken. Then she straightened her spine. I could practically see the determination building inside her. Cinder block on top of cinder block. "Well, you won't be spending any more time with that boy. He's not a good influence."

With the tines of my fork, I folded the potato skin over and over until it was a small brown parcel. I shoved back my chair. "I'm going to lie down," I said.

"You're not feeling ill, are you?"

"No, I'm fine." But I was tired. Tired of her.

She watched me walk down the hallway, called out, "I'll check on you later, dear. Bring you some warm milk."

I swallowed my anger, pushed open the door to my room. And she was right there, sitting on the edge of my bed. Hair in loose waves. She'd borrowed a pair of my gym pants and a faded sweatshirt. Her feet were bare, toenails painted a coral color.

I closed the door behind me. "Hello," I said. I hadn't been seeing her as much, but I tried to be understanding. She was working most days, and with the baby, she was extra busy.

"I heard the fuss out there. Everything okay?"

"Not really. She treats me like a kid." I sat on the bed beside her, felt her head leaning on my shoulder. "I'm sick of it."

"I get it. Being a mother is hard. But she's got to let go eventually."

"Doubt it."

Her warm breath spread over my neck. My skin erupted in goose bumps.

"Is there anything I can do to distract you?"

"Possibly," I said, smirking at her. "What have you got in mind?"

She pushed my shoulders with her palms, and I flopped backward onto the bed. Then she was straddling me. My shirt had turned into slippery silky pajamas. She gripped my wrists, slid my hands above my head, leaned down over my body. I could feel the tips of her full tits grazing my chest. They were a whole lot bigger than they were before. Probably from tons of milk. Then she brought her mouth close to my face, nipped my jawline with her teeth.

"Ouch," I squealed. "That actually hurt."

"Oh, I'm just getting started."

The weight of her bottom pressed on me, and blood rushed between my legs. I moaned, arched my neck. I caught a glimpse of her fingernails, longer, pointier than they were a moment ago. "You could take an eye out with those," I joked.

"Yeah. If I wanted to."

I was beginning to love her mischievous side.

She scratched at my ribs. I lifted my knees, laughter rippling through me. "That tickles!"

Just as her hands were working their way inside the band of my gym pants, the doorknob rattled. "What's going on in there? Why'd you lock it, dear? Who are you talking to? I know you don't have a phone jack. Is there someone outside your window?"

"I'm busy," I said.

"Busy how?"

"Doing homework."

"You need to open this door, mister. Right this instant. Your milk is ready."

"I don't want milk."

A huff. "Well, you should have said so earlier. I'm not going to waste it."

I heard her brushing her fingers along the ledge above my door-frame, then the ting of a metal pick being inserted into the center hole of the doorknob. A mechanical snap and my mother strolled into my room.

The lunch lady vanished.

"Really, Mom?" I sat up, placed a pillow over my lap. "Why do you have to bust in?"

"Because this is my house, and I can go wherever I want." She wandered around my room, peering into corners and checking behind the curtain. She even glimpsed into the closet. "What homework, then?"

"Nothing. I was just thinking about an assignment." Life sciences. Human anatomy. Mating rituals. "It's a presentation, so I was talking through some ideas."

"Oh, okay." She thrust the warm mug into my hand. "Now, down the hatch. Every drop."

She stood in front of me as I drank it. Hands on her wide hips. "That's a good boy."

I felt a thick heat spreading over my insides. Sourness sloshing around in the pit of my stomach. I hated when she said that. A good boy. I didn't want to be a good boy.

"Now, shall we go over your topic?"

"No."

"You sure, sweetheart? Didn't I tell you how bright I was in school?"

I wanted to put my face close to her face. Holler at her so loudly that her ugly fluffy hair lifted off her skull. Couldn't she see I wasn't the same stupid kid anymore? That I'd changed? That I'd grown?

"Yeah, you told me. But I got it, okay?"

"You look really flushed. You sure you're not feeling off?" She clamped her hand over my forehead. Then thrust it down the back of my shirt. Checking for fever. "Well, I'll let you get back to it. Love you, dear."

When she went out of my room, she left the door open a crack. Just enough so her dark eye could peer through whenever she passed by.

I fell backward on the mattress again, but as hard as I tried, the lunch lady refused to come back.

·

"And the dizziness has decreased?"

"Yes, Mrs. Fischer. A lot better, actually."

We were in her basement office for another session. She was wearing a lime-green skirt, and her bare legs were pale. I could see tiny black dots where the shaved hair was regrowing.

"That's incredible news. You've been using your strategies, I presume?"

"Totally. I thought it wouldn't make a difference, but it's actually helped." I wasn't saying that to make her feel good, either. She'd taught me how to breathe better. How to visualize that shaky cage in my guts. To see the door dissolving. The nervous bird transforming into a brave bird and flying into a clear blue sky. "It took a lot of practice." But I could do that now. Replace my apprehensions with a focus that was strangely sedate.

"I'm happy to hear it." She crossed her legs, and her left foot began to swing softly. The bottom of her sandal had a thick rubber sole. "And what else has been going on? Socially, things are okay?"

"I guess so."

"Making connections with your peer group?"

I studied the sad girl on the velvet painting behind Mrs. Fischer's head. Why would an artist want to paint a kid who was crying? Why would a person want to buy it and display it?

"I mean, there's been a bit of something. That's sort of bugging me."

Mrs. Fischer leaned forward in her chair. "Do you want to talk about it?"

"It's nothing really. I just met this girl."

Eyebrows up. "A love interest?"

"Yeah. I'd call it that. But the whole thing is kind of tough to summarize."

"Well, those feelings can be both exciting and confusing. When you're young and curious about each other."

Pink rose in my cheeks. *Curious* was an understatement. "All that's going good, but it's my buddies. They started talking about her. Saying stuff." The guys and I were hanging out in the alleyway when we saw her passing by on the sidewalk. I looked away, and she never glanced at me, as we'd agreed to do. But my friends wolf-whistled. Yelled crude things. "Come try my sausage!" "You wanna whip my potatoes?" Stupid lunchroom jokes.

Mrs. Fischer tapped her chin with her fingers. "Encroaching on your turf, would you say?"

"Kind of." It had actually happened a month or more ago, but it was still bothering me.

"And how does your girl feel about this unsolicited attention?"

"Well, we haven't talked about it." I didn't really want to tell Mrs. Fischer that I'd just stood there. Didn't pummel them like I should have. "It's awkward."

"Then I'd say that warrants a conversation with your pals, don't you think? About respect."

I picked at a hangnail on my thumb. "But how do I do that?"

"In my opinion, being straightforward is always the best approach. And keep the message simple. Explain that the comments toward your girlfriend are making you uncomfortable."

Your girlfriend. That was the first time anyone besides me had said it out loud. "What if they don't listen?"

"You need to keep trying. Being committed to someone is not always easy. It takes maturity that unfortunately most boys your age don't have."

"I guess."

"And your mom?" she asked as she uncrossed her legs. "Has she met this special person?"

I scowled. "Hardly."

"Well, that's quite a strong reaction, dear."

"She wouldn't get it. She'd probably scare her off."

Mrs. Fischer nodded. "Mothers worry. But we always have our child's best interest at heart. Why don't you try to broach the topic?"

"I really don't think I can."

More nodding. "That inner struggle is an integral part of growing up. You rely on your mother, but at the same time you need to establish your own separate identity. To individuate."

Individuate. I liked that word. "Reads about right, Mrs. Fischer."

"And sometimes it's a painful process. Not just for you. But your mom, too."

She checked her watch, then stood up. Our time was over. I handed her the wad of bills. As I was leaving, she touched my elbow, said, "You've made such astounding progress, and you'll find your strength with this. I know you will."

"Thanks," I said, and skipped up her basement steps.

Once outside, I lingered in her driveway. I didn't want to go home without my reward. When I glanced up at Mrs. Fischer's house, I saw Brad's bulky shape in a darkened window on the second floor. I knew he was keeping an eye on me. To see if I was going to be a Peeping Tom freak. So I made a show of marching down toward the street and turning onto the road, but then I crept through the leafy bushes on the opposite side of the lunch lady's house. Climbed a tree closer to the back of their property. Farther away, but even from that height, it still had a quality view.

I searched from room to room, but I couldn't spot her inside the house. Usually she was home when my session finished, and I could follow her during her early evening routine. Twice she'd left the curtains of her bedroom open and I'd watched her undress. Shoes. Knee high stockings. The flared pants and crocheted top dropping to the floor. I did not blink once as her hands reached up behind her back, fiddling with the fastener on her bra. I could have helped her with that if I was beside her. I'd practiced with my mother's bra secured around my pillow. A pinch of the two bands, releasing the hooks and eyes.

I waited on that branch. My legs dangling over the side, going tingly, then numb. But my girlfriend never appeared. She hadn't been to work the past couple of weeks either, which worried me. All I could see was her husband in the nursery. He was sitting on the carpet, curly haired baby dressed in pink balanced on his lap. He was smiling, reading to her from a picture book. Then he placed her in a crib and dimmed the lights. On the cool breeze, I could faintly hear the tinny pluck of a music box. Easily recognizable tune. "Twinkle, Twinkle, Little Star."

At some point over the past few months, I'll admit I'd forgotten about the baby. I tried really hard to work it into the story, though. Like those times the lunch lady used it as an excuse when she was late. Or never showed up at all. Or when she suggested creative ways to make things up to me, and I'd spend hours and hours imagining. Then gradually, she stopped mentioning it. So did I. And we carried on like we had before. Just the two of us. No mistake made.

From my spot up in the tree, I heard squeaking. Rubber shoes hurrying along damp stone. For a moment, I thought it might be her, running behind this evening, but then Mrs. Fischer appeared. In the yard. The irritating sound of her playful tapping on the back door. A yellow light popped to life and the screen was pushed open.

"I brought you these," she chirped. She handed him a plate covered with a cloth. Cookies. Sandwiches. A cold slice of lasagna. I couldn't tell and I didn't care.

He let her inside.

Then—then I watched them embrace.

My stomach came alive. The entire cage in my gut was rattling, full of agitated birds beating their wings. Beating against each other. I tried to center myself, tried to visualize, but I could find no door, no way to dissolve the metal bars. And let them out.

I wrapped my arms around the smooth trunk, and my sweaty hands ran over a rough patch. Scars cut into the bark. It was too dark to see, so my fingertips dipped in and around the indentations. Straight cuts. Two semicircles. The initials *B* and *F* carved side by side.

Mrs. Fischer's son had been here, too. Sitting exactly where I was.

I held my breath for so long, I nearly slipped out of the tree.

•

I did not know what to do about Bradley Fischer's encroachment, but I decided I'd have to say something to his mother. Demonstrate my growth. She should not be skulking over to her neighbor's house in the darkness. Inserting herself into a situation where she did not belong. Things were already complicated enough, and those inter-actions could only damage my lunch lady. Cause her pain. While I absolutely wanted the marriage to implode eventually, I needed to be ready to swoop in and catch her. And as hard as it was to acknow-ledge, I wasn't there yet.

That evening, after my mother was snoring, I crawled through my bedroom window and rode my bicycle to the grassy area across from Mrs. Fischer's house. I stashed my bike in a clump of trees and checked all the homes. Everything on the street was still.

Above me, the lamp was buzzing. Only offering the faintest erratic glimmer of light. Shoulders slumped, knuckles grazing the pavement, I darted across the road and up her driveway. Her car was an old VW beetle. Olive green. Crouching beside the passenger side, I retrieved a knife from my back pocket. I stabbed a single puncture near the rim of both the front and back tires. I skittered around to the driver's side and did the same. There was a soft steady hiss.

While certain things may require a conversation, as Mrs. Fischer had said, sometimes a single word would do. With the tip of my blade, I scratched *BITCH* into the hood of her car. I made the letters small and neat, but easily observable. I mulled over an exclamation point but decided punctuation was unnecessary.

I folded my knife and poked it into my back pocket. I'd never van-dalized anything before, but surveying my work, I was content with the effort.

After that night, I never went back to her basement. Instead, I took the therapy money and went to Main Street. Sometimes I'd buy myself a copy of *Tiger Beat*. Or a paperback of hidden word puzzles for my girlfriend. Sitting side by side on a bench, we'd share a double cheeseburger and a milkshake. I'd tell her if she had ketchup on her chin. She'd laugh at the rocker hairstyles in my magazine. We'd stay together until the required amount of time had passed, and then I'd wander home to my mother.

NOW

.

CHAPTER TWENTY-SIX

Molly

"GO. GO OUTSIDE!"

That was what the teenage boy shouted as Molly stood in the garage doorway. His eyes were strange and unfocused, and his bony frame was kneeling beside her dead mother. With the side of his hand, he scraped the pooling blood, as though trying to reverse the flow of liquid spreading over the concrete.

"Go, I said! Get out of here!"

And she did as she was told. Practically floating through the kitchen on a cloud of fear. Yanking at the sliding glass door with her skinny arms. The weight of it. When she reached the back of the property, she hunched down into a ball.

So many odd details of that afternoon were locked in her memory. She could recall sucking on the corduroy fabric covering her knee. The shrill caw of a crow in the trees overhead. And there was a beetle on the lawn, with an iridescent shell. Like a soapy bubble in the sunlight. She watched it crawling up a thin ribbon of grass, until the blade bent. The beetle vanished. Only to reappear a moment later, trying again to reach the end of nothing.

At some point, a pair of strong, certain hands slid beneath her arms. Then she was lifted through the air, brought closer to a warm chest. The scent of flowers and vanilla as Molly fused her body to her neighbor's.

When she was in her early twenties, Molly had requested a copy of the trial transcripts. She paid particular attention to Mrs. Fischer's short testimony. Reading and rereading multiple times. Undoubtedly because the woman's words gave Molly comfort. A sense of safety during the most frightening moments of her life.

Mrs. Fischer told the court that after she picked up Molly, she'd knocked on the back door of the Wynters house. But no one answered.

"And you weren't concerned?"

"Of course, I was concerned. But this wasn't the first time. Edie Wynters had a tendency to—"

"To what, Mrs. Fischer?"

"To do her own thing. I suppose that would be the polite way of putting it. Neglecting her responsibilities."

"And what happened next?"

"I took the child home, as I often did. My son and I kept her entertained. I figured the mother would pop over when she was ready. Or else Dr. Wynters would collect her whenever he returned home."

•

Molly spent most of that early November afternoon on the peer support line. Seated on the couch, with the awful painting of the overhang right behind her head. It was mostly quiet, except for the occasional hang-up. One elderly woman called to talk about the dull gray weather and wondered if she might be catching "the sads" again. Seasonal affective disorder, Molly assumed, and she suggested the woman make an appointment with her family physician. Have a blood panel completed, her vitamin D levels measured. "That's a starting point," Molly said, encouragingly. "Toward feeling better."

Outside the window, a small black bird swooped up to a feeder. Pecked once, twice, then fluttered away. Why was she continuing to waste her precious time? Slouched on a sofa waiting for a phone icon to shake and lift. Even though she knew it was irrational, she wanted to connect with that caller. Man, woman, teenager, or adult. Her thoughts kept circling to the unsettling mention of "paying her dues." No matter how hard she tried, she couldn't fully convince herself that the person was merely troubled. Or that the calls were simply pranks. Instead, she was left feeling both livid and helpless. She had the inane desire to confront, but also to make room for understanding.

Or perhaps this was an example of self-deception. Not about the details of her mother's death, but about her reasons for distracting herself with the helpline. Maybe she was avoiding the reality of her father's condition and the tasks that lay ahead. Inevitabilities so sad, the thought of them were a gash across the middle. Could it be possible she was punishing herself? Purposefully opening herself up to misdirected cruelty? An attempt to balance out some undefined guilt.

Then she considered the third point on the mental triangle. The most difficult one to examine. That the caller's words resonated. She had doubts. She had worries. She was curious.

Molly pressed her eyes closed for a moment. Pinched the bridge of her nose until she felt a dull throbbing pain. Occasionally she marveled at the fact she was paid to help others work through their thoughts. Their minds. When her own so often felt like a woolly snarl. Every loose end so deeply hidden away, there was nothing to grasp.

After an hour, Molly responded to an incoming call. A low hum in the background. She sat upright, adjusted her laptop. Here it was. Maybe this was the call she'd wanted. The call she'd dreaded. But after she introduced herself, nobody spoke.

"Hello," Molly said. She pressed her hands on her earphones. A rhythmic squeak. Of metal? Was the person leaning back in an office chair? "Can I help you?"

Molly edged forward, breath held, muscles tense. Finally, a woman began speaking. With a feigned cheerfulness that was mildly irritating. It took Molly several seconds to recognize her own voice. Repeating the same phrase with slightly different intonations, different speeds. The alterations made her words sound as though they were pulled through mud, or high-speed like a chipmunk. Both familiar and foreign. And oddly menacing.

"Hi, it's Molly. How can I help? Hi, it's Molly speaking. How can I help you? How can I help you? Hi, I'm Molly. I'm Molly. I'm Molly. How—how—how can I—"

Whoever was on the line had been recording her. Had created a bizarre compilation of her introductions.

"Who is this?" she yelled. "What the hell's wrong with you?"

Then she felt a stab of anger at herself. For seeking out discomfort. Clearly some part of her craved being unsettled by this offensive whack-job. Which made no sense, given how complicated her life was at the moment. She did not need a single thing more.

She would stop. Ask Russell to block the caller.

As her voice echoed in her ears, she made a note of the exact time. She was about to click "End Call" when the recording abruptly stopped.

The distorted tone. Deep and gravelly. Making her stomach drop. "There are things you need to know, Molly Wynters."

"And what exactly do you mean?"

"Once you understand, you're going to help me."

"Why would I help a coward?"

"You think I'm a coward?"

"I sure do. Hiding in your dark little bedroom behind a screen. Trying to scare people." Her breathing was shallow. Vision fuzzy, as though miniscule fireflies were zipping around her face. "Did you leave that newspaper in the mailbox?"

"I did, Molly. You weren't offended by my message, were you?"

"Wow. How old are you? Thirteen? Fourteen? Did you get a selfie on the front lawn, too?"

Laughter, then. "When you were a girl, you had a music box that played 'Twinkle, Twinkle, Little Star.'"

Her hand, hovering over the trackpad, froze. "Who is this?" she said again. Much softer this time.

"I've got your attention now, do I?"

She hesitated. She had owned a music box when she was little. Pink satin interior, ballerina that sprang upward when the lid was lifted. She could not recall the exact tune.

"What do you want from me?" she said. Five seconds passed. Then ten. Molly would have assumed the call had been disconnected, but the white noise was ongoing. "Are you still there?"

"I am." Several more moments passed. "You know what, Molly? As much as I enjoy our chats, I think it's time we really connect."

"What?"

"Let's meet. Tonight. In the alleyway that's next to the pharmacy. Around eleven."

Her palms were suddenly damp. She wiped them on the legs of her jeans. "You—you think I'm actually going to show up?"

"You accused me of hiding. So, I'll stop. And I think you're a smart girl, Molly. You'll be there. If not, I'll be forced to pay you a visit. When you're not expecting it."

That was undoubtedly a threat, and she tried to control the shake in her voice. "Don't bother waiting long."

"I won't. But we should both quit pretending. Don't you agree? You know what happened. And now it's time to make it right."

•

Molly stood at the mouth of the alleyway next to Wynters Drugs. Everything on the street was closed except for a pub at the end of the block. The door opened, and for a moment, country music seeped out into the night. A man emerged, stumbling over the sidewalk. He slumped against a parked car and lit a cigarette. "Yeah, yeah, yeah," he bellowed into the air. "All good. I'm all good."

When she took two steps forward, she was swallowed by the blackness. Digging around in her purse, she found her phone. Fully charged, and she swiped down to select the flashlight.

She had no intention of waiting in the alleyway for the caller to arrive. Though she was capable of impulsive behavior, like rushing up to the overhang that night, she was not entirely reckless. Instead, she'd arrived at the pharmacy a whole hour early and planned to find a safe spot to tuck herself away. Some nook or cranny where she would not be seen. And when she heard the person approaching, she'd take photographs. According to an internet search, if she had her camera in night mode, she'd be able to capture who it was. And then go to the police to report the harassment. The threat.

She edged forward. A garbage can was knocked over, and as she moved around it, she envisioned an animal or a person tucked in behind. Waiting to burst out and startle her. She aimed her light deeper into the alleyway. It was longer than she remembered. Narrower. A barbed wire fence blocking the end.

Stab of panic then. A slender needle in her chest. She could not identify a single spot to hide. Except for the indentations of doors on either side, the walls were tall and featureless. She was realizing her idea, which had seemed reasonably clever inside her kitchen, was ludicrous.

Molly took a step backward. Once again she was making a poor choice. A dangerous choice. What was going on with her? Why did she even care who it was?

But she knew. She knew. That third point on the triangle she'd considered earlier. Once she discovered who it was, she was not going to go to the police. Instead, she was standing in the pitch-black waiting for a stranger to arrive because she wanted to know if she'd made a mistake. Her memories felt like concrete. But even concrete could crack.

Someone was approaching behind her then. Coming from the direction of the road. Rapidly getting closer.

"Molly?" Soles scraping over damp pavement. "Is that you?"

She spun around. Raised her phone, shone it toward the noise. The glow reflected off a pair of glasses. Scratched lenses.

"Russ." She exhaled. "What are you doing here?"

"I was having a drink. Just down the street." He folded his arms across his chest. "I wasn't sure if it was you. Did you lose something?"

"Not exactly. No."

"Then might I ask why you're here?"

She stared at Russ. "I—I can't say for sure. I was out. Wanted to clear my head. And I thought I heard something. Or someone. But I think I imagined it."

"Even so, it's not worth investigating here." With the beam of his own flashlight, he traced the brick walls. They were covered in layers of graffiti. Declarations of love. Tags. A huge cartoon penis. Then he illuminated the ground just beyond her feet. A mess of litter and broken glass. A filthy towel. Two used condoms. He tut-tutted. "Obviously this is no place to clear your head."

Molly dropped her phone into her purse and pushed her hands into her jacket pocket. "I know, I know. I wasn't thinking. I was off in my own world." Which was true. If Russell hadn't shown up, what might have happened? The mention of a music box had hooked her. Made her think there was something to it. But that was a common item back then, found in the bedrooms of most little girls. Likely all playing the same simple tune.

"How about we head back to the house?" Russell said. "I'll make us a tea. And we can clear our heads together."

CHAPTER TWENTY-SEVEN

"YOU DID WHAT?"

"It's not a big deal, Mom. I read about her in the police file and went to talk to her is all."

They were in the kitchen of her father's house. Alex was pale, shaky, and was using a steak knife to hack a warm brownie from the tray Glenn had made. Molly had to resist the urge to take the blade from his trembling hand and do the job for him.

"You actually went to see that lady who used to work at the lake."

"Yeah," he mumbled. Mouth full. "That's what I said."

"The same lady who was supposed to testify." But who was deemed to be an unreliable alcoholic. So drunk that afternoon, her witness statement was ignored.

Alex gaped at her. There were crumbs on his lips. "Woah, you're really not listening today."

"I'm serious, Alex. Did you just walk up and knock on her door?"

"Why are you being so weird?" There was a sheen of sweat on his forehead, and he yanked off his hoodie. "So, I knocked on her door.

I told her I was doing a school project and asked if she still remembered anything. She said yeah, she totally did."

"And then what? You went into a stranger's house?" Molly paced back and forth beside the counter. "I don't think that's what your law teacher had in mind, do you? Putting yourself at risk."

She was irritated at his irresponsibility. But also peeved at herself. Just last night, she'd wandered into a dark alley alone. To meet a person with a serious grudge. She often wondered about various aspects of her personality, Alex's personality, and where those traits came from. Did Alex inherit his impulsivity from her? And if so, how did she come by it? Maybe her mother? Outside of the stories her father told, Molly really had no idea.

"Like, what was going to happen? She looks older than Grandad."

Molly remembered the rumors about that woman from when she was young. Whatever the kids wanted, booze, porn, weed, she would provide. Molly had bought beer from her a time or two, but for the boys, the price often didn't involve money. Her services were well-known and had been available for years. "Well, what did she say, then?"

"Nothing much, really. She was cleaning out a cabin and heard fighting. Arguing."

"Arguing?"

"Yeah, and when she went out, there were two people over there. Up on the ledge on the other side of the lake. One was bent down, and the other was hauling a piece a garbage, she said. That's what people did, dumped their trash." He glowered. "I mean, nobody had a clue about the environment."

Molly stopped pacing. "It doesn't matter what she says."

"And why not?"

"Because she was blitzed. Loaded. Three sheets."

"So? She's still got eyes."

"And seeing double through them. There was only one person up there. Besides my mother. And that was Terry Kage."

He took a deep breath and exhaled, as though sugar was finally flooding into his bloodstream. "Well one of those Terry Kages apparently yelled something, too. It echoed right across the water."

"I know, Alex. I read it all, remember? No one shouted 'knee deep' from the overhang. That's nonsense." That was what the lady claimed. Insisted on, in fact. She'd heard a man yell the words "knee deep." It was included in her police statement and reported in the papers, but ultimately dismissed as fiction.

"Maybe Terry Kage thought the water was shallow?"

"No chance. Everyone knew you couldn't swim to the bottom if you tried." Through her sweater, she scratched at the bend in her elbow. The blotch of dry, itchy skin was likely hereditary as well, but she didn't know about that either.

Alex peeled off his T-shirt and handed the damp clump to her. Then tugged his hoodie on over his head.

"Was that it, then?" she asked. "You left?"

He laughed. "Yup. Took off the second she started singing this dumb country song. Like she thought I'd be into it or something."

"What's that supposed to mean?"

Alex smirked, said, "Forget it, Mom. I'm joking."

Molly leaned her lower back against the counter. "Stay away from her, okay? I get that you're trying to cover everything and I'm not trying to dissuade you, but there are always people who insert themselves into situations. To get attention or feel useful. She's one of those."

"Sure, but just because a person has a shitty life, it doesn't mean they're a liar."

"I didn't say that, Alex."

"And just because someone lives a decent life, doesn't mean they're always honest."

Molly folded her arms across her chest. "Of course not. Things are never—"

"Sorry to interrupt," Glenn said, as he appeared in the doorway. He glanced at Alex, then at the half-emptied pan. "Brownies good?"

"Totally," Alex said, patting his stomach.

"You'd never guess there's a whole zucchini in them."

"What? Really?"

Glenn chuckled, then said to Molly, "Are you still okay if I head out for a few hours?"

"Of course, Glenn. You should go."

"Great. Dr. Wynters is resting, but you can call me anytime"— he lifted the cellphone he was clutching—"if you have a question or concern."

"I'm sure we'll be completely fine," Molly said.

"I'm headed out, too," Alex announced moments after Glenn left. "If that"—he bowed slightly in Molly's direction—"is agreeable with you."

"Of course, it's okay with me," she said.

He stuffed his feet into his sneakers. Popped a ball cap on his head. No gloves. No scarf.

"At least take your jack—" But her words were cut off by the slam of the door.

•

Once Alex and Glenn were gone, Molly sliced the remaining brownies into neat squares and piled them on a plate. She covered them with a clean tea towel and then wandered into the living room where her father was sleeping.

For a long while she stood in front of the bay window. Watching the wind scatter the fallen leaves. The days were getting shorter, and when she noticed the light disintegrating, a heaviness began to press around her. As though the air inside her childhood home had substance, had sound.

She wished Alex hadn't gone to see that old woman. It wouldn't surprise Molly if there was brain damage from all those years of abusing alcohol. Her recollections were likely nothing more than bleary distortions. A few particles of truth, perhaps, but with countless bridges to span the gaps. A cohesive story was surely soothing to her.

Hearing that she'd been singing to Alex aggravated Molly even more. Had she been acting provocatively? Moving her ancient hips toward him? Clearly, she did not realize whatever trade she'd offered thirty or forty years ago was a violation. Though everyone turned a blind eye. Laughed her off, to the point she was practically viewed as a rite of passage. If she'd been a man, she'd have gone to jail.

When the streetlamp burst to life, Molly noticed a car idling. At first, she thought it was Dr. Even, back yet again, but a girl climbed out. Long hair trailing down her back, patterned leggings. She flicked up her hood, jogged toward the divider, and joined the shapeless huddle of teenagers standing beneath the near-naked oak trees. They linked arms then, the group strolling away in a single tight line. For a moment, Molly considered that Alex might be among them. That his arm might now be connected with another's. The thought of his possible friendships gave her a moment of happiness.

After closing the curtains, she went to the chair beside her father's hospital bed. His body was not much more than a single long ripple in the felted wool blanket. The beige tube snaked up his right nostril, and the plastic bag, hanging above him, was slowly shrinking. Glenn had suggested a night feeding in order to add some much-needed calories.

She gently touched his forehead with the backs of her fingers. Smoothed his hollow bristly cheek. The soft drop of skin that formed his earlobe.

They were so different, the two of them. While she'd always grappled with an unsettling mix of uncertainty and rashness, her father was a man of constant calm. When she was young, she'd sought ways to test the limits of his patience. Saying "fuck" in front of her third-grade teacher or stealing a bag of frozen corn from the supermarket. One time he'd found her at the overhang, drunk on peach schnapps, legs dangling over the edge. "I feel bad inside," she'd slurred as she flumped back on the dirt, arms spread wide. "Like part of me is rotting, Dad. And I don't even know why." "Molly." He'd said her name so softly. "Please come away from there." Then he gripped her forearm, dragged her over the ground. As she stumbled home, her father holding her upright, he hadn't snapped at her with impatience. Instead, he'd offered encouragement, understanding, and affection.

Molly watched his face. Beneath his eyelids, his eyes did not roam. The only movement she could detect was a slow, steady breathing. She stroked his hand, blue veins prominent over the bones. "How can you do that?" she said. "Even with all this. You're peaceful."

As she folded back the top of his blanket, a dull thud pulsed up through the floor. Molly's hands jumped. A second clunk, then. Quieter this time. Like a plastic water bottle had rolled off the counter. She held her breath, listened. Glenn was out. Alex was out. No rodent could ever be that loud. Then the unmistakable *slish* of cardboard sliding over concrete.

For an instant, she forgot everything, and she reached forward, shook her father's shoulder. "Dad. Dad!" Her voice trembled. "Someone's in the basement."

Her father's eyes slowly opened.

"Dad! Someone's broken in!"

There was no alarm in his expression. No protective determination. He was not going to leap to his feet, clutching whatever was handy, and confidently tell her to stay put while he went to check things out.

As his eyes lowered, she felt a cold gush of anguish. As though a frothing wave had knocked her sideways. Wanting to drag her away.

More movement below, and she tamped down her panic, rose to her feet. Her father might be defenseless, but she certainly was not. Quietly, she moved toward the fireplace. Her fingers wrapped around the handle of a brass poker. She raised it, so the sharpened end pointed ahead of her. Then, with soft steps, she made her way out of the dining room. Down the hallway, toward the basement door.

She knew each wooden step. Where her weight would produce a creak. Or maintain her silence.

Halfway down, she bent slightly. Scanned the space. In the shadows, she saw a form, hunched over, rifling through her family's belongings. Terror was replaced by rage, and she rushed down the last stairs. Poker aimed into the dimness. Ready to strike. She cried, "What the hell are you doing?"

By the time she reached the landing, the shape was a frantic blur of jeans and puffy coat. A black hat. Or a navy hat? Head tight toward the body. Medium height and clumsy, tripping over a storage container, then out the basement door, scrambling up the concrete stairs.

A boy or a man. She knew that for certain. But what was he searching for?

Then, in the narrow window near the ceiling, she saw legs rushing past. Caught a glimpse of the sneakers. High-tops. Unlaced, tongues hanging out. Like a teenager might wear. Or an asshole adult.

THEN

·

CHAPTER TWENTY-EIGHT

Gil

ON THE WALL in the storeroom was a photo of a woman in a candy-red bikini. She was seated on an office chair, a single slender leg extended in the air. Seth had chosen the calendar, and at some point every month, he'd remove the thumbtack, lick his lips, eager for the big reveal. A long, low whistle, and he'd always say, "Ah. What I wouldn't give."

Last time Andrea had stopped by the pharmacy, she'd seen the June lady. "Really, Gil?" she said. "Wouldn't have guessed you were so juvenile."

"Yes, really, Gil?" Seth echoed. "You dirty old dog."

Gil checked the date. Marked a tiny red check in the upper corner of the white square. Edie had been gone for two full months. He'd received multiple updates from the head psychiatrist at BirdSong, but the assessments were cautious. With the strict schedule, plenty of fresh air, and the introduction of medication, Edie had made "subtle progress." Continued evaluation was crucial. Gil hoped that soon he and the baby could visit.

He would bring the memory book. Since Molly was born, he'd kept track of absolutely everything. Writing down her length and weight from every doctor's appointment. Making a note when Molly batted at the stuffed lion in her crib. Recording the date and exact time he'd caught her smiling, grabbing her feet, cooing, pulling herself to standing. Just last week she'd taken her first steps and spoken her first words. "Dada-dada-dada."

He would not mention that June Fischer had baked a delicious vanilla and strawberry cake for Molly's birthday. Or that Molly had finally cut her teeth and was now sleeping like a log. He would not bring up his arrangement with June, either. How they often shared a glass of wine in the warm summer evenings, and how he'd discovered a calming bliss in the ordinariness of their conversations.

As soon as Seth arrived that afternoon, Gil hurried to remove his white coat, pack up the remains of the lunch June had made for him. A thermos of leftover spaghetti and meatballs. A box of Sun-Maid raisins.

"She's already got you wrapped around her finger," Seth said, as Gil headed for the door.

He stopped. A faint heat invading his cheeks. "Who?"

"Little Miss Molly, of course."

For an instant, Gil thought Seth was somehow aware of the vivid dream he'd had last night. Where Edie was a spotty memory, and it was his neighbor who greeted him when he returned home. As he followed June into the kitchen, her clothes dissolved. He saw her shoulder blades, her spine, two dimples above her full backside. And he lifted her onto the countertop. Pushed apart her legs and tore away the stained apron that remained. She threw her head back as he pushed into her, said, "I've been waiting for this."

And then he'd woken up. Jumped out of bed and hurried to shower, like some sort of overheated teenager.

"Hardly," Gil replied. "Molly barely even knows she's got a finger."

On the drive home, Gil smiled to himself and shook his head. June was a kind and generous friend, and his dream was simply that of a lonely man. Missing his wife.

He pulled into his driveway. For an instant he didn't understand why his hands had grown slick on the steering wheel. Then he was aware of a car parked beside the front door of his home. He didn't recognize it. And he knew it didn't belong.

Gil shut off the engine and got out. The car had a dented fender with an "Impeach Nixon" bumper sticker. Rust bloomed around the wheel well, and one brake light was smashed. He peered through the driver's window. The interior was littered with empty soda bottles, crumpled papers. A duffle bag was opened, balled-up clothing spilling out. There was no rearview mirror.

He scanned his front yard. Nobody was loitering. Could the driver have randomly parked that piece of trash and then abandoned it? Could a prowler be waiting inside his home? Might June have noticed something? Were she and Molly safe?

Just as he was about to investigate further, he heard a man's voice. Booming out through an open window of his house. "Well, I'll be jiggered."

Gil tensed. There were no questions now. Someone had strolled through the front door in broad daylight. He rarely locked up the place, and even if he had, there were still two hidden keys. One beneath the front welcome mat, a second balanced on the doorframe of the basement door.

He'd have to call the police. Then the man was saying, "And that was when—" The ending of his sentence drowned out by cackling laughter. Familiar but surprising.

Edie.

Panic shifted to confusion. Just two days ago, the psychiatrist had recommended extending her stay, but she'd returned on her own? Apparently accompanied by a man?

Gil marched inside.

"Oh hon," Edie said as she rushed into the hallway and hugged him. "You're home."

"I am," he replied. "And so are you." Gil eyed the belt of her jumpsuit, encircling her wasp waist. She'd grown even thinner.

"I found a couple of steaks in the fridge and I'm about to put them on the barbecue. Should be enough for the lot of us. And potatoes, too. Do we have mushrooms?" She turned on her heel and went to the kitchen. Gil followed her, watched as she yanked open the doors, sorting through the cupboards.

"Edie?"

He tried not to stare at the young man who stood a few feet away. His dark blond hair was slicked back, with several oily hunks hanging over his forehead. He was wearing flared blue jeans and a plain white T-shirt. A cigarette behind his right ear.

"Um. Edie?"

Could she possibly have hitchhiked home? And invited some random man in for dinner?

She twisted her head. "We've got mushrooms. Two cans! Got to be kismet."

"Edie!" he said louder. "Who is this person and why is he here?"

"What person?"

"That one, for god's sakes." Gil pointed at the man, who was now grinning at him.

Edie bent at the waist with laughter, then clapped her hands together. "That's just Cal."

"Cal?"

"Yes, my brother, Cal. I totally forgot you never knew each other." Then she flicked her finger this way and that. "Cal, Gil. Gil, Cal. Now we're all friends. Oh, and hon? He'll be staying with us for a day. Maybe two at most."

"Hey," Cal said. He had several steel-blue tattoos on his arms. A three-leaf clover. A flying cherub with a bare rear end. A royal flush.

Gil coughed. "Hey," he said back. Then to Edie, "Can we talk for a minute? You know, over here."

"Sure can." As she walked with Gil, she called over her shoulder, "Cal, can you spark up the barbie? I'm famished."

They stepped into the dining room, and Gil closed the French door. "Edie, what happened? At the clinic?"

"I left."

"What do you mean you left? You were there to get help. So you'd get better."

"But I am better. Can't you tell? I feel fantastic."

He had to admit, even though she'd lost weight, she did seem upbeat. Exuberant, actually. Her eyes still had those dark circles, but she was organizing a meal. Even said she had an appetite.

"Then why didn't you call me?"

"Are you angry?"

He touched her elbow. "Of course not. I just need to understand."

"I mean, I don't know." She chewed her lip. "I just kept thinking about Cal and wondering how he was doing. And so I called the penitentiary."

"The what?" Gil's mind started skipping through his inner thesaurus. *Jail. Joint. Cooler. Slammer. Big house. Lockup.* He could find no alternate meaning.

"They switched me around from person to person, until someone finally told me he'd gotten out. Like a month ago. So I pushed a bit, and they gave me a phone number. That's how I reached him. And I asked him to swing by and grab me. It's not a big deal."

Gil could see Edie's mouth moving, but he hadn't processed a single word after she'd said *gotten out.*

Questions were springing into his head. What had Cal done? Had he stolen money? Or had he committed a violent crime? But before Gil could ask a single thing, Cal's tanned face appeared on the other side of the door. He was holding a barbecue fork in his fist, and with the two sharpened tines, he tap-tapped on a glass panel.

"Get grooving, missy, or this shit's going to be charred."

She laughed again, as though the prospect of burnt meat was the funniest thing in the world. She strolled out of the dining room, and the two of them headed across the family room toward the backyard. Shoulders touching, nonstop chatter.

"Or that time Dad made Mom sew carrots onto his jacket?"

"And that little horse followed him all the way home? Like he was the pied-fucking-piper of East Aymes."

"That was my birthday."

"Yeah, yeah. It was. You got ten good minutes before the fuzz showed up." Cal sighed. "I fucking miss him, man. And Mom."

"Yeah. Me too." Quiet for a moment, then Edie yelled, "It's not charred, Cal. You're such a fibber." A smacking sound.

"Ow, Edie! What'd you do that for?"

They were like two playful youngsters. Joking and snickering and prodding at each other. Was that the way adult siblings behaved? Gil had no point of reference. But it grated on him, that comfortable connection. Then Gil took a moment to remind himself what was important. Edie appeared in a much better place than two months ago. The lightness that enveloped her now was a good thing. A few days with her brother would be a good thing, too.

•

"So, Cal." Gil tore open a tinfoil-wrapped potato. "What'd they, um, get you for?"

"Really, Gil?" Edie frowned. "That's your first thought?"

"Sorry. Am I not allowed to ask? Is there a rule or—"

"Nope, you don't ask," Cal said through a mouthful of fried onions and mushrooms. "Especially if you're in the clink. But I'm an open book, buddy. It's actually a funny story."

"Oh?"

He swallowed, belched. "I was totally shit-faced, me and my guys, and we all rolled into this dive, right? But they wouldn't let us in. We had fake ID but—"

"You were underage?"

"Sure, but they were so fucking righteous. Acting like we were some loser kids, and all we were doing was trying to get some beer, score some shit."

"The nerve of them," Gil managed.

"And then this chump, the guy who owned the joint, saunters out into the parking lot like his shit don't stink and he starts messing with us. Shoved me right there." With a tight fist, Cal slammed himself in the shoulder. "And that's cause, right? You know, legally speaking. Him laying hands on me."

"I guess so?" Gil loosened his tie.

"So I reached into the box of the truck and grabbed this bottle and swung it at him. Got the cocksucker right in the jaw. And fuck me, but this tiny hunk of glass stuck in his neck. Well if the idiot don't yank it out. You never saw such a goddamn mess. Red squirting everywhere." Cal threw up both his hands. "Two minutes and he dropped dead. Like that. Poof. It weren't my fault. No, sir. My mother even said so, didn't she, Edie?" Edie was nodding. "But no one'd listen."

"Wow, Cal," Gil said, putting down his fork. His appetite had waned. "That sounds like really bad luck."

"Story of my life, brother. Story of my fucking life." He stuffed another forkful into his mouth. Chewed hard. "But brighter times ahead, right?"

"Sure, sure."

"Edie told me you offered a job in your shop. Stocking shelves or whatever."

"She said that?" Gil shifted in his seat.

"I'm grateful, good buddy, but I won't take you up on it. Around all those drugs? That's like dropping Casa-fucking-nova in a room of naked babes and telling him to keep his trousers zipped." Cal snickered. A drop of bloody juice leaked from the corner of his mouth. "Besides, that nine-to-five shit's not for me. You can't tie me down."

"Yeah, it's pretty dull," Gil said, relieved.

"But I got a business plan, though. Been working on it when I was inside."

"Can I ask?"

Fingers spread in the air. "In a single word: skateboards."

"Sorry?"

"I mean the whole industry's just beginning to hum. It's on the, what do they call it? The cusp of explosion."

"Skateboards. Huh. Wouldn't have guessed."

"He's not going hog wild, Gil," Edie said. "Just starting small."

"Yeah, I got a bunch of decks and trucks in the trunk. Wheels and shit. I figured I'd slap some together and head over to the high school. Hustle a bit."

"Isn't school out for the summer?" Gil shifted again.

"Sure, but kids are still hanging, no? And Edie knows them all, so that's my in right there. Then once I got enough cash, I'll open a store. Fully dedicated to custom boards. When that takes off, I can start a chain."

"I think it's a really solid plan." Edie tossed another chunk of meat onto Cal's plate, and Cal stabbed at it.

"Isn't it, though? And I've been looking for investors."

Gil felt himself blanch. Cal snorted, poked Edie with a wiggling finger. "Will you get a load of his mug, sissy?" Then to Gil, "Don't worry about it, brother. I already know you're strapped. That dump you stuck my sister in was a fucked-up money grab, weren't it?"

Molly began throwing wooden blocks out of her playpen, and Gil got up from the table, went and lifted her out. "Well, Cal. I wish you tons of success."

Cal continued eating with immense enthusiasm. Shoveling forkful after forkful. His lips and fingers were shiny from grease. Edie tossed a beer cap at his head. Cal tugged a strand of Edie's hair. She squealed. And he guffawed.

Gil slid open the glass door and, with Molly in his arms, stepped into the calmness of the backyard. June's honeysuckle was blooming, filling the air with sweetness. In the breeze, he caught the faintest tinkling of ice against glass. His neighbor was outside, relaxing on a patio swing, nudging it back and forth with her toe. As she lowered her drink, she waved to him. He waved back.

He resisted the urge to walk over there. Slide in next to her and tell her about the bizarre evening he'd just experienced. How Cal was like a bad-guy character from a comic book. How Gil's life was feeling more and more like a daytime soap. How Edie had improved, but somehow seemed different. Happy and light. Too light. As though not a single thread tethered her to the ground.

CHAPTER TWENTY-NINE

THE PHONE IN the stockroom was ringing. Gil put down the metal spatula. He'd lost count of the capsules, *Amoxicillin 500 mg*, and would need to start again. He tried not to sound annoyed when he said, "Wynters Even Drugs."

"Have I reached Dr. Wynters?"

"You've got him. Is this regarding a patient?"

"No, sir, nothing like that. This is Basil Reynolds from First Central. How are you doing today?"

There was something about the formalness of his tone that instantly set Gil on edge. "I've had better days, to be honest, Mr. Reynolds." He laughed nervously.

"I'm sorry to hear that, sir. Well, I won't keep you long. Just need to straighten out an issue."

"Issue? What's going on?"

Paper rustling in the background. "Seems you've reached your overdraft limit, and unfortunately, we've had to decline payment on several checks."

"What checks? The only checks I've written are for"—he squeezed his eyes closed, trying to recall—"the electrical bill, a repair on the lawnmower. Oh, and I bought a stroller. For my daughter." That was it.

"Oh no, sir. I can assure you, we have quite a hefty pile here. Let me refresh your memory. Gayle's Interiors. Aymes Pretties. Homelife Hardware. Jude's Burgers and Shakes. Nature's Dreams. Larson's Automotive. And I'm just getting started."

"Those aren't mine," he insisted. "I haven't been to any of those places." But as soon as the words left his mouth, he knew exactly how Mr. Reynolds would reply.

"Your wife, perhaps?"

Blood jetted around inside Gil's skull. He could see it all. Curtains and sheets and pillows and kitschy artwork. An ice cream maker and beaded plant hangers and a two-person hammock still in its box. In the corner by the front door, a mound of unopened parcels.

When he'd questioned Edie, she'd dismissed him. Explained it was only Cal, selecting a few gifts as thanks for their continuing hospitality. "Isn't that thoughtful of him?" she'd said. "He really appreciates us letting him stay all this time." Gil realized now he'd been deluding himself. Thinking Cal hadn't just chosen those items but paid for them as well.

"As I'm sure you're aware," Mr. Reynolds continued, "insufficient funds for a check does lead to a banking fee. Multiple fees, in your case."

"Fees?"

He cleared his throat. "We're suggesting you drop by today, so we can get this mess cleared up. Make a deposit."

"Um," he whispered. He'd made a deposit just two days ago. Sliding his salary across the worn wood toward the teller.

Through the earpiece, Gil could hear Mr. Reynolds breathing. It was easy to picture the man, leaning back in his banker's chair. Handlebar moustache, chocolate-brown tie, dull yellow dress shirt stretched tight across his stomach.

"Um," Gil said again. If more checks bounced, could Edie be charged with fraud? He'd sworn he'd never dip into their emergency fund, but what choice did he have? He instructed Mr. Reynolds to shift the money over from that. He explained his wife had been redecorating. "She's gone to hell with it," he'd joked. "If I'm honest."

Mr. Reynolds did not laugh. There was muffled silence on the other end, as though he'd covered the mouthpiece with a thick, clammy hand.

Gil pressed his ear harder, strained to listen. Then a pen clicking in, out, in, out, in, out.

"I think you'd better stop by," Mr. Reynolds finally said. "Can we expect you later this afternoon?"

•

Gil screeched into the driveway, slammed the car door, and flew into the house. Music was blaring from the kitchen. The air stank of caramel and burnt butter. He picked up Edie's purse and flipped it over. Out came her wallet, a metal tube of hand lotion, umpteen pens and pencils, a flimsy scarf. And a checkbook. Only a half-dozen checks left. He tore them to shreds.

Then he marched down the hallway. He needed to understand what had happened. Figure out a way to undo things. But as he rounded the doorframe to the kitchen, his muscles seized.

The floor and countertop were littered with cracked eggshells and cocoa powder and torn packets. The stand mixer was working on high speed. Smoke was seeping out around the oven door. Filthy bowls and pans overflowed from the sink. There were plates of cookies and brownies, and on the floor beside the cupboards, a platter held a tall rose-colored cake, half iced, splitting under the weight of itself. In the middle of it all were two fire alarms, torn from the ceiling, plus skateboard parts, silver nuts and bolts, rubber wheels.

Cal was standing at the stove, swinging his hips left to right as he stirred the contents of a saucepan. Edie was rolling balls of dough between her palms. On top of her head was a tall white hat with the words "Star Chef" embroidered in navy around the band.

"Could you turn that off?" Gil pointed at the radio.

Cal lifted his head, tapped his ear. "Can't hear you, my brother." His blue jeans were riddled with holes, and his T-shirt was scissored off above his waist. Bare stomach visible, and just below his navel was a slender tattooed arrow. Pointing down.

Stepping over a mound of spilled sugar, Gil flicked the knob. Then he unplugged the mixer. Edie kept working, but Cal whipped around.

"You got a problem, buddy? You're killing our groove here."

Gil could barely speak. Yes, he had a problem. His kitchen looked like a bomb had exploded. His couch reeked from the sweat of a grown man. His bank accounts, including his emergency fund, had been drained. And he barely recognized his wife. She'd left the treatment center feeling healthy and optimistic, and for the past few months, she'd been acting like an adolescent on speed.

"I need to talk to Edie," Gil said. "I'll deal with you later."

Cal shot the wooden spoon in the sink. "Woah, woah, woah. Deal with me? What's plucking your strings, dude?"

Edie kept counting the balls out loud. "Forty-nine. Fifty. Fifty-one."

"Edie, can you stop? We need to talk."

"Fifty-two. Fifty-three."

Gil caught sight of the playpen then. Tucked around the other side of the corner. Slowly he moved toward it, certain it would be empty. That Molly had to be in her bedroom, because no reasonable person would expose a child to the racket, the smoke, the utter chaos.

But there she was. Sound asleep on the padded bottom. Lying on her back, arms bent upward, hands in fists, thumbs hidden. Flour was sprinkled over her dark hair, a flick of raspberry jelly on her cheek.

Gil turned toward Cal. "Get out," he whispered calmly.

"What's that, pal?"

"I said, Get out."

Cal laughed then, his horse-like whinny ratcheting up to the ceiling before it drifted back down. "Do you hear that, Edie?"

"Oh, shit, shit, shit," Edie cried. She dropped the dough, then rushed to open the oven door. A gray cloud billowed out around her head. "They're ruined!"

"Take your belongings," Gil said. "Take your car keys. And leave my house."

"I'm just trying to help her realize her potential, man."

"Edie's doing just fine."

"Which part, buddy? Fine being your little wifey? Or fine in the fucking loony bin?"

Gil dashed to the couch, clutched the paper bag of clothes, and threw it at Cal's chest. Cal caught it, yelled, "She's bigger than that, you know. Hell of a lot bigger. I bet you didn't even know she had a fucking dream."

With oven mitts on, Edie was examining the cookie sheets, dotted with black lumps. "I'm going to open a bakery, hon."

Gil grabbed Cal by the upper arm, wondered if he was strong enough to drag him to the front door. "And every cent. You're going to give it back."

"What cent?"

"The money."

"My seed money? No can do, bucko. Already invested."

"You're going to return it."

"I thought you was supposed to be smart. Seed money don't come back."

Edie was in the hallway now. "I did that. I gave it to him. I did. I'm his sister and it was my choice."

When Gil yanked Cal's arm again, Cal tripped on the edge of the rug. "Fuck," he said as he righted himself. "I'm trying to be patient, here, chum. But you're starting to piss me off."

"Let him go, Gil."

Another yank, and the neck of Cal's cotton T-shirt stretched. Threads snapping. The paper bag burst open and soiled laundry spilled onto the floor. Balled socks. Underwear. A faded sweatshirt. Cal drew his free arm back, swung at Gil. Missed.

"I said let him go."

After tugging Cal a few steps farther, Gil opened the front door. From the bowl on the side table, he grabbed Cal's keys, tossed them outside onto the lawn.

"Sis, how did you marry such a fucking asshole?"

Then Edie yelled, "If he's going, I'm going!"

Dropping Cal's arm then, Gil turned toward her. He wanted to tell her she couldn't leave. She had a child. She had a husband. She had a home. But when he gazed into her face, he fell silent. Her cheeks were flushed. Eyes glassy, pupils dilated.

And it struck him, what had been happening. She'd returned home from the treatment center on a much better path. But as each week with Cal passed, she'd been twisted tighter and tighter. A spring that was about to snap.

She shoved past Gil, dropped to her knees on the grass, searching through the blades for the lost keys. "They're here somewhere. They're here!"

All those changes were because of Cal. How could Gil not have noticed sooner? "What have you been giving her? What is she taking?"

In the doorway, Cal stood still. He gawked at Gil, and for several moments there was complete silence. Then he slowly shook his head, and said in a calm, low voice, "All I was trying to do was make my little sister happy, you know? Make her smile." He cleared his throat and spat a greenish gob onto the doorstep. "But to say shit like that to me? You're a sicko, man. You're actually fucking sick."

CHAPTER THIRTY

GIL COULD NOT sleep. His neck was stiff, and his head felt as though it was stuffed with hay. He'd waited for hours, watching the street from the upper level office. The lonely smells of fall drifting in through the open window. He was angry, worried, but also ashamed. After Edie and Cal had torn off in the rusting junkheap of a car, he noticed one of his neighbors had stopped on the sidewalk. An older lady in a dark orange cardigan, mouth tight and frowning.

"What a tone to use with your wife, Dr. Wynters." Her black poodle strolled onto Gil's lawn and squatted.

"She's unwell, Mrs., um," he stammered. Her name escaped him, though he knew she was a customer.

"And that makes it better?" She kept her nose in the air as she tugged the leash and walked off. Without cleaning up after her dog.

Edie finally returned in the middle of the night, tripping out of a grumbling truck. When the dome light clicked on, Gil saw a man's tattooed hands on the steering wheel. Heard chuckling, a deep voice, "You good, honey? You alright there?"

The next morning, he packed Molly's things, carried her over to June's house. Then he drove to the pharmacy and went straight to the phone in the stockroom. When he reached BirdSong Wellness, Edie's doctor was not available, but he was able to speak with a nurse. She placed him on hold while she hunted down the file, which she said was now "inactive."

"As you know, her initial assessment was completed several months ago, Dr. Wynters. It indicated she was diagnosed with delayed postpartum depression."

"And her course of treatment?"

"We pride ourselves on a multipronged approach here. Talk therapy, nature therapy. We had a local painter come in for art therapy."

"Drugs," he blurted. "What were the drugs?"

"Oh, yes. I see she was prescribed Elavil, which is a tricyclic antidepressant that has shown solid re—"

"I know what Elavil is. I'm a pharmacist, for Christ's sakes."

She sighed. "If you could please remain calm, Dr. Wynters, I'm trying to assist you." Several moments of silence. Then, "From the notes on file, the doctor did notice more engagement, as well as improved communication when the medication reached therapeutic levels. It mentions an elevation in mood."

"An elevation? Well, it's been elevated right through the roof."

"Oh, dear. Clearly your wife needs further evaluation, sir. And I see here that's what we recommended. But our hands were tied, unfortunately, as she checked herself out."

"And why on earth would you permit that?"

"Permit?" Another moment of silence. "To be clear, Dr. Wynters, mental health treatment has made leaps and bounds. Our clients are never confined."

Gil slammed down the receiver so hard his palm stung. He paced back and forth in the stockroom. He had no idea what to do. He'd have to talk to Seth, though. Ask for a loan. To cover groceries, light bills, gas in his vehicle. Gil would create a story to sidestep Seth's inevitable questions. A close relative, house burned or flooded, unforeseen medical expenses.

He swallowed a pill. *Lorazepam 2 mg.* Then paced some more, waiting for the sedative effects to work their magic. Just as a mellow glow began to appear, the bell above the door jangled. Les Carpenter strolled into the pharmacy.

Gil covered a yawn as he emerged from the stockroom. "Playing hooky, Mr. Carpenter?" Even though he and Gil were the same age, Les appeared much older. A full head of coarse gray hair, deep wrinkles around his eyes and forehead.

"No, sir. Took the day off." Les worked as a telephone line repairman. He was the one who shimmied up the poles, messed with the wires. "Had to take the wife over to the hospital for X-rays. She's got this stubborn cough she can't shake." He placed the prescription on the counter.

Gil examined the chicken scratches. Two items. *Tetracycline 250 mg.* And a cough suppressant with codeine. He went to the shelf and took down the correct containers. Dumped a mound of black-and-yellow capsules onto his counting tray. Once he'd finished that task, he pulled a flat glass bottle from a cupboard, dropped a funnel into the mouth of it, and filled it with the bright red syrup.

While he clacked out the directions on his typewriter, Les asked how Molly was faring. Gil replied, "Great. Wonderful. Best ever."

"Exhausting though, isn't it? You look like you haven't sleep in a dog's age."

"That, too. Yup." Gil fake-laughed. Smoothed the prescription labels onto the bottles. "For the antibiotics, four times a day. And a teaspoon of syrup when she needs it. No more than every eight hours."

The lines between Les's eyes deepened. "Four for that and three times for that."

"Don't worry, all the instructions are right there in black and white." Gil pointed at the labels. "And of course, you can always call me or Dr. Even any time. We're—"

The sound of muffled screaming interrupted them. Followed by a string of loud guffaws and garbage cans striking each other. Bottles smashing.

"Cripes, Dr. Wynters. Sounds like an all-out bash."

The noises were coming through the side wall of the building. Teenagers had infiltrated the alleyway between the pharmacy and Happy Pets.

"They're early today," Gil replied. "Must be no school."

"What ever happened to raking up a few leaves or picking up some litter?"

Gil shrugged. "Not the same as when we were youngsters."

"You better believe it, buddy. My mother kept me on a tight leash. And when she took the collar off, she handed it straight to my wife."

Gil whistled as he carried the medications over to the register, punched in the prices. "And that's the damage, Mr. Carpenter," he said, gesturing to the total.

Les patted his pockets. "Well, I'll be damned." His cheeks flushed. "My wallet. I must've left it by the front door. How stupid can I be?"

This was not the first time Les Carpenter had feigned a missing wallet. But Gil understood the stresses his customer was under. He made only a modest wage. Both wife and mother frequently ill.

Plus a daughter with some sort of developmental issue that required Les sinking every extra cent into a special school.

Gil pressed the "Paid" button, and when the cash register door shot open, he gently pushed it closed. He carefully put the items into a paper bag and crimped the top. "We're all settled up for today, sir. Hope the wife feels better."

Les took the bag in one hand, wiped at his face with the other. "If you ever need anything, Dr. Wynters, you just let me know. New telephone? You got it. Extra line? Just ring me up."

"I'll keep that in mind," he said, even though he had no need of anything.

Once Les was gone, Gil went back to his desk and sat down in front of the typewriter. He ran the tips of his fingers over the keys. The sedative was having minimal effect, and he could still sense that edginess, aggravation rubbing at his seams. He wondered if he should consume another milligram to carry him through the rest of the morning.

Edie should not be taking the Elavil. He had no doubt it was doing more harm than good. But how could he stop her? Two days ago, he'd heard her telling Cal, "You know, I never wanted my mind controlled! But now I'm like a new me!" He could discuss it, but there was no reasoning with mania. That was the only description that fit. Her energy was boundless and frenetic, and the entire world transformed into glittery thrills.

He put his head in his hands. When her pill bottle emptied, she could easily get a refill. Her general practitioner would provide it, and she would go to a different pharmacy. She resented the fact that he'd been the one who took her to BirdSong, and no matter what he said now, he'd have zero sway.

Gil dropped his fists onto the keyboard and a dozen thin metal arms shot up and clumped together. Hoping he hadn't caused damage, he nudged them back one by one.

But what if she didn't need a refill?

The idea popped into his head. A teensy spark.

What if he created a refill for her?

He straightened his spine and slid a prescription label into the typewriter. Twisted the knob on the side. Once properly positioned, he typed in the brand name *Elavil*, below it in brackets *amitriptyline*, the correct dosage, the exact instructions that were on her medication at home. Then he affixed the label to a new bottle and hurried over to the shelves on the back wall. He found it. A jar full of *Lithium 300 mg*. He had no need for the counting tray, just shook the tablets into the container and secured the silver lid.

Both medications were small and white, though the ones he'd selected were slightly larger and had a different letter imprinted on one side. She would not stop to examine them. Why would she?

Him

THE SKY WAS overcast, threatening to rain. As I sat on the damp ground in the alleyway, I picked the knots out of my shoelaces. I wanted to appear occupied. Even though I was a full year older, I still had nothing to add to the conversation my friends were having.

"Rocket fuel."

"Wacky tabacky."

"Can't forget nose candy."

They were trying to list all the nicknames for drugs. Acting so confident in their knowledge, as though they were local kingpins. I doubt they'd ever laid eyes on most of that stuff. Whatever it was.

"Cow patties."

"That's revolting," I said. "Who'd want to ingest a cow patty?"

"You'd be surprised."

We'd just finished that unit in health class. The last one before summer break. And it was full focus on the dangers. Nothing about the fun. But who wouldn't appreciate a glass of joy juice while nibbling on a disco biscuit? If I had to guess, I'd say the drink was bright pink, and the cookie was a snappy vanilla wafer with rainbow sprinkles.

"Still could mess you up," I said.

"Exactly. How do we get some?"

"Just might be your lucky day." A hand reaching into a back pocket. Pulling out a clear baggie. Waggling it in the air. At the bottom, a dozen tablets.

"Where'd you get those?" I asked.

"Found them in the trash. Right outside there." He pointed at the door that the pharmacist occasionally shoved open to yell at them.

"Oh, yeah?" I thought that was unlikely.

He walked around holding the baggie, and everyone reached in, plucked one out.

"But what is it?" I asked as I stared at the piss-colored pill resting on my palm.

"For your head."

"My head's good."

He laughed, ruffled up my hair. "Yeah, but in a few minutes, it'll be extra good."

I closed my fingers around it and watched the others as they gulped theirs down with a mouthful of soda. Zero hesitation. I decided I wasn't going to take mine. I had plans to meet up with the lunch lady after dinner, and it would be too risky if I was whacked. What if my mother caught me? Discovered I'd snuck a guest into my bedroom without permission. Was engaged in—how would she phrase it?—adult activities. Besides, I had no idea what would happen to me. Or how long before I'd turn back into myself. My mother had told me she was cooking pork chops and broccoli casserole for dinner, and if I wasn't on time, she'd be stomping around town searching for me. She'd totally lose it if I was curled up in a corner somewhere, my brain drifting through outer space.

"Cool," I said, as I pretended to swallow it.

Things got rowdier when the drugs kicked in. Bottles smashing against the wall. Vicious sidekicks to the metal trash cans. Fists pumping the air, then pounding their chests so hard I could hear the hollow echo. They were having loud arguments about ridiculousness.

"No, the pads on the bottom of its feet."

"Magnets hang them upside down."

"Fingerprints are the same. Stick to anything."

Jumpy laughter. "That's bullshit, man."

"It's not, you asshole."

"Get up to the roof then. Go on. Climb the brick."

Then one of my friends tore his sneakers from his feet, peeled off his socks. Several attempts to claw up a vertical wall before he slumped down, hugged his knees. "I got nothing to prove to you, pinhead."

"We should keep it down," I said. How many times had they gotten into hot water over their raucous behavior?

No sooner had the words left my mouth than flashes of red-blue light shot down the narrow alleyway. *Whoop-whoop* of a police car.

While the others lolled about as though their legs were marshmallow, I raced to the end of the alleyway and slipped around the corner of the building. Crouched down and poked my head out just enough to watch. Two uniformed officers were approaching.

"Guess we found the party, huh?"

"Starting early, though. Not even suppertime, boys."

"Where do you fellows live?"

"Yeah, we're going to take you on home. Have a word with your folks."

I made my way along the back of the buildings. Then wandered down some house-lined laneways. For a time, I sat on someone's front lawn, using newly sprouted blades of grass as a whistle between my thumbs. I was in no rush to get home, worried that somehow my mother would have found out. When my stomach began growling, I turned up my street, and then my fears were realized. My mother was on our front step, wearing my father's old hunting jacket. The color was canary yellow, and it felt like warning. She was waiting for me.

"Well, that's the very last straw, my boy," she said as I approached. "Do you know what happens to kids who consume illegal substances?"

I shook my head. It was medicine from the pharmacy. How was that illegal?

"They run around naked. Or yank out their own teeth with pliers. One woman dipped her newborn into a fat fryer, for goodness' sake!"

I rolled my eyes. She had to be joking. Though I had seen one of my buddies moon the others.

"Don't give me that face. I read the newspapers. I keep abreast of things."

Abreast. I tried not to giggle. "C'mon, Mom. I'm perfectly fine. Here, look." I stood on one leg, closed my eyes, and touched a fingertip to my nose.

"Quit that this instant," she shouted. "What's wrong with you?"

"I'm trying to show you I didn't take anything. I swear."

"I couldn't care less what you took or did not take. The fact is, you've been exposed to an unsavory element."

"Exposed? But nothing happens if you just touch it. I mean—"

She put her hand up. "I won't compromise your well-being. And I won't compromise your safety. We're done in this pointless little hick town."

I blinked. "Done? What does that mean?"

"I've been mulling it over, and my decision is made. As soon as I get things sorted, we're moving. Starting fresh."

"Mom! That's not funny. You're trying to ruin my life!"

She lowered her voice to an eerie softness. "And you'll be eating dinner in your room, dear. I prefer my own company this evening."

I stormed past her into the house, through the kitchen and down the hallway. Slammed my bedroom door so hard the entire wall shook. I could not calm down. I wanted to punch holes through the drywall. Tear up my sheets. Rip the lamp from the wall. But I sat on the edge of my mattress, eyes squeezed closed, every muscle knotted. Tamping all the rage down, a shiny kernel in my gut. I tried to find the lunch lady. I needed to share what was happening. Needed her to explain how to handle things. But I was so angry, so upset, she wouldn't appear.

It took me forever to fall asleep. When I finally did, I did not dream of my girl, like I wanted. Instead, I dreamed of my mother. As old as I was, she was holding me folded on her lap. Something pointy pressing into my cheek. And as I turned, I saw her wrinkled hand gripping her tit, forcing the hardened nipple into my mouth. Rancid milk coursing down my wide-open throat, filling my insides, filling my mouth, spilling out the corners of my lips.

I woke up with a heavy sense of dread. She was taking me away and I was going to lose everything that was important. And no matter what I did, I was never going to escape her.

•

For several months, we barely spoke. At some point before summer vacation ended, boxes began to appear in the kitchen. A mound of blank newsprint. Piles of clean laundry sitting on the couch, on the coffee table. Then after school, a man arrived in a truck. I watched him through my bedroom window as he trampled over the soft grass, hammered a wooden post. Ten minutes later, a "For Sale" sign swayed in the breeze.

The painful compression in my chest was back again. Mrs. Fischer had taught me to identify it. Fear was not simply an emotion. It created physical sensations. Even though my brain recognized my mother, every other cell in my body reacted to the woman out there as though she was the most dangerous kind of predator. Having snuck into a home, threatening to destroy every semblance of happiness within its walls. She was no different than a criminal with a knife or a gun. A jerry can of gasoline and a single lit match.

I clearly needed to make myself heard.

When I came into the kitchen, she was standing in front of the book-shelf. Sorting through the rows of romance paperbacks. "What do you think, sweetheart? Should I keep these or pass them along."

I placed the kettle on the stove. "Will you read them again?"

"Mm, not sure." Then she dropped her hands, limp at the wrist. "I'll take them. Nobody does me any favors, so why should I?"

While she was filling boxes, I made her tea. Brought it to her in her special cup. Fragile china, a band of pink roses around the rim.

"Thank you, dear," she said as she sipped. "Glad that you're feeling better about things."

"Yeah. A bit."

"We're going to love life in the big city. Who knows? I might even meet someone."

I stayed close to her, slowly started wrapping the Hummel figurines in the corner cabinet. A series of perfect little boys frozen in everyday moments. Hiding under an umbrella. Holding up a red apple. Balanced on tiny wooden skis.

After a while, she began yawning. Then she folded the lid on a final box, patted it with her hand. "We've been productive, haven't we? But tomorrow's another day."

I closed the glass door of the cabinet. "And the house isn't even sold yet, Mom."

"That won't take long, I suspect. And you best tend to your room, darling. You certainly don't want your old mother sorting through your private belongings."

"I'll start tonight."

"That's my boy."

I told myself I had no plan when I entered her room two hours later. I was only going to sit on the edge of her bed. Ready to plead with her, should she awaken. But I knew she was sound asleep. Before I made her tea, I'd borrowed several of her sleeping pills from her night table. Obviously she shouldn't have left them lying around like that.

"I can't move away, Mom, not now. I wish you could understand."

She was lying on her back beneath a thin cotton bedsheet. I layered on blanket after heavy blanket, and with the warmth, she began to snore. After each inhalation, she held still for a single second. Then came an irritating puff of air. I lifted each of her arms and gently placed them under the covers.

"I'm in love, you see. I've never said that out loud to anyone besides her, but it feels good to announce it. I'm completely, desperately in love."

A ladies magazine was open on the bedspread beside her. An article about getting ready to sell your house. Another about packing up efficiently prior to relocating. "Your Smoothest Move Yet!"

"She's perfect, Mom. Sweet and kind and more beautiful than anyone else in the world. She makes me laugh so much. And sometimes"— I lowered my eyes—"she really turns me on."

On the carpet beside my mother's bed was a box of clear plastic bags. She planned to seal up our sweaters, our towels, our fluffy comforters.

"So I hope you understand, but I'll die without her. I need to protect myself. Protect her."

My mother never budged when I slipped one of those bags over her head. Gathered up the bottom edge. She barely shifted as I pressed the button on the vacuum cleaner. Inserted the end of the nozzle. Only when the plastic began to tighten over her face, her head, did she jolt. Mouth frozen in a wide-open position. Sealed so tight in the plastic, I could count her teeth.

"If you really think about it, you could call this self-defense."

The weighty bedding held her arms down. And I waited there, letting the vacuum suck out every molecule of air. I was shocked how small her head became when all her fluffy hair shrunk around her skull.

"Mrs. Fischer told me it's a painful process," I explained, as I flicked the vacuum switch to "Off," carefully lifted away the bag. I plumped up her hair, kissed her warm forehead. "But she was right, you know. I finally found my strength. It was in me all along."

•

In the morning, I dialed the operator. The woman then contacted the police, and they sent over an ambulance. While I waited on the line, I wept. But when I peered inside, took stock of what resided in my heart, all I found was a soaring sense of freedom.

NOW

·

CHAPTER THIRTY-ONE

Molly

WHEN MOLLY RAN onto the patio, she couldn't see anyone. Wisps of fog hung in the air, creating shadows around the lawn furniture, shadows beneath the trees. "You can stop hiding," she said.

A motion light attached to the side of the neighbor's house flicked on, casting an orange glow over the empty backyard. Blurred movement, and then a door creaking. Molly waited. The light clicked off.

He'd slipped inside. As though the safety of his childhood bedroom would be the end of it. Her hands formed into fists. Head thumping with indignation. She wanted an explanation as to why Bradley Fischer had been inside her father's home, rifling through old belongings. If she asked him, he'd likely grin and laugh, and act as though nothing happened. But perhaps he'd take the Aymes Police Department more seriously. She dug her cellphone from the back pocket of her jeans and punched "Emergency Call."

"I need to report a break-in."

"At your place, ma'am?"

"No, my father's. I know who it was. He lives next door."

The 911 operator asked her for the address. Then asked for the neighbor's address. "Hold tight," the woman said. "A car's on its way."

Standing on the grass between the two homes, Molly wavered. While the 911 operator had told her to wait until an officer responded, she could not stand still. Instead, she rushed along the walkway, stomping down the concrete steps to the Fischers' basement entrance. With the side of her fist, she banged on the door. "I know you're in there," she yelled. She banged again. When no one answered, she hurried around to the front of the house. Jabbed at the bell. Once. Twice. Three times. "Can you open up, Mrs. Fischer? It's important." Finally, movement inside. Jingling, as a metal chain slid over the lock.

"Is that you, Molly? Making that racket?" Mrs. Fischer's was wearing a quilted bathrobe and the ends of her hair were damp. "You've interrupted my bath."

"I'm sorry, but there's an . . . issue. A serious issue."

"Is it Gil?" She brought her hand to her cheek. "Has he . . . is he—?"

"No," Molly said, as she stepped inside. "He's okay."

"Then what, dear?" A hint of irritation in her tone.

Molly took a deep breath, blew it out through her nostrils. The house had an unpleasant odor. Like boiled cabbage. "I just discovered your son in my father's basement. When I caught him, he bolted."

"Someone was in your basement?"

"Not someone, Mrs. Fischer. Bradley."

She let out a tinkling laugh. "Oh, that's not true. It's some sort of—what do they call it? Mistaken identity?"

"Unfortunately, it's no mistake. He was just there. Seconds ago. I saw him." Or at least saw his ankles. "And I'm certain it's not the first time, either."

"Well, I'm not quite sure what to say. I can see that you're upset, dear, but he's been home all evening. Working away on a video game." She shook her head. "Such a colossal waste of time at his age. That constant shooting noise is terrible. I don't know why boys are so enticed by violence."

Molly wanted to tell Mrs. Fischer that her son was not a *boy*. He was middle-aged deadbeat.

"How about I call him up," she said brightly. "Get this little mix-up sorted." Then her smile faded, and she fussed with the collar of her robe. "Though I don't like to disturb him." She leaned toward Molly, whispered, "In case he has company."

"Well I think you might have to, Mrs. Fischer. I've already alerted the police." Molly shifted from one foot to the other. Her anger was not dissipating.

"Oh dear." She turned quickly and teetered down the hallway, fingertips grazing the worn wallpaper as she went. Then she disappeared around a corner. The sound of gentle tapping. "Bradley? Bradley, dear?"

"What is it now?" A throaty bark.

Rapid thumping as he ascended the basement stairs, and in moments, he was sidling toward Molly. Mrs. Fischer trailing behind.

"Oh, it's you, Moll." Tone downy soft. "What's up?"

He was no longer wearing the hat or the jacket. The toes of his sport socks were loose, flopping. As though he'd ripped a pair of snug sneakers from his feet.

"You're really asking me what's up?"

"Shit, were we supposed to connect or something?"

Mrs. Fischer touched his forearm. "No, Bradley. Molly says you popped by her father's house. A bit unexpected."

"With all due respect, Mrs. Fischer, that's not what I said at all. I told you he was in our basement. Going through my family's things. Which, last time I checked, was a criminal offense." She took a step forward. "What were you trying to find? What was so important?"

"Woah, woah, woah," Bradley said, holding up his hands. "You got it twisted, Moll. I've been home all night."

Mrs. Fischer nodded. "And I know you've been very into your computer work this evening." Then to Molly, "I can certainly vouch for that."

"If anyone's been in your basement," he said, "it was probably Glenn."

"Then that explains it." Mrs. Fischer nodded again. "That man nurse. He's never been particularly friendly . . ."

Molly looked at Mrs. Fischer, then at Bradley, and then back to Mrs. Fischer. A splinter of doubt appeared. *Could* it have been Glenn? She hadn't actually seen Bradley in the backyard. A squirrel could have triggered the light. Then she remembered the sneakers.

Harsh knocking behind her, and Molly jumped. Police had arrived, though she hadn't heard a car pull up. After she opened the front door, she noticed the color drain from Bradley's face.

"Jesus, Moll. You got Lyle out of bed for this bullshit?"

Officer Kage stepped into the foyer and stood beside Molly. "What's going on here?"

"Not a thing, buddy." Bradley twisted his head left, then right, several audible cracks.

After Molly explained the situation again, Officer Kage scratched his stubble, said, "Mind if I take a look in your room, Brad?"

"Okay, okay," Bradley said, hands lifted, palms outward. "I'm going to do everyone a solid and be totally straight, alright? Sure, I dropped over a few times. I didn't think it was a big deal."

Molly's mouth hung open. "How can breaking and entering not be a big deal?" Then to Officer Kage, "I hope you're hearing this."

"C'mon, Moll. We're neighbors, right? Pals. And the key is sitting right there. On the upper ledge. Same as it's been since, like, forever." Bradley sprang forward and playfully punched Officer Kage in the upper shoulder. "Right, Lyle? You remember."

Officer Kage spread his feet farther apart. Hooked his thumb into a belt loop. "No, Brad. I don't."

"Molly, please," Mrs. Fischer said. "He's trying to be honest. Give him a safe space to share." Then to Bradley, "Can you explain your reasoning? What you were feeling at the time?"

Bradley slumped, brushed the tile with his toe. "Kinda upset, I guess."

"And can you explain—"

"Listen," Molly said, interrupting this time. "Can we cut through the crap? What the hell were you doing?"

"Fine. Fine! I was—I've been selling shit online."

"What? What shit?"

"I don't know. Your mother's shit."

Molly was stunned. "I don't understand."

"There's a huge market for it. Whackos'll buy anything belonging to a murder victim. And your mother's case was popular, so you got a gold mine down there. And your dad didn't have a clue!"

"A gold mine?"

"Totally. I sold a sweater with this mildew funk. Then some letters. A few old paperbacks. Oh, and a pair of"—he cleared his throat—"undergarments. Those got the most bids."

Officer Kage was shaking his head. "Christ, Brad. You haven't changed a bit."

"You stole her things?" Molly's fingers were a cage over her mouth. "So they're gone?"

"Yup. In the mail. I got tracking, though. So no one can try to screw me."

Her head felt light, limbs weak, but her hands and feet pulsed.

"Hey, Moll. I'm real sorry. I didn't think anyone would care. I mean, not like she needed any of it. And just so you know, I didn't keep a single thing for myself. Totally not my jam. And if you want, I can—"

Officer Kage had a small black notepad in his hand. "I think you've said enough, Brad." Then to Molly. "Are you planning on pressing charges?"

"Wait. What?" Bradley's eyes were wide. "I told the truth."

"Yup. You sure did. And now the homeowner gets to decide how we proceed. As Dr. Wynters is unwell, I will defer to his daughter."

Mrs. Fischer gripped Molly's wrist and brough her mouth close to Molly's ear. She whispered, "Please, Molly. I can't handle this house on my own. I need him here with me. He's all I have. Please."

Molly took a deep breath. This Mrs. Fischer was not the same woman she'd known as a child. Confident, straight-talking. Wearing floral trousers and striped tees. Often no bra. Now she was a dried twig, easily snapped in two. The indignation Molly felt began to recede. She was still disgusted with Bradley, but pity for Mrs. Fischer was overriding it.

"Okay. I won't." It wasn't Mrs. Fischer's fault her son was an entitled brat. "I'll remove the key. He can't ever do that again."

"Thank god." Mrs. Fischer brought her hand to her neck. Spoke quickly. "And Bradley will return any items still in his possession as well as donate all proceeds thus far gained through this . . . misguided entrepreneurial endeavor. Now, Officer Kage, do you need my son for anything further?"

"No, ma'am." Notepad flipped closed. Slid into an inside pocket on his jacket.

"Then why don't you head downstairs, Bradley? Carry on with your projects."

Head lowered, he dragged his feet along the hallway and disappeared around the corner.

When Officer Kage left, Mrs. Fischer turned to Molly. "I'm disappointed," she said. "But proud of him for taking responsibility."

"Still, it was an unbelievable violation."

"I know, dear. And I'm grateful you're turning a blind eye. He feels awful about it. I can tell. And he's under so much pressure these days. His wife is taking him straight to the cleaners. She even wants support for their puppy."

"That doesn't excuse it. And to be clear, my decision had nothing to do with him."

"Don't you worry. I'll make sure there's no confusion."

Mrs. Fischer's hand reached to fiddle with the pendant on her necklace. Sitting in the dip at the base of her throat. Molly paused. It was tiny, some sort of insect, perhaps. A shell formed by two pieces of opal.

"Where did you get that?" Molly said.

"Oh, I've had it forever. I came across it today and wore it on a whim. Pretty, isn't it?"

"Yes, yes it is." Molly tripped over the rug as she stepped out into the cold air. Why did she suddenly have a prickly sensation spreading over her skin? Only days earlier, she'd been thinking about those moments after her mother was murdered. She could have sworn she was in the backyard. Alone and focused on a beetle. But the insect had not been climbing a blade of grass at all. It had been swinging from Mrs. Fischer's neck.

CHAPTER THIRTY-TWO

MOLLY SMOOTHED THE quilt, tossed two pillows against the headboard. "It's meaningless," she said, her phone nipped between ear and shoulder. "Though still disconcerting."

"Because the lady was wearing a bug pendant?" Casey replied. "And your three-year-old self remembered the insect was on a lawn?"

"I mean, yeah."

"It makes perfect sense to me. Consider it logically. Over time details shift and morph, but that doesn't negate your entire recollection."

"But what if it's not just the necklace. What if I mixed up other things?"

"And I'm one hundred percent sure you did. And that would be normal as well. Think of the kids you work with."

Molly didn't have to stretch too far. Just that morning, she'd been on a video call with a six-year-old client and his mother. The little boy had been carried from a house fire when he was sleeping and was now having night terrors. Whenever they discussed that evening, he told Molly that he saved his favorite stuffed animal from the fire. A panda bear that was blind in one eye. His mother gently corrected him, the bear was lost to the flames, and she'd purchased a new one. In a phone call later, Molly suggested that the mother allow the boy's narrative to continue. So that he viewed himself as a hero in his story.

"I get it," Molly said. "But it's a bit trippy, if you know what I mean."

Casey laughed. "And not the kind of trippy one wants."

"Well, that's been a while, hasn't it?" Glancing around the bedroom, Molly noticed a clean line through the dust on the dresser. As though someone had dragged a finger along it.

"Seriously, though. Would you consider talking to someone? It might help."

"Maybe? But to be honest, I think it's just being back here. People recognize me. If one more person tells me I look like my mother, I'm going to burst. Plus I'm seeing the same shitty crowd that I went to high school with. Or their shitty kids. And to top it off, Alex is still doing his deep dive into the murder. So much dirt is getting kicked up, it's hard to see."

"Make sure you're taking time for yourself. Otherwise, you're going to crash and burn."

Molly closed the bedroom door behind her and walked down the hallway. Crashing and burning didn't seem so far away. When she reached the kitchen, she said, "Oh, shit. I've got to go."

"Everything okay?"

"Yeah, yeah. Just another day in Aymes."

An enormous pool of water was spreading over the tiled floor. Tiptoeing around it, she grabbed her boots from the entryway and yanked them on. Then she went to the sink. Besides Alex's breakfast plate, it was empty. When she opened the lower cupboards, she saw the issue. A constant stream from the black tubing connected to the faucet.

She examined the supply lines. No shutoff had been installed. And the way the pipe was positioned, there was no way to even squeeze a bucket beneath it. The main valve for the house had to be located in the basement. She punched in Russell's cell number, once, twice, and left a message. "Can you call me? There's a slight leak. Well, more than slight. Call me back."

Standing in front of the door beside the refrigerator, she wavered. Scratched at her elbow. What were the chances that his basement apartment was unlocked. Though the very last thing she wanted to do was enter her landlord's home uninvited, didn't this constitute an emergency? The growing puddle had nearly reached her boots. Within minutes, it would begin trickling over the steps.

She felt along the wall and remembered there was no light switch at the top. No handrail either, so she pressed her palms against the drywall as she descended. At the bottom, she knocked loudly. Holding her breath as she waited in the pocket of darkness. Knocked again.

At once, the door flew open.

"Russ! You're here." The scent of chemical cleaners tweaked her nose. Bleach.

"I am, Molly. And as you know, this is not the proper door to reach me."

"I apologize. I tried calling. The kitchen sink is spurting water. I mean, a pipe." She caught sight of a substantial bulge in the ceiling of his kitchen. Like a great gray blister. "Look," she said, pointing upward.

"Well, that is a problem." He turned and went to a closet. Tugged open the slatted folding doors. His movement betrayed no sense of panic. He disappeared inside.

With the tip of her toe, she nudged the door open a few more inches. She'd never been in Russell's place before, but it was exactly as she'd expected. Neat and orderly. Every kitchen chair was pushed into the table, and a clean tea towel lay over the handle of the oven. The only item on the counter was a huge cutting board, its pale surface a crisscross of blade marks.

Above the couch was a large piece of artwork. Identical in size and style to the one in her unit. An expanse of black water in the forefront. A vertical sheet of rock, glowing in the setting sunlight, and a dense cluster of trees that topped the ridge.

"Found it," Russell announced from inside the closet.

She took a step forward. There was a subtle streak of yellowish paint in the lower corner of the painting. Was that a mistake with the brush? Or was that meant to represent a person? A ghost? Her throat was suddenly dry. Could that be another painting of the overhang? But done from the opposite vantage point?

"You know, some renters would have left it. Not batted an eyelash," Russell said when he emerged. Closed the closet doors. "I'll call a plumber this afternoon to fix the pipe. It's fine to go in, I presume."

"Of course."

"And actually, it's good that you're here. I wanted to speak with you about something."

His knitted brow prompted her to say, "You're making me nervous, Russ. Is it Alex?"

"Not even close. It's that caller you mentioned. The one you described as 'odd'? I tried to track it down."

"You did?"

"I assumed the individual was making you uncomfortable?"

"I mean, yes. But you really didn't have to."

"It was no trouble, but Shawna would have my hide if she knew I took a 'peek under the hood,' as you say."

"Well, she won't hear it from me." Molly smiled. "Did you find anything?"

"I did. It was all a bit strange. There were multiple calls with the same digital ID, originating from one of those cheap phones. Are you familiar with burners?"

"People actually use those?"

"They think they're untraceable, I suspect, but you can't believe everything you see on a cop show."

"Did you—did you try to trace it?"

"I probably shouldn't have, but yes. I was able to pinpoint an address, Molly. But here's what has me concerned."

The way he was watching her over the rim of his glasses made her shoulders tense up. "What do you mean, concerned?"

"I can't be completely sure, but it appears the phone calls originated from inside your father's home."

THEN

•

CHAPTER THIRTY-THREE

Gil

MILKY COFFEE, PIECE of honeyed toast. Glass of orange juice. And as he did every morning, Gil placed a flat white pill beside her glass.

"Breakfast is ready, Edie," he called out.

"Be right down!"

Since Gil had been managing her prescription, a sense of structure and stability had encircled their lives. Edie had been promoted at the cafeteria and was now in charge of setting the menus. Molly was thriving in her nursery school. Even though she was only two and a bit, she could already identify her colors and letters and shapes. The pharmacy was busier than ever, and Gil had recently given their one employee a small raise.

He refused to think about the past. It took effort, but he was able to lock away all those awful moments. What was the point in revisiting the missteps and betrayals? Or second-guessing the actions he'd taken to improve things? Only a weak mind would choose to dwell on misery.

"Did you hear my car when I pulled in last night?" she said as she slid into her seat.

"No?"

"The engine's making a terrible scraping noise."

"Take it to a mechanic, then." He'd been trying to get her to give up her old beater since they'd met. But she refused.

"Maybe." She took a sip of coffee and pushed the medication into her mouth. Swallowed. "Or I'll give it time. Sometimes things settle down."

Gil laughed. "I don't think automobiles work like that. But you decide." He'd given up trying to direct her. Edie was a woman who knew her mind, and she'd sort it out in her own time.

"You're dropping her off?" she said, nodding toward the family room. Molly was sitting cross-legged in front of the television set, transfixed by *The Jetsons*.

"Sure, and I can pick her up, too."

"I'll grab groceries, then."

Gil had invited Seth, Andrea, and their four boys for dinner that night. Barbecue. Beers. An easy fruit salad.

"Don't forget hot dogs," he said as he led Molly to the entryway, buckled up her white leather shoes.

"And I'll grab toilet paper, too." Edie appeared beside them at the front porch. Shoved a hairnet into her purse. "We're nearly out."

A dry kiss on Gil's cheek and she was gone through the door. A screech of metal as she backed her old car out of the driveway. He smiled to himself. Moments like these were the everyday interactions he'd always craved. The simple banter of existence. There was a predictable happiness to it all.

As he carried Molly outside, he paused in front of the brass knocker. "Bye-bye, lion," she said as she reached to bump its nose. Gil growled softly into her ear. "Bye-bye, lunch!" And she squealed and jammed her hands into her armpits.

He helped her into the booster seat so she could see out the car window. "All good?" he said.

"Good, good, Daddy."

Yes, it was. Life was *good, good*. And more than anything he wanted it to stay that way.

•

The Evens arrived at 6 p.m. sharp. When Gil opened the door, Andrea was standing to the side, the boys in a straight line down the front steps. They were dressed in identical blue-and-white-striped overalls and entered the house like a procession of train conductors. Once inside, they scattered, tearing through the family room and out into the backyard.

Andrea bustled past him, handing Gil a glass plate piled with cherry coconut squares. "Boys?" she yelled. "Boys? Did you say hello to Uncle Gil?" But they were already rolling in the sandbox, scrambling in the trees, popping the head off Molly's Chatty Cathy doll and firing it at each other.

"Holy hell." Seth limped in. "You can still cancel, you know."

"Not a chance." Gil smiled. Family life was supposed to be noisy and messy. "What happened to you?"

"Tripped over a goddamned dump truck. I think I twisted my knee."

"Come on, then. How's about a drink?"

"Sure thing, but first I should manage the pain." He winked, and then dug into his shirt pocket. Retrieved a pale green tablet.

The evening was a joyful ruckus. Gil grilled and Edie served. The boys settled in a circle on the grass, food heaped on plates balanced in their laps. Seth, much more relaxed, drank beer after beer while Andrea doted on Molly.

When the sun dipped and the temperature cooled, the boys came inside. Gil turned on the television set and the children gathered to watch *Happy Days*. Gil nudged Seth and Andrea toward the living room, a rarely used area with red shag, geometric wallpaper, and cro-cheted cushions on a hard-backed sofa. He poured whiskey into crystal glasses, handed one to Seth. Andrea shook her head said, "None for me, thanks." Seth lay back on the sofa and lifted his foot onto the coffee table. Edie brought a cooling bag and placed it on Seth's knee. He sucked in air through clenched teeth.

"You really did a number on yourself," she said. "You ought to be more careful."

"Maybe if he'd stoop to pick up a toy or two," Andrea sniffed, "this wouldn't have happened."

"What about if one of the boys stooped? How's that for a novel idea?" Seth leaned forward, adjusting the ice. "You know who I just thought of, Gil? Remember that kid who lived down the street from you?"

"What kid?"

"The one who had a crush on your mother. Ernie something or another. A real runny-nose type."

"Yeah, yeah. But I don't think it was a crush, he just—"

"You see, Gil's mother was something out of a fairytale." Seth chucked. "Baking cookies. Out on her front stoop, offering them up after school."

"She had time for that?" Andrea said as Molly toddled in, climbed onto her lap.

"She *made* time for that." Seth gave his head a tight shake. "Anyway, this kid Ernie was always first in line to get his cookie. Get a hug, too. And it pissed Gil off."

"It wasn't a big deal," Gil said. "I barely remember him."

"So what did he do? Sees the kid bicycling through the path in the woods, and buddy here tosses a stick right through the front spokes of his wheel."

"Come on, Seth," Gil said. "No one wants to hear this."

"Boof! Up and over the handlebars. Flew a good ten feet? Poor bastard knocked his front teeth out. Broke a wrist. Dare say he had a good concussion."

"Seth. Give it up, now. You're exaggera—"

"And Gil whistled all the way home."

"You're making that up," Edie said.

"See?" Seth clapped Gil on the back. "Nobody's got a clue about you. I caught a whooping for it, though."

Andrea frowned. "I'd say you caught a whooping because you deserved a whooping, Seth. Probably you threw the stick."

Seth laughed loudly, then opened his mouth wide and downed the remaining half inch of whiskey. Belched quietly. "You're right," he said. "Could've been me. Usually was."

The boys were bickering over which channel to watch, and the noise was growing louder. It was beginning to grate on Gil's nerves. He stood up. "It's been a slice. But I should get that little one to bed."

In Andrea's arms, Molly's head was beginning to nod, jaw working her thumb. Gil knew his little girl would soon be fast asleep. He also knew what happened after that. Every Saturday night he reached for Edie beneath the sheets. His hand sliding over her hip bone, the dip of her stomach, kneading the soft folds between her legs. She would tug up her nightdress, and he'd climb on top of her. Moving slowly, gently, until he heard her shudder beneath him.

Andrea gazed down at Molly. "Did you know Seth and I are trying again?"

"Really?" Gil said. "I wish you two lots of luck." Though he knew more than luck was needed. Late last winter, Seth had wide-leg-shuffled into the pharmacy, a brown paper bag in his hand. He lay flat on the floor of the stockroom and positioned a package of frozen peas over his groin. "Can you handle it today?" he'd said. "I need a few hours to recoup."

"Yes, fifth time's the charm." She laid a hand on Molly's scratched knee. Covering the tiny heart Gil had drawn in Mercurochrome.

"She's still after a little girl," Seth said. "And I told her, whatever makes her happy."

Andrea pressed her cheek into Seth's shoulder. "I thought I'd have to argue, but my amazing husband's in total agreement."

Edie yawned. Even though Gil cautioned against it, she'd sipped half a glass of beer. The combination of alcohol and medication had made her logy. "Wouldn't that be tough, though?" she said.

"With the brood I've already got? I'm sure I'll find some—"

"No, I mean, considering . . ." Edie held up two fingers, made a scissoring gesture.

Gil froze. He'd told Edie the story after it had happened. How Seth was groaning on the stockroom floor, chewing down Excedrin Extra Strength. At the time he'd assumed it was a joint decision between a married couple, only recently realizing the truth when

Seth swaggered into the pharmacy. Bragging about "the nightly baby bang" that was occurring in his bedroom.

"What's that?" Andrea looked from Seth to Edie and back to Seth. "What does she mean?"

"I'm not sure," Seth stammered, his cheeks pulsing red. "Someone's crossed some wires. Nothing intentional, I'm sure."

Edie stretched, then yawned again. "Not intentional? Can that happen by accident?"

"Edie," Gil said in a low tone.

As awareness bloomed, Andrea's face went pale. She got to her feet. Passed Molly to Gil. "I should have known," she hissed. "No argument at all. Every night with me on my back. You were so eager."

"Now, Andrea. Listen to—"

"No, not eager. Pretending to be!"

"Let me explain."

"What a fool I've been," she cried. "This really is the worst you've ever done. The very worst!" She stormed into the family room. "Boys? Get your shoes! We're leaving."

"But *The Waltons* are on."

"Not a squeak!"

Andrea swung open the front door and trotted down the driveway, a trail of boys scurrying behind her. She yanked open the back door of their station wagon, bigger children piling in first, younger climbing in on top. "I told him, will you?" she yelled. "For god's sake, get him up off the floor."

Seth hobbled out of the living room. Stopped on the mat, bending and straining to secure the straps on his sandals. When he straightened up, Gil said, "Listen, I'm really sorry about that, but I'm sure she'll—"

"Sorry?" Spittle flew out of Seth's mouth. "You're sorry?"

"Of course I am. I never thought you'd lie about—"

"You can be a righteous asshole, you know that?" The left side of his face lifted in a lopsided smirk. "I do what's needed to keep my house in order. Same as you, buddy. Same as you."

CHAPTER THIRTY-FOUR

"you've made a mistake," Gil said. "When I called to reserve, I explained that I needed the exact one."

They were stopped at the wooden lean-to that marked the entrance to Rabey Lake's rental cottages. Gil was certain it was the same woman working. Tanned leathery skin and scraggly ponytail high on her head. She looked like a washed-up go-go dancer.

"And how might I know what one that was?"

She was close to his open car window. Gil could smell her breath. The sickly scent of decaying apples.

"It was Number 16. Is that available?"

She scanned the clipboard's single sheet of paper. Tapped her pen on the page. "I'm not sure, mister."

Tugging his wallet from his back pocket, he retrieved a crisp twenty-dollar bill. Waved it toward her. "Is it available now, then?"

"Yup," she said, snatching it from his outstretched hand. "Opened up this second. But don't come whining to me if the roof leaks."

Gil rolled the car forward onto the narrow dirt road. Potholes jostling them left to right. Last time it was Edie who was commenting on the tall trees, the homey accommodations, the stillness of the lake. This time it was Molly. She was balanced on Edie's lap, her chubby hands planted on the dashboard. She read out the numbers on each sign. Squealing when she saw a squirrel leap from branch to branch. "See, Mommy?" she said. "See?" Edie was silent. Head lowered. Picking at the label that was sticking out the top of Molly's T-shirt.

Something had changed. Gil could not identify what had happened. Was happening. Over the past month, Edie had started skipping work, and she often forgot to buy groceries. Her hair was so greasy, it was plastered to her scalp. When Gil reached for her in the evenings, she stiffened, turned away.

"Well, here we are," he said as he parked beside the cottage. "It hasn't changed a bit."

"It's changed a whole lot." She pushed the car door open with her foot. Released Molly onto the ground.

Edie had a point. It was early autumn this time instead of midsummer. Though it was unseasonably warm, there was a scent of woodsmoke in the air. The trees were a brilliant display of fiery reds and golden yellows. And the lake appeared even blacker, colder. Deceptively still.

"I doubt you can swim this time."

"Why would I want to swim?"

Gil brushed it off. He could picture her clearly. Diving into Rabey Lake. Her long white limbs, delicate back, gliding beneath the water. Had she forgotten?

Molly was popping around the grounds. Plucking up red maple leaves. Examining acorns.

"Not too close to the water," Gil called.

Edie stretched, scratched her fingernails along her ribs. "I'm tired," she said.

"From what? It wasn't a long drive."

"Does it matter? I'm going to lie down."

Gil had expected the dark clouds to vanish as soon as they arrived. He thought she'd be enthusiastic about his surprise. Maybe even appreciative. "How about you relax outside. So Molly can play."

She shrugged. "Sure. Fine. Whatever."

"But before that, I want a photo of you two." Gil reached for his brand-new Kodak camera, already loaded with film. "Molly," he said as he lifted the body to his face. Assessed the frame. "Go to Mommy."

When Molly raised her arms, Edie did not bend and lift her into an embrace. Instead, she put her hand to her forehead, blocking out the sunlight. "Can you hurry up? I told you I'm tired."

"Okay, okay." He forced some light laughter as he took the snapshot. Then said, "Good enough."

From the trunk, he pulled out the thick quilt and brought it to a patch of dried grass. He carried over some board books and a few of those long-legged dolls that Edie insisted on buying. He continued to unpack, and the girls settled in on the quilt. Edie reading her magazine while Molly played beside her, chattering to herself.

As he lifted the cooler into the cabin, he heard the soft growl of a motor coming into the driveway. It was the clipboard woman on a dirty golf cart. A jumble of bedding balanced on the seat beside her.

"This one wasn't made up," she said. She looked him up and down. "You got a head on your shoulders. You don't need me, right?"

"Nah." Gil jogged toward her. Gathered up the pile. "I got it."

"Got to love a modern man," she said with a grin, before driving away.

Inside, he placed the towels in the bathroom. In the bedroom, he strained to stretch the fitted sheet over the mattress. Every time he pulled one corner, it popped off the opposite side. Once he'd conquered the bedding, he went to the kitchen to boil the kettle. Two mugs, with two generous scoops of coffee crystals. A heaping spoonful of sugar for Edie.

While he waited for the kettle to whistle, he peered out the front window. Edie was lying on her back now, the magazine covering her face. For a split second, he marveled at her ability to relax. He was always anxious around Molly, trailing behind her, ready to catch every fall. Then an electrical jolt shot up his spine. The blanket beside her was empty.

Gil flew outside, yelled, "Where is she?" She was not beside the blanket. She was not on the dock. She was not scampering near the edge of the lake. "Where'd she go?"

Edie rose up on her elbows, the magazine sliding into her lap. "How should I know?"

Whipping his neck left to right, he scanned the water. His daughter might be screaming and flailing beneath that smooth surface. And he couldn't hear a single sound.

"Molly?" he called. "Molly, where are you?" She did not answer.

"There's her shoe." Edie pointed at the sparsely wooded stretch that separated their cottage from the one next door.

Gil raced toward it. Grabbed it from the ground. Then he tore down a path. Calling Molly's name over and over. Light dissolved and the forest loomed all around. His eyes were slow to adjust. It was difficult to see. "Molly? Molly, where are you?"

He caught the sound of whimpering. And his legs shot in that direction.

She was there. In the middle of a copse, the ground a spongey marsh. She was lying in several inches of murky water. Her skin and clothes were covered in muck and flecks of dirt. When her small fists pushed against the moss and she lifted her head, she was gasping.

Gil scooped her up and she coughed and sputtered as he patted her back.

"I flipped, Daddy," she said between sobs. "I flipped down."

"You slipped, sweetie. But you're safe now."

With long strides, he carried her out of the woods and straight into the cottage. The kettle was hissing and spitting, and he dashed to the kitchen to turn off the stove. Then he brought Molly to the bathroom and removed her wet clothes. When he eased her into a tub of warm water, the crying subsided. "You're better now, right?"

"I'm okay."

Gil worked shampoo through her hair. Dug a compact from Edie's toiletries bag, clicked it open, and handed it to Molly. She was mesmerized by her reflection as he transformed the bubbles into a shark fin, an antelope, a monster with spikes.

Soon she was giggling and splashing. The scare of near drowning had begun to recede, replaced with brightness, silliness, jubilation. The only emotions that should braid together to form the stuffing inside a child.

Gil sighed with relief. He could lose everything else. His home. His work. Even Edie. If she abandoned him, he would find a way to survive. But if anything ever happened to his daughter, he would never recover.

Edie appeared in the doorway. "She seems happy enough."

"How can you say that?" Hands curling into fists. He hadn't been this furious since the whole fiasco with Cal. "You can't do that." He kept his tone low, controlled. "You can't take your eyes off a child."

"She was sleeping."

"Really? Or you were?"

"I said I was tired. I don't feel well."

"Well, you need to get untired, Edie. She deserves better, you know." He pulled the metal chain, freeing the stopper. The drain gurgled as he bundled Molly into a starchy towel, hugging her to his chest.

"So you think it's my fault then? Whatever the kid does?"

"Who else's would it be?"

"You don't get it, do you?"

"Get what? Am I supposed to read your mind?"

Edie rubbed her eyes. "I stopped taking your stupid pills."

The walls in the cottage bathroom suddenly felt too close. Ceiling too low. He chose his next words carefully. "You mean the medicine you were prescribed? Was that the doctor's recommendation?"

"And by doctor, you're referring to yourself, correct?"

How did she find out? How long had she known? "But they were helping you," he mumbled.

"No. They were helping *you*."

He slipped past Edie, a squirming Molly still gripped in his arms. He had to think. This was fixable if he could explain his reasoning. He regretted the deception, of course, and he'd honestly never intended it to go on for so long. Just a month, maybe two. But hadn't their family life improved significantly? Weren't they finally content?

"Where are the keys?" She was kneeling on the floor, rifling through his overnight bag.

"Why?"

"Give me the keys. I need some air."

"You've got all the air in the world here. With us."

"I don't. I don't." She jumped up, rushed at Gil. Patted his upper legs, dove her hands into the pockets of his trousers.

"You need to calm down, Edie." He shouldn't have let her see his anger. "I'm sorry. We both made a mistake."

"We've made a lot of mistakes," she said as she found the keys. "And we're going to make a lot more."

Then she was running, like a doe clipped by a bullet. Dazed, injured, weaving back and forth on rickety legs as she darted through the cottage and out the door.

CHAPTER THIRTY-FIVE

ONE EVENING IN late winter, when Gil was passing by the bathroom, he noticed the door was open a crack. Edie was inside. She was naked and standing in front of the mirror, gazing at her body. Her hair was pinned up, and she turned her face side to side. With a finger, she touched her jawline, and the bumps of her trachea. Hands trailing down, she cupped both her breasts, nipples pinched between thumb and forefinger. She pushed them up her rib cage, forcefully, and then let them drop. Her right palm slid down over her white stomach, found its way to the space between her legs. She drove her fingers through the thick hair, the sound of nails on damp skin. Then she angled her left leg slightly before reaching to hold herself. A sharp breath and her eyes fluttered. She stayed like that, mouth slightly open, eyes locked on her own reflection, her palm rubbing back and forth. Gil could tell by the rise and fall of her chest that she was breathing faster.

He was about to quietly step away, pretend he'd seen nothing, when she said, "Wait." Both hands were on the counter near the sink now.

He cleared the saliva that clung to his throat. Croaked, "Yes?"

"I have a question. I need to know the answer now."

Now? "Okay."

She was surely going to ask why he'd been spying. Or if he'd liked what he saw. In the early days, she'd often said things that made Gil embarrassed and aroused at the same time. And at that moment, he was both once again. Not surprising given that intimacy between them was practically nonexistent. Only three times in the months since the cottage, and that was after he'd begged.

"Why'd you marry me, Dr. Wynters?"

Gil blinked. "What? What do you mean?"

"You know exactly what I mean."

"Well." He nudged the door with his foot. As it slowly opened, the hinge creaked. "I married you because I love you."

"Then why do you love me?"

"Because I do. I've loved you since the moment I saw you."

"I asked why. Not when."

He had no answer to offer. How could he explain to her what he could not explain to himself? Something happened when he'd met her in that driveway. He could recall every detail. The artificial light making her thin dress transparent. Toothpick legs stuck inside a pair of men's boots. Her face set in a stony way. Irritated almost, but doing what needed to be done to boost his car. Her smile had felt like a blow to his skull. Stunning him.

"Because of who you are, that's why."

She snickered then. "Can't you see who I am? I took your name, but inside I'm still Edie Paltry."

"And that's okay," he insisted. "It really is. It's okay to be you."

"Do you ever consider what the word *paltry* means? Pointlessly small. Utterly worthless. Mean. Contemptible. It suited us all, you know. My father. My sister. Cal. Me. Even my mother made no difference in this world. We're all nothing. We're all empty."

"Stop." Gil shook his head hard. "Stop saying these things. None of it's true."

She lifted a sweater from the hook on the back of the door. Slid it over her head.

"Do you want to know what I think? With all the sensible options, why you'd choose someone like me?"

He stared at her. Saying nothing.

"I think," she said, her voice low and steady, "there's actually something wrong with you. I think you're empty, too."

His eyes began to sting. "There's nothing wrong with me, Edie."

She laughed then. "Well, an idea to mull over while I'm gone."

"What? Where are you going?"

"For a drive." She tugged on a pair of panties. Flared jeans patched at the knees.

"People have gone to bed. You can't go."

"No?"

"You're not even wearing a bra, Edie."

"My car won't mind."

•

Gil taped a small sign to the front door of the pharmacy. "Stepped away. Be back in fifteen minutes. Please wait."

He stopped his car a block away from the high school. Walked the rest of the way and paused beneath a oak tree. From his vantage point, he could see the front of the school as well as the entire parking lot. He used to look forward to this time of year, the cooling temperatures, the changing leaves. When it began to get dark a little earlier. But now the shifting season rattled him. It was another reminder of the instability that had infiltrated his life.

He glanced at his watch. Two minutes left before class ended. Over the summer, he'd started snooping through her things. Checking her purse for receipts and rifling through the dirty laundry. Now that school had started up again, he'd begun leaving work to check on her. Sometimes trailing behind afterward, as she ran errands. A stop at the corner store for cigarettes or a stroll through the supermarket. Several times she drove over the tracks and slowed on the gravel shoulder beside her old house. She'd sit there, engine idling for ten or fifteen minutes before driving away. Even though she never did anything out of the ordinary, it did nothing to calm Gil's agitation.

It gave him no pleasure to invade her privacy. But for nearly a full year, she'd been shutting him out even more. Since Rabey Lake, she barely looked at him. Rarely interacted with Molly. Refused to have Seth and Andrea back for dinner, even though the vasectomy misstep had long been smoothed over. He'd asked repeatedly what he needed to do to repair things, make it up to her. And her response was "Leave me alone." She'd gone to her family doctor, she said, and from now on she'd handle her own health. Her own medication. She didn't need him prying into her personal business. Those words stung.

As time passed, he'd hoped the contempt would eventually fade. She'd realize his intentions were well-placed, and then things would improve. But she became even more distant after he'd shared the news about her brother, Cal.

Gil received a telephone call at the pharmacy from the police sometime during last spring. Cal had been killed. Not from drinking or a violent altercation, as Gil might have predicted, but because he did a favor for a friend. They'd been moving an old freezer, and Cal lost his footing. His chest was compressed beneath the appliance.

"How long ago?" he asked.

"It's been several months," the officer said. "We had a tough time locating next of kin."

It took Gil ages before he found the courage to tell Edie. At some points he'd seriously considered not mentioning it at all.

There was no hysteria, like he'd predicted. In fact, she barely displayed any emotion at all. "My whole family's gone, now" was all she said. "The lot of us. Dead."

Before he could contradict her, explain that she was still very much alive, and so were he and Molly, she closed the door to the bathroom. Ran a bath, washed her hair, and then she'd left their home for another drive. And as usual, where she went, or with whom, he had no idea.

A muffled bell reached Gil's ears. The front doors of the school flung open, students tumbled out, leapt down the concrete stairs. Squeals and raucous laughter, a mess of bell-bottoms and knitted ponchos. Gil was aware of the height of some of the boys. The breadth of their shoulders and thickness of their sideburns. A couple of them he recognized, troublemakers who loitered in the alleyway beside the pharmacy. These were the young men Edie interacted with every day.

Minutes after the teenagers dispersed, Edie appeared. Strolling around the side corner of the building. Her coat was unbuttoned, an orange felt tam balanced on her head. With speedy steps, she strode across the parking lot. She was nearly at her car when a boy trotted toward her. Gil's spine lifted off the trunk of the tree. Who was that kid? What was he up to? He was too close to her, and though Gil could not hear a word, he noticed the shuffling feet.

The awkwardness in his gangly arms. The way Edie tilted her head, reached up to adjust her tam.

Gil teetered slightly, dug his fingernails into the bark of the tree. There was no denying the body language. An intimacy existed between them. He was only a teenager. Maybe sixteen? It was suddenly obvious to Gil. This boy was her secret. He was her lie.

When Gil returned to the pharmacy, Les Carpenter was standing outside.

"Waiting long?"

"Nope, just got here, Doc."

Gil unlocked the door, took the prescription from Les's outstretched hand. *Dilantin-125 oral suspension.*

"I can pay about half now. Can I get you the rest later?"

Gil attached the label to the glass, put the bottle into a paper bag. "You still working for the phone company?"

"Probably 'til the day I die."

"Remember how you offered, you know"—he cleared his throat—"a favor if I needed it?"

"That I do, Dr. Wynters. You want to upgrade your gear?"

"Not quite," he said. "Not quite."

Gil sealed the mouth of the paper bag with three narrow folds. Pressed his thumbnail back and forth over the layers, creating a sharp crease. Then he pushed the item toward Les Carpenter, waved away the bills in his customer's hands.

"Let me tell you what I have in mind."

Him

SHORTLY AFTER THE funeral, the "For Sale" sign came down. As I was now a responsible young man, it was decided I could remain in my home. Be independent. My sibling lived away, but my aunt would do frequent checks to ensure I was looking after myself. Had ample groceries. Was maintaining my exemplary grade point average. I could not have constructed a sweeter outcome to the sudden tragedy of my mother's death.

Those next twelve months were, in many ways, the very best of my life. Things really blossomed between me and my lunch lady. There were no limits on when we could be together. We had our routines, school and work, of course, but we tried to connect over dinner every single evening. She preferred it when I cooked. Usually I heated up a frozen meal from my aunt, or made something simple like macaroni and cheese or meatloaf. She never once complained, even when the sausages burned or the instant potatoes were lumpy. Sometimes I'd light a candle and place it in the center of our table. She was even prettier in that soft glow.

Afterward, we usually watched television or read books side by side on the couch. I'd make popcorn with extra butter and salt. She insisted on drinking grape juice with it. I told her she was quirky, and she said it was charming to be a little peculiar.

At some point during the winter, I finally began to settle in. I chucked out my mother's clothes and romance novels and ugly knickknacks. Then I moved my belongings into that big bedroom. The first time I surprised my girlfriend with the larger bed, the thicker sheets, she was thrilled. Stripped off her skirt and sweater right away. Took a bath first, an extra capful of my Mr. Bubble. The foam rising up to her neck. I sat on the edge of the tub, reached my hand through the suds into the scalding water. Found the gap between her legs, and as I rolled my knuckles back and forth over that fleshy area, she panted hard. I watched her tits moving up and down through the bubbles, and I couldn't wait to get her into my mother's bed.

If we'd had a particularly busy night, sometimes I was exhausted at school. Dozed off in class. But the teachers never called home to rat me out. They understood that I'd been juggling a lot, and besides, there was no one there to answer.

Another wonderful thing happened that year as well. My friends circled around me with an unwavering amount of support. Most afternoons, they came to my house. Friday and Saturday nights, they usually stopped by to hang out. We were no longer relegated to the basement, and unlike my mother, I was always set for company. I didn't mind the mess too much either. The spilled beer and overflowing ashtrays. Circles were melted into the carpet, and there was vomit beneath the cushions on the couch. I understood they were trying their best to ensure I wasn't lonely, and I was happy to provide a location for a bit of revelry.

Sometimes, though, I worried things might go wrong. What if my aunt popped in at the wrong time? Or a neighbor called the police because the music made the ground vibrate? Or the skunky stench of weed was wafting out and alerted a passerby? Last weekend, one of my friends got up on the roof and crowed like a rooster. He'd accepted another pill from the sandwich baggie, and it took nearly an hour to coax him down.

On a Sunday night, several weeks after school was back in, I ordered three extra-large pizzas. Loaded with toppings. I'd already bought a half dozen bags of chips and Cheezies. Plus Ding Dongs and Ritz Crackers. Pop Rocks and Bottle Caps. I filled the fridge with Hires and Dr Pepper, the freezer with Drumsticks and Fudgsicles. I used up half my monthly food budget on supplies.

"I wanted to say thanks," I said to my friends, as I dropped the steaming boxes on the coffee table. "For being around, you know. It's been kind of a tough year. After losing my mom." Which was mostly a lie. It hadn't been tough at all. Except for the annoying parts like doing my own laundry and cleaning up bacon grease. Or that morning when the toilet got clogged and I couldn't find the plunger. In those moments, I really did miss her.

"Man, that's decent of you. I love pizza."

They threw open the cardboard lids. Grabbed hot floppy slices, jammed them into their mouths. The hiss of bottles openings. Metal caps tossed at the ceiling. Cellophane bags popping, potato chips flying everywhere. They were having a good time.

"You got it made in the shade. Having your own pad like this."

"And cash at your fingertips."

"I wish," I said. "I only get so much at a time."

"Still, if I knew I'd get a house to myself, I'd toss a hair dryer in my mother's shower. Like yesterday. Stand back while she sizzled."

I looked down. He wouldn't get away with that method, but I didn't share my thought. Instead, I brought my thumbnail to my mouth, chewed.

"That was a shit thing to say, loser."

"Yeah, his mother's actually fucking dead."

"Sorry, man. I was only joking."

"It's okay," I said. "We all say dumb stuff. And I get it. It's good having my own space. Where I'm free to be me." With my buddies and with my girlfriend. When the pizza boxes were nearly empty, I said, "Don't forget, I got ice cream, too."

"No shit!"

I watched them rolling over themselves, like puppies, racing to the kitchen. They yanked on the freezer handle, hauling out the packages. Frozen treats torpedoed across the room.

Lately I'd been feeling so much more relaxed. I figured perhaps it was time to show more of myself. To expose my secret. That would be the ultimate relief, to share what had transpired in my personal life. It might be difficult for them to grasp my relationship at first, but I knew they cared about me, accepted me, and they would eventually understand.

Quietly, I reached my hand under the side table. Moved my fingers over the carpet until I found what I'd hidden there. I lifted it out and set the metal frame on the table. Adjusted the angle so it faced my friends.

It took a full seven minutes before it caught anyone's attention.

"Woah. Is that the lunch lady?"

"What?" I asked innocently.

"That babe in the picture. Isn't she the one who serves up the food?"

"Yeah," I said. "I figured it was time to start making this place my own."

"Ripping a page out of the yearbook? How's that making it your own, buddy?"

"I don't have a real picture . . . Yet." I'd pasted my girlfriend over a snapshot of my mother kneeling in the garden. Floral gloves, holding up a handful of dirty carrots with feathery green tops. My mother had been a pleasant person then, and I didn't want the reminder.

"That's totally weird, dude."

"No, it's not." I took a deep breath. The cage in my gut was wide open. Not a fluttery bird to be found. "We've been seeing each other."

A hoot of laughter. "You've been what?"

"Spending time together," I said. "For a good while now. Her and me. Mostly in the evenings when you guys aren't around."

"No way. She wouldn't look at you sideways."

One of them was chuckling so hard, he slipped off the couch. "What are you smoking? She's married. Even got a kid."

He didn't need to remind me. That he lived next door to her. I hadn't forgotten that he had also climbed that tree and spied. We were chums and all, but there was also something disgusting about him.

"Don't believe me, then. I don't care." A hunk of vanilla ice cream was melting on a throw pillow. Spreading outward, soaking into the woven fabric. "I'm tired. You guys should probably leave."

"Cool, man. This shit's getting weird, anyway."

They all stood up, grabbed their jean jackets. At the door, one of them said, "Prove it."

"Yeah," a second friend chimed it. "Prove she even knows who you are."

They were all gaping at me. I regretted opening my mouth. How could I have believed they'd be able to comprehend something so ethereal. Delicately constructed between two people over years. They were only immature twits. Had no sense of intimacy or romance or the nuances of communication. It wasn't easy to march up to a practical stranger and let her know how I could see her so vividly. That she took up so much room inside my skull, there was an aching pressure on the bone.

"Fine," I said. "Tomorrow. I'll prove it."

•

I saw her before she saw me. Striding across the high school parking lot toward her car. Her beige trench coat was billowing in the breeze, and on top of her head, she wore an orange tam.

"Hey," I called. "Hold on a sec."

She stopped, turned. I skipped to catch up to her. As I stood in front of her, I smoothed my hands over my button-down shirt. I hoped she couldn't see the burn mark on the cuff. I'd tried to iron it that morning.

"Did I drop something?"

"No." I smiled at her. Her real eyes were slightly different than her other eyes. Not soft brown, but green with flecks of gold. Prettier, actually. "I just thought we should talk."

I'd been awake most of the night, ruminating over how I was going to approach this. It would sound ridiculous at first, but if she listened to me, it would make sense. A person's thoughts were not without power or meaning. They were legitimate experiences. Not quite tangible moments, but the connection she and I had formed was still deeply valuable.

She lifted a hand to shield her eyes from the sunshine. "About?"

I swallowed. "About us. I mean. Everything that's going on." I felt a staticky shyness building inside me. If I touched her skin, I'd release a spark. "You probably already have an inkling."

Her eyebrows knitted together. "An inkling?"

"A sense of things." It was impossible to fathom that after all this time, she might be oblivious. Hours upon countless hours she'd been fully present with me, even though she was miles away. In the very center of herself, there had to be an awareness. A continual sensation of being split in two. One side longing to reconnect with the other.

"Hey, I think you've got me mixed up with someone else."

I knew all her favorite things. Granny Smith apples. The color violet. Irish setters. I knew she was afraid of narrow flights of stairs and over-inflated balloons. I'd studied every fold and crevice of her entire body. Understood exactly where to stroke and flick and pinch to bring her to the edge. And all of that was reciprocated in kind. How could a person possibly summarize that in a single sentence?

"—okay? You're really spaced out."

I blinked. "What?"

"I need to go," she said, pulling her purse closer. "Maybe you should go see the health teacher. She can be a real help."

"What?" I said again.

"Mrs. Fischer. She deals with teenage issues or . . . whatever your problem is. She can help you."

I lowered my head, gazed up at her. Mrs. Fischer was the last person I wanted to see. "You don't understand." This was not going as planned. I was rambling, acting weak.

"Why don't you go to the office? Mrs. Even'll call your mother."

"She's not around," I said. I never used the word *dead* when I described her. It was far too permanent. While I understood people often did crazy things for love, I did not want the responsibility of my mother's fate on my shoulders. Or on my girlfriend's shoulders.

"Oh, well." She took two steps backward. "I've really got to get home."

I took two steps forward. I didn't want to scare her. I only wanted to get closer. Then I flung out both my arms. "Don't you remember? It's me. From the ditch."

"From what?"

"I was in the ditch that night. You pulled over in your car and saved my skin."

"Listen. I've really got no clue what you mean, okay?"

"Gosh," I said. "I guess it was quite a while back."

She looked at me for several moments. "Like a really, really long time ago?"

"Yeah. That's right!"

Gradually came a nod of recognition. "Oh, I remember now. You look different. Older. Less drippy."

I laughed lightly, scuffed at a leaf on the ground. "Totally older. And way less drippy." Our banter was finally commencing. "I never really said thank you."

"Don't mention it." She was walking away quickly now, her heels clipping on the pavement. Then she called over her shoulder, "Anyone would've done it."

No, anyone would not have done it. A million people would have driven past. Ignored my distress. Never even tapped their brakes.

I watched her scrambling into her car. "Goodbye," I yelled. "See you later. Gator!"

She lifted her hand. Open palm. How I willed her to touch her lips with her fingertips, shake the kiss into the air so I could catch it. But she didn't. Not this time. Perhaps she was aware my friends were close by and was resisting doing something so blatant.

After she tugged the door closed, she plucked the tam off her head. Tossed it onto the passenger seat. She had trouble starting the engine. One, two, three twists of the key. Oh, if only I could help her with that. Help her with everything in her life. But eventually the cough morphed into a growl. And she was gone.

I glanced back at my buddies, who were leaning against the brick wall near the lunchroom exit of the school. They were snickering, punching each other. I raised both my thumbs. They raised their middle fingers back. I assumed that sort of camaraderie meant I'd risen to the challenge,

even though the interaction wasn't quite as warm as I'd hoped. I understood what was happening, though. And why. Aligning my inside world
with the outside world was going to take a little time.

•

In the days after the parking lot, I thought she and I would start building
something substantial. All it would take to get things rolling was a basic
hello. A friendly wink. A subtle brush of her hand as she dumped limp
fish sticks onto my plastic tray.

But instead of getting closer, I noticed the opposite happening.
Unexpected cracks weakening our bond. When I tried to speak with
her at lunchtime, she never replied. I wasn't sure if she was ignoring me
or if she simply couldn't hear me, so I spoke louder. Still no reaction,
except from the guy in line behind me. Jabbing my shoulder with the
handle of his fork, "Out of the way, bonehead."

I waited after school, too. Assuming she might be more relaxed
outside of her stressful work environment. Though when I rushed
toward her in the parking lot, she did not slow to greet me. Instead, she
increased her speed, leapt into her car, and slammed the door. With
jumpy fingers, she pressed the metal button to lock herself in.

I rapped on her window with my knuckles. Offered a toothy grin.
"It's me," I yelled. "The guy from the ditch."

Engine struggling, and when her car finally came to life, she reversed
out of her spot. Careening away so fast, she nearly ran over my foot.

Even at home, when it was just me and her, I detected a shift. She
complained about the sour milk forgotten in the back of the fridge and
whined that the television program we'd selected together was boring.
She stopped touching me, too. No more nails crawling down my back,
or a playful hand slipping into the front of my joggers.

That night, when she took her usual bath, she locked the bathroom door. I leaned my forehead against the thin wood, whispered to her. "What's going on with you?"

When she finally came out, she had her wet hair twisted up in a towel and was wearing my mother's fluffy bathrobe. Zipped all the way to the neck. I thought I'd thrown that ugly thing away.

"Can we talk at least?" I asked.

She shook her head as she went to the bedroom. "Nah. I don't want to."

"Is it the boys hanging out? I can put an end to it, you know."

"It's not that." She sat on the bed beside the rolled-up bundle of sheets and blankets. "It's got nothing to do with you."

"Certainly seems like it." I was bewildered. Upset, too.

She pulled the towel from her head, her damp hair falling around her shoulders. I went to the thermostat. Cranked up the heat so she wouldn't catch a chill.

"I've never met anyone like you before," she said. "You're sweet and handsome. So generous and thoughtful. Super intelligent, too."

"Oh, come on." I shuffled my feet. "I'm not all that."

"But you really are. Mark my words, you're going to be something someday. You're a nurturer. Plus"—she glanced up at me—"no one's ever made me as horny as you do."

She usually didn't employ that sort of coarse language, and I blushed. "Then what's wrong? Why is everything going sideways?"

Her chin was twitching. "It's just complicated. Can't you see that?"

I shook my head. "Yeah, a bit. Maybe—"

"I want nothing more than to be here with you. But dividing my time is exhausting."

I sat down beside her. "I get it, but I thought we were figuring things out?"

"If only I'd met you before. There'd never be a question."

Tears welled up in my eyes. Everything was breaking too quickly. "You can't quit trying. You can't! I don't want to be alone."

I wrapped my arms around her, and while she didn't resist my embrace, she didn't return it, either.

I breathed her in. The bathrobe still smelled a lot like my mother.

NOW

•

CHAPTER THIRTY-SIX

Molly

MOLLY LEFT RUSSELL'S house immediately. The only person who could have made all those phone calls was Glenn. She was shocked that he was capable of doing such a cruel thing. His references had been impeccable, and from her observations, he'd been nothing but a conscientious caregiver for her father. Why would he want to torment her?

"What? What did you say?"

As she repeated Russell's statements, the color drained from Glenn's face. He leaned forward, gripping the edge of the kitchen island.

"This is total garbage, Molly. I would never." His eyes were shiny. Fearful. Reminding Molly of those dead rabbits.

"So you're saying you haven't called the support line."

"Why would I?"

"That's not answering the question, Glenn."

"Absolutely never. Not a once."

"Okay then. I'm not sure where to go from here."

"Well, I am." He flipped his phone over on the counter and, with his jaw clenched, punched in a number. "I'm getting Russ on the line. He needs to explain himself. This is practically slander."

Glenn tapped the button for speaker.

"Russ? Glenn here."

"Sorry, Glenn." An audible sigh. "My hands are covered in blood. I'll have to call you later."

"No can do, pal. This is more important than cleaning out a carcass. What's this business you told Molly? About me harassing her?"

A metallic clatter. As though he'd dropped a knife. "I certainly never accused you. I simply outlined my discovery."

"And you're suddenly some sort of investigative expert, are you?" A fleck of white spittle struck the screen of the phone.

"No, Glenn. I simply know my way around the software."

"Not as well as you think, obviously."

Several moments of silence. Then he said, "Perhaps I misspoke. I shouldn't have been so definite. Location is approximate."

Molly brought her mouth closer to the phone. "How approximate, Russ?"

"Oh, hello, Molly. I hadn't realized this was a group conversation."

"Yes, I'm at my dad's now. You're on speaker."

"Hmm. Well, to clarify, it would be a radius of sorts."

"What does that mean? Of sorts?"

She listened carefully as Russell reframed his earlier statements. The location transformed from a precise pinpoint on a map to a wonky dot of indefinable size. The caller could have been on the front lawn, parked in a car in the road, sitting beneath a tree in the divider. Down the road, across town, on the other side of the tracks.

"Or what about," Glenn stammered, "a different city? Country, even? How's that for a possibility?"

"I made an error, Glenn. Perhaps I may have misinterpreted things."

Glenn mumbled to himself. "Knows his way around some software, my rear end."

"As I politely mentioned, Glenn, I'm occupied at present. I will return your call at a later time. And Molly, I do apologize if my statements were misleading or created cause for concern."

Glenn tapped at his phone. Several strikes before he managed to hang up.

"Unbelievable," he said, folding his arms across his chest. "He's always been like that, you know. Positioning himself as somebody important. He probably has zero idea what he's talking about. Or maybe he's trying to freak you out."

Molly brought her hand to her cheek. "Why would he want to do that?"

"Who knows? He doesn't think. Some people are just . . . vacant."

"I'm really sorry, Glenn." She felt warmth beneath her fingertips. "I rushed in with my mind made up, and that was wrong. He was so confident. I believed every word."

"You don't need to apologize. I shouldn't have gotten so riled up over nothing. I've just been under a lot of stress lately."

"From being here? All the hours with my dad? I fear I've been taking advantage of your generosity."

"Oh no. Nothing like that at all. I love my job. Looking after Dr. Wynters." He pulled out a stool, sat down. "It's more personal."

"Gotcha." He'd just separated from his wife. Of course he'd have issues to navigate. "You don't need to explain."

"No, I want to, though." He exhaled slowly through his mouth. "You see, my wife and I split because I wanted a family and she didn't. We married kind of late, and I thought we'd adopt, same as my brother did. She was always on the fence, but eventually told me we were too old to chase after a kid. I disagreed. So for the past months, I've been going through this process of becoming a foster parent on my own. Let me tell you, it's super intense."

"Really? That's fantastic, Glenn. You'll make a wonderful foster dad. And there's endless need."

"If it happens. And that's a big if. I'm currently a single man with no permanent address. Certainly not the picket-fence-nuclear-family they've got in mind for this sort of thing."

"But surely they look at character. History. Stability. And you'll provide a loving environment while the child's life hopefully gets sorted."

Glenn laughed lightly. "Oh, it's astounding what they look at. That time I got caught drinking underage up on the overhang? The chip in my front tooth? Why my wife kept our cat? All open to scrutiny."

"Better than the opposite, I suppose. These kids are so vulnerable. Often traumatized. I currently have a couple as patients."

"I know. Some of the stories are gut-wrenching. And that's why I was so upset. If a rumor got around that I'd been terrorizing you? It would screw up my chances for sure. Why would Russell do that? Seems like an outright lie."

"I'm sorry, Glenn. I really am."

"Just be careful, Molly." He stood up, slipped his phone back into his pants pocket. "For all you know, it was him making those calls."

•

That evening, as Molly lay on the sofa, she could hear Russell through the vent. Bustling around below her. Kettle screaming and dishes clanging. A woman was chattering, as though a talk show was on top volume.

Why would he lie? Or perhaps *lie* was too forceful a word. At the very least, he had misled her. She'd nearly fired Glenn, with no discussion. When instead, that man deserved an award.

Earlier, over dinner, she'd sheepishly told Alex what had happened.

"Mom," he said. "Nurse Glenn's pretty cool. He wouldn't do that."

"I know, I know. It was a bad mistake."

"And Mr. Farrell's a bit of a freak, but he's no hacker genius. He literally makes rabbit sliders for a living."

"You're right. Though the two aren't mutually exclusive, you know."

"Besides, it's easy enough to fake an IP address. Mess with your location. Everyone does it."

"Well, I don't."

"That's because you're old, Mom."

She'd chuckled, then. When he ribbed her, he seemed more like his previous self. Since she'd overheard the truth about his charges, and explained that she wasn't going to push things from a legal standpoint, the tension between them had begun to soften. He was laughing more often. Was occasionally playful. A couple of times, he'd even left his bedroom door open an inch. Perhaps, given enough time, the two of them would eventually recapture that easiness that had always existed between them.

Molly spread a throw blanket over her legs. Even though Alex's explanation was logical, she couldn't resist making a mental list of everyone who'd been within close range of her dad's house. Teenagers who were always loitering on the grassy divider. Kids horsing around and mothers with toddlers. She'd even seen Russell a couple of times, once on his own, and also strolling with Shawna. How often had she noticed her father's friend, Dr. Even, parked across the street? Were there other times that she'd missed him? She'd also seen Officer Kage driving past on multiple occasions. Had Bradley called about the trespassers as he'd said he would? Or was his offer of help just more manipulation. His being involved in something questionable was not a stretch. Though it couldn't possibly be Mrs. Fischer. The thought of her making calls on a burner phone was ludicrous. But did that mean impossible? And what about Glenn? Had she accepted his explanation too quickly? Was she being gullible?

A throb had developed behind her temples. Obsessing over a random person's identity was not helpful. Nobody she knew was overflowing with resentment. She was a therapist, trained to pick up on nuance; surely she'd have detected that emotional intensity. Even if efforts were made to disguise it.

The caller was a stranger. It had to be. As Bradley said, people are fascinated by murder victims. Even spent money on their old T-shirts and underwear.

Her laptop sat on the coffee table in front of her. Molly stared at it. She'd been avoiding the peer support line for a few days. To gain a little distance, she told herself. Put the whole thing out of her mind. The calls. The alleyway. But that tension inside her, that desire to *know*, would not subside.

Before she could talk herself out of it, she bolted upright, lifted the lid, and logged in. She had to wait only seven minutes before her ears filled with the soft hum of white noise. She recognized it instantly.

She did not introduce herself. Instead, simply said, "Hello."

"Hello."

That gritty voice.

Calmly, she said, "You didn't show."

"No?"

"I was there. Like you asked."

"As I knew you would be."

"So, what was the point then? Some sort of test?"

"Nothing that calculated, Molly. Maybe I just changed my mind. A person's allowed to do that, you know. Reassess things."

"Sure. But just so you're aware, you don't get a do-over."

Feathery laughter. "Oh, Molly. Do you really think you set the rules?"

"What rules? For participating in this mindlessness?"

The caller's tone changed then. Lower, deeper. "Have you tried hiking up to the overhang and yelling out those two little words?"

"What two words?" Though she knew exactly. *Knee*. And *deep*. Just that morning, she'd whispered them into the watery spray of the shower.

"It echoes, you know. In a most illuminating way. Sometimes I stand there and scream."

An image fluttered into her mind. A faceless head, its mouth like a ragged hole. Leaning precariously over the edge of the rock. Wailing at water below like an animal in pain.

"Do you think that bothers me? Mentioning a single fact you read in a police report? Or a newspaper article. So what?" Then with soft mockery, she said, "If you'd like some help, I can suggest some resources."

"Very kind of you to offer, but I'll pass." More laughter. "Do you know where I am right now, Molly?"

She hated the way the person kept repeating her name. "Of course not."

"Come on. Why don't you take a guess?"

"Listen," she said. "I've indulged you for far too long, but I've reached my limit. I hope you find what you're—"

"I'm standing directly across from your childhood home. That blissful place where you grew up. Without a concern in the world."

"I don't believe you," she breathed.

"I'm beneath the streetlight. Near some trees. There's a lamp on in one of the front rooms, Molly. Is your father sleeping?"

She shifted forward on the sofa. Held her laptop in both hands. This was getting too messed up. Had ventured away from disconcerting and was now in alarming territory. "I think you have serious problems."

"Should we settle—"

"And I refuse to let my family's tragedy be a source of entertainment a second longer."

"Molly."

"I'm hanging up now."

"That's not a smart choice."

"And don't ever call the peer support line again."

"You're going to regret this, Moll—"

She moved the cursor, clicked the trackpad. The phone on the screen gently settled into its cradle, as though that call was no different than any of the dozen others she'd answered. She tugged off her headphones, tossed them onto the couch. She considered calling Lyle Kage, but resisted. It was only last week she'd bothered him about the break-in. Instead, she called Glenn.

When he answered, he sounded groggy. Or was pretending to sound groggy? "Molly? Is everything okay?"

Had she actually woken him? "Can you check to see if anyone is outside?"

"Outside where? What's going on?"

"Can you just go and look out the front window? Across the street."

"And what am I supposed to be looking for?"

"A person, under the streetlamp. On the grass divider."

Shuffling, then. "What? Who's under a streetlamp?" A door opening and closing. More footsteps. The scrape of metal curtain rings sliding over the rod. "Nope, no one. It's empty. Like it should be at this time of night."

"Thank you. I'm sorry to bother you."

"Molly, what's this about? Is it related to those calls? I'm starting to get concerned."

"Just a prank, Glenn. It's nothing at all." But she was certain that if she checked beneath the streetlight, the dying grass would be tamped flat.

CHAPTER THIRTY-SEVEN

PEA GRAVEL POPPED and crunched beneath her wheels as she pulled into the tree-lined driveway of the nursing home. The place, surrounded by evergreens, looked more like a grand home than a facility for the infirm. Red brick, turrets, and on the shingled roof, a pair of fat gray doves nestled side by side.

Eventually, her father would need to be transferred from his living room, from Glenn's care. The duration of his life was uncertain. Doctors said he might live a few weeks, or several years, and would require around-the-clock support until the end. Molly would have to budget. He'd left no instructions, no insight into his wishes. That meant every decision was her responsibility. His savings needed to be evaluated. His home sold. His care arranged.

An intake counselor, in seafoam-green scrubs, greeted Molly at the wooden front doors.

"Patients receive daily rehabilitation," she explained as they began a tour of the facility. "A doctor's always on call, and we have nurses here twenty-four seven. And, of course, communication with family is a main priority."

"That's reassuring."

They moved through an airy foyer and down a long hallway. Pristine floors, pristine walls. White wainscotting lining the lower half. An elderly man, smartly dressed, was taking slow steps with a metal walker. As they passed, the woman touched his arm, said, "Getting your exercise, I see." And he replied, "Yes, miss. Got to move the leggies every day."

She laughed and then said to Molly, "As you know, we are a smaller community of residents here. A family of sorts. And we try to select our activities based on their interests and level of ability. There's an art room for creative types and a library for our readers. We also have assisted hikes arranged daily." The woman paused outside a set of double glass doors, gestured to Molly to enter first. "And here's our classics room."

Molly stepped into a bright open space with warm oak floors. A concerto quietly played from speakers in the ceiling. Two ancient women sat in wingback chairs, gazing absently through the enormous windows facing onto a hillside of trees. Most of the fall color had been drained, but there were still patches of scarlet and yellow that caught the sunlight.

"My father isn't . . . he's not communicating very much."

"I understand. We're accustomed to supporting residents no matter the challenges. I'm sure your father would enjoy the music, the fresh air."

"I'm sure he would," she said, though she wasn't sure at all.

"I'd be delighted to answer any questions. As I mentioned, we have a place available."

A place available. The phrase was so innocent, so inviting. As though Death had not stopped to take a loved one. The only reason for a vacated bed.

"Would you like to see the actual room?" the woman said, gesturing toward a white door. "The gentlemen's sleeping area is through there."

"Um." Molly brought her hand to her neck. She was suddenly hot. "I'm not feel—" All at once she began to gasp, then wheeze. She patted her face. Expecting to discover a wet woolen cloth pressed to her mouth and nose. She reached out, smacked her sweating hand against the wall. "I . . . cantbreathe."

The intake counselor held Molly's upper arm and, with a firm grip, guided her out of the room and down another hallway, until they reached a sunny office. "Here," she said, "take a seat. Everything's fine, okay? You're fine."

A paper cup full of lukewarm water appeared in Molly's hand, and she gulped it down.

After a minute, the palpitations slowed. Her ribcage loosened. And a shivery chill replaced the heat that had pulsed through her body only moments earlier.

"Your first visit to a care facility?"

"Yes," Molly stammered, wiping her palms on her thighs. "I'm so sorry. I don't know what happened to me."

"Your reaction is fairly common," the woman said gently. "Making this choice is not easy."

"No, it's not," Molly said. How could she bring her father here? Even though the environment was warm and welcoming, they were still a cluster of souls waiting to leave the earth. Strangers to each other, maybe strangers to themselves.

She wasn't ready to let him go.

"I'll have to think on it," Molly said as she stood up.

"You certainly don't have to make a decision this instant, but unfortunately we can only hold the placement for forty-eight hours."

"Of course. I'll let you know soon."

On the return trip, Molly debated with herself. The nursing home was actually idyllic. Scenery beautiful. Staff competent. Glenn could not stay on forever, and her father would have a private room there that she'd fill with familiar things. She considered whether her indecisiveness was less about the care and more about the inevitability. She could no longer pretend, even for a second, that he would recover. There was no going backward.

There it was. The hardest part. Absolute acceptance. Not the few words she told herself when she faced that brass lion knocker every morning, but the full weight of the loss. Her ailing father needed her to make the right choice, even though signing those papers would crack her heart in two.

As she was traveling the winding road toward Aymes, her phone began ringing through the car speaker. Since Alex's last low-sugar episode, she'd kept Bluetooth on at all times.

She cleared her throat. "Alex?"

Papers rustling, and the clatter of the receiver. "No, it's just me. I'm glad I caught you. You got a quick min?"

Molly recognized that birdlike chirp immediately.

"Hi, Shawna. Everything okay?" Perhaps Russell had told her about the confusion with Glenn, and that Molly had suggested breaching the anonymity rule. Or she could be wondering why Molly hadn't logged into the network for over a week. The volunteer of the month was demonstrating poor dedication.

It had been the right choice, though. Interacting with that troubled caller had become a morbid distraction. She'd spent too much time with the voice in her head. Making her question things that were in the distant past. Since she'd stopped engaging, she'd had fewer thoughts of Terry Kage, her mother's death, and everything else associated.

Molly thought it likely the caller continued for a while. Perhaps the efforts to reach her even increased in frequency. That was common, but without the reward of her response, behavioral extinction would eventually occur. By now the person had surely conceded. Faded into oblivion.

"Absolutely no need to worry," Shawna said. "This is just something I like to do. Have a little chitchat with parents, and I said to myself, there's no time like the present!"

Molly hadn't considered it would be school-related. "That's thoughtful. Alex is keeping up?"

"Like a champ, actually. He's found a fantastic peer group. And I've checked in with all his teachers. They're singing his praises, of course. His law teacher, especially. Mrs. Eliason says he takes to a task like a dog to a bone. You might have a future lawyer on your hands."

"That's wonderful to hear, Shawna." Even though their conversations had improved, Alex still didn't share much about his days.

"On a more personal note, Molly, how's your dad doing?"

"About the same. It's difficult, but we're making the most of this time with him."

"Well, I'm glad you have support."

Hard drops of rain clinked against the windshield. Molly flicked on the wipers, slowed her speed. "Yes, Glenn's been an absolute superstar." How could she have doubted him?

"No, I meant your husband. It's good he's here to pitch in."

"I'm sorry? My husband?"

"Yes, he came to pick up Alex a little earlier. Called the office and said he was waiting outside. I spoke with him myself."

"What?" That made no sense. Leo, her *ex*-husband, had such minimal involvement in Alex's life. Surely if he had planned a trip to Aymes, he would have reached out to Molly first. Not simply show up at a high school. "He didn't come in? Didn't sign him out?"

She tittered. "No, we're all friends around here. We don't need those big-city rules. But I believe your dear husband has one heck of a head cold, Molly."

"He sounded sick?"

"If you're concerned, there's a place on Main Street that makes the ultimate chicken soup. What's the name? Oh, it's right on the tip-tipity of my tongue. The silkiest broth you . . ."

But Molly was not listening anymore. She was certain it wasn't Leo who'd called the office. Molly and Alex were always slotted in the lowest drawer of that man's mind. There had to be a logical explanation. A new friend horsing around. Pinching his nostrils. So he'd sound old enough to get Alex out of class.

"Listen, Shawna, I actually have to go."

"Of course. Let's have another catch-up soon, okay? Your treat this—"

Molly pressed the button to disconnect. Then pulled onto the shoulder of the road, dug her phone out of her purse. There was only a single notification on her lock screen. A message from Glenn. Her father was sleeping, and he was dipping out for an appointment with family services.

She called Alex. It went straight to voicemail, which he'd never set up. Then she sent a text. "Where are you?" Bringing the phone closer to her face, she watched the status beneath her message. *Sending*. Then *Sent*. But not *Delivered*. He'd either shut off his phone or run out of battery.

He was probably at the rental, but that didn't have a landline. She tried her father's but there was no answer there either. He wasn't at the community center. A secretary said Officer Kage had canceled Alex's hours for the afternoon; she didn't know why. In desperation, she called Russell. Twice. But he did not pick up.

As she was about to pull onto the road, Molly's cellphone rang again. This time, a blocked number appeared on the screen. She pressed to answer. "Hello?"

"It's me, Mom." His voice boomed through the speakers.

She felt a bloom of relief. "Thank god, Alex. What's going on? I got this weird call from your school. Some sort of mix-up about your father?"

"Mom."

"If you wanted to skip, you could just tell me. I'm not so hard-nosed that—"

"*Mom!*"

"What? Where are you?"

"I'm in a car, Mom." His words were jittery. Nervous jittery or hypoglycemic jittery. She couldn't tell.

"In a car? What car?"

In the background, she could hear a radio playing. A twangy song. Like country music.

"I'm supposed to tell you something."

Her fingers tightened around the steering wheel, back lifting off the seat. "What, Alex, what?"

"I'm supposed to tell you to come meet us."

"Who do you mean? Who's *us*?"

"We're headed to the overhang, Mom. Just go, okay? Just go there."

THEN

•

CHAPTER THIRTY-EIGHT

Gil

THE AIR IN his car had grown cold and stale. Gil was half a block away from home, a flat gray box sitting on his lap. When he flicked the plastic switch, the box emitted only dull static, like a radio not tuned to a station.

Les Carpenter had explained the simple setup. He'd hidden a bug inside the receiver of the telephone on their kitchen wall. An incoming or outgoing call would produce sound waves, and those waves would be transmitted to the receiver now clutched in Gil's hands.

"I've never done this before," Les said. "I hope I didn't mess up the wires."

Gil shook the metal contraption. Les was probably right; he'd messed up the wires. Edie was home alone again, and in all the afternoons Gil had waited, the machine had not detected a single call.

He twisted the volume knob as far as it would go. The car was flooded with a harsh hum, and he tossed the box onto the passenger seat. Started his car. He needed to return to the pharmacy. That boy Edie had insisted he'd hire was minding the place on his own. Plus, he needed to finish filling the prescriptions before Seth arrived.

As Gil adjusted the gear shift, a soft pop came from the box. Then a click. The static vanished, replaced by a different noise. Like a breeze coasting over the mouth of a cave.

"Of course I'm here."

Edie's voice erupted from the speaker, and Gil grabbed at the box. As he fumbled with the volume, a neighbor wandered past his car. That older woman who allowed her annoying poodle to soil his property time and time again. Last spring he'd reached his limit and used a sledgehammer to force wooden pickets into the hard ground along the front border of his lawn. A makeshift fence, which he would replace even though Edie said she liked it. Reminded her of East Aymes.

She paused by his car, rapping with a knuckle as her doughy face filled up the passenger-side window. Gil tried to wave her along just as Edie said, "Where else would I be?" But the lady knocked again.

He twisted down the volume and reached over to lower the window a crack. "I'm busy," he stammered. "I'm on a call."

"What sort of call?" She eyed the box in his lap. "What's that contraption?"

"Nothing. It's, it's . . ." His heart was firing, and he couldn't think of a single response. He just wanted her gone. "Sort of a phone."

"You park yourself out here every day, Dr. Wynters. And I don't think that's right." She sniffed. "Or normal, for that matter."

"Duly noted." He attempted a warm smile, hoping it didn't appear sinister. Then he closed the window and lifted his foot off the brake, inched his car forward. Slowly, slowly, until the woman disappeared from his rearview mirror.

"—have you been?" Edie said as Gil stopped, readjusted the volume.

Silence followed her. He played with the green knob, the white knob, but he heard no reply.

"You know I do . . . No, there's no chance of that." A puff of air, as though she was aggravated.

He was only hearing one side. Her side. Though Gil knew, deep in his bones, the individual on the other end was not some female friend from the cafeteria.

"You're teasing me," she said. The giggles were high-pitched and excited.

Gil shifted in his seat, tugged at the collar of his shirt. Had she ever used that tone with him? Even in the earliest days of their marriage?

"I do. Yeah, totally. When we—"

A flurry of electric crackles distorted the end of her sentence.

"No, tell me," she said. "Every detail exactly. What're you going to do?"

He could hear her breaths. Slow, deep, steady. "Oh . . . Oh!" Then, "Yes. Over the back of that chair."

Nothing for several seconds.

"Don't even mention that wet rag. I don't want to think about him."

Gil's hand shook as he flicked the tiny switch to "Off." The box in his lap was suddenly quiet, and he pressed his damp back against the driver's seat. Stunned.

Was he the wet rag?

"Don't ever settle," his father had always said. And he hadn't. Instead, he'd waited nearly forty years to meet the woman who made his feet lift off the ground. Since then, he'd done everything he could to build a life for her. To create a family. To make her happy. Now, it was clear: he'd become the punchline to a lame joke.

An icy rush moved through him. He pushed open the door, leaned his head out, and vomited on the pavement.

•

"How about we plan a vacation. A real one. Somewhere exotic?"

A weak attempt, Gil recognized that. Thinking he could wriggle back into her heart with the promise of travel. Excitement. Something no teenaged boy could ever offer.

"Nah," she replied. "Too much money."

He looked up from his dinner. Fried hamburger patties, lumpy potatoes. Canned green peas, barely warmed. "Not if we save. It's certainly manageable."

"Well, we need to pay for something else."

"And that would be?"

"I'm buying a headstone for Cal."

"What?"

"Yeah. I was thinking to get him one in marble. He'd be so jazzed. Something a bit showy."

Gil put down his fork. "I don't understand. You don't even have his ashes." He'd already explained this to her. As Cal's body had gone unclaimed for a given duration, he was cremated. His remains interred in some sort of collective disposal. That was the way the officer had described it, though Gil wasn't certain what that meant.

"So? No reason he can't have a grave marker. In my family's plot."

There it was again. *My family.* She used it consistently when referring to her parents, her siblings. Never once including him or their daughter.

Molly was concentrating on the green peas, transforming them into a snake curving around the potatoes. "Can we talk about this later?" he said. He didn't want a three-year-old listening to a morbid conversation about death and headstones.

"What's there to talk about?" Edie's knife clanged on her plate.

"I'm buying a proper headstone for my brother."

"Sure, then. Marble sounds about right." He did not want a debate. He did not have the energy for it. Since he'd heard her talking on the phone that afternoon, he'd felt unwell. As though he'd overmedicated, or ingested some contaminant, and it was slowly leeching into his bloodstream.

"What's gotten into you?" she said. "You're acting so sour."

"Am I?"

"Yeah. You're such a downer."

Wet rag. Downer. These days she was sounding less like an adult and more like a student from the high school. Gil would bet money that the boy from the parking lot used those sorts of expressions. He'd also bet the boy had been on the other end of the line. His words causing her breathy giggles. How many afternoons had Gil seen him rush toward Edie? Each time there was a furtive exchange of words. Just long enough to solidify plans, while not drawing attention to themselves. There was no way Gil could even ask. He'd have to admit to what he'd done. And planned to continue doing.

"Isn't your daddy a sourpuss, Molly? Huh?"

Gil lowered his head. Nipped his upper thigh with his thumb and forefinger so he wouldn't embarrass himself with a display of emotion. His mother used to say, "So what if you're sensitive, darling. There's nothing wrong with that." It was the only time she ever lied to him.

Molly was wiggling in her chair. Her fist gripping a small spoon. She brought her ear close to her food and smashed a pea.

"Pop," she squealed.

Edie bristled at the shrillness. "Stop that."

"Pop!" Louder this time.

Gil touched the back of Molly's hand. Gently said, "The pop is even better with your teeth."

She picked up a pea and put it in her mouth. An exaggerated chomp. Delight in her eyes as Gil clapped his hands.

Edie scraped back her chair. "The nosy shrew from next door was right, you know." She brought her plate to the garbage and dumped the contents. "Your daughter is a hundred percent you."

"She didn't mean it like that." Gil couldn't remember such a comment, and even if June Fischer had said it, she'd certainly meant no harm. But that was what Edie did. Took tiny slipups and tucked them away. Like boring leftovers in the back of the fridge, festering until the time was right, and then she'd lob them at him with force.

When she was gone, Molly tugged at Gil's sleeve so that he shifted closer. She placed a warm hand on either cheek. Stared at him sternly. "You're not a down daddy," she said. "You're an up daddy."

He smiled. "Thank you, sweetheart." Then he picked up her spoon. "Do you want to join the clean plate club?"

Perhaps she was a small female version of him. Their mannerisms were identical. The same eye color and tiny little cleft in their chins. Their personalities, a match. That was why it was so easy to love her. Be loved by her. With Edie, it was the exact opposite. Every interaction was fraught, as though their relationship served some other purpose for her that he could not identify. All Gil knew for sure was that since the blustery night he'd met her, he'd been constantly failing. Constantly falling.

At some point, he was going to strike the ground.

CHAPTER THIRTY-NINE

WHEN SETH ARRIVED that afternoon, he was aggravated at the mound of boxes in the storeroom. "We both need to carry our weight, Gil. What are you doing all day?"

Gil had been letting work pile up. Unfilled prescriptions for customers. Incomplete accounting. A long-overdue inventory of stock and supplies. But he was too ashamed to explain why he was unable to focus. All he wanted to do was sit in his car, to wait and wait for a few minutes of a one-sided phone call. To hear the brazenness in her tone. The playfulness. The plans to meet, though a location was never revealed.

During the first few conversations, his brain had worked to spin reasons that had nothing to do with that boy from school. Perhaps she actually was chatting with her friends from the cafeteria. Or a neighborhood pal from where she grew up. Gil had never viewed himself as particularly cool, even when young, so maybe it was just youthful banter that was slightly beyond his comprehension. When he could no longer sustain that self-deception, he tried pretending he was the person on the other end. Gil replying to her comments, his shaky voice bouncing around inside his car. He tried talking with a foul mouth, saying things that would encourage her saucy replies. Then, disgusted with himself, he shifted tone. Imploring her to listen. Clutching the metal box and begging her to stop. He'd do whatever she asked to make things good between them.

Two days ago, he'd smashed the cold chunk of technology against the steering wheel. But it did not break. Her crystal-clear words continued to emerge from the speaker. He could not control himself, and he left his car, rushing into the house. Found Edie in the kitchen. Her head in the fridge, crisper hanging open, first bite of an apple in her teeth.

"Why're you home?" she asked calmly.

The long cord from the phone was still swaying side to side.

"Forgot my umbrella. Supposed to rain later."

"Is it? Who's at the store?"

"Just Lyle," he'd said. "Sorting the shelves. Doing a wonderful job, he is. A really wonderful job."

"Well, you best not leave him too long. You know how teenagers are."

"Yes," he'd replied. He knew exactly how teenagers were. He heard them most afternoons in the alleyway beside the pharmacy. Abhorrently rude. Gil had wondered if the boy from the parking lot was like that? Had wondered if that was what Edie preferred?

In the crowded stockroom, Gil stepped around Seth. He picked up a box and tore open the cardboard flap. "I'll stay for a while longer," he said. "Get a few things sorted."

"Sure, sure, but you got to get a hold of yourself, buddy." Seth punched him lightly in his upper arm. "Seems like only yesterday you couldn't wipe that stupid grin off your face. And now you're like a glum chum."

Gil tried to take a deep breath, but the muscles in his shoulders, his ribs, were cricked so tightly he could barely inhale. "Things aren't good," he managed.

"With the missus?"

"Yeah. Lot of problems."

"What sort of problems?"

"I don't want to get into it." He rubbed his eyes, sore from lack of sleep. "I do love her, you know. But I can't stand her at the same time."

Seth chuckled, though not in a gloating way. Gil perceived it more as an effort to comfort him. "We've all been there, buddy. It'll get better. Promise."

Gil began organizing the bottles. Recording the names and quantities, noting which ones needed reordering. As he filled the containers on the shelves behind the counter, he paused to swallow two lorazepam tablets. He could manage that way. When a sedative pushed his glaring deficiencies outside of himself. A blurry place where they did very little damage.

He slit the top on another box. Ran his fingers over the contents. Had they needed an additional supply of penicillin and gentamicin? When he noticed the phencyclidine, he realized there had been a mistake. That was not a medication they carried at the pharmacy. That was permitted only for use as an anesthetic for animals. He examined the label.

He carried the box out to the pharmacy counter. "Delivery error," he said, handing it to Lyle. "It's for Happy Pets next door."

"Do you want me to bring it over?"

"They're closed on Saturdays," Gil replied. "Just do it Monday."

"No sweat, boss."

"But fix the tape first. If he thinks we opened it, he'll have a conniption."

No love was lost between Gil and the owner of Happy Pets. The veterinarian often called the police for the most benign reasons. When the teenagers were acting up. When Gil placed the tiniest table on the sidewalk with a few sale items. When the nose of a customer's car was too close to the vet's Chevrolet Vega.

"Gotcha." Lyle winked. "Guy's a jerk, yeah?"

"Yeah. Guy's a jerk."

Gil returned to the stockroom. There were still a dozen or so boxes that needed sorting and shelving. Women's hair dye. NyQuil. A vertical display of L'eggs hosiery that he should have constructed weeks ago.

"I'm heading out," he called to Seth as he slid off his lab coat. "But don't touch anything."

Seth stuck his head into the storeroom. "If you insist."

"I'll come in tomorrow afternoon. Get it cleared away. I'll finish the inventory, too."

"On a Sunday? You sure?"

"Yeah. If I start around two, I'll be done for dinner." He pulled on his jacket. Wrapped a thin wool scarf around his neck. "You're right, you know. I need to get it together." He could not keep spying on Edie. Hearing her was only a torment to him. It would not solve anything.

•

The next day after lunch, Gil had intended to go to the pharmacy and finish emptying the boxes and stocking the shelves. But when he was backing out of the driveway, he noticed Edie's face in the living room window. She'd pulled back the curtain and was watching him leave. She'd never done that before.

An anxious feeling began to intensify in his chest. It reminded him of when he was a child, shuffling across the floor of the cellar to retrieve a bottle for his mother. He'd swing his arm through pitch-black, trying to locate the dangling string attached to the lightbulb. In those moments before he could see, the darkness held every possibility.

Gil braked, then looped his car around and returned to his side of the street. Parked two doors down. He took the metal device from the glove compartment and flicked the switch. Just once more, he promised himself. And then he would never listen in again. He'd make up some reason for Les Carpenter, tell him the bug was no longer needed. Could Les stop by and undo what he'd done?

Only white noise sputtered from the speaker, and Gil adjusted the volume to low. Laid it on the seat beside him. As he waited, he leaned the back of his skull against the headrest. Closed his eyes. His stomach growled. He hadn't touched his breakfast or his lunch. He felt continually sick. Armpits clammy, his mouth bone-dry.

In less than two minutes, Edie was on the phone. "For a while at least," she said.

Gil's eyes opened, and his spine straightened. Her voice was different this time. Perhaps because Molly was close by. He'd left her in front of the television, a bowl of dry Cheerios in her lap.

"Of course you'll love it."

Then she said, "Really smooth. Yeah."

He pressed his knuckles into his forehead. What was *really smooth*? He could think of several parts of her body fitting that description. Nothing anyone else should know about. Besides him.

"You won't be disappointed."

When the telephone call disconnected, Gil threw the box at the dash. It struck the stereo and the 8-track ejected.

This was not the way to pull himself together. As he took a deep breath, he heard a cry of joy coming from the grassy divider. A young father was playing catch with his son, exclaiming each time the ball slid into the youngster's leather glove. Off to the side, the mother clapped her hands. Even their golden retriever seemed contented. Leaping and snapping at the first of the season's snow-flakes falling from a dull November sky.

Gil noticed a boy then, about a dozen feet away from the family. He might have been sixteen or seventeen, and he was alone, his hunched body partially obscured by the branches of an ever-green tree.

With his sleeve, Gil swiped away the condensation on the car window. Why was that kid standing there? What was holding his attention?

Gil was distracted by a rusty sedan. Muffler popping as it rolled along the street, slowing in front of his house. Two teenagers stumbled out of the passenger side, the smaller one kicking the door closed with his foot. Gil recognized Bradley Fischer, who swaggered toward his own home, but the second boy did not follow. Instead, he paused on the sidewalk as the dilapidated car chugged away. Gil leaned forward until his chest was touching the steering wheel.

The boy began moving up Gil's driveway. His gait uneven, uncertain. He kept peering upward, then rapidly ducking his head, as though something besides snow was careening through the air around him. When he reached the front door, he patted the face of the brass lion with his fingertips, and then stepped back, shook his right hand. Jammed his fingers into his mouth, like he'd been bitten.

Gil was too far away to see clearly. Was that the same boy from the school parking lot? Was he brazen enough to enter Gil's home? Do whatever was planned with Edie, all while Molly was right there?

Seconds later, one of those questions was answered. The front door was opening. Gil could not see Edie, just her arm scooping the air. Welcoming the visitor—the intruder—inside.

Gil glanced across the street at the green stretch that separated the two lanes. The boy who'd been hiding in the trees was gone.

Him

IT WAS MID-AFTERNOON when my friend announced that he had to leave my house because he was meeting the lunch lady. "The hot one," he said. "I've got a date." Those were the exact words he used. *Hot*. And *date*.

"That's not true," I whispered.

"Fuck, yeah it is. If he says it is."

"She might blow him the second he's in the door."

"Especially if he brings pizza. That shit happens to those guys all the time."

"It won't," I said. "She wouldn't do that." She just wouldn't.

When it was time for him to go, the boys told him to ditch. Stay and hang out. But after he downed a pill from the sandwich baggie, he was up, tugging his jean jacket on over his hooded sweatshirt. Talking about being responsible. Giving the broad what she wanted. He stuck his tongue out, wiggled the tip. Everyone snickered at that. Except for me.

One of the boys said, "You'd better be in and out fast. Before that kicks in."

The phrase *in and out* caused a fresh release of laughter. I glared at them all.

"I'll drive you," my friend's brother said as he shook his car keys in the air.

"Yeah, I'm going to jet, too." Bradley Fischer grabbed up his infamous baggie and stuffed it into his backpack. "I'll grab a ride with you."

The three of them left my house. I left a minute later. The rest of the guys stayed behind. Someone had brought beer, and they were warming up a supersized bag of frozen French fries in the oven. No one asked me where I was going. I was beginning to suspect that none of them cared.

●

As I biked toward her house, I reviewed the developments from the past two weeks. I'd stopped trying to chat with her in the cafeteria. Refused to continue chasing her across the parking lot. Instead, I'd opted to step back, hoping my lessened efforts might draw her closer. Though it led to the converse. She seemed more distant than before.

I'd shifted tactics then. Started watching her house from inside a cluster of evergreens across the street. I was confident in my disguise. Green jacket, brown corduroys, black sneakers. No different than a patient, watchful tree. Twice, she arrived before me. But the other times I had to wait a full hour or more. I wondered where she went in between. All that time unaccounted for. She never carried groceries or had a child gripped by the wrist. Reality was kicking me in the guts. I couldn't deny that a wall of secrets now existed between us.

One evening in the darkness, I climbed the oak in her backyard. Brought a slim blade and shaved away the B and the F until there was only the smooth damp flesh of the tree. I should have done that when I first discovered it. Perhaps leaving his mark there had caused some bad luck. Obliterating Bradley Fischer's initials might be the message Fate needed.

All the lights were on in my girlfriend's house, and I could see her and that man she'd married in the kitchen. Though I could hear nothing, I knew they were arguing with each other. Reddened faces. A fist lowered onto the countertop. Arms throw up in exasperation.

When I witnessed those moments between them, I began to feel hopeful again. Excited, even. I considered it was only a matter of time until she realized where she belonged.

But then there was more upheaval. Yesterday, I'd become aware that my friend was making moves. Positioning himself as a wedge in my relationship. I realized the severity of things when I noticed him in Mrs. Fischer's driveway. He'd dropped his sports bag on the pavement and was leaning over the hood of her car.

Mrs. Fischer appeared on her front porch. Handing him something in a paper towel. A muffin, perhaps. Or a pile of cookies. He took three animal bites, and the snack was gone.

"Teenage boys are always hungry," she'd said.

I'd rolled my eyes, then. Stoned boys are even hungrier.

"Can you point out the damage? I don't see anything major."

She gestured with her hand. "Under there. I covered it over when it happened and just forgot about it. But now that I'm giving the car to Bradley, he wants it repaired."

He peeled away several strips of what appeared to be dark green tape, then swiped a hand across the back of his mouth. "Cripes, Mrs. F. Who'd scratch that into your car?"

Me. It was me. With the tip of my knife.

"I'm not certain. Someone with quite a lot of rage, I suppose. And no outlet."

Which was utter fiction. If a person made a statement, why must it be associated with an emotion? Ire or bliss. Why couldn't it just be the truth? Mrs. Fischer *was* a meddling bitch. Simple as that.

"I'll apply some filler. Sand it down. Match the color." He coughed. A rattly bark of young lungs exposed to too many cigarettes. Too much pot. "Better to work in your garage, though. In case it starts to storm."

As I listened to their banter, I felt a flash of hatred toward my friend. Jealous that he'd received valuable knowledge from his father. Transforming him into someone who was needed, useful.

Then, as Mrs. Fischer dashed inside to grab her keys, my girlfriend opened the front door of her house. Waving her hand and calling to him. I held my breath, strained to listen. She said she had something she wanted to show him. She said she needed him.

At that moment, my mind began to reel. *Needed?* Were the two of them strangers? Or were they more?

The very thought of him brushing against her body made the metal bars on my inner cage strain and bend. They should not have been conversing. Should not have been interacting. There was no way to innocently insert that friend into my story without messing everything up.

"Can't today," I heard him say. "But I'll come back tomorrow."

And that was exactly what he was doing. Riding in the passenger seat of his brother's car. Soon to be arriving for his "date."

The entitlement in his tone was revolting. How could everything in my world tilt that quickly?

I pressed the pedals faster. My thigh muscles were on fire by the time I reached the manicured divider. I took up my usual position among the trees and watched him arriving. Then he just stood at the bottom of her driveway. A full minute passed at least. It was cold for early November, and he must have noticed the first snowflakes that were beginning to fall. He kept batting at the air. Once he straightened himself, he weaved up the stone pathway. His right arm held out at his side, running his hand along a hedge that was not there.

Whatever he'd consumed allowed him to still place one foot in front of the other, but just barely. When he reached the front step, his hand formed a fist. Hard knocking on the door.

"Oh, there you are," she sang in a way-too-sultry tone. "I've been waiting."

He mumbled something, but I couldn't make out his words.

I saw you, then. Upstairs. With your tiny palms pressed against the glass, you were full of awe and innocence.

I never expected her to let him inside, especially given his state. But she did. I wondered how normal he was acting. Was he slurring his speech? Did he have cartoon spirals in his eyes? Was he yawning, his muscles sleepy? Or had a feral desire to fuck overtaken him? And though I loathe that term, that was all it would be. Fucking.

When the door closed, so many images burst into my brain. Him ambling into her kitchen. Filling the space with his cheap aftershave. Her leaning over him, her tits pressed into his chest as he reached up, groping her clumsily. Could he glimpse the edge of her bra down the front of her shirt? Were her lips pressed to his? Was her thigh rubbing at the rigidness beneath his joggers?

I could never have anticipated the pain that coursed through me. While I had reconciled that she might sometimes screw her husband, this was altogether different. She was cheating with my buddy. Right in front of me. Like a taunt, a direct strike, meant to cause damage. Destroying what we had built.

Part of me wanted to rush in there. Rip him off her. Pound his drugged-out face to a bloody pulp. But I didn't.

I glanced up at you one last time.

Then I picked up my bike and rode away.

NOW

•

CHAPTER FORTY

Molly

FOOT PRESSING ON the gas, Molly skidded off the gravel shoulder and sped down the road. Cutting the curves, wheels crossing the yellow line. *I'm supposed to tell you something, Mom. We're going to the overhang. We're going. We.* Alex was not with his father. He was not with a classmate. The fear in his voice was undeniable.

When the town sign with the dancing corncob loomed over the ditch, Molly held her breath. Just around the next bend, she jerked the wheel, veering across the pavement. Slam of the brakes, and her car came to an abrupt stop in front of the overgrown path that led up the hill. The entrance was blocked by a familiar car.

Molly rushed toward it, peering through the windows. Alex's book bag had been tossed into the back. Sitting on the driver's seat was a set of keys with a metal octopus keychain.

She recognized that trinket. Recently watched it dropping from a hand. Landing on a tufted stool. The keys belonged to Mrs. Fischer.

"Alex?" Molly called out as she hurried through the long grass. The blades tearing with each forceful step. "Mrs. Fischer?"

She was in the woods, now. Clambering up the steep slope. She cupped her hands to the sides of her mouth. "Alex?" she cried again. "Answer me!"

When she reached the crest, she saw them. Dangerously close to the lip of the overhang. Alex was sitting on the ground. And standing beside him, an elbow hoisted onto a painted sign—"Danger! No Dumping!"—was Bradley.

Molly's panic vanished, outrage rising up to replace it. "What's going on?" she yelled. "Just what do you think you're doing with my son?"

Was it possible he was so deluded that he was attempting to befriend Alex? Thinking he'd get his greedy hands on more murder victim paraphernalia?

"Well, it's nice to see you, too," Bradley said, his fingertips grazing the sign. "How's your day going so far?"

There was something about his low shoulders and loose jaw. The friendliness in his tone. So out of sync with the situation. It made Molly slow her approach.

"Fine. Just fine," she said, trying to sound a little softer. "But this excursion is over now. I'm taking my son home."

He let his elbow drop to his side. Took a step toward her. "Not so fast, Moll. I didn't hike all this way to turn right around. Have you forgotten all the history here? We should at least appreciate the view."

She looked at Alex. His face was ashen and he was curved forward over his bent knees. "Listen," she said. "I'm not sure what you were thinking. Obviously, a misjudgment we can sort out later. But right now, I'm feeling pretty uncomfortable."

He chuckled. "You're uncomfortable? How do you think I feel? Living in my mother's fucking basement again."

She caught it, then. A caustic bitterness simmering beneath the surface. "I'm sorry, but that's got nothing to do with me. Or Alex."

"No? You sure about that?"

Even from several feet away, she could see the tremor in Alex's hands. "Look at him. He needs to eat something." She began digging through her purse. Trying to find sugar.

Bradley moved in front of Alex. "Why don't you cool your jets, huh? Stay right where you are."

"Now this is starting to feel a little threatening, Bradley."

"Don't get it twisted, babe." He laughed again. "I'm not threatening anyone. I don't see a knife or a gun. We're just three friends up here. Hanging out. And I really need you to listen to me."

Molly's hand located a chocolate bar. "We'll meet up another time, okay? Go have that second drink. Whatever you want. I'm just going to toss some sugar to Alex."

"I already tried talking to you, Molly. A whole bunch of times."

"What? When?"

She threw the chocolate. It plopped on the ground beside Alex, but when he reached for it, Bradley kicked out. A spray of dirt, and the bar sailed off the overhang. A quiet gulp when it struck the water below.

"This is not a joke, Bradley." She stuck her hand in her bag again, searching for more candy. "He's diabetic. If he doesn't—"

"Put your purse down."

Alex's face was gray now. Shiny from the sweat. "Don't be an imbecile," she blurted.

Bradley stared at her, his tongue poking the corner of his mouth. Then he lurched, grabbing Alex by the collar, yanking hard. Alex tumbled sideways, a mess of skinny arms and legs scrambling as Bradley dragged him within a few feet of the edge.

"Mom?" Alex whimpered. "I don't need anything. I'm good, I'm good. Just do what he says, alright?"

Another step and they would tumble over the side. Drop into a freezing lake in November. In his condition, Alex would not be able to swim.

"I'm sorry, I'm sorry," Molly whispered, gently placing her purse by her feet. "I didn't mean to call you that. We can talk. Right now. Okay?"

"Now that's better," Bradley said as he released Alex. "There's no need for us to fight, Moll."

"I don't want to fight either. And I honestly didn't know you were trying to reach me. I apologize. I would've made the time."

"Oh, you made the time. You just didn't make the effort."

"I don't understand what you mean."

"That stupid support line. I heard you bragging about it to my mother." He sucked air through his teeth. "Do you know how often I called? How many times I had to hang up on some stupid skank named Shawna?"

Molly froze. "Why would you do that? Why not just reach out? Or stop over?"

He hesitated. "Man. I don't really know. I didn't want to be so obvious about shit, I guess. Figured I'd try, you know, planting a seed. So you'd think. And come to your own conclusions."

What conclusions? Had she missed something obvious? "I'm really confused, Bradley."

"When you realized what I'd done to help you, you'd want to help me."

"I'm—"

"You know, we were all into your mother. And she knew it, too. The way she'd act when she was in the cafeteria. I'd say every dude in high school ate lunch with a boner."

"Brad—"

"Then this fucking geezer comes along, and the dumb bitch marries him. Bet she got tired of his wrinkly dick after week one. And you know what? He hated her for that. Hated that he couldn't keep her happy."

A thin film of cold sweat now covered Molly's body. "You're being crude." Her parents had had a good marriage. Her father told her time and time again.

"You really got no clue, do you?" Bradley chuckled. "Did you even know it was me who gave Terry the drugs? Took them right out of your father's place. Lyle didn't stop me."

Molly nodded. While trying to hide her surprise.

"Christ," he continued. "That kid was so gullible. And then he went off the fucking deep end."

"That makes sense, Bradley. If you feel some guilt. That's normal."

"Me?" His head flicked backward. "You think I did something wrong?" Hands closing into fists. "That day your mother died, I did what I was supposed to do. And . . . and I've continued doing that, every day since."

He was rambling. She still couldn't grasp what he was trying to communicate. But she wanted him to hurry along. Get to his point, so she could help Alex. "What was it you were supposed to do?"

Bending his head, he pinched the bone at the top of his nose. "I've had a shitty life; do you know that? Raw deal after raw deal. I know my mother's ashamed of me. My friends are laughing behind my back. Glenn. Rusty. Lyle. Hell, if Terry was still here, he'd be doing the same."

"No one's laughing. I can assure you."

"And none of it's my fault. Eventually, when nothing ever gets better, you start to feel a little desperate, right?"

"Of course you do."

"I know what happened, Molly. Up here on the overhang. And I've never told a soul. I protected my mother. I've been a good fucking son. Protected you, too. Like a good fucking neighbor."

"Protected us? You were here? With Terry Kage?"

But that made no sense. Molly remembered him being home. His antics helping to calm her fear. How he'd lifted her onto his shoulders and stomped around his kitchen, pretending to be some sort of wild beast. Grunting and gnashing his teeth as Mrs. Fischer prepared dinner. Molly had clung to him, squealing, her fingers locked in his shaggy hair as they swayed together.

"No, not me. But somebody else was."

"Who? Who else?"

"You know, Molly. You've always known."

She looked around the clearing. When she was younger, she used to imagine those moments. A boy talking gibberish to the sky, the trees. Hauling a limp body over the ground. That instant when her mother teetered on the edge. Then the drop. The splash. A flash of color beneath the surface as her body drifted down and down until it disappeared.

But now, there was a second person. Another teenager? A man? Or a woman?

"Go," Bradley said. "Move over there."

"I'm sorry?"

"Go closer and yell it out. Those two words. Like that old slag said."

"I don't—"

"Go to the fucking edge!" Spit flew from his mouth.

Molly inched forward. Being so close to the drop gave her vertigo. "Knee deep," she said.

"Yell it!"

"Knee deep," she repeated. A little louder.

Bradley stomped toward her, clutched her upper arm, and shoved her backward. "You're useless. You've always been useless."

He yelled then, the words bursting from his mouth. Skimming over the water. Bumping, dipping, morphing. Disguised by the time the echo reached another's ears. Molly heard it clearly now.

All those years ago, a stricken heart had stood on the ledge and cried out. Not *knee deep*, as the woman had claimed. But a name.

Eeedeee!

"My dad," Molly whispered. "It was my dad. He was here, too."

A memory shot through her mind. Like a missing parcel appearing on the front porch. Lid flipped up, a sepia light shining on the contents.

"What did you see, Molly?" Mrs. Fischer leaned closer.

"Daddy. I saw Daddy in the garage."

"No, no, dear. That's not right. Your daddy's at work. What did you see?"

Slowly, slowly, with Mrs. Fischer's coaxing and gentle correction, Bradley's smiling and clapping, the involvement of the unknown boy grew larger. Blocking out the person behind him. Blocking out the truth.

"I was coloring," she'd said. "I heard a man downstairs."

Molly sank to the ground, drove the tips of her fingers into the dirt to stabilize herself. Everything that happened on that Sunday afternoon was still there. Even though, for years, it had been folded and hidden away from view. She'd always sensed the puzzle had been rearranged. And that a corner piece was missing.

Her father.

"I knew the entire story, and I couldn't breathe a fucking word. I stayed noble like that." Bradley lit a cigarette, took a long drag.

"Why? Because my mother would do anything for your loser dad. She loved him. Loved him more than she ever loved her lame-ass son."

Molly's body teetered back and forth. She'd lied on the stand. While those lies had saved her father, they'd destroyed somebody else. Fractured an entire family.

"And I spent my whole life holding it in. That secret. Do you know how hard that's been for me? Watching you grow up, happy and fucking oblivious to all the bullshit. While one of my best buddies hung himself for something he didn't even do."

"I made a mistake," she said. "A terrible mistake."

"But it was too late then, of course. If I told, my mother'd go to jail along with your fucking father. I'd probably go, too."

Molly stood up on shaking legs. "That's a lot of burden for one person to carry. I see that now. I do."

"Mom," Alex breathed. "I don't feel good."

"I figured you'd understand, Moll. The damage that did to me, I mean, you can't even calculate."

Molly straightened her spine. She'd detected the slightest shift in Bradley's tone. The surliness had receded, replaced by a vulnerability. A pleading for sympathy, perhaps. "Brad? I heard you, and I get it's been rough. But this isn't going to fix anything. You've kidnapped a child."

"That's not—I only meant . . ." He tossed his cigarette, a flurry of sparks when it struck the ground. "He caught a lift, is all. I didn't force him in the car. Did I, buddy?"

"Mom?"

"But you didn't take him home, did you?"

"It's a pit stop. So we could figure our shit out. You get that, right?"

"I don't feel good, Mom." Alex was slurring.

"I need to check on him," Molly said. "This has surpassed serious."

Bradley leaned down and patted him on the shoulder. "You're okay. You're fine."

"He's not fine. You can see that."

"Shut it, will you? Give me a second to fucking think!" He gnawed at the skin on the side of his thumb. "Okay, okay. He can go as soon as we've made our agreement."

"What agreement? That an awful thing happened? That I was a gullible three-year-old?"

"Nothing like that." More gnawing. "Fuck planting a seed. I'm going to lay it all out for you, okay? You'll be selling that big house soon, right?"

"My father's?"

"Yeah. And it's not like I want half or anything, Moll. Just what I deserve. For the suffering I endured. You got to see that."

There it was. The primary reason behind every action he'd taken since she'd arrived in town. He didn't want validation or resolution. He wanted money.

Revulsion rinsed through her. Bradley Fischer was not a man. He was an incompetent and manipulative grub.

"And besides," he continued, "your dad already agreed. Ten thousand, he said."

"He did what?" Then she recalled the cashier's check in her father's desk.

"Oh, yeah, but the fucker wanted to play chicken. Wouldn't hand it over."

He'd been blackmailing her father. Her stomach dropped, and an instant later, anger filled the hollow. She clenched her fists, controlling herself. Accusing him would only amp up his agitation. Instead, she spoke clearly. Quickly. "Listen to me, Brad. We can figure—"

"Totally pissed me off. Like royally. I mean, I was right there in front of him, fucking pleading, and he wouldn't bend. Even got up in his grill. I thought he was going to break. I did. And then the bastard keeled over."

"He what?"

"You heard me."

All Molly could see was her father. Eighty-three years old in his creased trousers and pressed linen shirt. Making his way up his front steps, and Bradley Fischer storming toward him. And when her father refused the demand, Bradley loomed over him, threatening him, until something inside her father's brain broke open. Blood spurting into places it did not belong. Creating pressure. Causing damage. Completely destroying the man who'd loved her all her life.

"Mom?" Alex was starting to retch.

Snapping back, then. To the overhang. To her son, whose blood sugar had plummeted to dangerous levels.

"Bradley. He could go into a coma any second."

"Please can I get some juice? Please, Mr. Fischer."

"What?" He turned his head sharply. "What did you just call me?"

"Mr. Fischer, please. Please?"

Bradley's head slumped forward then. His shoulders jerked up and down several times, as though he was chuckling. But when he looked up, he wiped the back of his hand across his cheek.

"Shit," he said. He smacked his palm to his forehead. "Fucking shit."

"Mr. Fischer?"

"I really fucked up, didn't I? I don't know, man, I don't know what I was thinking. How could I fuck up so bad? So fucking stupid." He wrapped his arms around his chest, then bent at the waist, emitting a high-pitched wail. Like a stray dog with its tail caught.

Then he righted himself, sniffed hard. "Mr. Fischer, huh? Little buddy just called me Mr. Fischer. Like I deserve that." His voice cracked. "My dad'd be so fucking embarrassed of me." He waved his hand. "Go on, little buddy. I'm real sorry for being such a dick. Go to your mom and get yourself a snack."

On all fours, Alex scrambled toward Molly. Turned her purse upside down, shook it. He grabbed the second candy bar, tore off the wrapper with his teeth. Pressed the squares of chocolate into his mouth.

Bradley wiped his hands over his face. "I know you're going to call Kage, Moll. I don't blame you. But could you give me an hour? So I can talk to my mom? She'll know how to sort this out. She always does."

Even though Alex was safe beside her, there was a crushing sensation lodged inside Molly's chest. Resentment. Repulsion. Hatred. Building, twisting, tightening. Restricting her breaths at the very tip of her lungs. She couldn't speak, but it didn't matter. Bradley just kept talking.

"I totally fucked up. But I didn't mean any harm. I really didn't. And I know you, Moll. You understand shit. You're a fucking therapist, for fuck's sake. Plus, aren't you glad I brought you up here? I can't believe you forgot that shit about your dad."

He dug around inside his jacket pocket. Retrieved another cigarette. His lighter next. Flick. Flick. Flick. But the flame would not appear.

"Fuck me," he yelled. "Fuck me!" He threw his hands up in the air. Then sighed, said, "We can still be friends, though. No reason things got to go sour."

Molly cracked. She bolted forward. Lunged. Pummeled Bradley with both hands. He stumbled backward, feet caught in the loose laces of his high-top sneakers. Arms flailing, fingers raking the air, but there was nothing for him to clutch. Until he hooked the hem of Molly's jacket. And yanked her. They tumbled together. Solid ground beneath her one moment. Then air. Only air.

Bradley's wailing in her ears. The cold smack of water, enveloping her. An explosion of bubbles. Light above, darkness below. Her body shocked into absolute stillness, and she dropped down and down into the icy depths of Rabey Lake.

THEN

•

CHAPTER FORTY-ONE

Gil

GIL CLIMBED OUT of his car and onto the quiet street, crept alongside his house and into the backyard. His heart was pounding as he slid open the patio glass door and stepped inside.

Heel to toe, heel to toe through the family room. When he reached the kitchen, he heard the faintest singing coming from behind him. It was Molly. Was she upstairs? Had his wife put their daughter in his office? He paused to listen when a ripple of boyish laughter curdled the air. A strange mechanical warble that made the hair on the back of Gil's neck stand up. Then Edie's voice. "So? Are you impressed?" They were in the garage. His wife and Bradley Fischer's buddy. Together.

Silently, he inched along a short hallway. He paused in front of a mirror and caught sight of a man with dark circles under his eyes. Thinning hair. Mouth open, panting. Loose knot in his tie. Wrinkled collar. The person looked disheveled. Unhinged. Gil barely recognized his reflection.

The door to the garage was ajar. The boy was leaning against Edie's car. She was standing close to him. Too close.

Was that where it happened? She'd pick him up at night in that piece of junk she drove, and they'd find a secluded road. She'd pull onto the shoulder; they'd move into the backseat. Or did she straddle him in the passenger seat? Her open palm pressed against the steaming window. His backside sticking to the cracked vinyl seating.

"Should we try it?" she said. "Should we give it a go?"

Bile rose in Gil's throat. It was going to happen right in front of him.

"Uh. Not with the . . . the door closed." The boy rubbed his hand to his forehead. "Fumes."

The leaden weight of awareness appeared in Gil's skull. If only he had a sedative. He could picture the label. *Bromazepam 6 mg.* He would ground it to a powder with his molars and lick every bit from the cusps. No water needed.

That laughter again. Bouncing around inside the garage. The boy pressed his fingertips into his face. "Fuck. My cheek. My, my gone." He opened and closed his jaw. An audible popping. "Only bone."

"Are you alright?" Her fingertips were resting on his arm.

"No, no, nuh-oh." He placed his hand on the roof of the car. When he lifted it away, a print of sweat remained.

"Do you feel sick?"

"Woah," he said. "Fuck, man, woah." Then his body tilted as though a sneaky wind had knocked him sideways. He stumbled, striking his elbow on the passenger-side window.

Edie reached toward him, catching his sleeve. "We can do this later, you know."

Do this later. If Gil was still gone, of course. Or would she sneak him in again? Maybe these little visits were a common occurrence.

He could not wait a second longer. He slammed the door open. "And so!" he yelled. "Here we are!"

Edie turned around slowly, looked up. "Here we are?"

"Or should I say, here *you* are." Then he sneered, "In this little situation."

Her eyes narrowed. "What's going on with you?"

"With me? It's basic, Edie. I've caught you."

The boy was crouching on the ground near the front wheel. His gaze lifted to meet Gil's. At first Gil thought the teen was going to challenge him, but instead he stayed where he was, his eyes wide, full blue iris, pinpoint pupils. Gil realized the boy was on drugs. Probably took something moments before he'd arrived. And now the effects were hitting him full force.

Edie laughed. "Caught me what, Dr. Wynters? Checking the engine before I sell my car?"

He couldn't stop himself. Blurted, "I heard you on the phone. Talking filth to him." He jabbed a finger toward the boy. Curled up now, arms squeezed over his head. "It's bugged you know."

Her mouth parted slightly, but she did not speak. Just stared at him. Blinking. Then, softly, "What did you just say?"

"The phone, Edie, I had it bugged. I heard your dirty conversations; they came through a transmitter. I . . . I needed to know."

A small smile. "Then you deserve it. You deserve hearing every single word we spoke."

"You can't do this me. You just can't." His breath was coming in short gasps. So little oxygen, he was growing light-headed. "You're my wife. It's not supposed to be like this."

She shook her head. "I wish I'd never listened."

"Listened to who?"

"I never wanted any of this. A shiny life in a shitty place. I've loathed every single minute of it."

Gravity pulled all of Gil's blood down into his legs. His trunk and head were suddenly numb, weightless. He'd been certain, given enough time, they would have the same relationship his parents had. A perfect, playful love. He'd tried so hard to force that connection into existence. All his efforts had made him into a horrible husband. Doing horrible things. Now he realized that none of it made a difference.

"Why, Edie?" His voice cracked. Tears welling in his eyes. "Why would you do it then?"

"I was all she had left, you know. My dad gone. My sister, too. And Cal was in jail, so he didn't count."

"That doesn't make any sense."

She shrugged. "My mother wanted me in a safe place. With a safe person. She was old and sick and so I said yes. I married you to make her happy. Then she died. And I was stuck."

"Stuck?"

"Stuck with you. Stuck with her." Edie jutted her chin out and Gil turned. Saw Molly in the doorway. A colored picture gripped in her small fist.

"Daddy?"

His daughter had heard the vitriol spewing from her mother's mouth.

Gil turned back toward Edie. He felt something straining against the inner curve of his ribs. Like a putrid rubber balloon. Displacing his stomach. Compressing his lungs and cutting off every wisp of air. So massive his chest could barely contain it. He pressed his hand into his sternum. Pushing pushing pushing. And it burst.

He grabbed Edie's arm and twisted it. Her mocking laughter ricocheted off the garage walls, the ceiling, and he shoved her. He didn't mean for his hands to have such force.

She flew backward, tripped over a tiny pair of yellow rubber boots, and slammed into the wall of the garage. So hard the gyprock shuddered. A stud loosened. A bracket shifted. The shelf he had installed years ago sagged ever so slightly on one side. A second bracket began to groan and bend. Then the sledgehammer that he'd safely balanced up there last spring teetered.

Edie was standing beneath it. A steely gaze, a satisfied smirk. As though she were pleased to be in the middle of turmoil. Delighted that she'd damaged him. Her tongue darted out, licked at the thin line of red seeping from her nostrils.

There was not a sound when the hammer tumbled off the shelf. The steel head struck the very top of her crown. Driving into her soft bone. Forcing her knees to buckle. Her body to collapse.

It happened in an instant. It took forever.

Gil could not grasp the scene in front of him. His wife now suddenly on the floor. The unnatural angle of her knee. Odd twist of her neck. The hammer was lying beside her, wooden handle resting on her shoulder. Slowly, slowly, bright plumes of red began to seep out from beneath her.

He leaned forward, palpated the skin beneath her jaw. No pulse registered in his fingertips.

A muffled slur. "Aw fuck. Aw fuck."

Gil had forgotten the boy was even there, huddled on the concrete floor. He crawled through Edie's blood, the bottom button of his jean jacket snagging her hair. Then he reached up and opened the passenger door of the car. Slithered inside, his slender legs hanging out.

Awareness flooded Gil. Rapid thoughts tripping through his brain at lightning speed. It was an accident. A terrible, terrible mistake. Yet entirely his fault. He would be taken into custody by police. Likely held. The shove would be considered assault. His version of the events that followed would sound preposterous. *Deadly hammer falls at opportune moment. Kills cheating wife.* A trial would take place. Who would testify? Neighbors? Lunch ladies? That old woman with the poodle? Was it last year that she'd witnessed he and Edie arguing? Could she identify the metal box he was holding in the car? And he'd confided in Seth, too. Had Seth told Andrea? Gil would be portrayed as a jealous and controlling husband. Unstable and violent. Who'd fed his wife lithium. Who'd kept tabs on her every move. Who'd traded free prescriptions for surveillance gear.

He'd be convicted. He'd go to jail.

"Daddy?"

Gil twisted around. Molly was still in the doorway. Sobbing.

And Molly. Molly! She would enter the system. Be taken in by strangers. Possibly kind. Possibly malevolent. Beyond that, Gil did not know. Though he'd heard horror stories about foster care.

Or maybe Seth and Andrea would look after her. But then, she'd be raised by an overbearing woman, a disinterested man, and a brood of rowdy boys.

Gil could not allow it. That was not a choice.

"Go!" He had never yelled at his daughter before. "Go outside!" He had to think. He had to think.

Her sobbing ceased, and she toddled away.

Gil edged closer to Edie and knelt down near her. Avoiding the halo of blood. Her skin was pale and perfect. Furrows in her brow smoothed. How long he studied her face, he could not tell. But for the first time in years, she appeared peaceful. Maybe even happy.

"Gil? What on earth?"

June Fischer was in the doorway, holding Molly by the hand. Her eyes moved from him to the battered mess that was his wife to the boy's legs jutting out of the open car door. "Should I call an ambulance?"

He shook his head.

"Well, what then?"

And an idea arrived. A monstrous solution. Instructions rising up through the droning in his mind.

He spoke three words to June. "I'm not here."

As though she instinctively knew what to do, she clasped Molly's hand, softly said, "Aren't you a brave girl." They turned around, began walking down the short hallway. "Such a brave girl coming to find me."

"I'm a brave girl."

"That's right. You are. Outside your house all by yourself. Somebody bad was there? What has he done? He hurt your mom."

"My mom's hurt."

"Oh, I wonder where your daddy is. I wonder where your daddy is."

"Daddy's in the garage."

"Your daddy is at work, dear. He's going to be so sad when he finds out that a bad man hurt your mom."

•

Using all his might, Gil tugged Edie over the lip of the car trunk. Her warm body flumped onto the hard ground, her face lit by the orange of the setting sun. He dragged her to the sharp edge of rock. Paused there. Gazed across Rabey Lake at the tiny cabins that dotted the other side. He'd been so full of love and hope when they'd stayed there that first time. Believed nothing would ever break the bond they'd forged.

But he'd been fooling himself. Edie had never loved him. Had never loved the child they'd created. She'd loved her mother and her father. She'd loved her sister, and her delinquent brother, too. Beyond that, there was no more room in her heart. The circle around the Paltry family, drawn in thick permanent ink, was closed. He and Molly were on the outside and would have always remained there.

Gil fell to his knees. "Oh, Edie," he whispered. He placed a palm on her shoulder. A palm on her lower spine. Warmth was leaving her, and he could feel a coolness moving in. "Edie, I'm sorry, Edie. I'm sorry." She was on the very edge. Only requiring the gentlest push. In that instant when she dropped, he wanted her back. Wanted to undo it. His body lurching, hands reaching, mouth crying out her name. "Edie!"

A single sharp splash. And she was gone.

Gil left the boy lying on his side in the dirt, twitching and incoherent. Blood covering his hands, his clothes. Glassy eyes flicking left to right at the water, the sky, the lowering sun. He was mumbling to himself, "Can I take a look at the motor?" Then he sputtered, "I can't. I can't. The car is empty. The engine's totally gone."

•

In the darkness, Gil crept along the backs of the buildings on Main Street. He slipped into the empty alleyway between Wynters Even and Happy Pets.

His fingers shook as he used the silver key to unlock the door of the storeroom. Once inside, he peeled off his coat. His cardigan and stained shirt. His plain cotton undershirt. Shoved the lot of it inside an industrial garbage bag. Then he went to the sink, squeezed a cake of soap in his fist and ran warm water. Rubbed at the red streaks on his hands, his wrists, his neck. He scraped the darkness from beneath his fingernails. The stream turned pink, and Edie's blood swirled down the drain.

He always kept a spare button-down at work in case of lunch spills, and he slid that over his back. As he dressed, he told himself he'd been at the pharmacy all afternoon. Sorting boxes. Noting the inventory. Doing exactly what he'd said he'd do, exactly where he'd said he'd be. In his mind, he replayed a kind of film of himself fulfilling his role, and those thoughts began to feel like the truth. Everything with Edie had been nothing more than a terrible imagining. Brought on by the effects of mixing two medications. Whatever he'd taken, he'd have to figure that out, but he needed to be more careful.

The bell hanging over the front door jingled then, and Gil's muscles seized. The police had already arrived. June had called. Molly had told them what she'd seen. In a minute, his wrists would be bound behind his back, and his life would be over.

He took a deep breath and opened the storeroom door.

"Hey, pal. Saw the light on. You making any headway?"

Gil steadied himself, sputtered, "Hey, Seth. Yup. Snail's pace, but I'll get there." Even though he'd changed his shirt and washed his skin, his trousers were still soiled. Shoes, too. The metallic stench of blood stuck in his nostrils. He wondered if Seth noticed. "What are you doing downtown on a Sunday?"

"Just out for some fresh air." Seth unpinned the thumbtack holding the bottom of the October calendar. Lifted the page to November. A woman in a tiger-striped bikini. He ran a finger down over the center of her chest. "Was supposed to meet my chum, but I was stood up."

"Anyone I know?"

"Nah. Doubt it."

Gil forced his mouth to smile, his head to nod. He had to act normally. "You've got something on your face," he said, tapping his own mouth.

Seth's tongue darted out, licked away the whitish streak beneath his lip. He grinned shyly. "Nothing sweeter than a bit of stolen ice cream."

"Stolen? How'd you manage that? The parlor's not even open."

"Nope. Got it from the high school, if you can believe it. The back door's been broken for years. Just need to jiggle the lock." He patted his stomach. "Makes me feel like a kid again. Sneaking in there."

The frenetic chatter inside Gil's head ceased. Leaving room for alarming clarity. "And how—how did you know how to jiggle the lock? Did someone show you?"

"Well, gee. I don't quite recall." Seth's neck flushed, and he scratched at his stubble. "I mean. I—I just did."

•

As he walked back in the early evening darkness, Gil's shoes scuffed the snow-covered street. Each step was becoming more difficult than the last, and his movements were growing slower, stiffer. Once he arrived at his house, he knew what he would discover. His wife and child gone, a sticky red stain on the garage floor, a missing car. He could wait a minute or two, but then he'd have to alert the authorities.

What were the chances his delicate mixture of truth and lies would be accepted? Yes, he'd left Edie at home with their daughter while he caught up at the pharmacy. Yes, it was unusual to go in on a Sunday afternoon. No, there'd been nothing strange about Edie's behavior lately. No, she wasn't prone to running off. Yes, they had a wonderful relationship.

At some point after the police arrived, June would appear with Molly. He'd have to speak with June prior to that, of course, but afterward, all he could do was hope. Would she detail the frightening scene she'd witnessed? Would Molly? Had that nosy neighbor seen anything suspicious? Noticed him in his car? Or saw that he'd left on the road? And if those things didn't ruin him, what would happen when the cops located the teenager? His glassy eyes had followed Gil the entire time. What would he remember? He was drugged out, no doubt, but what if he'd sobered partway? It was even possible that the police would discover no one at the overhang. The boy, in his stupor, could have stumbled over the edge.

There were so many loose threads. And the outcome of either possibility was unimaginable. Either he would be found out and taken into custody. Or the boy, who'd been visiting Gil's home to assess Edie's car, would be arrested. He had been so certain the boy had been on the other end of the phone calls. But when he realized his error, and the circumstance he'd created for an innocent teen- ager, guilt struck him like a boxer's punch.

Hard flecks of snow swirled through the night air, and Gil's eyes were watering from the cold. He tried not to think about Edie. He tried not to think about Seth. His best friend since high school, betraying him, and everything that could or might mean. Instead, he focused on the image of Molly's face, shiny and smiling, and some- how his feet continued to take steady, tired steps.

He located his car. With the sleeve of his coat, he brushed away the thin layer of snow from the windshield, then climbed inside.

The cold engine grumbled as it turned over, and the wheels crunched as he eased the automobile into his driveway.

Gil paused on his front steps before opening the door. In the shadow, he could see the brass lion. Nearly every day, he lifted Molly up so she could bump its nose. Gil wondered if he'd get the chance to do that ever again.

"Hello?" he called softly as he stepped over the threshold. It felt better to pretend. "Anyone home?" He flicked on the light in the hallway. Saw tiny shoes and Edie's purse. A limp plant on the side table. "Seems everyone's out."

He wandered into the kitchen. Turned on the light over the stove. A coffee mug sat beside the sink. Crusts from a peanut butter sandwich were left on a wooden cutting board. Molly's coloring page, an orange pumpkin, was on the floor. Gil plucked it up and attached it to the fridge with *M* and *W* magnets.

Now, not a single thing was out of place.

"Hello?" he said again.

Even though he knew he wouldn't find one, he scanned the countertops for a note. Edie's scratchy handwriting. Alerting him to an errand. A visit with a friend. There was nothing.

He took two steps down the narrow hallway. The garage door was open. The faintest draft glided past him. He would do it. He would go and look inside. But instead of continuing, his legs froze, then began backing away. Long strides through the kitchen and across the family room. Into the backyard. He went quickly along the stone pathway, crossed the snowy driveway, and clambered up the front steps of June's house.

He caught the comforting scent of a roast cooking. He could hear Bradley joking loudly. Followed by a child's tinkling laughter. Time would heal, wouldn't it? But only if he was permitted time.

He made a silent promise that if, by some miracle, his actions were not detected, he would dedicate the rest of his life to being a good father. He would never expose Molly to the anguish he would feel over his cruel actions. Instead, he would tell her a thousand stories of her mother. Of bath time and warm pajamas. Puppet shows and tea parties. Snuggling in a chair reading board books. His daughter would sense a deep and abiding maternal love, instead of the nothingness that had actually been there.

"Please," he whispered, as he leaned his forehead head against the coolness of the door. "Please."

All around him, thicker flakes were falling. The sight made him wonder. If he could go back in time, would he have gone across those railroad tracks to deliver the ointment to Mrs. Paltry? A different choice, and he'd never have met Edie. Never have married her. Never have invited her madness into his life. And never have discovered such madness within himself.

Those thoughts about snowstorms and deliveries were pointless, of course. If he erased the worst of his past, that would also mean erasing the best. And for that reason, he would drive toward Edie, drive toward all those mistakes, every single time.

"Hey," he called out as he pushed open the door. "Hello? Where is everybody?"

"Daddy!" Molly raced toward him.

"There's my girl," he exclaimed as he scooped her up, swung her around.

NOW

·

CHAPTER FORTY-TWO

Molly

A CAR SLOWED and stopped. Slam of the door cutting through the midday calm. Molly sat up on the blanket. "Hey, Casey?" she said, phone pressed to her ear. "I've got to go. He just arrived."

She'd suggested a picnic. In the grassy area across from her father's house. Though it was March, the weather had been unseasonably warm and dry, and the trees that lined the street were already flushed with bright green buds.

Alex was seated on the blanket beside her. Fingertip pricked, he squeezed a drop of blood onto the end of a test strip.

She ran her hand over the smooth crook of her elbow. That patch of scaly itchiness had finally healed. "All good?" she said when the machine beeped.

He smirked. "Functioning within normal parameters."

Then Glenn was striding toward them, arms full.

"Sorry I'm late," he said, as a little girl squirmed against him. "One minute I can't find a shoe. Next minute I forgot where I put the snacks."

Molly squinted in the sunlight. "But you wouldn't change a thing, right?"

"Of course not. And luckily Rusty's place is the size of a thimble."

In December, Molly and Alex had moved into her father's house, and though she told Glenn he was welcome to stay, he decided to rent Russell's two-bedroom. "A switcheroo," he called it. Russell had frowned. "Given the circumstances, I won't protest. But you should know the internet is shared by the entirety of the home, Glenn. I expect you to be judicious with your streaming."

Glenn had only been settled for three weeks when he received a call from Children's Aid. His foster parent application had been approved, and a three-year-old girl named Agnes would be placed in his care. Apparently, the single mother had died from an overdose, and friends had brought the child to a church. To date, no father or other relatives had stepped forward. Glenn was already hoping that no one would.

"I won't complain." Glenn knelt on the blanket. Released the little girl. "Rusty's been a real help. Ags called him Uncle Russ last week, and that actually got a smile out of him."

"He's got a soft heart," she said. "Beneath all that sandpaper." Shawna had said something similar when she and Molly first met. And she'd been right.

Alex rolled a purple ball toward Agnes. "How 'bout a game of catch?" He often babysat on evenings and weekends and had quickly become one of Agnes's favorite people. For a child who'd experienced so much turmoil, she was surprisingly trusting.

The little girl nodded. Reached up and took his hand. They toddled a few feet away, and Alex gently tossed the ball in her direction. But each time Agnes caught it, she did not toss it back. She squeezed it, twirled with it, heaved it all directions.

When the ball bounced off Alex's forehead, Glenn chuckled. "No major league pitcher there, I'm guessing."

"You never know," Molly said. "His head could have been the exact target." She twisted the cap off a bottle of sparkling wine. Filled two plastic cups and handed one to Glenn.

Glenn tilted his head to the right. "So, it's true then."

Molly gazed across the road at her father's house. Then to the house next door. A "For Sale" sign stood in the very middle of the lawn.

"Yep. It's been there a few days. She's selling."

"I heard she needs the money. Still searching for Brad." Glenn tut-tutted. "So much denial there, I'd say."

Molly took a gulp of the wine. Felt the liquid spread over her insides. "I haven't spoken to her, actually. Not . . . since." She'd wanted to talk to Mrs. Fischer. So that she could explain what happened. In a delicate way, of course, but one that might offer some closure. Yet in the months since Bradley had drowned, neither woman approached the other. There was simply too much to unpack, and though Molly had had hours-long discussions with Casey, she still could not process the truth of her mother's death. Or how fully manipulated she'd been as a child. By Mrs. Fischer, by Bradley. But also by her father. But what was the alternative? Where would Molly be if she'd been separated from the last member of her family? Most children without parents did not fare nearly as well as young Agnes.

Glenn leaned a little closer. Lowered his tone. "She'll waste her last dollar looking for that loser. Even though it's pointless. Mark my words. She's not giving up."

The two of them sat side by side. Glenn watching his daughter. Molly watching her son.

"I don't know," she said. "I don't suppose I would give up either."

•

It was Russell who'd saved her. He'd been hiking, checking his snares, and had heard the shouting, witnessed the last moments of the altercation with Bradley Fischer. With total disregard for his own safety, he'd leapt off the rock and plummeted to the lake below. Diving down, he grasped the collar of Molly's jacket and brought her to the surface. With his arm secured around her torso, he'd swum across Rabey Lake. Two dead rabbits still secured to his belt.

As he pulled her up onto a dock near the cabins, the old care-taker hurried toward them. Wrapped a blanket around Molly. Another around Russell. "I heard the ruckus," she said. "Noise carries around here."

Molly could not stop sputtering and shivering. Her body in shock from the fear and the cold. But also the *closeness*. In those moments when she was sinking, she was certain she was going to die. That she would settle on the bottom. She and her mother, prac-tically mirror images of each other. Their bones eventually scattered among the massive heap of trash.

"You're okay now, Molly," Russell said, firm grip on her shoulder. "An ambulance is on its way."

He removed his blanket and placed it on top of the other one. She was shaking so fiercely, she could not speak to protest.

Across the lake, Alex was standing on the overhang. "Mom!" he yelled, waving his arms. "Are. You. Oh. Kay?" She could hear him clearly.

"Will you look at that kid?" The lady pointed at Alex, shook her head. "I always tell the youngsters not to go horsing around up there. Accidents happen, right?"

Molly pressed her forehead into her bent knees. She needed to calm down. She needed to think. What had happened with Bradley Fischer was not a mishap. There was no way to justify what she'd done. The situation had deescalated. Alex had been safe beside her. He had even been eating chocolate so his blood sugar would rebound.

How could she ever explain? The fury and the panic that had accumulated within her. She hadn't thought of the consequences. She'd only wanted Bradley gone.

"Where's the other one?" the lady said.

"We don't know." Russell gripped Molly's shoulder. "I didn't see him."

Molly scanned the lake. The water was still. No one else was swimming across.

.

"He was threatening us," Molly said. She held a mug with both hands. Steam from the lemon water rising up on her neck, her chin.

Alex agreed. "When I came out of school, he told me to get in his car. Or else."

"Or else what?"

"I don't know. Was I supposed to ask?"

"No, no." Officer Kage looked up from his notepad. "I'm not suggesting that at all. You did everything right, Alex."

"He wanted money," Molly said. "To support a drug habit. But—but I'm surmising. I don't know for certain."

"So he brought you up to the overhang to demand cash?"

The heat from the mug was burning Molly's hands. "It seems preposterous, but yes. That's what he did."

"I've heard stranger stuff," he said. "And how exactly did you end up in the water? That's a dangerous drop."

Molly squeezed the mug. Her palms felt as though they were shrinking onto the pottery. Every time she glanced at Lyle, she was overwhelmed with emotion. Not just from the tangled mess with Bradley, but what she now knew about her mother's death. She'd have to tell Lyle the truth. But first, she needed to explain the confrontation on the overhang. Explain what she'd done and hope it did not completely derail her life. Derail Alex's life. "I was so—" she stuttered. "I just couldn't see—I—"

A light tapping interrupted them. The door beside the refrigerator creaked open, and Russell's face appeared. "I don't mean to intrude," he said. "I wanted to check in on my tenants."

"We're doing okay." A shiver moved through her, even though she was no longer cold. "Thanks to you."

Molly owed her life to Russell Farrell. Felt an immense gratitude for the courage he'd displayed. But at the same time, the sight of him made her heart flitter. How much had he actually heard?

"Come in, Rusty," Officer Kage said. "I'd like to talk to you, too."

Beneath the kitchen table, Molly's knee bounced up and down.

"When I encountered them," Russell said, "I immediately determined it was a crisis situation. And if I stepped forward, it'd only antagonize things."

"You didn't announce yourself? Try to help?"

"Not a chance, Lyle." Russell folded his arms across his chest. "You know Bradley as well as I do, and if I'd intervened, it would have riled him up."

He proceeded to describe it all. How Bradley seesawed between affable and aggressive. How he dragged a weakened and frightened Alex to the very edge of the rock. How he demanded money like the world owed him yet another favor.

"Molly stepped between him and her son. To protect the boy. And also out of concern for Bradley, would be my guess. That's the therapist in her. Putting others before herself."

"Then what happened?"

Molly braced herself. Once Russell's statement emerged from his lips, everything would change. Officer Kage would have no choice but to take her to the station. Press her further. Alex would be left alone in the rental. Worried and waiting. What would happen when she admitted it all? Would she eventually be allowed to leave? Who would look after Alex?

"Well, I was taken aback by it, I'll say that for starters."

As Russell explained those last moments on the overhang, Molly gaped at him. Was it possible he'd looked away at the exact second she'd lunged? Or was his view obscured by branches, and he was presenting his assumptions as facts? Telling Officer Kage that Bradley had shoved her, and not the other way around. And as Molly tripped backward, she'd caught the hem of Bradley's coat, causing *him* to lose *his* balance. The two of them tumbling into the lake together. An alarming tangle of limbs.

"You jumped in after them?"

"I certainly did."

"And Bradley never surfaced."

"Nope. And to tell you the truth, Lyle, I wasn't inclined to hang around and search for him."

Whatever the reason behind Russell's statement, it did not matter. He'd spoken with clarity and confidence, while Officer Kage scribbled every word onto a fresh page in his notepad. There would be no further questions.

•

One night in mid-December, Molly's father fell asleep in his living room bed and never woke up. On the day he died, there was a snowstorm. School was cancelled, businesses closed. Roads were impassable. She and Alex had been waiting most of the morning for the plow, and eventually trudged over from their rental through drifts up to their knees.

Shortly after they arrived, Molly wheeled her father to the sliding glass doors that faced the backyard and pulled up a chair beside him. Together they sat watching the thick fat flakes that tumbled from the sky. There was an endlessness to it. A comforting depth. He seemed more alert than usual, gazing out into the diminishing light. She wondered what he was thinking. Or if he was thinking anything at all.

Likely he didn't understand a word she'd said, but still, she told him she forgave him. Though she didn't know exactly what happened, and never would, she knew he'd made a monstrous error. Followed by a cowardly choice. At first, it had shocked her, but now she realized it made perfect sense. Before Russell interrupted her interview with Officer Kage, she'd intended to tell the whole story. But even in those moments, she'd stammered, her mind working at high speed, assessing the possible outcomes. If Russell hadn't conveniently appeared, would she have actually confessed? Or would she have told a version of events that prioritized the security of her child?

As she replayed her own struggles, she told her father that she hoped he hadn't suffered the pain of that choice every day. That the guilt hadn't festered into something hard and matted inside his chest. Though she was certain it had. That was why he'd remained in Aymes his entire life, instead of moving away and opting for a fresh start. It made sense, now. The daily reminders were his punishment. His penance.

She placed her palm gently on the top of his head and told him he was the best father, the best man, the best person she'd ever known. And that she hoped her son would grow up to be just like him.

"I love you, Dad," she whispered. "I love you."

Late that evening, after Nurse Glenn had moved her father into his hospital bed, Alex stretched out beside him. Their heads tilted slightly toward each other. Their bodies, though so different in age, were still strikingly similar.

"And then the guy, like, opened his throat and shoved down three entire wieners. Isn't that gross, Grandad?"

She could have been imagining things, but as the two of them lay there, side by side, she thought she saw her father's hand moving. Slowly inching over the blanket, crawling up onto Alex's hand. Then their fingers, young and supple, old and gnarled, lay knotted together.

•

Glenn pulled the bottle of wine from the basket. Refilled Molly's cup. He put his hand to his forehead, shielding his eyes from the sun as he watched Agnes running headlong toward Alex. "They need us for everything, don't they? The responsibility of it is kind of scary."

Molly understood. Children, trying to make sense of the world, were constantly seeking reassurance. Absorbing every fragment gathered to build a solid foundation. Sometimes misunderstandings were incorporated into the mix. Sometimes outright lies. But if layers of goodness were piled on top, those broken bits did not have to weaken the structure. Or define a person. They didn't have to define her.

Telling Lyle Kage the truth about her mother's death had been the most difficult conversation of her life. They'd sat in the small living room of the rental. He in the wingback chair, and she on the couch, the painting of the overhang on the wall behind her. She held nothing back, detailing as much as she knew. That her father had been responsible. That Terry was a teenager in the wrong place at the wrong time. And that the testimony she'd given in court had originated from a narrative created by Mrs. Fischer. Molly told him that she'd somehow kept those memories hidden from herself. Like a cassette that had been recorded over. Even though she'd always sensed something was wrong, she'd been too afraid to examine it. And she was deeply sorry for that. For not having had more courage.

Lyle nodded. Face expressionless. "Okay," he'd said as he stood up. "Okay."

They'd crossed paths since. On Main Street's sidewalk, twice in the grocery store. He was polite, always pausing to say a kind word about Alex, who was finishing up his community service hours. Molly wondered if, at some point, he might feel forgiveness. If not for her father, then perhaps for her.

She'd been working on that as well. Had made the decision to remain in Aymes while she healed the damaged parts inside. At first it felt indulgent, but gradually she recognized how necessary it was, if she intended to be a strong and present mother. At some point over the past months, she'd begun to discover a curious stillness growing within her. Something she hadn't experienced before. As though she was slowly accepting the parts of the story that belonged to her. And letting go of the parts that did not.

During the quiet evenings in her childhood home, she occasionally caught herself thinking of that doe she and Alex had seen on their drive last September. How it blocked her route until its offspring had disappeared into the thick woods. Molly had been initially struck by the beauty of the animal, the quivering fear. But she'd also noticed something else. The quiet defiance.

She recognized that within herself, too. And as she often did, she wondered if there was a family path to the characteristic. Surely that trait had come from her father. They'd both done abhorrent things, and the deception that followed enmeshed their lives with another. Her dad with Mrs. Fischer. And now Molly with Russell. But there was no other option. At differing points, both she and her father had stood in the road. Facing oncoming dangers. As the person they loved passed safely behind.

EPILOGUE

NO MATTER HOW many decades pass, a man never forgets his first love. The intoxication, that syrupy sweetness. I might even suggest there is a certain delirium to it. With my lunch lady, I always felt a sense of endless time, endless possibilities. We'd caught hold of the tail of infinity.

After she was dead, we saw each other only on one final occasion. It was a short visit. She was standing in the bathroom when I pulled back the shower curtain. I was wet and naked, and her sudden appearance startled me. I draped a towel around my waist.

Several moments of awkward silence passed, and I finally said, "I don't want to lose you."

She slowly shook her head. Her eyes were full of resignation. "Oh, Russell," she replied. "What makes you think you ever had me?"

Those were the last words she ever spoke. She turned and left the bathroom. Disappearing from my life and shattering my heart.

·

As ridiculous as it may sound, I've often employed the techniques I learned from Mrs. Fischer when I was a teenager. Her careful guidance helped me regulate my emotions, corral my anxiety, and use thoughtful action to express myself.

A few nights after the lunch lady's death, I visited the place where she and I first met. I climbed down into the ditch and knelt in the water. The cold soaked into my boots, through the fabric of my pants. While I knew she would not return to save me, I still watched the road. I wept until I was bent from exhaustion.

Some days later, I built a simple white cross. In the middle of the night, I erected the structure near the mouth of the trail that led up to the overhang. A deep hole, two bags of fine gravel. I knew you would see it, and I hoped it gave you comfort. Let you know somebody cared.

I attended every single day in court, too. On the afternoon you testified, I sat as close to the front of the galley as possible. Leaning forward, I was transfixed by each word you spoke. I was in awe of your determination, your eloquence. Your mother would have been so proud of how you told her story. As your almost-father, I was proud, too.

Relief flooded me when he was convicted of the crime. But that became rage when, three years later, he was released on a technicality.

I was compelled to follow him. Day after day after day. Unsure of what to do, but also certain that I had to communicate effectively. How could the legal system be that ignorant? How could your testimony, so compelling, be brushed aside? My opportunity to right the wrong finally arrived a few months after he left prison.

One evening, Terry was walking around Aymes, head down, dragging his feet. He seemed aimless, despondent, and I trailed him through the streets and then up behind the high school. I hung back in the shadows as he climbed on top of a metal storage shed.

Initially, I was confused. Why was he removing his shoes and why was he mumbling to himself in that pathetic blubbering way? When he pulled a length of dirty yellow rope from his backpack and tied his sneakers to one end of it, I had an inkling. And I knew I was right when he swung those sneakers up and over the lamp post beside the shed. He actually caught it first try. Some people just have natural luck.

He tried but was unable to tie a proper noose. Finally settled on a knot and slipped his head through. Crept forward, toes at the lip of the flat roof. As he relaxed his legs, the rope pressed into his throat and his face began to darken. But after several seconds, he scuttled backward. Waited. Then tried again.

This continued for an interminable amount of time. To the point of being vexatious. I assumed he was scared and uncertain. He was crying, too. Breathing in hard. Blowing out even harder. In the orange glow of the evening, I could see clear strings of snot flying from his nostrils. Although he was working himself up to the task, all that hesitating was not productive. I decided to be a good friend to him, then, and help things along.

The sounds of his sobbing disguised my approach. The low sun was in his eyes, casting our overlapping shadows in a fortuitous direction. I was able to inch up behind him, completely undetected. A single sharp nudge and my friend, your mother's murderer, lost his balance. Pitching forward, socks slipping. He only fell three feet off the side of the shed before the rope went taut. Bouncing slightly, he scratched at his neck with his fingernails. Legs kicking back.

His feet found empty air. I stood at the lip of the roof, staring down. Eventually his arms dropped to his sides. His kicking ceased. The purple in his upturned face was like the worst kind of bruise.

It was not an easy thing to watch. I can say that with sincerity.

•

Soon after that I sold my house and moved into the city. Went to college, before dropping out and working a flurry of odd jobs. A landscaper, a dog walker, a dishwasher, and once even a potato chip inspector in a factory.

I was well into my forties, if you can believe it, before I managed to open my shriveled heart again. She owned a bakery specializing in buttery pastries. Had thick black glasses and wore her hair in a messy bun on top of her head. Our interactions began innocently enough. She told me which muffins were still warm, or if I bought five, the sixth was free. But in time, our bond deepened to something powerful and profound. She was a little like my lunch lady, actually. Warm hands. Quick with the wit. Charmed by my quirkiness.

As I developed that relationship, I remained as patient as could be. I was utterly convinced that we were of one mind and destined to marry someday. I even envisioned our children. Her perky nose, my high cheekbones. When I couldn't wait a second longer to show her—the real her—my commitment, everything went awry. My overture was badly misinterpreted, and no matter how hard I tried to explain the connection we had, she refused to understand. I was sentenced to seven years in prison. Served three and a half.

I returned home to Aymes. I felt a sense of rightness when I found my new home and settled in. A fresh start. I was on the opposite side of the tracks this time, where memories of my past, my mother, barely existed.

When you contacted me, it sent me into a tailspin at first. A full-on tidal wave of unresolved emotions. But eventually I realized we were supposed to reconnect. I was present at the very start of your creation, and the cord between us, though stretched and frayed, had never broken. The universe has a way of sorting things out.

I was anxious when you and your son arrived. People can change, and being estranged for so many years is undoubtedly difficult. Though it wasn't my intent, our reunion was peppered with small white lies. Mention of my recent divorce. Stating my late mother was in a retirement home. That you had the only key to the door beside the refrigerator.

I've been keeping tabs on you. Not in an obtrusive way. I simply want the same as any paternal figure would. To ensure your health and well-being. Though no one in town has forgotten your bravery when you were a child, not everyone has the best of intentions.

Take that moron Brad, for instance. When you met him at the bar, I sipped a beer outside on a nearby patio while you socialized. Through the front windows, I saw him tampering with your drink. My suspicions were confirmed when you teetered out. Barely able to focus. You were obviously in a vulnerable state, and unfortunately I didn't reach you before that nosy reporter from the local rag asked his questions. But at least I intercepted Brad. Before he could slither out of the bar, I'd ushered you into a cab and sent you home.

I could not let him get away with what he'd done. When he discovered your absence, he retreated to the village green across from Main Street. He was seated on a bench in the darkness, and I'm sure it was his mother who paid for the woman kneeling before him. I waited until the transaction was complete, and then pulled a black balaclava over my face. Rushed up behind him and punched him squarely in the side of his head. Dragged him over the damp grass and kicked him. He curled on the ground like a slug dowsed in salt.

That night you dropped your phone at the overhang? I was there, too. You went so close to the edge and I was ready to stop you. Reach my hands through the black and turn you around.

And when you mentioned a concern about the peer support line, I began listening in immediately. My cousin would be appalled, of course, but it was a necessary intervention. I had to know what was causing you alarm. I soon found out. Someone playing games, making insinuations and threats. Trying to throw you off-kilter. Although I tried, my tracking skills are, I confess, limited. I suspected Glenn, simply due to his proximity to you, as well as his buffoonish behavior as a teenager. But clearly I was stretching, and I made an error. For which I apologized.

Setting that minor misstep aside, fate has not let me down. Though I'd done my best to insulate you from harm, it was merely coincidence that I was checking my snares near the overhang that afternoon. I waited, watching it all as it happened. I couldn't hear what he was saying, but it didn't matter. The angle of his body, the jut of his jaw told me everything. There was no justification for his behavior. When he caught hold of your coat, and you plunged into the lake, I didn't hesitate for a single second.

I've never been a strong swimmer, but adrenaline took over. I dove down, grasped your collar, then hooked an arm around your chest. As I began pulling you upward, I saw him trying to reach the surface. I struck out, my foot pummeling his nose. Red clouded the water, and his mouth opened wide. A huge bubble emerged, and it still gives me pleasure to remember that wobbly pocket of air rising past me. His last breath.

When I spoke with Lyle, I was already aware of everything you'd said to him. Your conversations travel through those vents, from upstairs to downstairs, with a particular crispness. The moment you were about to incriminate yourself, it was necessary for me to step in. I described a sequence of events with precision and inserted a minor lie.

From my past mistakes, I've learned I'm better when I am giving. Not when I want something in return. Though my path to understanding has been rife with despair and heartache, I finally know what real devotion is. Generosity, without expectation of reciprocity. My way of caring may not be loud. It may not include a garish display or verbose declarations. Love can be subtle. Invisible. Entirely singular. And still completely authentic.

·

It's nearly dinnertime, and I can see you through the kitchen window of your father's home. Your home, now. You are filling a vase of yellow flowers with water. Tulips, maybe. Your son is behind you, saying something that makes you laugh. The sight of your head lolling backward, mouth wide open, causes joy to course through my body.

You turn your back now, likely carrying the flowers to the dining table. Placing it among the three plates already there. Three sets of cutlery. Perhaps you'll check your watch, as you are expecting me to knock at any moment. I've been invited to join you for a meal.

You may not see it yet, Molly. But in time, you'll grasp the connections. Between you and me. Between me and Alex. A second chance was needed to reestablish the profound love that links us together. Has always linked us together. We are family. Whether you like it or not.

ACKNOWLEDGEMENTS

While working on *A Man Downstairs*, I have also been processing major life events. It has been a period of significant upheaval and devastating loss, but there have been many moments of growth, beauty, and unexpected warmth. I know this book would not exist without the tremendous support that came from so many different corners.

The initial spark for *AMD* arose during multiple brainstorming sessions with my agent, Danielle Egan-Miller, her former assistant Ellie Roth, and her foreign rights manager, Mariana Fisher. I'm so thankful these creative women gave me the building blocks I needed to begin this story. And whenever I encountered (oh so many) bumps on the road to completion, Danielle was always available, sharing her tireless optimism and brilliant guidance. She is a wonder.

AMD is the third book I've worked on with my phenomenal editor, Lara Hinchberger, at Penguin Canada. I continue to marvel over her uncanny ability to see clear paths among my tangles.

It bears repeating—she truly does help me discover the story I'm meant to tell. This is such a special partnership, not just because of her expertise but also her genuine kindness.

Writing is often an intensely isolating endeavour. The encouragement of others means so very much, and the depth of gratitude I feel for those people is difficult to express. My daughter, Ella Deák, is an avid reader and has been offering valuable and astute feedback on my manuscripts since she was old enough to manage the dark and disturbing bits. My niece, Madolyn Lundrigan, during a time of immense strife, demonstrated a strength and perseverance that left me in awe. I frequently called upon the memory of her grit when I hit the creative wall. These four friends for too many reasons to mention: Palmina Ioannone, Doris Dadoun, Jane Stollar, and Samira Mubareka. And Simon Archer, who sees in me what I often struggle to see in myself. Every writer I know needs that sometimes.

Finally, a sincere thank-you to the Ontario Arts Council for supporting this project when it was still mostly sticky notes and lofty ideas.

© ArnaLena Seemann

NICOLE LUNDRIGAN is the author of several critically acclaimed novels, including *An Unthinkable Thing* and *Hideaway*, both of which were shortlisted for the Crime Writers of Canada Award for Best Crime Novel, and *The Substitute*. Her work has appeared on "best of" selections from *The Globe and Mail*, Amazon.ca, *Chatelaine*, *Now*, and others. She grew up in Newfoundland and now lives in Toronto.

nicolelundrigan.com
facebook.com/njlundrigan
Instagram: @nicolejlundrigan